# REMNANT

## THE PALIMAR SAGA: BOOK ONE

K. R. SOLBERG | C. R. JACOBSON

*Remnant* is a work of fiction.
Names, places, and incidents are either a product of the authors' imaginations or are used fictitiously.
Any resemblance to actual events, locales, or persons, living or dead, is entirely coincidental.

2023 Epic North Publishing Paperback Edition



Published in the United States by Epic North Publishing, LLC.

Paperback ISBN 979-8-9863498-0-0
Ebook ISBN 979-8-9863498-2-4
Hardcover ISBN 979-8-9863498-1-7

Printed in the United States of America on acid-free paper.

epicnorthpublishing.com

*Book design by K. R. Solberg*

*Cover art by Kaia Bakken*

*To Kevin Jacobson and Sean Solberg,*
*who have supported our imaginings*
*for a very long time.*

*To Owen, for being our most enthusiastic reader.*

*"Fantasy is escapist, and that is its glory. If a soldier is imprisoned by the enemy, don't we consider it his duty to escape?"*

J. R. R. Tolkien

*Remnant* is filled with complex characters, intricate plots, magic, intrigue, and high-stakes adventure. This is not a light read. **For your benefit, an index and appendices (page 383) are included at the back of this book** detailing characters, places, and terms. These references are also on our website: palimarsaga.com

# CONTENTS


1 Death of an Immortal . . . . . . . . . . . . . . . . . 1
2 Vultures. . . . . . . . . . . . . . . . . . . . . . . . . . . 8
3 Handshakes. . . . . . . . . . . . . . . . . . . . . . . 14
4 The Storyteller. . . . . . . . . . . . . . . . . . . . . 25
5 The Red Watch . . . . . . . . . . . . . . . . . . . . 34
6 Trinkets and Trespassers. . . . . . . . . . . . . . . 44
7 A Bitter Homecoming. . . . . . . . . . . . . . . . . 53
8 Questions . . . . . . . . . . . . . . . . . . . . . . . . 63
9 The Spire Lords . . . . . . . . . . . . . . . . . . . . 67
10 A Change of Plan . . . . . . . . . . . . . . . . . . 76
11 Crossing the Door. . . . . . . . . . . . . . . . . . 84
12 Meetings and Manners . . . . . . . . . . . . . . . 93
13 Curfew . . . . . . . . . . . . . . . . . . . . . . . . 104
14 Harry . . . . . . . . . . . . . . . . . . . . . . . . . 112
15 A Farewell. . . . . . . . . . . . . . . . . . . . . . 116
16 The Cook . . . . . . . . . . . . . . . . . . . . . . . 126
17 Rendal . . . . . . . . . . . . . . . . . . . . . . . . 132
18 The Stolen Sister . . . . . . . . . . . . . . . . . . 139
19 The Hunt . . . . . . . . . . . . . . . . . . . . . . . 146
20 A Prospect. . . . . . . . . . . . . . . . . . . . . . 156
21 The Harvest Temple . . . . . . . . . . . . . . . . 162
22 Encounters . . . . . . . . . . . . . . . . . . . . . . 167
23 The Rogue Master. . . . . . . . . . . . . . . . . . 175
24 Lair of Immortals . . . . . . . . . . . . . . . . . . 180
25 Behind the Curtain . . . . . . . . . . . . . . . . . 186
26 The Bronze Ring . . . . . . . . . . . . . . . . . . . 196
27 Ghosts of the Deep Wood. . . . . . . . . . . . . 205
28 Sidras . . . . . . . . . . . . . . . . . . . . . . . . . 215
29 Forest Demons . . . . . . . . . . . . . . . . . . . . 226
30 Debt . . . . . . . . . . . . . . . . . . . . . . . . . . 239
31 The Cellar . . . . . . . . . . . . . . . . . . . . . . . 246
32 Brimholt . . . . . . . . . . . . . . . . . . . . . . . . 257
33 The Well . . . . . . . . . . . . . . . . . . . . . . . . 266
34 The Hall of Prophecy . . . . . . . . . . . . . . . 273

35 Manhunt. . . . . . . . . . . . . . . . . . . . . . . . . 279
36 The Godkiller . . . . . . . . . . . . . . . . . . . . . 282
37 The Specter . . . . . . . . . . . . . . . . . . . . . . 291
38 The Banshee . . . . . . . . . . . . . . . . . . . . . 296
39 Infiltrators. . . . . . . . . . . . . . . . . . . . . . . 301
40 The Battle at the Gate . . . . . . . . . . . . . . . 308
41 The Summons. . . . . . . . . . . . . . . . . . . . 315
42 Between Brothers . . . . . . . . . . . . . . . . . . 320
43 The Poisoned Road . . . . . . . . . . . . . . . . . 328
44 The Arch Purifier. . . . . . . . . . . . . . . . . . 335
45 Fire Wielders. . . . . . . . . . . . . . . . . . . . . 340
46 Remnant. . . . . . . . . . . . . . . . . . . . . . . . 345
47 Making Plans . . . . . . . . . . . . . . . . . . . . 353
48 A Scolding . . . . . . . . . . . . . . . . . . . . . . 358
49 Uninvited Guests . . . . . . . . . . . . . . . . . . 369
50 The Other Gate. . . . . . . . . . . . . . . . . . . 376
51 A Spoil of Victory . . . . . . . . . . . . . . . . . 379
Index . . . . . . . . . . . . . . . . . . . . . . . . . . . . 383
Appendix A Races of Ethar. . . . . . . . . . . . . 390
Appendix B Nations and Regions. . . . . . . . . 392
Appendix C Character Directory . . . . . . . . . 396
Appendix D Roles and Occupations. . . . . . . 408
Appendix E Craft and Sorcery . . . . . . . . . . . 411
Appendix F Culture and Environment. . . . . 414
Note from the Authors. . . . . . . . . . . . . . . . . 421
Book Two. . . . . . . . . . . . . . . . . . . . . . . . . . 423
A Palimar Saga Novella . . . . . . . . . . . . . . . . 424

THE DEVOURER'S WASTE
Grater Continent of Urlas
THE DRAKE LANDS
THE OLD WASTE
Once the Kingdom of Gravos
THE DEEP WOOD
Theron River
Utheran Ocean
Estbye
Lorinth
TARIA
A Province of Corigon
Virin River
Depbas
Nine Tribes of
tSOLAN
Ruled by the Great Rajiv
Syres River
tSolorilis
Cathyn Sea
Obaris
COSTA
Pelton
Rotira
Port Selta
Cazan River
Sheval
Osrin
Dothra
Bay of Songs
Drawl
Laria
Palim
Howling Sea
CORIGON
YVENEA
Setmal
Zeree
Theen
THE FREE LANDS
Theron River
Niryen
Oboran
Lake of Tears
Lake Everen
Darsa
Temple of Ize
Syres River
Memladra
Corre
Mogryn
AGINOM
A Province of Corigon
Kor'Vol Ruins
Doness Ruins
SHARDLING ISLANDS
750 MILES »
THE DEAD LANDS
Once the Kingdoms of
Kartha and Ruvia
N
W
E
S

# PALIMAR
LAST LIVING LANDS OF URLAS

# 1

# DEATH OF AN IMMORTAL

*The Temple of Ize, Southern Corigon*
*May 7, 1189 PT (Post Tyrannus)*

*Mavell*

The stench of decay stung Collector Mavell's throat. He tightened the black scarf over his nose and mouth, stepping aside as another collector dragged a guard's petrified body by the ankles.

"Wait." Mavell's monotone voice echoed in the marble room.

The collector halted, wiping sweat off her forehead with her own scarf.

Using his bloodied boot, Mavell knocked a dart loose from behind the guard's ear. The smell of rotting fruit rose from the hollow tip—wraith poison.

Like all the fallen guards in the room, this man's rifle remained slung across his shoulder, his pistol in its holster. Fifteen armed men, but not one had fired his gun.

The scene reminded Mavell of a knacker's yard with no care given to quality butchering. This, however, was the Hall of Hoven in the Temple of Ize, a sanctuary of Drawlen. After examining the room, Mavell knew this was no haphazard slaughter. Just a gruesome work of art.

He nodded to the woman.

She grunted, heaving the stony body over the threshold. Two other collectors cleaned the remaining gore with buckets of steaming water. The distant whimpers of a child melded with the clamor of sloshing mops, boots on stone, collectors exhaling their nausea.

"Collector Mavell." His partner stepped into the room and stood at attention. Grime smattered her usually pristine uniform—an assemblage of black clothing, scarf, and belt ordered with lethal accessories. She stared with blank lavender eyes.

"Collector Detoa," Mavell said, sparing her a glance.

"He is here."

An ominous man appeared in the doorway as Detoa moved aside. He was unnaturally tall and draped in dark, silver robes, his face covered by a glittering fabric rippling like water.

Mavell dropped to one knee and bowed. Detoa and the other two collectors imitated him.

The Veiled Man stood, unmoving, for several minutes. Then he entered the room, one foot mechanically following the other. By the time his lord passed, Mavell's knee throbbed.

"Rise," came a nasally voice from under the silver veil. "Show me the body."

"Bodies, Your Eminence." Mavell gestured to the carnage. "There are twenty-three—well, almost twenty-three."

The Veiled Man regarded Mavell.

Even with the immortal's face covered, Mavell tensed under his piercing stare. "Seven of them are just heads. They were killed elsewhere and brought here as a message."

"Blood for blood." The Veiled Man pointed his gloved finger to the dais, above which the phrase SANGUINIS PRETIUM SANGUIS dripped in crimson letters. The Veiled Man's arm disappeared into his robes like a stone sinking in oil. "I have no interest in the mortals, Collector. Show me Hoven."

Mavell bowed and led the Veiled Man to the end of the hall while the other collectors resumed their work. At the other end of the space, a golden throne hid beneath a cloth, and crusted blood lined parts of the exposed metal. Mavell peeled the fabric off the upper half of the corpse entombed on the seat.

The Veiled Man stepped back. "Is that—" He pointed to a bloody mass stuffed inside the corpse's mouth.

"Hoven's heart, yes." Mavell removed the remaining cloth, displaying Hoven's erupted chest. "This was done by someone with an intimate understanding of an immortal's regenerative power."

Curling his long fingers, the Veiled Man balked.

Mavell replaced the sheet. "We have a genuine godkiller on our hands, Your Eminence."

"Indeed." The Veiled Man stretched his neck. "Why Hoven? What was the motive?"

"Vengeance, I'm sure." Mavell pointed to another covered mass in the corner while motioning to Detoa. Walking past him, she and two collectors pulled off the black fabric. It slithered to the floor, revealing the massive dragon-like head of a great-horned wyvern.

Three sets of eyes reflected the blue light of the sunrock lanterns. One of its onyx horns, curled back from the wyvern's flat nose, had been broken in half. The scales of its bruised face had withered and grown pallid. Within its gaping mouth, skewered onto its long teeth, sat seven petrified human heads. And the smell . . .

"Cover it. Burn it," the Veiled Man said. "Explain, Collector Mavell."

"According to the keeper of this temple, Hoven's clerics dispatched the wyvern to clear the way for a mining venture sixty miles east, across the border in Yvenea." Removing his knife, Mavell tapped the creature's mouth. "These seven heads are those of the clerics and a few Yvean conspirators. Other than Hoven, there were fifteen guards, an oracle, and her young daughter—all present in the room at the time of the incident."

"Why so many guards?"

"The oracle must have told him something was coming."

The Veiled Man nodded. "All were killed, I presume."

The corners of Mavell's cheeks lifted behind his scarf. "Two survived—the girl and the oracle. Although the oracle was unconscious, they were mostly unharmed."

"Bring me the girl," the Veiled Man said.

Mavell signaled to Detoa, who bowed and left the room. Standing rigidly, Mavell waited with his master. He glanced at the throne where Hoven had ruled the south with notorious cruelty for three hundred years. That immortal legacy ended abruptly, and a child was the only living witness to his death.

Detoa returned with the witness, who shuffled into the room with her neck drooping. As they approached the Veiled Man, the girl held fast to Detoa's arm.

Placing two spindly fingers under her chin, the Veiled Man raised her head. "Show me what you have seen, child." He lifted his veil. For a moment, the girl's eyes widened, their light returning. She trembled with her mouth agape. When the Veiled Man dropped his covering, the girl resumed her limp posture.

"It seems our killer is plagued by a small conscience," the Veiled Man said. "He spared the woman and her child."

"Killer?" Detoa said. "A *single* killer?"

"There was an accomplice. Both, I believe, were ralenta. But most of the killing was done by one man."

"How is that—"

"Impossible," drawled a voice from the doorway.

Mavell's teeth clenched when Selvator Kane, a dark-haired boy in an embroidered purple justaucorps and polished boots, strode into the room.

Not really a boy. Just a monster in the skin of a boy.

"How indeed, Lord of the Veil?" Sel approached, crossing his arms like a parent waiting for a child to explain his misbehavior.

The Veiled Man snorted. "Are you not the Lord of Whispers, Selvator? Did you come to be of help, or to act as your revered father's errand boy again?"

Sel bristled, but his voice remained steady. "I'm simply here for the child. Young Haana has latent shade craft, so for your sake, I hope you did not harm her."

"Indeed not," the Veiled Man said. "I have lifted the burden of this horrific event from her mind. She will henceforth have no memory of it. So, if anything, I have helped her."

Sel narrowed his eyes. "And what have you done with that—burden?"

The Veiled Man tapped his temple. "It is safe and waiting for his lordship to witness for himself."

"Then I shall take you to Lord Refsul immediately. I will meet you on the wraith gate." Sel took Haana's hand and escorted her through the door.

Once again, the Veiled Man stood, silent and still. Once again, his servants waited, just as silent, just as still. Only Haana's footsteps echoed down the stone corridor.

At last, the Veiled Man faced Mavell. "We shall speak in private, Collector."

Mavell nodded, calling his shades to cloak them. Wisps whirled like smoke from an extinguished candle, encasing them in a soundproof cocoon of darkness.

"I am giving you a secret assignment, Collector. Find this godkiller."

"Dead or alive?"

"Oh, trust me, young hunter, you and any mortal in all the Drawlen ranks are no match for this creature. He is *mortari*, a Shard Keeper, a reincarnation of Agroth. You will find him alive, and you will leave him alone."

The words *mortari* and *Agroth* swirled in Mavell's mind. They sounded familiar, but he nodded rather than risking ignorance before his master.

"You will tell no one what I show you, Collector, other than your partner. There are pieces of the child's memory only you and I will see. Not even Lord Refsul, himself, will know the nature of this adversary. Do you understand?"

"Yes, my lord."

His master put two fingers under Mavell's chin and lifted his own veil, revealing a pair of solid, white eyes. A vision of this room before the present gore flooded Mavell's mind.

*He was crouched behind a pillar near the dais. No, not crouched. Beneath him, Haana's face reflected in a water basin.*

*Hoven, in all his obese glory, reclined on his golden throne. A red-haired woman of immense beauty, Tessa the oracle, stood rigidly at his side. Her perfection was only tarnished by the look of disgust on her face.*

*"You broke your word," she said.*

*"I am a god, Tessa. I get whatever I want, no matter what deals you try to make. You say someone is coming to kill me. I say let them try." He thrust out his sagging arm and surveyed the guards posted along the walls.*

*"No. You won't be getting anything you want," Tessa said.*

*"Why is that?" Hoven's hand snaked up Tessa's thigh, slipping under the gold fabric of her dress.*

*"I told you. I saw your death."*

*"You lie."*

*"A foreseer cannot lie."*

*The crystals in the sunrock lanterns extinguished, a shadow falling over the windows like a curtain. Muffled screams erupted while the power of a ralenta's shades momentarily blinded Haana. A minute later, fifteen dead guards lay exactly where Mavell first found them.*

*Tessa struggled to free her wrist from Hoven's fat-handed grip. He grunted and tossed the slender woman. Tessa's head struck the wall, and she fell unconscious and bleeding. Hoven drew a gaudy blade as he barked in horror.*

*In front of him sat the head of the wyvern with seven human heads skewered on its yellow fangs. Haana's eyes moved toward two hooded figures in the middle of the hall. A tall, lanky ralenta held a curved, bloody knife in each hand.*

*Next to him stood the godkiller. His eyes blazed behind the shadow of his hood. A long, glittering red knife protruded from his sleeve. He stepped forward with preternatural speed, then vanished. After a low, quick buzzing, he reappeared in front of Hoven. He lifted the knife and—*

*Haana buried her face in her arm. When Hoven's laughter filled the room, she lifted her head, eyes widening. Hoven clenched the godkiller's forearm, fending off the knife.*

*"So glad we're all enjoying ourselves," the accomplice said.*

*With overwhelming strength, the godkiller thrust the knife forward, and Hoven's cries erupted. A red glow filled the room, intensifying with Hoven's screams, followed by silence. Enveloped in darkness, Haana wept.*

When Mavell resumed reality, he was lying on the floor. His shades no longer cloaked him, having lost connection with their master. Detoa's hands rested on his shoulders, but she jumped when he shook her off and glared.

As Mavell rose, his legs quaking, the Veiled Man leaned closer. "Find him. And when you do, don't let him know. Report to me and me alone."

Brushing a greasy yellow lock off his forehead with a bloody glove, Mavell bowed. The Veiled Man faced the throne. "He won't be missed." Slowly and silently, he walked out of the room.

Mavell watched until his master was out of sight, then whispered to Detoa, "That's probably true of most immortals." As they left together, they passed through the atrium garden along the mid-level balcony. Sel and Haana came into view beside a fountain on the ground floor. The collectors slipped between two planters at the edge of the balcony to listen through the power of Mavell's shade.

"I have a gift for you from your mother." Sel draped a gold chain with a pendant over the child's neck.

The girl squealed nervously as she clutched it.

"Now we shall return to Shevak," Sel said.

"Lord Sel, what about my mother?" Haana sounded rather mature for one so young, but being a Drawlen harem child often meant growing up quickly.

"The oracle will recover." The immortal tucked Haana's blond hair behind her ears. "You'll be mine someday, when you're old enough and have come into your ralenta power. Then no one will touch you. No one but me."

Detoa scoffed. Mavell pulled back his shade as Sel, the Eternal Child of Shadow, led his unsuspecting charge through the glass doors into the courtyard. The two collectors moved along the balcony for a closer view below. In the courtyard, the Veiled Man occupied the octagonal platform of the wraith gate. Sel ascended the eight steps, holding Haana's hand.

Three bronze rings rotated within the gutters upon the wraith gate and eight bronze poles rose from holes at each corner, grinding and spinning against their stone housings. Attaching to each pole like a net, a fog of shadow solidified for a second before vanishing, along with the three people. The poles sank, disappearing beneath the intricately carved platform. The bronze rings slowed to a stop.

The two collectors stared at the empty gate from the balcony. "I never thought Selvator Kane to be sentimental, or a child-lover." Wrinkling her nose, Detoa picked at a blotch of dried blood on her sleeve.

"He's neither." Mavell leaned against the railing. "He's grooming her for a convenient binding. He'll be quite disappointed when he finds out she doesn't have a shred of ralenta power. Too bad for the girl. Sel is a wolf among wolves."

"How can you know she has no shade craft when she's only five?"

He pointed to his forehead. "I've seen through her eyes. By the way, what do you recall about the name Agroth?"

Detoa stared, her brows wrinkling. "Agroth. Man or immortal?"

"You tell me."

"I think . . . hmm. Something to do with the Fires. Or maybe the Devourer."

He licked his crooked teeth. "Ah yes, the ancient terrion king who was given the power of Absolute Death by Sovereign. When he died, priests divided his power among his warriors to continue fighting the Devourer."

"They were called the Order of Mortari, weren't they?" she asked.

Mavell adjusted his scarf. "Indeed. Supposedly, Agroth reincarnated during the Fires and killed the first legion of immortals."

"Perhaps he's returned." Detoa tapped a finger against her mouth. "Perhaps he killed Hoven."

"The dead remain as they are, Detoa. But the power Agroth wielded was enough to kill countless immortals. That power may indeed live on, and it appears someone has started using it again."

# 2

# VULTURES

*Lorinth, Taria*
*May 3, 1190 PT*
*One year later*

*Jon*

Jon Therman's shoulders sagged under his damp wool coat. He shifted on the wagon bench, loosening the reins of his wood ox. The stout creature shook its shaggy head and trudged through the mud. Wind beating against Jon's aching back, he stood to stretch.

Sitting beside him, Shane zem'Arta slept while leaning on the brace, his boots resting on the rail. The hood of his tattered coat partially covered his face, exposing his open mouth full of pointed teeth. Water dripped from the silver-blond scruff of his neck; it trickled under his collar. Despite the cold rain, the mercenary relaxed as if basking in the sun.

Must be a troll thing. Jon smirked.

He thought of the sunrock furnace in his parlor as the fog of his breath rolled into the May air. After a month of traveling, Jon longed for his wife's warm embrace. The ghost of her laughter played upon his ears, and his fingers tingled at the memory of her silky auburn hair. Ahead of him, however, a mining caravan stretched for several miles.

Wood oxen pulled wagons loaded with sunrock. One of the animals stumbled, its belly sinking into the mud. The convoy stalled. While cursing and kicking, a worker yanked on the animal's upturned horns, only for his foot to tangle in its mane. He slipped. The creature dragged him a few steps before he rolled free.

Drawlen militiamen in tan uniforms accompanied the caravan transporting smith-grade stones. These heat-bearing rocks were worth stealing if one was daring enough.

Jon urged his wood ox over a rise, Shane jostling next to him.

The dreary town of Lorinth lay in the valley before the Deep Wood bordering Taria. As if some force held it back, the forest of tall, twisted trees arced north. A barren field stretched for a half mile between the woods and Lorinth.

The slate roofs and stone streets held a sheen with murky puddles dotting the square. Like Jon's wagon and the caravan, the black paint on the buildings peeled, evidence of a temperamental winter.

From Jon's vantage point on the west road, the southern highway stretched like a bending river across the hill-dotted landscape. Merchant carts clogged the road, fighting through muddy trenches. Only a few vendor tents populated the market square. The impending Life Harvest—the twice-per-decade Drawlen pilgrimage—usually drew a bustling business to this sleepy village.

Then he saw it. There was no mistaking the gray-clad rider galloping across the field from the north. A Drawlen ranger advanced, skirting the town and picking up speed. Jon pulled the reins of his wood ox to a mewling halt.

Shane woke, planting his feet for a pounce and placing a gloved hand on the pistol at his belt. At the same time, a crash came from within their covered wagon.

Jon swiveled at the noise.

His teenage daughter emerged, pulling open the canvas flap. "What's the deal, Papa?"

Ella's coat rested loosely over her shoulders, her curly brown hair matted and pressed to one side.

"Stay in the back, mouse," Shane said.

She glared, pursing her lips much like her mother. "Stop calling me that!"

"There's a *vulture* coming, Ella." Jon gently closed the flap.

Shane clenched his fists.

Jon nudged him. "You'd better get back there too, you know. These are Drawlen rangers. A troll in these parts will mean a lot of questions."

Shane scoffed but obliged, lifting the flap. "I thought you said your town was quiet." Then he disappeared inside the wagon.

Jon sighed as he tied the bonnet. He scratched the back of his left hand, where his open-fingered glove covered the Drawlen brand once marking him as a slave. A familiar anxiety flooded his mind: This new life was a dream. He would wake up, a slave boy in the mining barracks, chained to a wall.

His chest tightened as the rider's face came into view a few yards ahead of him. Joran Wilde returned Jon's cautious stare. The metal emblem of a hawk glinted on the sleeve of his uniform. *A lieutenant.* It had been years since Jon had seen his brother-in-law; he'd been deemed bad company for a Drawlen officer. Joran's jaw was set, his lips drawn tightly, his eyes harder than what Jon remembered. He looked like a true soldier of a Drawlen order as he sped past on his sweating brown steed.

Jon shivered.

Children's laughter cut through the moment. Jon's two sons leapt and ran along the wagon caravan toward him.

Jeb arrived first, loose russet curls bouncing over his eyes. He dove onto the bench and linked his skinny arm with his father's, whispering, "Nate got into a fight with Will Loren again."

Jon chuckled, brushing grass from the eight-year-old boy's coat.

"Jeb, you traitor!" Nate yelled.

Jeb stuck out his tongue just as Nate's foot sank into a puddle.

Nate sported a cracked lip and a purple bruise on his left cheek. His wool coat now donned as much mud as it did patches, and he skipped with a limp. Having freed his boot from the mud, he scrambled into the cart and beamed at his father. "It was a . . . friendly sorta fight."

"Did you shake his hand with your face, then?" Ella emerged from the back of the wagon and wedged herself between Jeb and Nate on the bench. She met her father's gaze and discreetly glanced at the floor of the wagon, indicating Shane had hidden himself in the smuggling compartment.

"Hey, I was defending *your* honor, ya know."

"Oh? Does my honor need defending by an eleven-year-old boy when I'm out of town?" Ella smiled and poked Nate's bruised cheek, but he swatted her hand.

Jeb giggled. "Will said he was going to give you a kiss for your fifteenth birthday, El. Nate knocked him right to the ground." He swung his fist through the air.

Ella's face flushed as she shoved her hands into the mass of her coat. She fumbled for a reply when a rustling in the grass disrupted their conversation.

A pale, sickly man broke through the sagebrush and stumbled across the road. Clad in a worn smock and metal wrist cuffs, he was sweat-soaked and bloodied. A bang echoed over the valley with the man's next step, accompanied by the thud of a round shot. Blood spattered from his chest as he collapsed into the mud.

Lieutenant Joran sat on his horse further into the field, rifle aimed and still smoking. He steered his horse to the body and began the tedious task of reloading the weapon. When finished, he slung the gun across his back and sat at attention while his horse sidestepped away from the bloody corpse, whose skin dulled and grayed with each second. Glancing briefly at Jon, Joran bowed his head and turned his eyes to the road.

Ella gasped. "Papa, isn't he—"

Jon raised a hand. "Look away, children."

Ella and Jeb stared at the floor planks, but Nate glared at his estranged uncle while another soldier on horseback trotted by and halted next to the body. Jon scowled as the man frowned at him. Captain Percy Duval was a man people went out of their way to avoid.

"Third North Rangers," Ella whispered with her head bent downward.

She really was well suited for this business.

The captain sneered at the body lying in the mud. "I would have preferred him alive, Lieutenant. This wretch had made a contract with forest demons."

Joran saluted. "My apologies, Captain. Your orders were to catch him at any cost. I aimed for his legs, of course, but the scoundrel ducked."

Jon stifled his laughter, too afraid for himself and his children. The fugitive had certainly not ducked.

Duval gritted his teeth. "Bring him to Lorinth and hang him over the temple stage. He'll get no burning. Superstition is going out of fashion, Lieutenant. We must replace it with fear."

"Yes, sir."

Duval flashed Jon a wicked grin, sending a tremor through Jon's chest. Joran steered his horse between them. "Just some bystanders, Captain."

As Duval's gaze lingered, Jon feared the ranger's schemes. He considered Shane's loaded crossbow stowed under the bench. He relaxed when the captain nodded and kicked his horse into a trot, heading toward town. Letting out a long breath, Joran dismounted next to the fallen man, now a rigid corpse.

Jon flicked the reins. The children huddled silently as the cart jostled into the ruts of the narrow highway.

Once they entered the town square, Nate jumped off the cart, skirting a puddle. "I promised Powet I'd help him in the shop today." He ran to the smithy next to Donfree's Trading Post.

Although he dodged the wheels of a passing cart, he crashed into a lamppost. The housing shook, the door flung open, and a spray of bright, blue sunrock powder spilled, glittering in the wind. Several identical lampposts lining the streets of Lorinth cast a haunting light against the overcast sky.

"Watch your left side." Jon waved. Before disappearing into the smithy, Nate waved back.

Jeb said goodbye and ran after his brother, leaving Jon and Ella to steer the cart around the trading post and into the barn. The boys seemed eerily unaffected by the scene they had just witnessed.

"Papa, shouldn't we shut the door?" Ella hopped off the wagon and tugged the barn door along its rusty tracks.

Jon shook himself and stepped off the cart. The door scraped along the wall as he pushed, sending flecks of black paint swirling like falling ash. When the latch clicked, Shane slipped out of hiding.

"Stay here tonight." Jon pointed to the loft.

"Abad is in town. His horses are out back," Ella said. "He could leave with you at first light."

Shane pulled his hood back, frowning. In the dim light, his eyes held their own glow, and the horizontal scars on his cheeks, one on the right and two on the left, could pass for smears of dirt. His dull, silver braid matted against his thick neck. "What about leaving tonight? I'd rather not risk a tangle with more Drawls."

"Really? I thought it was your hobby," Ella said, earning a scoff from the mercenary.

"You'd be walking *into* a tangle leaving at night with vultures in town," Jon said. "It's less suspicious to leave in the morning." He dug in his pocket and handed his daughter a coin. "Get Shane some dinner and blankets. He's going to lay low until he's *well* out of Taria."

Shane grumbled while removing his bedroll from the wagon.

Ella patted Shane on the back and left through the side door.

Jon opened the tailgate of the wagon. Removing crates and burlap sacks, he stacked them against the wall under a shuttered window. Shane shed his coat and pushed back his sleeves, revealing intricate tattoos. His leather vest still had streaks of blood from their disastrous smuggling acquisition in Estbye.

Jon moved the last crate from the wagon. "Shane?"

"Yeah, Jon?"

"Don't ever ask me to do this burning kind of work again."

"What? You're not having fun?" Shane snickered and opened the smuggling compartment. Inside lay an unconscious man—bound, gagged, and blindfolded.

"No, Shane. I'm not having fun."

# 3

# HANDSHAKES

*Lorinth, Taria*
*May 3, 1190 PT*

*Jon*

"Still out cold," Jon said.

Shane pressed his boot into the comatose man's waist, shoving him to the side of the smuggling compartment. "Essence of Alunen. Burning good stuff. This fool won't wake up 'til I want him to."

Jon fitted a plank along a groove in the middle of the compartment, snug against the man's back. "And when is that, exactly?"

"When he's in a Freeland gallows." Shane sported his fanged grin.

"Won't he die of starvation before then?"

Shane laid a burlap cloth over the body. "There's a reason it's known as the Deathless Sleep. Expensive stuff."

"Speaking of expenses." Jon held out his hand. "I think I've earned my payment."

Shane pulled a vial of glowing blue liquid from his pocket and handed it to Jon. "I won't lie. Somulet Elixir doesn't live up to its reputation, or its price, in my opinion."

Grabbing the vial, Jon dropped it into his vest pocket. "It's a last resort."

The side door of the barn opened, prompting Jon to shut the compartment of the cart. Ella entered, laden with blankets and a clay bowl of steaming stew. Her hair had been retied, her face scrubbed pink. "Cameron says Mom wants to see you right away. She's at the sick house."

Jon nodded. "See that Shane gets whatever else he needs." He gave her a kiss on the forehead and headed toward the door.

"How about a foot rub?" Shane leaned against the ladder and lifted his leg.

"Sure, right after I poison your dinner." Ella shoved the bowl of stew into his hand, spilling some on the ground.

Jon strode to the sick house, which stood opposite Cameron Donfree's Trading Post. Atop the limestone building sat a crumbling steeple, the husk of a Creedan church—a remnant from before the Drawls' invasion two hundred years earlier.

The corroded hinges on the sick house door creaked when Jon heaved it open. Patients crowded the long room, lying in beds or scattered along the dusty floor. Jon stepped around a Drawlen priestess from the Order of Eruna as she chanted over three dying patients. Clay urns lined a high ledge along the walls. They sat empty, waiting patiently for the nearly dead that populated the cots. After hollow-eyed priests filled the jars with ashes, children too young to comprehend their contents would paint colorful interpretations of a desolate world on them.

When Jon spotted his wife measuring medicine, he shook that macabre picture from his mind. Ruth lifted a patient's chin with her right hand, branded with the Drawlen seal, much like Jon's own.

After the priestess left, Jon slipped behind Ruth. He smiled when she flinched. Even a retired thief was hard to surprise. He kissed her on the neck and dropped the flask of blue liquid into her apron pocket. "Fifty drams of Somulet," he whispered. "Made strictly by the Yvean recipe."

She spun, kissed him firmly, and cupped his face. "Thank you, love. It's so good to see you." Then her smile faltered. "What's wrong, Jon? What happened?"

Jon glanced around the room. A tension hung here, the same tension hovering over the whole of Lorinth. "Vultures are in town."

Ruth stroked Jon's beard and sighed. "They've been here all week."

"Have you seen your brother?" Jon asked.

Her gaze darkening, Ruth looked away. "Only from a distance. I figured it wouldn't look good for Joran, associating with me while he's on duty." Her voice cracked, but she cleared her throat, pointing to the door. "Never mind now. Abad is waiting for you at the tavern." She kissed him again, her soft lips lingering. Jon's hands wandered down her hips before she pulled away. "Later, my love. I'll be leaving soon with the boys. I want to start David on this as soon as I can." She patted her apron pocket concealing the vial.

"You should stop in at Cameron's before getting the boys," Jon said. "Someone would like to see you."

Adjacent to the sick house, the vast iron doors of the Drawlen temple swung open. A procession of soldiers and priests of Refsul, chief of the Drawlen immortals, emerged from the doorway onto the platform.

Jon stepped farther into the square, void of pedestrians.

Superficially, the temple was the most beautiful building in town. A masterpiece of marble walls, hard lines, and bronze molding, it stood three stories tall, each tier smaller than the last. Stained-glass windows lined the building, and silver and bronze inlaid the eight-pointed Star of Sovereign, a repeating border along the door and window frames. Ten-foot bronze statues of Refsul and Eruna faced the square on opposite ends of the platform.

Captain Percy Duval supervised from the doorway as the soldiers hoisted a petrified corpse onto a post in the middle of the stage and secured it with ropes. They granted no courtesy of a pyre. The body would be left to rot instead of burn, condemned to hell, giving it no path to paradise according to the Drawls.

Jon swallowed hard, suppressing his nausea. Across the square from the temple, he quickly ducked through the door of Loren's Inn and Tavern. He shouldered his way through the noisy crowd, a strange mixture of drunken songs and nervous murmurs ringing in his ears.

Some off-duty temple guards were drowning themselves in ale and lamenting the presence of the Third North Rangers. When Jon reached the bar, he received a hard, enthusiastic slap on the back from Arik Leir, a lieutenant of the temple guard. "Welcome back, ol' boy. You look like you've had vultures—hick—circling you." Usually a temperate man, Arik wobbled on the stool, red-faced and slurring.

Jon returned the gesture. "Well, their party seemed rather dull compared to this."

Arik waved to the boy working the bar. "Ha! Willy, get this soggy sod a drink. Something strong. I'm buying. At least this uniform is good for wages."

William Loren, a tall boy of fifteen with a pale face set off by deep brown hair and a lanky build, nodded to Arik and Jon. An impressive bruise encompassed Will's right eye. "Evening Mr. Therman. What'll you have?"

Jon grunted. "Have any brandy?"

"Sure do. Good stuff . . . I mean, so I'm told." Will fumbled under the bar, glass clinking against metal. He stood, pouring from a brown bottle into a dented mug. When he slid the full drink across the counter, Jon caught the boy's wrist and raised his brows.

"You should have your old man teach you to wrestle properly, William. And also"—he let go of Will's arm and leaned back—"if you're to give my daughter any kind of birthday greeting, make it a handshake."

Will forced a laugh. "I wasn't—I haven't . . . I mean, yes, absolutely, sir. A good old-fashioned handshake." He exhaled and scurried away when a patron called for him.

Arik lifted his mug, clunking it against Jon's. "He's a fine kid, ya know. Keep scaring off the nice ones and Ella will have to marry a scoundrel like you."

Jon chuckled and took a sip. A few guardsmen approached, clapping Arik on the shoulder and dragging him into the crowd. Arik stumbled forward, still grinning, and performed an off-key and off-color version of a nursery song.

Carl Loren, the pub's proprietor, appeared across from Jon at the bar. He was a soft-faced fellow, stout with cheery eyes and wiry blonde hair—nothing like his son. "Abad and Cameron are in the back." Carl's forehead glistened with sweat, hands running along the bottles at the rail.

Jon nodded and grabbed his mug, ducking through the canvas curtain into the kitchen. He nodded to Margaret, Carl's wife, who tended to the oven. She smiled and waved, pulling out a loaf of bread. Abad il'Dani waited near the doorway to the back room at the end of the hall.

"How did t'ings go in Estbye?" he said in a rolling Aginomian accent.

Jon approached and shook his hand. "Good enough." He resisted divulging the troublesome acquisition he and Shane had made in the lower docks, or the bodies of the three hired guards floating in the canal. "Although, if you're ever inclined to steal from a Freeland bank, don't."

Abad nodded, scratching at his tidy charcoal beard. "Al'dough being on dis side of it is certainly good for business. Cameron just gave me de lad's deposit. Maybe we should set up an operation in Palim?"

Jon raised his brow. "This little job is as far into Freeland dealings as I care to go. It's all politics, and I don't want to meddle in that. Not to mention, it's a country full of mind-reading terrion."

"Right. Well, might want to keep an open mind on dat first point. Politics is de only business left dese days, smuggling or not." He ushered Jon into the back room, locking the door behind them.

The space served as Carl's office, storage for dry goods, and a discreet meeting place for Jon and Abad's smuggling operation. Four sunrock sconces cast a pale blue light, silhouetting two women seated at the table. The light contrasted with the red glow from the furnace stones in the small hearth adjacent to the door. Abad grabbed the tongs and turned the stones, creating a warm draft.

Across from the hearth, Jon braced himself against the shelves lining the wall and scowled at one of the women. He fidgeted with the silver lettering on a book, one of many occupying the space. Carl's love of literature had grown into an obsession. He owned most every legal book in this Drawlen territory, and some illegal ones.

Cameron, a stout woman in her fifties, sat at the red table in the center of the room. Her hands shifted to the brace of pistols at her hips, and she glared at the person across from her, Krishena Dantiego.

Krishena, Rogue Master of Rotira and one of Drawlen's most wanted criminals, paid her no mind, leaning forward in her chair. The beads woven into her dreadlocks clinked together. They accented her coal-colored coat spotted with steel rings while her pale eyes contrasted against her dark skin.

"Jonathan Riley," she said in a brassy voice with a subtle tSolanian accent. If she was going for friendly, her choice of words was a bad start.

Jon took a long gulp from his mug. "That's not my name, Dantiego."

"No matter where you go, Jon, you can't change where you come from." When she smiled, her white teeth and the long scar running from her brow to the base of her jaw caught the lantern light.

Abad placed the tongs on their hook and joined the women at the table. "Rogue Master, you came here to make a proposal, not open old wounds."

Krishena nodded, the metal cuffs on her neck clanging like a far-away chime. It was a mystery how she managed thieving while wearing all that jewelry.

Draining the last of his mug, Jon slammed it onto the table. "So, what brings you to this exotic destination?"

"I'm here on behalf of the Ruvian Protector, Alistar Soral."

Cameron sighed, rolling her eyes at Jon. "Knew this was a bad idea."

"Ruvians." Jon spat the word like something rotten.

"He's asking for your help, Master Smuggler," Krishena said.

Jon shook his head. "You know my answer. And this certainly isn't a conversation to have in a town crawling with Drawlen rangers, where my *family* lives."

"My shades protect us." Krishena waved a hand in the air, and for a few seconds, the swirling, smoky vapor surrounding them appeared, like a dome of fog within the room. "No one can see or hear, even if they burst through the door."

Jon glowered at Abad. "Did you know Ruvians were involved in her little proposal?"

Abad huffed. "Jon, hear what she has to say."

"You know I want *nothing* to do with my father's business."

Krishena rose and stood eye to eye with Jon, every bit a rogue master despite being only thirty. "I care nothing for Lucas Riley's business. But surely you saw the little show your friend Duval put on today? The Mortal Reform Act has passed in Pelton and Depbas. Clerics need only the suspicion of a contagious illness to sentence anyone to the Life Harvest. They will be lining up political dissenters by the hundreds. Duval could be putting *you*"—she jabbed a finger at him—"on the caravan if he wanted."

A tremor rose in Jon's hands and moved to his shoulders. He gripped the edge of the shelf behind him.

Krishena leaned back, crossing her arms. "And have you forgotten who pulled your daughter from the clutches of Lord Hayden, or who got your family to this quiet little town while collectors sniffed around in Estbye, or who watched over your children while you were locked up in Langry?"

Jon shoved her against the stone wall, grabbing her dusty lapel. "You burning fool! I don't need Drawlen's enemies clamoring for my attention while Duval sniffs around like a hungry wolf! Do you think working with you and your Ruvian cronies is going to make me less a target for Drawlen's death game?" He stepped back, wringing his hands and gritting his teeth. "I knew Soral would come slinking around for something like this. Back then, you told me his aid was an act of good will." He poked his index finger at her. "So, go tell him to burn in a fire."

Cameron jumped up, head and shoulders shorter than anyone in the room, and Abad moved behind Jon. Krishena leaned against the wall and flattened her collar with gloved hands. "Feel free to tell him yourself."

Jon startled when another man appeared in the far corner of the room, shadows drawing away from him like curtains. Krishena was notorious for this kind of dramatics. Abad leapt for the door while Cameron pulled her flintlock pistols, pointing one at Krishena and the other at this tall, bronze-skinned man. For a moment, everyone held their silence.

"Cameron, put them down." Jon pointed at her holster.

"I knew this was—" Cameron withdrew her guns.

"*Dis* is why I don't like bringing rogues to meetings." Abad took a seat.

"*This* is sorcery!" Cameron threw up her hands as she sat.

Krishena cleared her throat and jutted her chin. "I am a ralenta, not a sorcerer."

"Enough." Jon addressed the man, who had remained quiet and pensive. "What in the fires are you doing here, Soral?"

The man stepped forward. He had the weathered face and posture of a seasoned soldier. Dressed in a simple brown justaucorps and matching waistcoat, he wore his shoulder-length black hair bound at his neck in a southern Corigish style. A sheathed cutlass rested at his side, and an unpainted crossbow hung over his shoulder.

Jon had seen many depictions of this man, the one Drawls had labeled the Arch Traitor. Mostly, they were demonic caricatures on murals or puppets in street shows. The Drawlen clerics hated—and hunted—no one more than Alistar Soral.

"You must be getting desperate if you're coming to me in person, Arch Traitor," Jon said.

Alistar laughed. It was a warm, amused sound—nothing like the villainous cackling urban puppeteers assigned to him. "I suppose introductions are unnecessary, Master Smuggler. Shall we get to business?"

Jon shook his head. "I have no interest in your business."

Alistar let out a long breath. "You have no idea what I've had to do these past years to keep your family out of Drawlen claws, Jonathan. All I'm asking is for you to listen."

"Whatever you want with me, I'll have none of it, so be on your way—quickly." Jon pointed to the door. "I want nothing to do with you or any Ruvian."

Alistar bowed his head, then regarded Jon with piercing eyes.

Jon's upper lip twitched. And there loomed Drawlen's villain.

The Arch Traitor spoke in a measured tone. "One day, you may find that sneaking around under Drawlen's nose to fill your family's bellies is not enough. However much you dislike us, we are your blood, Jonathan Riley." He rested his hand on the pommel of his sword. "I'm asking you to be a part of something greater than smuggling sunrock or helping a Freelander spy nab a bank robber. You rely solely on your own luck and cunning. Both will eventually fail you."

Rage coursed through Jon's veins. He ripped off his leather glove and displayed the Drawlen brand on his right hand. "This is the result of your *greater* cause. My father died in a cave somewhere because he was more interested in chasing old relics than caring for his own burning family." He smacked the table with his glove. "Then your people tried to use me to start a war when I was but a child! My mother died getting me away from your power-mad cult. I spent six years in the bottom of a Drawlen mine, and now your little recruiting operation has brought the vultures down on us, Forest Demon!"

Alistar's hard gaze fixed on Jon. "That man on the temple steps outside, he was mad. Nothing to do with us at all. But the Drawls don't care. They will use any means, any lie to keep power. Yvenea and tSolan have slipped from their grasp, so they are coming down hard on the territories they still have. The west will suffer dearly for eastern freedom."

"So move your people to Yvenea. Why must you bother me?"

"You've a gift for moving things around without anyone noticing," Krishena said.

"It's good long-term business, Therman," said Abad.

Jon closed his eyes and ran his hands over his face. "David put you up to this, didn't he?"

"He said you'd throw a tantrum," Cameron said. "His words."

Jon let out a long, slow breath and opened his eyes. Finally, pragmatism won over his grudge. "What do you need moved . . . where and when?" he said. "But"—he held up a finger—"don't mistake this for an agreement. I just want to know the scope of the job."

"We have sixty thousand souls to move from various secret locations. After that, we hope to bring the Ruvians from Pelton and tSolan. They number almost two hundred thousand." Alistar held out both hands. "We are preparing a place suitable for our numbers and with room to grow. But we need supplies brought there—discreetly."

"What kind of supplies?"

"The kind you build a city out of."

"And your timeline?"

Alistar planted his hands on the table, leaning forward. "As long as it takes."

"And what are you offering us?" Abad asked.

Alistar nodded to Krishena, who pulled a leather pouch from her jacket, laid it on the table, and rolled it open.

Cameron exhaled slowly. "Holy burning fires."

Jon and Abad leaned closer, golden light warming their faces as they gazed at the most beautiful object they, and probably anyone alive, had ever seen. A glowing necklace lay before them, the likes of which surpassed the worth of all the jewels in the world. It was as if the morning rays of the sun had been strung together. Solisite gems were the subject of many rumors and legends. Supposedly, they adorned the crown of the Emperor of Greq across the Utharen Ocean and made up the wealth of the royal Yvean vaults.

"This is the smallest piece." Krishena stroked the gems on the necklace. "A good-faith deposit."

Abad gazed at Jon with bewilderment and delight. "Let's build a city, eh, Jon?"

"Well, we should probably . . . authenticate this first."

*Shane*

On the shallow loft in Cameron's carriage house, Shane yawned as he sprawled in the hay. He folded and unfolded a penny knife Ella had picked off one of the thugs they'd dispatched in Estbye. He leaned forward, considering how else to vent his nervous energy, then grunted and tossed the knife in the air. Thurse—or more commonly, trolls—were a rare and unwelcome sight in this northern territory.

When the side door creaked, Shane froze. He expected Cameron or her shop manager. But the woman who stepped into the barn was neither. Once he recognized her, Shane pocketed the knife. Her hair was the same deep red mass of curls he remembered, her most distinctive trait. In the last seven years, she hadn't aged much, but there were more lines on her pale face, more weariness in her eyes.

It took her only a moment to spot him. Her hazel eyes widened. "Well, I certainly wasn't expecting you, lamb."

When she grinned, Shane noted the features she shared with her daughter. He huffed at the nickname. It made him feel like the boy who had once crouched on the ground at the mercy of this cold-eyed ex-rogue with a knife to his ear. "Hey, Ruthie," he said as he stood.

Ruth climbed the ladder and hugged Shane in her usual motherly way while he awkwardly kept his hands at his side. "What brings a sharptooth Freelander to our humble and overly superstitious little hamlet?"

"Espionage."

"Ah," Ruth patted her cheeks while they both sat. "And you were having so much fun, you decided to share it with my husband and daughter?"

Shane put a hand to his chest. "Coincidence, honest. I needed to move something without turning heads. Jon's good at that. El's a lock-picking prodigy, by the way. She's got a bright future."

Ruth laughed. "She's also got no regard for danger. I'd appreciate it if you don't drag her into a fight next time."

"Sorry about that."

They sat quietly for a while.

"How are they—Tessa and Remm?" Ruth asked.

Shane took a deep breath. "Your sister is—she's in deep. I don't hear much other than what Liiesh tells me. I wish I could say more. But Remm is his usual self. Restless for a fight. Making things messier than they need to be. I swear he's made for this work."

"Hmm. Well, tell him to write when you see him. El and Nate love your letters, but they're always disappointed they're not from their brother. Threaten him if you must. You're good at that."

Shane snorted. "Will do."

"I need to head home." Ruth swung her legs onto the ladder. "I think if the boys saw you, they wouldn't be able to keep their mouths shut. Maybe next time when vultures aren't circling all over town."

"Yeah, I guess. Later, mother bird."

"Good travels, Red Wolf."

Shane watched her leave the barn, then picked at the hay. Seeing Ruth Therman brought back memories both painful and wonderful: *"Don't waste your life being that pirate's lackey. He'll turn you into a wolf. Choose your own fate."*

He had become a wolf, regardless of escaping a life of piracy. Still, Ruth's words had changed his life.

*Jon*

Jon entered the yard behind the tavern. Instead of calming him, the cold night air only energized his seething. Sure, Alistar's offer was, well, irresistible. But that didn't mean he wanted to work with Ruvians. He tugged at his beard and kicked at the gravel.

Both moons—the pale blue Vitaeus and its giant red neighbor, Mortemus—shone full and high, bathing the town in eerie threads of silver and crimson.

Jon tracked past the yard, where two silhouettes appeared at the end of the alley near the front of the tavern. The profiles of Will and Ella drew nearer to one another.

Jon's breath hitched, his body tensing and heart pounding.

Will moved slowly, like a foal taking its first steps, and reached out. Jon bit his lip, torn between pretending he wasn't there and leaping between them—until Will finally closed the gap and shook Ella's hand.

They spoke briefly, but Jon was too far to understand. Then Will walked away, leaving Ella alone, her head drooping. Jon beamed but concealed his approval as he approached.

Ella jumped when he put a hand on her shoulder.

"I'm bushed, El. Let's head home."

"Uh . . . sure." She avoided looking at her father and pointed to the small, open-topped wagon she had pulled from Cameron's barn, their wood ox hitched and mewling quietly.

When they hopped onto the bench, Jon took the reins.

As the wagon jostled along the east road, Ella glanced over her shoulder. She glared at Jon, a scowl on her pink face. "*You*—you got to him, didn't you!"

Jon shrugged, failing to hide a triumphant smirk.

# 4

# THE STORYTELLER

*Lorinth, Taria*
*May 3, 1190 PT*

*Jon*

Jon prodded the wood ox east toward the Therman Farm. "Won't it be nice to sleep in our own beds tonight?"

Ella bit her bottom lip and plunged her hands into her pockets. She had sat silently the entire three miles home. As they turned onto their property, she sprang from the bench and marched to the house, leaving Jon to park the wagon.

He yawned and pulled the animal into the pasture between the barn and garden. Most of his frustration had waned into exhaustion. The glint from both moons cast bluish-red shadows across the stone shed as he trudged by.

The house had remained the same since his teenage years. His stay then had been brief but memorable. Now, thirty years later, the single-story building still stood securely, nestled into a hill with an exterior wall of fieldstone. The roots of hemlock trees held the roof intact. Cool sunrock light streamed out the windows framed by limestone arches. The smell of fresh bread greeted Jon as he opened the door and stepped onto the flagstone of the parlor next to the kitchen.

Ruth turned the sunrocks in the furnace, which bridged the two rooms. She removed a loaf pan from a narrow oven next to the furnace, then stepped through the archway to meet Jon with a lingering kiss. Jon pulled Ruth closer and traced her jaw with his lips as she giggled.

"What's bothering El?" she whispered.

"Being fifteen." Jon turned his attention to the kitchen, where his surrogate father lay on his cot. "How did David do with the elixir?"

Ruth shrugged. "It's medicine, not a miracle. He wanted to talk with you, but . . ."

David's snores filled the room.

"Speaking of, I'm off to bed." She yawned, kissed the back of Jon's hand, and started down the dim hall toward their bedroom. "Don't be long." She looked over her shoulder and winked. Jon stared after his wife with a stupid, boyish grin. He was quite ready to follow when a gravelly voice called from the kitchen.

"I'm not sleeping." David struggled to sit on his cot, rubbing his thickly bearded cheek with a calloused hand.

Jon trudged into the kitchen.

David's wrinkles appeared more pronounced in the month since Jon had left for Estbye than in the entire thirty years he'd known him. Though an impressive age for a Tarishman under Drawlen rule, the man's physical resilience had waned in his mid-eighties. His sallow skin and haggard breath gave further evidence. How long before the Drawls decided David Therman had outlived his usefulness?

Jon pictured the urns in the sick house. Another scene flashed in his imagination: *Urns, filled with ash and painted with the whimsical illustrations of a child's mind, rattled in nets hooked to the side of an iron-caged cart. In the cage, ashen-faced people sat crowded together, and death, a faceless figure clothed in shadow, drove the cart with an air of leisure.*

As he sat on the bench next to the cot, Jon disguised his inner turmoil under a layer of sarcasm. "Resting your eyes, were you?"

"Praying and waiting for you, Jonathan."

"Praying I wouldn't strangle our new business partner?"

David rubbed his wrapped ankles. "Ach."

Jon pushed his hands away. "That'll only make it worse, old man."

"That's the problem. I'm old."

"You waited up for me so you could complain?"

"No, I want to speak with you."

"We had an agreement. You said you wouldn't involve me with the Ruvians."

"I haven't. I told Alistar you'd refuse."

"You told Cameron I'd throw a tantrum."

David grinned. "Oh, yes. I did, didn't I?"

Jon shook his head. "I'm not happy about it, but—"

David's brown eyes twinkled, and he nudged Jon playfully with his bony elbow. "Quite the little trinket, isn't it?"

"Was it stolen? They said they found it in the Dead Lands. I find that unlikely."

"Why not? It's a whole country of ruins. And even if they robbed it from a Dead Land tomb, it would technically be a Ruvian treasure. And speaking of trinkets and treasures." David rose and jostled over to a far corner of the kitchen, digging through cluttered shelves and returning with an unpainted wooden box.

Jon ran his hand through his hair. "You could get arrested for having a thing like that."

"I could be arrested for a great many things, and so could you, Master Smuggler." David traced the engraving on the cover, a seven-tongued flame surrounded by Ruvish writing. "Your father asked me to save it for you. I never opened it. That privilege is yours." He pressed the box into Jon's hands. "I had thought to give it to you sooner, but, well, you've made your opinion of your heritage quite clear, and I've respected your wish. But frankly, I'm running out of time. We are running out of time." Then David collapsed on his cot.

Holding the box, Jon rose. "Get some rest, old man." He walked down the sloping hall leading to the bedrooms, the contents of the box clanging with each step. Confirming his decision, he paused at the open door of the cellar. He would work with the Ruvians, but he would not be one of them. He tossed the box onto a pile of crates, where it tumbled next to the wall. When Jon closed the door and made his way to the bedroom, his shoulders slumped as he watched Ruth sleeping soundly. He crawled into bed and kissed her forehead.

Jon spent the next few weeks in turmoil. He felt simultaneously trapped and enthralled by the potential of working with the Ruvians. Although he had resolved to forget the box, it nagged him. His frustration soon changed to worry, however, as David's health declined while the Third North stalked the Lorinth countryside.

The creak of the front door, followed by Ruth's weeping, awakened Jon just after sunrise in late June. He clambered out of bed and rushed to the parlor, where she sat crying on the floor.

He knelt and wrapped his arms around her. "What is it, love?"

He followed Ruth's gaze toward the kitchen, where David lay snoring on his cot. She shuddered and whispered to Jon, "The elixir—it isn't working. Joran came to the sick house last night and told me Duval is coming to take David on the Life Harvest. The caravan leaves *today*." She buried her face in Jon's shoulder, trembling with sobs.

After a few minutes, David cleared his throat and called for them.

Ruth wiped her eyes as she and Jon entered the kitchen. "I didn't mean to wake you."

David lifted himself upright and patted Ruth's back when she sat next to him. "Not to worry, dear. Duval's intentions are no surprise. Besides, Sovereign's ways are at work. We all knew this day would come, and I'm ready to face my final journey. I've been ready for quite some time."

Jon pulled the bench next to the cot. "You . . . you could go to Sidras, David. You could live among the Ruvians." The thought appalled him, but the idea of David in the grim procession at the Life Harvest in Drawl was far worse.

David sighed. "To what end? Death will come to me soon, no matter where I go. Besides, wouldn't Duval find it suspicious that only after his lieutenant's warning do I hide myself? Joran took a great risk. And surely, your family would reap awful consequences if I avoided this fate. You know, long ago, I decided not to hide from the world. Why should I turn back now?"

Squeaky hinges interrupted them as Ella stepped out of the bedroom she shared with her brothers. When she entered the kitchen, she met her mother's tear-filled eyes. "They're coming to take him, aren't they?"

David motioned for Ella to come closer. He took her hand and met her gaze. "Yes, the officers will come soon, and I'll go with them. Don't be troubled, Ella. Think instead of all the very lost and frightened people I'll meet along the way. Think of the hope I could bring them before the end." He brushed a brown curl away from her face. "Now, wake up your brothers for breakfast so we can finish our story."

Rubbing tears from her eyes, Ella sniffled and nodded.

When she left, David lay back down, and Ruth started frying bacon slabs. Unable to bear the heavy mood, Jon tucked himself in a worn chair near the furnace.

The children rushed past him and planted themselves at the side of David's cot as he sat up. Jon fumbled with his pipe and found himself enraptured by David's masterful storytelling.

"Let's see. Where did we leave off?"

Jeb screeched. "Regem the Selfless was facing down the general of the Tyrant's vanguard!"

"Yes, yes." David clasped his hands and leaned forward. "So, the young hunter, wounded from an arrow to his shoulder, weary from battle, faces his final foe. The towering, heavily armed Karthan warrior looms before him." He drew his arms over his head. "The monstrous creature looks down at the boy and laughs. 'You would stand between the great Faust Dragonsbane and his throne? Drop your sword, and I will offer you a merciful death!'

"But Regem is unafraid. 'I am but a vessel of Sovereign. As long as he gives me breath, I will be like a mountain between your false king and his prize.'"

As David spoke, Nate and Jeb sprang from the floor and sparred with imaginary swords. They settled down after Jon scolded them.

David smiled and placed a hand on his chest. "'So be it,' says the general, and he raises his claymore, bringing it down upon Regem's head. The boy lifts his humble blade to block the blow, but it shatters." David raised his hands to block a phantom blow, and the children squirmed. "But Regem's faith is not in his sword. It is in the words of the Saint who has charged him with this great task. And so, Regem lets the broken blade fall and takes the Saint's gift from his pocket."

"Oh! The dragon's fang," Nate yelled.

"Yes. He lunges forward and thrusts the fang into the skin of the general's ankle. Sharper and more deadly than any weapon of man is the tooth of a dragon. Even for the ogres of Faust's wicked horde, the dragon's poison brings death. The general quivers, howls in anguish, and falls dead.

"But Regem's victory is brief, for the world gate is opening. Its great golden rings cease their spinning and stand upright. A cloud of mist spills from its center. For a moment, all is silent." David thrust his fist to his mouth and coughed violently. He waved a hand as he recovered. "Then, the thrum of metal against metal and boots on stone fills the valley. The mist clears, and through the magical gate, Regem can see into the land of Greq many thousands of miles away. There, on the threshold of the gate, is Faust the Tyrant, seated on his fiendish dragon, with the whole of his forces marching behind him."

Ella handed David a mug of water.

Mumbling his thanks, he took a sip and went on. "And so, with the life already leaving his lungs, Regem picks up a jagged rock from the ground. He rushes to the pedestal at the base of the gate, tosses aside the sunstone that powers it, and smashes the mechanism with the rock in his hand, forever ending the age of the World Walkers. The golden rings quiver and sway. Faust lunges forward, but he is too late. The last human voice Regem hears is Faust cursing him in anger. Now, Regem is trapped in the solitary Valley of the Gate with no help for his wounds and no way home. But it is a worthy sacrifice, for he has saved his beloved Palimar from falling once more under the cruel thumb of Faust the Tyrant."

Jeb and Nate whooped and took up their imaginary duel once again. Ella laughed and shook her head.

"So, dear ones," said David as the boys settled down. "That is the end of our final tale. But tell me, why do you think our hero turned out to be Regem, the lowly huntsman, and not the king or any of his knights, or even the mighty shapeshifter? What did the Saint see in this young man that the others lacked?"

With oohs and grunts, Jeb and Nate competed for David's attention, but it was Ella's calculated answer that won over the commotion. "He trusted in the wisdom of the Saint instead of his own power, even when it seemed foolish or hopeless."

David applauded, and they spent a few minutes discussing the story.

Jon leaned forward in his seat. "Children, help your mother with breakfast."

Nate moaned, but Ella dragged him to his feet and Jeb followed them to the table.

David joined Jon in the entry room, and they sat across from each other in their worn straw chairs for the last time.

Jon's gaze flitted to the front door, sunlight filtering through the wide gap at the bottom. He pictured himself at fifteen, standing in that very doorway and looking back at the old man in the straw chair with disdain. "Burn in hell!" he had shouted before walking out of the house and out of David's life. The next time he stood there, eleven months ago at age forty-four, he'd been newly released from prison.

"We've spent many hours in this room, you and me," David said, breaking Jon's reverie. "I taught you to read in here. And your children as well. In fact, your father and I spent many hours here, sitting, just like this." He patted his armrest and grinned, though his eyes were sorrowful.

After several minutes, Jon took a deep breath and made the request he had vowed never to utter. "Tell me—about my father."

David smiled as if Jon's words had lifted a burden he'd been aching to shed. "Lucas Riley was an impressive young man, full of passion. Most Ruvians were very closed off from the world for a long time. Others lived in slums and had forgotten their heritage. We were dying out when your father was born.

"He was one of the last descendants of the old kings. Every clan wanted him as their own. When he was a boy, he was moved from one of the strongholds in the mountains to Sidras to escape a local epidemic. On the way, he saw the long line of journeyers heading to the Life Harvest to be sacrificed. That image haunted him.

"He was determined to make his people strong again. Strong enough to aid Drawlen's castaways, those deemed too weak or old to be of use. Strong enough to reclaim a place of our own, to live freely without the fear of Drawlen oppression." David curled his hands into fists. "He risked not returning to you and your mother. But it was worth it, Jon. It was worth the risk if it meant he was one step closer to realizing that vision.

"Your father died when his work had barely begun. Don't get the impression I wish you to take up his fight. Vengeance, while it makes for a good story, ruins a man like no other ambition. But the Ruvians are without their rightful leader." He pointed at Jon, his eyes darkening. "Without you and your family, the bloodline of kings is lost."

Jon leaned back and sighed. "Kings and bloodlines don't mean much these days, David. Everything is about power."

"And who, but you, has the power to give the Ruvians a new home?"

"Just because I can build a house doesn't mean I want to live in it."

Horses whinnied outside, disturbing the tension. Ruth rushed into the room and peered through the distorted windowpanes. "They're coming."

David struggled to his feet and faltered.

Jon grabbed his arm and helped him up. "David, I just—"

Fists pounded on the door, echoing through the house. When Jon opened the door, Percy Duval greeted him. The captain's eyes alighted in satisfaction as he regarded David's feeble form.

David boldly stepped over the threshold and hobbled up to him. Outside, Joran stood at attention next to a horse-drawn cart, where a sergeant waited in the driver's seat.

"Nice of you to join us, Therman," Duval said.

David straightened. "Must be getting slow if they have rangers working the Life Harvest."

Duval spit at his feet. "Silence, Therman. Respect is still in order."

David grunted and spun around. The three children, now standing in the yard, rushed to him. He hugged Ella and kissed the tears on her cheek. "Cling to hope, sweet girl." He turned to Jeb, who gripped his sister's hand. "Courage, Jebadiah. Find your courage. Understand?" Jeb nodded, tears swelling his round, soft eyes. David then put a hand on Nate's shoulder. "Remember our lesson today, Nathaniel. Put your hope in Sovereign's truth, not in your own strength." Nate nodded, jaw quivering. Finally, David faced Jon.

Before he could speak, Duval whacked David in the back with the flat of his sword. "Move it!" He pushed the old man against the cart, but David struggled to climb in.

Duval sneered at Jon and Ruth. "You've come a long way from crawling on the streets. You are now the official holders of the Therman property. Don't waste it." Duval tossed a brown envelope at Jon, who fumbled to catch it.

Behind Duval, the sergeant cursed and shoved David face-first into the cart.

Nate charged past Duval, screaming profanities. Duval stepped toward him, but Joran moved between them. Jon ran after Nate and grabbed his collar. As the sergeant drove the cart away, David clutched the rails.

His eyes wide, Joran stood face-to-face with Duval. Despite this, his voice was even. "Captain, let me take charge of these whelps. Father Ferren is waiting for us at the temple."

Duval scowled at Nate with such hatred, Jon feared he'd be holding his son's corpse before the day's end. In silent desperation, Jon offered a prayer to David's god, the Ruvian god, his father's god: *Sovereign, David says you are the Great Protector of the weak and broken, so here we are. Protect us.*

To Jon's astonishment, Duval relented. "Very well, Lieutenant." He mounted his horse and followed the cart.

Once Duval disappeared down the road, Joran addressed Nate. "You fool! He would've run you through without a second thought."

Jon put his arm around Nate's shoulder. "Please, he's just a boy."

Joran glanced down the empty road. "Keep your boy in line. There's no need for you to lose another one. Listen, I'm being reassigned to Shevak, so I'll accompany David as far as the Modrian Mountains. He'll be well cared for."

"Either way, he goes to his death. What does it matter?" Jon said.

"One day, you and I will rise above this, Jon. Until then, I'll look out for you as best I can." Joran nodded to Ruth. "Goodbye, sister." Then he mounted his horse and rode away.

Nate pulled back from his father, shaking his fists. "How could you let this happen?"

Jon caught him by the arm. "We don't have a choice, Nathaniel."

"We do. You're just a coward!"

Jon gripped Nate's shoulders. This child of eleven had the fog of a war-weary soldier in his hazel eyes. For a moment, Jon remembered five years ago, staring into the dark eyes of his then fourteen-year-old son, Remm. His shirt had been torn and there was blood on his hands. Jon shook the image and narrowed his eyes at Nate. "Listen to me, boy. I take risks every day to keep this family together."

Nate glared, then spat on the ground. "I'd rather be alone and free than together and waiting to die!" He pulled himself out of his father's grip and stormed into the shed, slamming the door.

Ella smiled at Jon sympathetically and led Jeb toward the house. The boy rubbed at his tear-streaked face as he looked over his shoulder.

Ruth put a hand on her husband's back, squeezing his shoulder.

Jon hung his head. "He's . . . just a boy, Ruth. He doesn't know what he's saying."

# 5

# THE RED WATCH

*Setmal, Yvenea*
*May 22, 1190 PT*

*Shane*

As Shane zem'Arta entered Setmal, the capital of Yvenea, the sunset turned the sky a dazzling magenta. He drove his horse-drawn cart toward the Freeland embassy, a large manor of pearly stone, stained-glass windows, and steep hipped roofs. From the pillars of the front porch hung seven flags representing the coalition city-states of the Freelands, bordering Yvenea to the east. The largest was the Palim flag, a golden sun silhouetting a crescent moon on a black expanse.

Shane rode through the marble archway of the carriage yard. Stopping the cart alongside the embassy, he saluted the two watchmen on either side of the drive by pressing his left arm into his right shoulder. The two black-clad guards mimicked him.

The doorman, dressed in a gold-trimmed red coat, scowled as Shane hopped off the ramshackle wagon onto the cobblestone. When the troll dropped his hood, however, the servant immediately stood at attention. "Good evening, Captain," he said. "I didn't recognize you in that—"

"It's called blending in, Hemley."

"Yes—thoroughly done, sir."

A large, gold-trimmed carriage drawn by two steely white horses rolled into the yard. Hemley scurried to the carriage door and opened it with a flourish. A middle-aged woman and a teenage girl exited, picking up their brightly colored skirts and stepping around a puddle. They resembled each other as mother and daughter, right down to their wide, golden eyes, pointed chins, and pale-yellow hair.

The brightness of their eyes and long, narrow pupils identified them as thurse—or trolls as they were called in Palish. Their kind normally frequented the Freeland embassy, but it was wholly uncommon to see women and children. Their outfits, which put them right at home in the Yvean courts, rarely appeared on Freelanders.

"My ladies." Hemley held the door open and smiled. "Your room is ready. I'm sure you are quite tired after a long day at the palace."

The mother lifted her chin. "It's not so much the royal court as it is these ridiculous outfits, Mr. Hemley. I will never understand Yvean style. Vastly impractical."

The daughter giggled and twirled as she stuffed a loose curl into her elaborate hair pinning. "I think it's marvelous, Mother."

Shane chuckled, earning a scowl from the mother.

"Venna, dear. You're here for your razt'vos, not to twirl around in corsets. Focus."

The girl tripped out of her spin and dropped her gaze. "Sorry." When she looked up, her attention settled on Shane. She momentarily froze, her eyes widening.

"Venna! Come along." The woman snapped her fingers, and the girl nodded fervently.

"Ladies." Shane inclined his head. He wondered how quickly a lovely girl like her might be devoured by predatory noblemen while she completed her traditional Karthan rite of passage. Her claws and fangs wouldn't deter the aristocrats of the Cilé Faíl from preying on her obvious naiveté.

The mother grabbed the girl's elbow, pulling her toward the manor entrance.

"He had three marks," Venna said. "Three!"

Her mother huffed. "I don't know what your uncle is doing, hiring thugs and murderers. Hurry along."

Hemley closed the great green door behind the women. "You really should get out of those rags, Captain. Folk are already mistaking you for riffraff."

Shane scratched at his cheek. "Even in a uniform, the scars are all a Freelander will see." As he rounded the cart, he motioned to Hemley. "Come here. I have a present for Leron, and I need your help delivering it." Shane climbed into the bed of the cart and forced open the secret compartment, revealing the comatose body of Daeven Kritcher.

"You have . . . a distinctly morbid taste in gifts, Captain."

The nearby district clock chimed in the tenth hour before Leron Novelen finally came through his office door. He carried his dusty blue coat tucked under one arm, and his chest-length gray hair fell loosely around his shoulders. Alight in the shadow of the room, his clever golden eyes appeared bloodshot and puffy.

Shane perched on a stool in the corner near the door. He relished the Red Watch Commander's startled expression at the unconscious body propped in his desk chair.

When Leron slammed the door behind him, the many framed paintings and documents on the walls rattled, and Kritcher's body slumped forward, face slamming into the stack of papers on the desk.

Leron drew in a frustrated breath. "Zem'Arta . . . you fiend."

"You're welcome." Shane folded his arms over his chest and smiled.

Leron jumped and fixed Shane with an annoyed glare. "You left your crew behind." He then threw his coat over an armchair, stepped around the mahogany desk, and closed the heavy curtains. For a moment, he examined Kritcher's body with clinical interest, then tipped him onto the floor and collapsed into the seat.

Shane walked across the room and sat in the armchair facing the desk. "I work faster alone. And Remm has a hundred wanted posters in every city west of the Modrian Mountains."

"Your crew has been a nuisance." Leron moved stacks of parchment and thick envelopes from his desk to a growing pile on the floor. "Leo banned them from his house weeks ago. They've been terrorizing the embassy staff ever since."

"Why do you think I left them all behind?"

Pointing at Shane, Leron glared. "Zem'Arta, that is on you. They're your crew. Train them or replace them."

Shane pulled at a loose thread on the chair's upholstery with an extended claw and blatantly changed the subject. "I heard you were in Shevak. Trouble in Drawlen paradise?"

"I was on assignment."

"Look at you, working the field. I thought you just told the rest of us what to do."

Leron leaned forward. "I was managing the rather sensitive mess you and your crew made, actually."

"You mean the Setvan informant I secured for you?"

Leron shook his head. "She's fickle and skittish. And her price is high."

Shane folded his arms, leaning further back in his seat. "Then use one of your other temple spies." He threw up his hands. "Oh, right. You don't have any others. The Red Watch hasn't had ears in the Setvan Temple in its entire existence."

"Was it worth nearly exposing our entire operation?" Leron asked.

Shane narrowed his eyes. "You tell me. I turned a disaster into the best chance the First Lord's ever had to gather intelligence on Drawlen."

"Hindsight is a poor defense." Leron sighed and gestured to Shane. "But you're right. Foolish, reckless, and *arrogant*—but you're right. We've never been this close to having an upper hand before."

Licking his sharp teeth, Shane smiled. "So, I get a raise?"

Leron arched a brow. "I recall you telling Harry you wanted to be paid in Drawlen blood."

"I was being funny." Shane plucked a wide-brimmed hat from the side table and flicked the outrageously long plume stuck in its brim. "Nice hat. Doesn't really seem like your style, Novelen."

Leron reached across the desk and snatched the accessory from Shane's hand. "I'm preparing for my next assignment. The Freeland ambassador to Yvenea has taken ill and retired. I've been appointed to take his place."

Shane tilted his head.

"Don't give me that look! It'll be a healthy change of pace for me. Besides, my son, Orin, is entering his first year of university here in Setmal. And my niece Venna is staying with me to complete her razt'vos. She's studying ancient languages."

"The blonde girl?" Shane asked, receiving a nod from Leron. "Might want to keep her away from the courts. They'll eat her alive."

"That's why I'll be assigning Sid to Orin's guard. You'll have to find yourself another enforcer."

Shane suppressed a groan. Sid was the only member of his crew he liked, even though the man's affinity for young women often landed him in hot water.

"Why not Morgel, or even Remm? They're human. You'd have less trouble getting approval from the Yvean constable. Besides, that womanizer will be just as bad as a Yvean arist—hanging around a pretty little thing like her."

"Sid vel'Forr knows better than to cross me," Leron said. "My son trusts him. I trust him. And Constable Asteryn trusts me. He was one of the officers who helped me during the Three Days' Night."

"Will I be taking orders from Harry, then?"

"No. You'll be returning to Palim." Leron grinned and jutted his chin, his blunt fangs glinting in the cool lamplight.

Shane sprang to the edge of his seat. "Why?"

"The First Lord's order." Leron folded his hands and leaned back. "He didn't say why. I suspect that you and your crew—especially Remm—wandering around the Drawlen territories like vagabonds makes him nervous."

Bending over the desk, Shane pointed to Kritcher's heaped form on the floor. "I was snatching this fool on *his* orders."

Leron waved a hand. "You certainly took your time with it."

"Do you know how hard it is to move an unconscious body across twelve hundred miles of highway crawling with Drawlen rangers and collectors?"

Leron settled into his chair. "How *did* you manage that all by yourself?"

Shane leaned against his armrest. "There's a Tarish smuggler I know."

"And how are you acquainted with this fellow?" Leron squinted, always wary of Shane's outland connections.

"He's Remm's old man, and a mutual enemy of Henrik Lowe." Shane spat the pirate's name, scowling.

"Very well. You depart tomorrow. Get your crew ready."

Shane left the room with a sigh and headed to the second-floor parlor. He found Remm sprawled on a chaise lounge, his awkwardly long legs bent over the back of the chair. He clutched a voluminous, ancient-looking edition of *The Rise and Fall of Vulta: Thurse of the Motherland*, written in tall Karthan letters.

"Can you even read Karthan?" Shane asked.

"No," Remm admitted in his high, chipper voice. Along with his tSolani dark skin and slender frame, he must have gotten his mannerisms from his late mother, for he seemed nothing like Jon. "But the illustrations are quite lovely." He flipped the book to show Shane a detailed wood print of a severed head on a pike. Then he slapped it shut and rolled over, kicking his legs behind him and folding his hands under his chin like an eager child. "So, how was your little solo adventure?"

Shane slumped on the plush couch next to the hearth stacked with bright yellow sunrocks. They held no heat but gave the room a homey glow. "Fine."

"How's ol' Jonny?"

"Could have found out yourself if you wanted."

Remm flipped back, tucking his hands behind his freshly shaved head. "Pretty sure I wasn't invited."

Shane gave a bitter guffaw and tossed a pillow at him. "It's never stopped you before. Although it was nice not having to clean up bodies after you. You'll be pleased to know that when we get to the Freelands, you can kill all the Drawls your twisted little heart desires."

Remm stuck out his bottom lip. "There aren't any Drawls in the Freelands."

Shane kicked his feet onto the lounge table. Bits of dirt and gravel fell from his boots onto the shiny surface. He dug an envelope from his vest and tossed it at Remm. "Some mail for you. Your siblings would appreciate a reply now and then."

Remm's eyes lit up as he plucked the envelope from the floor with a hum. "How is our little mouse?"

"Snarky as ever." Shane pursed his lips. "She misses you."

Remm stroked the envelope with his thumb. "Hmm. Just her?"

"I'm sure Jon has a tragic lack of trouble-making in his life. Ruth asked about you too. I didn't see the boys. I had to get out of town pretty fast."

Remm huffed, then sprang to his feet. "C'mon. I've got a little surprise for you."

Shane shook his head. "Is it the same as last time?"

"You know, zem'Arta"—Remm put his hands on his hips and cocked his head—"you won't explode if you have a bit of fun now and then."

Exhaling, Shane settled deeper into the sofa and closed his eyes. "Just tell me."

"Since dear ol' Sid is ditching us to chase Yvean skirts, I got us a new recruit."

Shane slowly opened his eyes. This was bound to go poorly. "Okay . . ."

"He's a ralenta, one of the strongest I've ever seen." As if it somehow helped his point, Remm waved his hand, prompting one of his shades to swirl around the room, momentarily snuffing out the light from the hearth.

"Remm," Shane groaned. "I'm too tired for this. I'll meet him in the morning."

"He's ten."

Shane jolted upright. "What?!"

Remm quivered. "I've never even heard of a ralenta coming into their craft that young. And he's so burning strong already."

Shane slammed his fist on the table, glaring at Remm. "You. Recruited. A *child?*"

"Purchased, technically."

Shane jumped to his feet. "What in the fires, Remm Therman?"

Remm folded his arms. "Burning hell, Shane! What was I supposed to do? Let the Drawls have 'im? He could be the most powerful ralenta in all Palimar, and there he was, on the slaver's block in Drawl, *eighty-six* marks. They didn't have a damn clue what they had."

"Where is he?"

Remm gestured over his shoulder. "In the carriage house with Carris and—"

Shane's patience evaporated at the mention of the kobold mercenary. "You left him with Carris!" He stomped toward the door.

Remm fell back onto the chaise lounge, mumbling, "No appreciation," and cut open Ella's envelope with a throwing knife.

Shane stormed out and marched through the halls of the Freeland embassy, causing the few servants still going about to cower from his path. When he reached the open door of the carriage house, he heard familiar voices and the steady thud of metal hitting wood.

"Blazing fires, kid," Carris's gravelly voice said. "You've lasted twice as long as anyone." *Thud. Thud.* "Maybe he's blind." *Thud.* "Don't you think his eyes are bit weird? The whelp's not even blinkin'."

Shane steeled himself, resolving not to murder the goblin no matter what stupidity she was engaged in. He pushed through the door just as a knife sank into the far wall, an inch from the ear of a small, blank-faced boy.

"Ey, Captain. Want a round with the rookie?"

Carris, a muscular kobold woman with long, sharply pointed ears, offered up two small knives, one in each hand. Several more lay on the ledge of the half wall beside her.

Morgel, the Greqi ralenta, who surprisingly had a shirt on for once, lounged on a hay bale in the corner.

Shane rounded on Carris but stopped short when a sleepy voice drifted from the loft.

"Bad idea, Carris." Sid stuck his big head full of long brown dreadlocks over the edge. Blotches spread across his tan face—apparently sleeping off several evening drinks. He grinned at Shane, showing off his sharp, pearly teeth.

"Out. Now!" Shane ordered.

Carris shrugged and threw her two remaining knives into the wall behind her. Morgel rolled to his feet and backflipped off the haystack. He followed Carris to the door, pointing at the woman and twirling his finger in the air, as if to say, "She's crazy."

Carris snickered and smacked her husband in the rear. "You love it."

Sid fumbled down the ladder and followed Carris, hands in his pockets and ducking through the door.

With the crew gone, the boy against the wall tottered forward.

"Not you," Shane said.

The boy froze, his dark eyes wide. If he'd been with Remm since he was purchased in Drawl, then Sid and Shane were probably the first thurse he'd seen. And the two of them fit well with the bedtime horror stories so popular in the outlands.

Shane approached the boy and dropped onto a dusty trunk next to him. He motioned for the boy to sit on the bench along the wall. The child, who looked distinctly tSolani with his tightly curled black hair, sat hesitantly.

"Did they feed you?" Shane asked.

Keeping his eyes on the stone floor, the boy nodded.

"What's your name?"

"Bren," he whispered.

"You from Drawl?"

Bren shook his head. "tSolan."

"Do you know what you are?"

With his head tilted, Bren raised his eyes. "Shadow friend."

Shane nodded. "What did Remm tell you about us?"

"You're Freelanders. Assassins."

"I don't deal in slavery, Bren. You're not staying."

Bren's eyes flashed between relief and fear. "Will you—will you sell me to the clerics?"

"I'm not selling you, kid. I'm taking you home. Back to your family."

A smile crept onto Bren's face, but then it fled, and his shoulders fell, his gaze returning to the floor. "No family."

Shane rubbed his eyes and exhaled. "Well, if you want, you can come along with us. You need to learn to use your power. Remm's a whelp, but he's a decent teacher."

Bren lifted his head. "Where are you going?"

"Back to the Freelands, to Palim."

"The Dragon City?"

Shane laughed. "Don't get too excited, kid. There aren't any dragons. Just ornery old terrion." When Bren wrinkled his brow, Shane added, "Fliers."

"What will I do there?"

"You can work with us if you want." Shane's stomach turned at the prospect of enlisting a child this young. "Or you can get a job as a message carrier. I wouldn't blame you if you wanted to ditch this crazy circus."

Bren paused, frowning. "I think—I think I'll stay with you." He glanced at the door. "They're not so bad."

"You've had worse things thrown at you than knives?"

Eyes still on the door, Bren nodded.

Shane slapped his hands on his knees. "All right, kid. Get some rest. You can bunk with Remm." He rose and assessed the boy's outfit: an ill-fitting smock covered his slender frame. "We'll find you some decent clothes before we leave in the morning." Then he headed to the door.

When Shane waved him along impatiently, Bren followed. Before they left the carriage house, the boy pulled on Shane's sleeve. "Sir, the woman said she's kobold. What—?"

"Goblin. Elf. But don't ever call her an elf. She'll aim for your throat, and she never misses."

The boy gulped. "What—what are you?"

"Thurse," Shane said. Bren's face wrinkled, so he added, "I'm a troll."

"Like the big fellow, Sid? And the master as well?"

Shane swiveled. "The master? Leron?"

Bren nodded.

"He's half-troll," Shane said. "But he's not your master."

"You are, then?"

"No one owns you Bren. I'm offering you a job."

Bren grinned briefly before his face resumed a blank stare. He followed Shane out of the carriage house and remained in his shadow until Shane brought him to Remm's room.

Despite his exhaustion, Shane's restlessness drove him to wander the halls of the embassy. When the district clock sounded the second hour after midnight, he entered the third-floor conservatory, a converted balcony at the back of the manor. The glass room usually offered a spectacular view of the city, especially with the crystal-blue streetlamps alight in the darkness. But rain poured from the sky, and the windows were fogged, making the urban scene look like a blurry painting. In the room, stone benches dotted the narrow paths between small fruit trees and tiered beds of exotic plants.

Shane rested his forearm on the brick ledge of a flower bed, his tattoos contrasting with his skin in the dim light. Deep in thought, he spun a dainty silver wedding band between the fully extended claws of his thumb and forefinger. The creak of the glass door echoed in the vaulted conservatory. A moment later, Leron strolled around a thick hedge. Wearing a blue sleeping robe, the older man leaned against the half wall next to him. Shane turned his attention back to the ring.

For a few minutes, they stood silently, listening to the rain. Leron leaned his head back and stared at the glass ceiling. "The pain never goes away . . . but it does get easier. You should find something to believe in other than vengeance."

Shane retracted his claws and stuffed the ring into his pocket. "Tell that to my dead wife." He strode out of the conservatory, glad to be leaving this city—this whole burning country—in the morning. Too many memories remained here. Too much of *her*.

# 6

# TRINKETS AND TRESPASSERS

*Lorinth, Taria*
*July 28, 1190 PT*

*Jon*

After sunset in late July, Jon wrestled with convictions he had resisted his whole life. He sat alone at the green kitchen table, resting his hands on a wooden box—David's last gift. The Ruvian seven-tongued flame adorned the lid.

Alistar had said he would send a message after the Life Harvest caravan left town. Now, several weeks later, Jon's impatience grew like gnawing hunger.

Since David's departure, malice crept into Jon's heart. What would this new smuggling job mean for his future, for Palimar's future? What damage could he do to Captain Percy Duval and the Drawlen radicals of Taria and Corigon with a smuggling network built to move cities?

Finally, Jon flung open the box. Perhaps his father had left a solisite bracelet to match the jeweled necklace Alistar used as payment. Jon's face fell. Inside lay a leather-bound book, three agate pendants fastened with silver wire to leather cords, and a dagger in a bronze sheath.

Jon examined the stone pendants. He imagined using the set to afford a death mark on Lord Bruce Hayden, the man who had turned his family's lives upside down five years ago. The items weren't worth a death mark—or even a ten mark. Still, they seemed unique. Ribbons of red, yellow, and gold weaved through the oval pendant, the innermost design resembling the flame on the lid. The second gem featured brown veins twisting like roots digging into the earth. The third resembled a sprouting seed in shades of green.

Jon pushed the stones aside and lifted the iron dagger. It had a narrow pommel and a double-edged blade. The sheath was stamped with intricate filigree and symbols. The metalwork and worn condition suggested an ancient origin. Perhaps it was a Ruvian heirloom, but the runes along the hilt and sheath weren't Ruvish.

Jon set down the dagger and retrieved the book, weighing it in his hands. Lighter than expected. He ran a finger across its black leather spine, strangely warm to his touch. He then leafed through the hundreds of thin pages. Each section concluded with a different signature. In red ink, the date 7 June 903 PT scrawled across the opening page, making this diary about three centuries old.

The entry, written in Old Ruvish, lamented the Ruvian's flight from their dying homeland in the south, when they met a legion of Drawlen purifiers at their northern border. Jon skimmed the rendition, having already heard the story countless times, until he reached the last line.

> *Thus, the cursed Immortal secured Palimar for himself and began his reign as the Second Tyrant. Our only hope now lies in secrecy and faith that Sovereign will one day raise us from the ashes of this injustice.*
>
> *~ Jacob Mathis III, last living heir of Ruvia*

Jon flipped through pages of packed text; sketches of cities and creatures both common and unreal; maps of Palimar and the wider world; and even orders of battle. Finally, he came to the last entry but refused to read beyond his father's signature—*Lucas Riley*. He shut the book and leapt from the bench, heart pounding.

"Thrilling read?" came a stranger's voice.

Spinning around, Jon faced a thin man standing in the kitchen doorway. Jon stumbled over the bench and backed against the wall with fists raised. "Who are you?"

The stranger bowed, his gray tunic scrunching at his rolled sleeves, revealing a gruesome scar on his left forearm. "I'm an old friend of David's."

Jon glanced at the dagger on the table. "How did you get in here?"

"This isn't exactly a fortress. Is it, Master Riley? Or is it Therman?" When the man laughed, his eyes twinkled. But the creases around them held the burden of an old soul. His posture and his set jaw seemed oddly familiar.

"*Who* are you?"

"You don't remember me? We met when you were very young. I showed your mother the way out of Sidras."

Jon's brow furrowed. He was only six when he and his mother fled in the night from the Ruvian hideout. He remembered an old woman—his tutor—smuggling supplies for them, and a cloaked man leading them into the wilderness. As the memory flooded his senses, Jon gasped when he recalled a name. "Richard."

"Hello, lad."

Jon's hand moved instinctively to his waist, but his pistol lay on the side table in his bedroom. "You can't be Richard. You would be an old man by now."

"But I am. I was your guardian when you were a child. I've been watching over your ancestors since before the land of Ruvia died, before the Fires, before Faust the Tyrant fell."

Richard no longer seemed ordinary, but something ancient and dangerous.

"A Blessed Immortal." Jon's eyes widened, his hands shaking at his sides.

"It's a bad joke, you know, calling us Blessed. It's more a curse."

"Did Alistar send you?"

Richard seated himself at the table, resting his hands on the chipped surface. "Right down to business. Very well, Jonathan. I've come to escort you to Sidras."

Folding his arms, Jon huffed. "What in the fires makes you think I would ever go back there?"

"You fled from Sidras at its lowest point. It's quite different now. And did you not already agree to Alistar's proposal?"

"Why can't he come to me?"

"This venture requires the blessing of the entire Sidrian council. We can't risk bringing them here." Richard examined the dagger and pendants.

"Do they mean something?" Jon asked.

"I've never seen them. Lucas liked to collect things." Richard grasped the dagger. "This is a Vultan knife."

"Vultan?"

"An ancient thurse empire that's long dead. They brought our human ancestors to Palimar as slaves thousands of years ago. The rift between men and trolls goes much deeper than Ruvia and Kartha."

"And the stones?" Jon asked.

Richard set aside the knife and held the red pendant. "Ordinary, perhaps. And yet, they're remarkably reminiscent of three of the Monuments of Sovereign." He returned the pendant and tapped each stone in turn. "The fire of purity. The roots of strength. The seed of life."

"Sentimental trinkets, then."

"Symbols of the divine," Richard countered. "And important enough for Lucas to ensure they passed to you. He carried this journal almost to his death. It's been passed down to every generation of the Mathis bloodline since the end of the Drawlen-Terrion wars."

Jon shoved the book into Richard's hands. "It's all yours. I have no use for dead men's musings."

Richard held the book in front of him. Black tendrils of shadow wrapped around it and disappeared with the book.

"You're a ralenta," Jon said. "An *immortal* ralenta."

Richard smiled. "Yes, some people have all the fun. Come, Master Riley. It is a fine night for a walk in the Deep Wood. Don't you think?"

Apart from his early childhood, Jon had avoided the forest. The Drawls forbade entrance into the Deep Wood bordering the Drawlen territories. He remembered liking the forest as a child and missing it when he left with his mother. Now, sweat trickled down Jon's forehead as he trespassed. The occasional chill washing over him told him shades encircled them. He shivered. Richard was cloaking them.

With each step, the forest thickened, the moonlight diminished, and the hoots of owls intensified. As Jon walked, the silhouettes of branches and underbrush taunted him. The smell of pines mixing with the fresh breeze offered minor comfort as he tripped on roots and rocks. Buzzing crickets and whistling wind drowned out his curses.

Jon huffed, struggling through the underbrush a few strides behind Richard. "Can't you just use a shade to trace us through this mess?"

Richard stopped and smiled. "Patience. Take a breath. Time in the woods will serve you well."

They trudged through a marsh, wound down fern-filled ravines, and hiked under sumac canopies. Emerging from a grove, Jon stepped into a breathtaking scene. Fireflies filled the clearing with their golden light. High branches provided shelter, and gnarled tree roots bound together, forming natural benches around a campfire.

The last time Jon saw a campfire, his mother had been alive. The aroma of woodsmoke thickened, and the sparks danced among the fireflies. As Jon and Richard approached, the three men sitting by the fire narrowed their eyes.

The smallest man, who wore a hooded coat, stood and drew a bow, aiming at Jon. The metal arrowhead glinted in the flames' light. The man to his left sat with his arms crossed. His red hair was cropped short on the sides, accentuating his pointed ears, and a fringe fell across his forehead. He scowled.

Jon's heart thrummed as he regarded the third man: an enormous, dark-skinned troll. His leather armor stretched over taut muscles, gleaming knives and hatchets strapped to his back, belt, and legs.

"Now here's something you don't see often," Richard said.

The red-haired man stood, still shorter than the seated troll. "Good old Richard."

"Halas." Richard nodded. Then he addressed the boy on the right. "What brings you all the way out here, Arimal?"

The boy set aside his bow and dropped his hood. He looked about seventeen, a younger replica of Alistar Soral. "Keeping the peace." He pointed his gloved thumbs to the men beside him.

The troll growled, displaying sharp teeth. "I've been perfectly agreeable, lad. Can't say as much for this whelp." The troll pointed to Halas.

"You're in *my* wood, ogre," Halas said.

Across the clearing, growls reverberated from behind the roots of a large oak. Three gray hounds slunk out, fangs bared, lips quivering, and hackles raised. They stalked toward the fire, lifting paws high over the roots.

Halas gritted his teeth.

"*Lezhat*," the troll commanded, snapping his head so sharply his thick dreadlocks swung over his shoulder.

The dogs retreated.

Richard and Arimal chuckled, but Halas crossed his arms and furrowed his brows.

"Jonathan Riley," Richard said with a twirl of his hand, ushering Jon forward. "Meet Halas Gorvenah, Lord of the Deep Wood. He usually has an unruly band of sprites running about, but I assume the Master of Hounds has frightened them off with his bad jokes."

The troll laughed and rose, easily standing seven feet tall. His leather boots crunched on dry leaves as he stepped around the fire. When he reached Jon, he grasped his wrist with the force of a vise. "Well met, Master Riley. Torok Missien, Master of Hounds."

Jon shifted on his feet. "I—um—nice to meet you, Master Missien."

"Just Torok." He slapped Jon on the back.

Jon hid his grimace with a toothy smile.

"And the lad is—" Richard looked around, but Arimal had disappeared. Halas immediately lunged into the darkness.

A yelp sounded as Halas jumped back into the clearing. Trailing him, Arimal and his bow skidded across the ground. The boy sported a bloody lip and dirty face. Halas bounded over him, plunging into the shadows once more. Grunts echoed, along with boots scraping on rock.

Torok whistled for his hounds, who circled the group, growling and pawing at the dirt.

Halas emerged with a hooded figure in a chokehold. The captive thrust a leg out and hooked a boot behind Halas's knee before twisting him around.

As the captive spun Halas onto his back, her hood dropped, and Ella's brown curls tumbled over her face. From his place on the ground, Halas kicked his foot toward her. But Ella sprang out of his reach.

"Enough, Ella!" Jon shouted. All eyes turned to him.

"You know this sneaking little whelp?" Halas spat as he rose to his feet.

"That's his daughter, you fool," Torok said. He and Richard burst into laughter.

Ella picked up the bow and returned it to Arimal.

He took it and nodded. "So, Ella Riley?" He thrust out a hand. "Arimal Soral."

Ignoring Arimal's offered hand, she tilted her head at Jon. "Um . . . Riley?"

"Later," Jon said.

Torok called off his hounds and bowed to Ella. "You know me as The Hound Man, lass. But call me Torok. An honor to see you again, and well met."

Ella returned the smile and flashed a clenched grin at Jon. "He was, um, in Estbye—one of the rescuers."

"So I've gathered," Jon said. "What in the fires are you doing here, Ella?"

"Mom thought—she thought you might do something rash, so she sent me to check on you."

"Something rash?"

"Well, I'm sure she meant drinking with Carl or burning down the barn. Not—whatever you're doing here in the woods." She studied each man in the clearing.

Halas chuckled. "Your wife sent a child to look after you?"

Richard strode up to her. "You followed us?"

Ella rocked on her heels and bit her bottom lip. "Yes."

"How?"

"She can see shades," Jon said. "Even though she's not a ralenta."

"And disarm Ruvian sentinels, apparently," Halas said.

"Sorry about that." Ella waved to Arimal.

He blushed and rubbed some dirt from his cheek. "Yeah, I could have done without your boot in my face. Clever, though, getting downwind of the hounds."

"That was just luck, to be honest," she said.

"Ella," Jon cut in. "You should *not* have followed me."

Pulling thistles from her hair, she glowered at him. "Well, I'll just ignore you the next time I see you wander into forbidden woods with some mysterious ralenta!"

"She's a fiery one," Torok mumbled, plopping back on the log.

"Her mother's daughter." Jon scratched his beard. "I'm serious. You could have—no, you *did* get caught. You're lucky they aren't—"

"Collectors? Hired thugs?" She shook debris from her boot. "What should I have done instead?"

Jon took a deep breath. "Well, it's done." He faced Richard. "She's here, so whatever arrangements you've made with Alistar, my daughter comes with me."

Ella brushed dirt from her coat.

Richard nodded. "Understood. Halas will take you to Sidras. Torok and I have a different journey ahead of us. It's a long way to the Devourer's Waste."

Halas sighed. "I think it would be better for Master Soral to take them."

"Oh? Sadiona toss you out again?" Richard smirked.

"Ha! She threatened to burn his tail too," Arimal said.

Ella cocked her head and peeked behind Halas. "You have a tail?"

"You're a very rude little girl, aren't you?" Halas said. "Kicking and tripping strangers and asking ridiculous questions."

Ella's eyes lit up. "You're a dryad?"

"I'm a skin-changer."

"Like the Drawlen Beast Barons?"

"Exactly like them," Halas said. "So be careful, *little* girl. I could transform into a wild beast right here and claw that smirk off your face."

Jon twitched, but Arimal put a gentle hand on his shoulder. "He's probably kidding."

Halas stepped forward and bent down on all fours, morphing into a large red fox. He turned his canine head and regarded the group with shining eyes. "Good day to you, good masters." He raised his black nose when his gaze fell on Ella. "Girl."

Smiling, Ella curtsied with the fringes of her coat. "Farewell, Lord of the Deep Wood. Try not to get pushed around by any other sneaking little whelps."

*Ella*

For over two hours, Ella and her father followed Arimal. A whisper of fog settled in the predawn light. They traveled upstream beside a rushing river in a ravine. Ella concentrated on matching the soundlessness of the Sidrian sentinel, suppressing the urge to ask questions.

When they came to the edge of a shining pool at the base of a waterfall, Arimal balanced along a ledge and disappeared behind the falls. Skepticism shadowed Jon's eyes as he followed, but Ella reveled in the adventure, skipping after Arimal.

While water splashed around them, Arimal heaved a flat stone and pulled a hidden lever. Next to him, a slab rolled back to reveal a dark, damp world beyond. Ella stepped over the threshold into a cave. Jon walked behind with a hand on her shoulder, keeping his balance. Inside the cave, Arimal pulled a similar lever, closing them into the passage.

A swishing accompanied the roar of the falls, and torchlight flooded the cavern. Ella flinched, still uncomfortable in the presence of fire. With the space illuminated, the camouflaged door proved to be a thin sheet of rock fastened to the cliff by wooden beams.

Arimal held the torch aloft and entered a low tunnel. As they navigated the passageway, intermittent dripping replaced the echoing of the falls.

The tunnel opened into a narrow gulch. Soon, a wooden gangway spanned the gap where the rocky ground had fallen away. Many times, they ducked under and stepped over bulges in the rock. A clear stream trickled far below the gaps in the planks. Once the morning sun brightened, Arimal doused the torch in a crevice of rainwater. Ahead, the ravine turned sharply.

"Seems your mother's been teaching you more than just medicine," Jon whispered to Ella. "How long has she been training you?"

Ella kept her attention on the path, but his judging tone nagged her. "Don't be angry with Mom. It was my idea. It's just that Remm was gone. You were gone. And when those men came—"

"You were only a child."

Ella glared at her father as they continued walking.

His expression softened, his gaze downcast. "You're still a child. You could not have hoped to save yourself."

Ella quelled the tightening in her chest. "So, I should just live in fear?"

Jon waved his hands. "No! No. I'm not angry. Not at Ruth, and not at you. I just—" He took a deep breath. "I don't want you to live in fear. And just as much, I don't want you to fall into a life of violence."

"I'm not violent!"

"Oh, not at all." Arimal stroked his bruised lip as he spoke.

Ella threw up her arms. "I was only defending myself!"

Arimal chuckled. "They all say that. Anyway, we've arrived."

Ella and Jon followed Arimal around the corner. The walkway ended at a balcony overlooking the most spectacular sight Ella had ever seen.

Arimal backed against the railing, spreading his arms toward the valley behind him. "Welcome to Sidras."

# 7

# A BITTER HOMECOMING

*Lorinth, Taria*
*July 28, 1190 PT*

*Ella*

"Oh, my fires," Ella said as she jumped toward the railing, startling Arimal and her father. "Have you ever seen anything so amazing?"

Steep cliffs encircled the Ruvian settlement and plunged into an island-spotted lake. Gigantic gray trees with fanning limbs and silvery-green leaves filled the valley. Wooden structures with thatched roofs blended with the lush landscape. Most of the dwellings circled tree trunks or else had been affixed to high branches, accessed by ladders and lifts. Some were nestled into the wide crooks of tree roots and others rested on the forest floor. Narrow bridges arched over the water, connecting the many islands to the shore just beyond their view on the balcony.

Her father's words cut through her wonderment. "It seems . . . smaller than what I remember."

Ella clutched his arm. "You've *been* here?"

He sighed and turned to the sentinel. "Arimal, could you give us a moment?"

"I'll wait at the bottom." Arimal tucked his weapon and bowed before descending the wooden steps.

Jon gripped the weathered railing, his knuckles turning white. "Ella," he began slowly. "The name you heard—Riley—it was my father's family name. He was Ruvian."

Ella's eyes widened, her jaw going slack. "Like David?"

"Like David."

Her mind blazed with questions, but her father's uncomfortable expression made her cautious. "So . . . the forest demons that Father Ferren's always on about? Those are just Ruvians hiding in the woods?"

His stony expression softened. "I think Halas and his kind might be more what Ferren imagines. But yes, they are hiding in the woods."

"Why?"

"They're trying to preserve their heritage, something that would be impossible in a world run by Drawlen clerics."

"Aren't Ruvians from the Dead Lands? Why are they so far from there?"

He tapped his fingers on the rail, one of his trademark habits. "Dead Lands, sweetling. Nothing lives there."

"Maybe that's a Drawlen superstition too," she said. "Like evil spirits in unpainted wood and soul-sucking forest demons hiding in the trees."

"I doubt these people would be here if going home was an option."

"I suppose. But you've been here. When?"

Jon's honey-brown eyes grew cold and distant. "I was born here."

She gasped. A fiddler played on the shore, his tune drifting toward them like the wind whispering through trees. Combined with the incredible view, the crisp woodland air, and the soft chatter of happy voices, it felt like a page from a story book. She studied her father, who seemed utterly unmoved by this scene. "And you left?"

He pressed his back against the rail and peered into the cloudless sky. A gentle wind ruffled his curls. "Ella," he said in a sharp tone. "This—this isn't something I'm prepared to speak about. Lucas, my father, was a descendent of old Ruvian nobility."

Ella stared at her father as if for the first time. Instead of the fiercely determined, calculated man she'd always known, he now seemed weary and immeasurably bitter.

He glanced over his shoulder at the scene beyond. "These people have been living in seclusion for so long, they're trapped in old ways of thinking, obsessed with bloodlines and prophecies. Lucas wanted to modernize them and increase their dwindling numbers by taking in outsiders. He married a Tarish girl, my mother, against his family's wishes. It divided them—divided their whole colony. Then he went off on some prophecy-chasing adventure and never returned. My mother was left alone, surrounded by people who thought she had tainted their kingly heritage. So, she ran."

Ella put a hand to her mouth.

Her father leaned forward and cracked his knuckles. "I was six at the time. They were going to take me and cast her out, probably kill her." He sighed and stroked his beard. "I am no friend of the Drawls, but I will not be a brood sire for these cult worshippers of a bygone empire. I will not let them treat my wife and children like—"

"Okay!" Ella said, louder and harsher than she'd intended. She took a deep breath. "Okay. I understand. So why did you come back?"

He laughed bitterly. "They've hired me to smuggle for them."

"Smuggle what?"

"Them." He waved toward the settlement. "I'm to smuggle them somewhere else."

Ella soaked in the far-off buildings and folk wandering the islands. On the shore, under an open-sided tent, people arranged wooden benches. "There's probably a few hundred here."

Jon nodded. "And apparently thousands more elsewhere."

"Where do they want to go?"

"They haven't told me. But they have a lot of work to do first. Which means before we start moving people, we need to move supplies."

"They're going to build a city?" she asked.

"Essentially."

"That will take years."

"Maybe."

Ella chuckled. "You seem more eager about this than you want to be."

Jon scoffed, his growing smile melting into an ugly scowl. "I most certainly am not."

Ella sprang from the rail and pounced in front of him, pointing a finger. "I saw that glint in your eyes! You were locked up in a Langry cell for years, and you've been doing run-of-the-mill, tax-evading sunrock shipments since. Then you run into a shady bounty hunter who has you carting bodies under Drawlen's nose, and it's got you all hot and bothered. You're craving a challenge!"

Jon waved his hands. "The price was—they pay well." He straightened and cleared his throat.

"You've never cared about money."

"Abad cares about money."

Ella laughed. "You've never cared about his opinion much either. This is about you." She jabbed her finger into the lapel of his jacket. "This is about being the *Master Smuggler*. And probably a little bit about revenge too."

Her father folded his arms. "Why would I help them if I want revenge?"

"Doing someone a good turn *is* the best revenge."

"Where did you hear a ludicrous thing like that?"

"Mom." Ella bit her bottom lip and fiddled with the red pendant necklace that had flipped out from under her collar.

Jon stared at the glossy agate in her hands. "Did she also tell you it's fine to take things that aren't yours?"

"Um . . ." Ella inspected the striking oval stone. "There were three. I thought you'd picked them out for me and the boys."

Jon sighed, a smile now gracing his features and softening the hard lines on his face. Warmth returned to his eyes. "Taking things that aren't yours, sneaking off into the woods, getting into scuffles . . . El, you're turning into your mother."

"Why, thank you."

Her father groaned. "Okay. Let's get this over with."

Ella and her father joined Arimal along the mulched path leading out from the gully. They passed a stable tucked under the ledge of the cliff, where Ella spied the muzzle of a mountain deer among the horses. She resisted the urge to dash off and explore every crevice of the valley.

Women in belted tunics with richly embroidered hems strung wildflowers and foliage to tent poles, rigging, and a wooden arbor near the lake. Many men and women darted to and from bridges, buildings, and a sparring ring. Most were clad—like Arimal—in forest-green tunics. They carried short swords at their belts with bows and quivers of arrows slung across their backs.

"I don't see any guns," Ella said.

"We have some," Arimal said. "But guns are loud. Easy to track. Besides, the powder is hard to come by."

Ella raised a brow at her father. "I thought you said they paid well."

Arimal laughed. "It's not the expense, Miss Riley. It's the logistics."

Beyond the crowd sat a tent where cooks loaded cauldrons with vegetables and slabs of meat.

"Is there some kind of festival?" Ella asked.

"Colas and Hazïr's wedding." Arimal grinned. "It's been a long time coming, those two. Ruvian weddings are incredible. They last seven days! There's dancing and feasting—and tournaments!" He pointed to a row of narrow birch-skin boats. "Today, they'll have canoe races and—"

"Arimal," Jon growled. "We're not here for a tour."

Arimal's cheeks reddened. "Right. This way."

He led them to one of the largest ground-dwelling structures. It was a two-story hall, with a bank of windows facing the reedy shore of the lake. On the opposite side stood an immense wooden door, a masterpiece with figures of warriors and kings carved into its face.

A man whose posture and outfit resembled one of the carved figures leaned against the adjacent wall. He looked like an aged version of Arimal, save for the many scars on his neck and forearms. "Master Riley." The man offered his arm.

Jon gripped the man's wrist. "Protector."

The man smiled at Ella. "And you've brought a bodyguard."

"Careful, Father," Arimal said. "She might be qualified for that. This is Ella, Master Riley's daughter."

"Welcome to Sidras, Miss Riley. I am Protector Alistar Soral." He offered a shallow bow.

Arimal whispered to her, "A protector is like—like a field marshal."

Ella hesitated but bowed in return. "Pleased to meet you, Protector. Aren't you—"

"He's the Arch Traitor," Jon muttered.

Ella's eyes widened. Alistar did closely resemble the propaganda illustrations she'd seen in Estbye and Depbas.

Alistar chuckled, deep lines creasing his face around his mouth and eyes. "Don't worry, miss. I'm much nicer and better looking than what the Drawls say of me. And I promise, I don't breathe fire or eat children."

Ella scratched the back of her head. "Of course you . . ."

Jon cleared his throat. "I've been told your council is waiting to meet with me."

Alistar gestured to the front door. "They are. Most of them are gathered in the Wisdom Hall. In fact, here comes the last one."

A short, elderly woman clothed in linen robes approached, hobbling with her cane. Her flat nose and shallow-set eyes marked her as Greqi. She mesmerized Ella with her kind smile and graceful beauty. The woman pulled back her hood to reveal softly pointed ears and silky gray hair pinned in a braid.

"Sa—Sadiona," Jon breathed.

Her eyes twinkled and her smile broadened. "My, oh my, Jonathan Riley." She dropped her cane—which boasted carvings like the Wisdom Hall door—and threw her arms around Jon's waist.

Ella's father stiffened, pursing his lips. He patted her on the back. When she stepped away, she studied him like a mother appraising her wayward child. "You've kept your appetite for trouble, I've heard."

"And you're still chasing folk off with threats of pyromania."

Arimal and his father laughed.

Sadiona frowned. "You must have run into Halas." She retrieved her cane and gestured to Arimal. "Did he cause any trouble for Torok?"

"Only insults, revered lady."

Sadiona closed her eyes. "I pray for the day he will eat his words, and that Sovereign will grace me in witnessing it. Then I can go to the urn in peace. And this—" She glanced at Ella. "This is your daughter, Jonathan?"

"Yes. Ella, this is Sadiona. She was . . . well, much like David was to you and your brothers. She was my tutor."

"Sadiona the Wise, we call her," Arimal said. "She's a deacon of the Serenity Creed."

Sadiona smiled at Ella. "Has David taught you our language?" she said in Ruvish, instead of the Palish they'd been speaking.

Ella grinned and replied in the woman's native language, "Yes. We speak it all the time."

Sadiona's hand flew to her heart, and she sighed. Her eyes shone when Ella spoke Ruvish. "Oh, bless him, that old bookworm!"

Tears filled Ella's eyes. "He—well . . ."

Sadiona put a hand on Ella's shoulder. "I know, child. He has seen his conviction to the end: to live in the open world, unafraid." She set her calculating gaze on Jon. "And you? Do you remember your mother tongue?"

Jon hesitated, then spoke in Ruvish. "Some—a bit."

Sadiona continued in Palish. "Perhaps this assembly will jog your memory. Shall we?" She nodded to Alistar, who moved toward the double doors.

Arimal bent closer to Jon and whispered, "I can give Ella a tour while you meet with the council. I don't mind."

"I do. She stays with me."

"Oh, please, Papa!" The Wisdom Hall looked intriguing enough, but Ella couldn't imagine being stuck in a logistical meeting while a fairytale kingdom awaited exploration. She gestured to the scene behind her. "This place is amazing. And I'll probably never see it again. Isn't this the place the priests call the lair of the forest demons? Is it true it moves around, that it's never in the same spot twice?"

Alistar chuckled as he pushed in the doors, revealing a bright, long hall. "Well, I don't know about any forest demons. We're all human here. And a few fae." He waved at Sadiona. "They move the trees and rocks around. It's how we stay hidden."

Ella clasped her hands and blinked at her father. "Please. I'll be very well behaved. Perfect, even."

"I'm not worried about you—well, a little. But it's these people I don't trust."

"You and your daughter have nothing to fear from any Sidrian, Master Riley," Alistar said.

"Papa, they need your help. They're not going to bother me and risk that!"

"If I may." Sadiona clutched her cane near to her chest. "I understand your concern, Jonathan. I am . . . deeply humbled that you've entertained the possibility of this partnership, and more so that you would step foot into this place again. However, it may be prudent not to introduce your daughter to the council. We don't want to encourage these old dogs to entertain grand ideas."

Jon took several deep breaths before turning to Ella and sighing. "Fine. But if you're not standing right here when I get back—"

"On the spot. Promise."

An hour later, Ella felt sure there wasn't a more enchanting place in the whole of Palimar than the humble Ruvian hideout of Sidras. They did, indeed, have mountain deer in their stables, as well as a litter of frost hounds just weaning from their mother.

Arimal took her along as many paths, bridges, ladders, and lifts as they could cover in their short time. He showed her inside the common halls and even his own house, which he shared with his father and younger sister, Amara, a quickwitted girl around Nate's age. Ella found her as peculiar and amazing as this secret world of the Deep Wood.

Amara joined them when they toured the village garden before returning to the Wisdom Hall.

Ella ran her hand over a stone column carved with runes at the garden's center. "What's this? I've never seen these symbols before." The column towered above them, its jagged top partially crumbled.

"We call it the Storm Stone," Arimal said. "It was here before us, before Halas and his people. The runes are Vultan. The tales say a trollish temple stood here thousands of years ago. Sometimes we'll pull up old bronze and iron tools or pottery when we plow the gardens or dig latrines. This pillar is all that's left."

"What does it say?"

Amara batted her hand. "It's a silly prophecy."

"Don't be so dismissive," Arimal said.

Amara placed her hands on her hips. "It's a prophecy about a storm that will give birth to a man with bloody eyes. He'll destroy the gods, burn cities, and grow really great fields of wheat or something like that." She shrugged, twirling her long black hair between her fingers. "At least, according to Sadiona."

"It's much more poetic when she says it." Arimal glared at his sister.

Before Ella could further ponder the Storm Stone, Jon called to her from the doorway of the Wisdom Hall. His eyes shone at the sight of her, but mixed with a frown as he shook wrists with Alistar when the Wisdom Hall doors closed behind him. Whatever they had discussed in the meeting with the Sidrian council had his smuggler's mind buzzing. He rushed toward Ella and motioned to the balcony where they had first entered the settlement.

After they said their goodbyes, Ella paused on the balcony, capturing a last look at Sidras. Jon cleared his throat and steered her toward the walkway, following Arimal.

*Jon*

Later that evening, Arimal bowed to Jon and Ella at the edge of the Therman farm and disappeared into the thicket.

Jon gripped Ella by her shoulders. "Remember, this is like any other smuggling job: You discuss it with no one. Especially your brothers. They know nothing of . . . what is it?"

Her hand fidgeted in her pocket, and she rocked on her heels. "Papa, I want to help the Ruvians."

He sighed and tugged his beard. "Then you'll be pleased to hear we're starting work on their supply runs next month."

"But I mean—I believe in what they're doing." Ella scraped her foot along the pebbly ground. "Uniting their clans. Building a place where people can live freely."

Her father huffed and swatted a mosquito on his neck.

Ella stuffed her hands deeper into her pockets. "Look, I know you have problems with them, and I don't blame you. But they've changed from when you were a child. Alistar and his children, they're outsiders. Alistar was a Drawlen general. Half the people in Sidras have no Ruvian blood at all. They—they also have a troll. Ruvians and Karthans living side by side."

He shook his head and wagged a finger. "They have one troll."

"And fae." She pushed her hand down over a bulge in her coat. But it was too late.

"What is that?" Jon glared as Ella's coat wiggled furiously.

She fidgeted with something in her pockets again, pursing her lips. "Please, Papa. It'll cheer up the boys."

He tapped his foot. "Ella."

She pulled a silvery-white puppy from her coat pocket. The tiny creature mewed and quivered in her grasp. "It's a frost hound. I'll just say I found it on the riverbank."

Jon took a deep breath, then ran his hands over his face. "All right, all right. Let's just go home."

Ella beamed, stroking the dog and snuggling it under her chin. She ran ahead of him when the boys opened the front door.

Nate and Jeb squealed upon seeing the animal in their sister's arms.

While the children sat in the kitchen fawning over the smuggled puppy and their new agate pendants, which Ella claimed were parting gifts from David, Jon sulked in the parlor. For one thing, his own daughter had concealed a live creature in her coat for several hours while walking two steps behind him—the Master Smuggler.

Ella and the boys debated about a name for the pup. Nate insisted on Ezron, referring to the Karthan rebel who helped the deposed Ruvian king overthrow Faust the Tyrant during his second reign.

Ruth stood at the hearth, broom in hand. "After today, that dog is not allowed in the house."

Jon buried his head in his hands. Once more, he wrestled in a tug-of-war between his life-long bitterness and this new unwelcome desire to reconcile his familial misgivings. The meeting with the Ruvians had gone surprisingly well. Instead of the panel of arrogant, pedigree-obsessed old men he remembered, these were humble refugees longing for the simplest of treasures: a home. Despite a host of reservations, he believed these people had changed. That didn't mean he had any interest in being one of them.

He shifted in the chair, causing his pistol to dig into his thigh. He took it from its holster, and then headed for the bedroom. When he opened the bedside cupboard to stash his gun, his father's heirloom diary laid on top a pile of books.

"Burning ralenta," he muttered. He set his gun aside, opened the false floor of the cabinet, and stuffed the diary inside.

# 8

# QUESTIONS

*Temple Setvan, Shevak*
*March 11, 1195 PT*
*Five years later*

*Mavell*

Inside the Temple of the Tree, Mavell leaned against a nude statue of Gathos the Mighty. A priestess murmured prayers while kneeling a few feet from an adjacent statue. She scowled at Mavell's sacrilegious stance. He wanted to be noticed. In particular, he wanted Tessa, one of the Eternal Oracle's fore-seers, to notice him.

She stood by a fountain beneath the broad shadow of the Tree of Eruna—a petrified structure enclosed in a glass atrium. Near her, five harem children—those born to servants of immortals and clerics—played a lively game of knuck-lebones. Haana, Tessa's daughter, laughed among them. Her defined cheeks and graceful movements showed the maturity of an eleven-year-old.

Six burning years. Six years of dead ends and denials in his search for Hoven's killer. Yet Mavell's quest for the godkiller always came back to this foreseer. Tessa knew something, but she continuously rebuffed Mavell's efforts to riddle it out.

Throngs of worshippers, servants, and clergymen bustled about the temple square just beyond the doors of the atrium. It was a festival year, a time of celebration and culling of the frivolous dregs from the populous.

Even now, three months before the Life Harvest, the frail and faithful queued at the gate between the Temple Setvan and the city of Shevak. They hoped to die within the temple rather than risk the tiresome journey to the Harvest Temple in Drawl.

A child's frustrated squeal drew Mavell's attention. Two of the children scuffled alongside the fountain. They splashed at the water until one retrieved a knucklebone.

The other child swiped for it. "My turn," he said.

"You dropped it," the other said, waving the bone overhead.

Haana stood and crossed her arms. "Mother of Dryads. Let's just reroll."

The two boys continued their tussle. The knucklebone ricocheted to land midway between them and Mavell. They chased it, halting when they saw Mavell. Their eyes widened as they stared at his black uniform and the scarf obscuring his face. They backed away. Haana held his gaze and stepped forward.

"Haana." One of the children pulled her by the sleeve. "That's a collector."

"I'm not his collection." Haana yanked her shirt from the child's grip. As she reached for the bone, Mavell used a shade to snatch it.

She followed the shade's tendril zigzagging through the air. Clever girl.

"Beautiful, isn't it?" Mavell let the shade hover before her.

Haana held out a hand. "The knucklebone, please."

Mavell used the shade to deposit the game piece into her waiting hand.

Stepping between them, Tessa scooted Haana toward the other children. "Collector, why are we graced with your presence this time?"

Mavell smiled beneath his black scarf and waved away the shade hovering before him. "How the girl has grown."

"My daughter is no concern of yours."

Mavell twirled his finger. "Yes, favored among our betters. A resident of the House of Prophecy. Future apostle of the Eternal Child."

Squaring her shoulders, Tessa drew closer, further blocking Mavell's view of the children. "And far outside your rank, Collector."

Mavell narrowed his eyes. "For now."

Tessa tilted her head, her long red tresses falling over her shoulder. "What do you want this time? More questions?"

"Oh, I have so *many* questions, oracle," Mavell whispered. He called up a shade to cloak them, blocking them from view of the bystanders. "I wonder how you have convinced the Master of Secrets of your daughter's false potential."

Tessa blanched and backed away, breaking the shade's spell. "Are you calling Selvator Kane a fool? Haana passed her trial before the entire court of apostles." She placed her hands on her hips. Behind her, Haana and the children huddled as they gathered their game pieces into a burlap sack.

Mavell let a shade manifest in his hand. It writhed over his palm, pulsing and growing to the size of a head.

Tessa remained stoic, either unable to see the shade or unaffected by Mavell's display.

"You see, Tessa, I've looked through your daughter's eyes. I know what a ralenta would have seen in that chapel the night Hoven died. She didn't see it."

Tessa lifted her chin. "She's late to her craft."

Mavell hummed and dismissed his shade. "If there is any at all. You play a dangerous game, oracle. You've secured the protection of a high immortal under pretense. But I don't blame you. This place is a snake pit, and you are a mouse. Your daughter would be one of Fenris's whores by now were it not for the protection of Mylis and Kane."

Tessa pursed her lips, hands clenched at her sides. "I foresaw the godkiller's coming."

Mavell stepped closer. "Come now." He brushed his hand along the waxy leaf of a fig tree. "Six years, and not even the inkling of another prediction? Are you not a foreseer? Foresee something."

She turned up her nose. "I have perceived only his absence, not his presence. Foresight is a delicate craft, Collector."

"When it exists," Mavell said. "Perhaps your daughter is not the only fraud."

"I know the high station of your order will be tested soon. It will not go well for you. Is that enough foresight for you, Mavell?" She looked beyond him, eyes hopeful yet cold.

Mylis, the Eternal Oracle, glided toward them, robes billowing over the ground like waves. Her two servants scurried behind. "Collector Mavell," she said. "Good morning."

"Lady Mylis." Mavell nodded and stepped back, clasping his hands behind him and curling his fists.

Tessa moved to Mylis's side, smiling at her. "The hour of the Tree approaches, Collector." Tessa's voice hinted malice. "All men must leave the atrium."

"Of course." With a bow, Mavell exited.

Outside, his partner Detoa waited. They weaved through the crowd, heading to the Temple of the Veil.

Detoa paused before the black façade of the temple and fiddled with her scarf. "How did it—"

"The same as always. Nowhere. Curse that woman to the Devourer's Waste! I'll cut the memory from her head if necessary."

Detoa looked back at the Temple of the Tree once more, her eyes bright. "What if she truly knows nothing?"

Mavell opened the doors to the Temple of the Veil. "She knows something. Maybe everything."

# 9

# THE SPIRE LORDS

*Palim, the Freelands*
*May 29, 1195 PT*

*Liiesh*

Liiesh Romanus, First Lord of the Freelands, remained stoic on his ivory throne. His eyes strayed from Tres, the man standing in the judgment circle below him, to the seven Arbiters of the Spire. The arbiters lingered atop their pillars surrounding the circle in their meditative poses: arms and legs crossed, heads bowed, and eyes closed. Their wings stretched around them like half-open leather cocoons. On the rims of their pillars hung their limiters—long necklaces affixed to silver talismans, each bearing the symbol of a family spire or station. This freed them from the psychic bonds of their limiters, allowing them to participate in a congress of thought.

The arbiters' minds murmured, echoing over the empty risers in the atrium. If this went on much longer, Liiesh would have to contend with a headache. To him, the matter was simple, but the arbiters deliberated exceedingly with all their judgments. Being men of the old world, even the youngest had wings of withered gray. Forty years ago, it took them three weeks to congress on naming Liiesh the First Lord. Time had only slowed them down.

Liiesh stifled a sigh and discreetly stretched his black wings. Seven hours was a long time to sit still, even for a terrion. Once more, he gazed at Tres. Black eyes as cold as steel stared back at him. *'This is where your arrogance gets you, little brother,'* Liiesh thought.

The edge of Tres's lips curled down. *'This is an insult to my station.'*

His brother's mental reply drowned out the hum of the arbiters in Liiesh's mind. They were connected by blood, a bond even a limiter could not dampen.

The folding of wings replaced the psychic buzz filling the atrium. All seven pairs receded behind seven dark shoulders, and seven pairs of black eyes gazed at Liiesh.

After he nodded, each of them reached for the ivory hooks to retrieve their limiters. With his fist-sized talisman once again around his neck, the First Arbiter addressed the defendant. "Tres Romanus, son of Tyris, Second Lord of the Freelands, brother to the First Lord, we have counseled on the matters of your conduct. In question are your many deeds of cruelty toward the groundlings in your service, the most recent resulting in the death of one of your human servants."

He unfurled his wings, then drew them in again. "You have brought dishonor to your house, your station, and your people. We find you guilty of excessive acts of cruelty and vanity. We sentence you to ten years of reparation fealty to the First Lord. During this time, you will be subject to him, not as his brother or his Second, but as a common servant." The First Arbiter stood, the rest following. Their blue robes draped past their feet, swirling about the rims of their pillars.

The First Arbiter extended his right hand. "This is our judgment upon you, before the First Lord, before the Spire Watch, and before Sovereign." He looked to the high glass dome above.

The sentries of the Spire Watch, one stationed between each pillar, unsheathed their sabers and lifted them high. They stretched their wings, black and strong with youth, remaining still with obsidian eyes fixed on Tres. The rest of the arbiters mimicked the First Arbiter, right hands held open and level with their faces, heads pointed upward at the clear night sky. Both moons hung above the center of the dome, casting red and blue reflections off limiters and blades.

Liiesh stood, relieved to stretch his legs and to hear the arbiters' verdict. Although it was a slap on the wrist, it suited his purpose. "I accept your ruling, Arbiters of the Spire. This trial is concluded. Fly in peace."

With a rush of wind, the arbiters departed, leaving the atrium through the large archway crowning the rows of raised seats across from the throne. As Tres lifted his boot, nine sabers pointed at his throat.

Liiesh smirked before waving, signaling the sentries to stand at ease. Tres glared at his brother.

*'A little subjugation won't kill you, Tres,'* Liiesh said in his mind as he turned to the Spire Watch and nodded. "Fly in peace."

The sentries followed the arbiters, their wings sending rushes of air swirling around the white stone atrium.

Tres glowered at his brother for a long while. Liiesh smiled with subtle satisfaction.

"Is this a game to you?" Tres said through gritted teeth. "The assembly will not be pleased with this secret trial."

Liiesh shook his head and pressed his lips together. "This is no kind of game. You spilled innocent blood."

"She was a thief."

"Thief or not"—Liiesh raised a hand—"the measure of a Lord of Palim is not in his popularity among the assembly, but in his regard for the least of men."

Tres stepped out of the judgment circle toward his brother, fists clenched at his sides. His boots echoed across the marble floor. "Most of the spire lords have done worse things. Will you put them to trial? Is this the start of a moral reckoning?"

"The spire lords are not my brother nor my Second. You are held to a higher standard. You took the Oath of Ivory. They didn't." Liiesh descended the steps of his throne and, with one strong flap of his wings, left the ground. Tres followed as they flew nearer the archway.

Once past the first arch, Liiesh turned sharply and glided down the wide corridor that wrapped around the atrium. He passed through another arch to soar into the open night sky, high above the city ground. Tres flew beside him.

The Assembly Spire, holding the atrium at its summit, stood tallest among the spires in the center of the vast city of Palim. A tower of shining white granite, its balconies and archways were inlaid with ivory. The city was a masterpiece of terrion architecture—one of the last of its kind—built on the peak of a seaside mountain.

The night sky shone like a clear onyx bowl of glittering stars, and the lights, flickering from hundreds of spire windows, mirrored it. Liiesh weaved past the dark towers, relishing the cool wind on his face as he sped toward his home spire in the northern district, the city's oldest quarter. He arrived at the topmost balcony and floated onto its obsidian surface.

The wind rattled him when Tres landed at his side. "Name your sentence, First Lord. Or have you not thought that far ahead?"

Liiesh fastened a button on his red cuff that had loosened during flight. "Of course, I have. Do you take me for a groundling? Lady Praya is leaving for

Setmal tomorrow. You will escort her." He stepped through the arched doorway, his brother at his heels.

Tres rounded on him. "That is Refsul's territory."

Liiesh stopped and faced his brother. They matched one another in height, but where Liiesh carried a regal air, Tres held the bearing of a warrior. He had exchanged the silk shirts and ornate coats of the spire lords for the black leather armor of the Spire Watch.

"Human politics change often, brother." Liiesh rolled his shoulders and focused on his limiter. He folded his wings, using mind craft to make them disappear. "Refsul does not have hold over that land as he did in our father's time."

Tres's black braids—bound with gold thread in the tradition of the Spire Watch—fell over his shoulder as he peered around the balcony doorway. "What business does Lady Praya have in Yvenea?"

"She is substituting for our ambassador. We've kept Leron Novelen's disappearance a secret so far. The post will allow Praya to assess Yvean resources we could not otherwise inspect." Liiesh straightened the lapel of his trademark red justaucorps. "Your primary responsibility will be helping her find evidence for Brealla's research. But you must also do what you can to help the Red Watch discover what became of Novelen."

Tres crossed his arms and glared at his brother. "Was this whole arbitration just so you could make me your lackey?"

"Do not confuse spire justice for scheming, little brother," Liiesh said. "If I wanted you as my errand boy, I'd have done it without the arbiters or the Spire Watch. And it would have been a permanent post. This is not a task for an underling. You have a talent for finding things long lost." He patted the hilt of Ironmaw, the ancient sword at his side. "If I were to die, the Freelands would be left with you for a ruler. Your ill-informed opinion of the other races has made you haughty and dangerous."

Tres retracted his wings and scowled. "I do not desire the First Seat."

"Neither did I." Liiesh marched through the foyer to his private office.

His steward waited at the door. The man bowed and ushered them inside.

Liiesh approached his ornate high-top desk towering over the center of the office. To his annoyance, his aunt already occupied the room.

Brealla Romanus, the First Scholar, stood casually, gazing out the long bank of windows opposite the door. She had a stately appearance, nearing her third century, but held a spark of youth in her eyes. Brealla turned and bowed her head, pulling her long gray locks over her shoulder. "Good evening, my lords."

A rustling across the room startled Liiesh. He bit his tongue and glanced at the two fireplaces on opposite walls adjacent to the door. Praya Aldonus sat on the plush couch before one of the hearths. When she shifted out of the shadows, the firelight rimmed her dark face. She rose and bowed. As Brealla's apprentice, she usually wore a scholar's uniform, but she now dressed in a blue tunic, black leggings, and boots—the outfit of a traveler. In exchange for a traditional updo of braids, she had donned a simple leather tie binding her hair at the back of her head. The look suited her.

Liiesh leaned on his desk and nodded politely.

Tres approached Praya. "I see you did plan ahead, brother. What would you have done had the arbiters not ruled in your favor?"

Liiesh narrowed his eyes. "Prepare yourself, Tres. You will not see your mother city for the term of your sentence or until your task is finished."

Tres bowed to Praya. "I shall prepare for the flight, my lady."

Praya's dark eyes widened, and she pivoted toward Liiesh. "You didn't tell him?"

Liiesh smirked. "Forgive me, young lady. That detail must have slipped my mind."

Crossing his arms, Tres stiffened. "What *detail*?"

A voice came from the doorway behind them. "That this will be a journey made on foot."

Orin Novelen, son of the Red Watch Commander Leron Novelen, entered the room and bowed. He was a strange creature, being one-quarter thurse and of the royal Yvean family. Liiesh didn't particularly trust either race. However, Orin, like many of Liiesh's associates, proved a necessary pawn on the board.

Liiesh nodded at Orin, then faced Brealla and Praya again. He caught his aunt's mischievous smile before she could hide it.

"Lord Orin Novelen," Tres said.

Orin bowed his head. "In Yvenea, Arist is my title. I am honored that you will be joining us."

Liiesh glanced at the crystal glass on the desk before him. The water within sparkled and spun of its own accord. He met Orin's gaze. "Arist Novelen, your new companions will meet you at the west gate at seven tomorrow morning. I trust you can leave as discretely as you came." He signaled to his steward, who remained at the door.

Bringing a hand to his chest, Orin bowed low. "Of course, First Lord." He turned on his heels and followed the steward.

Brealla grinned. "Fascinating, is he not?"

Liiesh shot the First Scholar a hard look. "I don't appreciate uninvited guests wandering freely through my house, dear aunt."

"My apologies, First Lord."

"Out." Liiesh pointed at the door. Brealla obeyed, and Praya scurried after her.

"Not you, Lady Praya." Liiesh held out his palm.

Spinning around, Praya widened her eyes and furrowed her brows. Liiesh waved his other hand at Tres, who scowled before following Brealla into the hall and closing the door.

Praya stilled. Her gaze shifted from the door to the fire to the windows—everywhere but the man before her.

Liiesh stepped around the desk. He clasped his hands behind his back and approached the couch.

Her eyes settled on the fire.

Stretching an arm, Liiesh motioned toward the couch. "Sit."

She slid onto the cushion, her rigid posture relaxing as he stood behind the other end of the sofa.

He pressed his palms into the back of the cushion and leaned forward. Silence settling between them, they both gazed into the flames. Liiesh's limiter dangled from his neck, glittering against the firelight. With calloused fingers, he gripped the talisman. It was forged the day he was born, and for ninety-one years it remained smooth and polished. No limiter ever tarnished except upon the death of its master.

"I have not forgotten our agreement, but they will expect things of us soon, Praya."

She stiffened before catching herself and settling back into the couch. "I know—my lord."

Liiesh turned his eyes back on the fire. It would be a few years before they had to honor that part of the agreement which had brought him, reluctantly, into power as the First Lord. Praya had been only a child then, too young to understand the meaning of betrothal. Now in her early decades of adulthood, their families expected heirs. "How much did Brealla tell you about what you are to accomplish in Setmal?"

Praya pursed her lips. "Other than cover for Leron Novelen? I assume she told me what I need to know."

"I'm sure she did." Liiesh moved around the edge of the couch and propped himself against the arm opposite her.

Praya jerked and clutched at her limiter—a set of three roses representing the Aldonus family.

He smiled, and to his surprise, so did she.

"Is there something else I should know, my lord?" she asked.

"It will be dangerous."

"Yes. I will be in Drawlen lands. I understand the risks."

Sliding across the cushions, Liiesh leaned toward her.

She pressed against the arm of the couch, eyes wide.

"Do you?" he whispered. "War is coming, Praya. Palimar will erupt in war. If we don't have what we need, our enemy will devour us. That is why your assignment is so important. Do you understand?"

She closed her eyes and shook her head. *'I'm not some child.'* The thought was faint, but her limiter could not fully contain its power. "Of course, I understand," she said aloud, glancing at him.

Liiesh cupped her cheek in his hand. Her skin was like charcoal against his bronze palm. "At no cost should your life be forfeited, not for anything. Do you understand?"

Her eyes softening, she nodded curtly.

Releasing her, Liiesh scooted back. "Now go." He cocked his head at the door, the hardness back in his gaze.

Without warning, Praya leaned forward and pressed her lips to his cheek. Chaste and brief, it wholly lacked affection. "I'll be careful," she whispered. Jumping from the couch, she spun on her heels, striding from the room.

On the desk, the water in the glass swirled and spilled from the container as though caught by a great wind. It splashed to the floor. Liiesh watched with a raised brow as the puddle rose, solidifying into the familiar figure of a water sprite. His shaven head glistened, and he sported a braided white goatee that reached to his collar bone, contrasting with his russet skin. Silver cuffs and earrings adorned his sharply pointed ears, and his eyes shifted continually from murky black to crystal blue, like the waters of the Howling Sea. He wore only a pair of baggy trousers that changed hue along with his eyes. An inch-wide multicolored tattoo encircled his left bicep.

"Why send one so precious into the grip of the enemy, young lord?" The man's voice resounded like a crashing wave.

"I have reason for everything I do, Raza." Liiesh rose from the couch.

"Reasons I certainly do not understand." Raza folded his arms. Standing a head shorter than the First Lord, he appeared almost youthful. But Liiesh knew better. The water speaker was an ancient creature.

Liiesh sauntered to the desk. "You've come with news, I assume."

Raza hunched over the desk. "They've done it. Rather successfully, I'd say. Shane zem'Arta joined forces with Zereen arbitrators to go after Henrick Lowe and his slavers."

"Really? The arbitrators must have been rather desperate."

Raza pressed his hands together. "Lowe's snatchers had captured Izen, the young Zereen prince and a few other warriors. They surely would have perished without zem'Arta's help."

Liiesh suppressed a satisfied laugh. "I'm sure zem'Arta's help rubbed the arbitrators in a bad way."

"They tried to kill him at the end. But Rodden intervened."

"And Lowe?"

"Escaped." Raza walked to the window, gazing at the harbor lights in the far distance. "No one is sorer about it than zem'Arta. We had to stop him from running off into the Dead Lands after Lowe."

Liiesh tapped a finger on the desk. "Where is he now? He's due to escort Arist Novelen to Setmal tomorrow."

Raza's eyes gleamed, like sunlight shining through clear water, and he smiled. "I'm here to tell you he arrived this morning. We came aboard the *Keol'ife*. Since you've been occupied, we took the liberty of dropping off our snatcher guests—including Jex ren'Turen—with the Spire Watch at Shayhem."

"Very good." Liiesh pulled a thick envelope sealed with his personal brand from the desk drawer and handed it to Raza. "Deliver zem'Arta's new assignment dossier. He need not bother to visit me in person. I'm sure he's tired, and his crew is probably burning down a bar by now."

Raza nodded and tucked the envelope under his arm.

"After that, go back to Shevak. Don't wait for the others. You can get there much faster. And keep watch over Tessa—we'll need her soon. Report back using the Red Watch when you can."

Raza raised a thick, white eyebrow. "The Red Watch has reached that far, young lord?"

Liiesh peered out the bank of windows. A cloud formed around the city, concealing the nearby spires, now only evident by the lights flickering through their windows. "The Red Watch reaches everywhere."

# 10

# A CHANGE OF PLAN

*Palim, the Freelands*
*May 30, 1195 PT*

*Orin*

The city bells tolled once for the first hour of morning as Orin and two Spire Watch escorts navigated the crowded streets of Palim, one of the last terrion dwellings of Palimar. Behind them towered spires and steep switchbacks as they reached the harbor tucked between a natural peninsula and a man-made breaker. This portion of the city was built to accommodate groundlings. Constructed from wood and brick, the tallest buildings reached only four stories, all with shallow roofs of slate.

The eerie, still weather cast an odd backdrop to the exuberant celebrations brimming in the streets and taverns along the main road. An impromptu festival had risen in the wake of news from the south: The vanguard had decisively purged Shardling pirates and snatchers, who had long harassed the Utharen shores of the Freelands. Even some terrion, who usually remained in their spires, mingled among the groundlings. A fog settled, and the flickering torchlight high above the streets marked the only evidence of the looming city wall.

The stony-faced escorts ushered Orin to the open door of the Broken Spire Inn. They bowed stiffly, then soared into the sky on their black wings. Orin stepped into the parlor, grimacing when his shoe sloshed in a puddle of beer. The air reeked of alcohol, pipe smoke, and boiling potatoes. He vowed never again to let Sid choose overnight accommodations.

After ordering a whiskey at the bar, Orin searched for a dry corner. He sagged onto a vacant bench and gazed wearily at the chaos. Young men and women danced on the banquet tables. Two gray-skinned kobold youths tap danced across the fireplace mantel. While a group of scar-faced thurse men squatted next to a barrel and threw dice, a fiddler jumped onto the bar and feverishly stroked his bow across the strings. Behind him, the barkeeper juggled glassware and eggs.

Orin rubbed his ears, annoyed at the clashing sounds. In the far corner, an inebriated woman banged tunelessly on the spinet. She smiled toothily at him and ran her hand down the keyboard. Orin scowled and turned away, emptying his glass in a single gulp.

Sid vel'Forr—Orin's friend and bodyguard—sat at a table in the middle of the room, engaged in a ferocious arm-wrestling match with a red-faced human. Sid thudded the man's arm against the table.

The man sprang from his seat. "Burn you to the Waste," he muttered.

With growling enthusiasm, a sharp-faced kobold woman grasped Sid's offered hand. "I think all that time wallowing in Yvean luxury has made you soft and fat, vel'Forr."

"Prove it, *elf*." Sid squeezed her fingers as his bicep bulged.

To Orin's surprise and the roaring delight of the crowd, she slammed Sid's huge, clawed hand against the table after seconds of vein-popping struggle. Then, she leapt onto the bench and threw up her hands. "Which one of you sods will face the mighty Carris, goblin queen of the Palim groundlings?"

Orin shook his head and set his glass on the bar before slipping through the crowd. After trudging up the stairs, he entered their room. The city lights from the window illuminated one of the four beds, where his cousin Venna lay sleeping. As Orin shed his coat and boots and collapsed onto his mattress, he wondered how anyone could sleep through the racket rattling the floor. He didn't wonder long though, for his exhaustion muffled the noise as he faded into a dream . . .

*His mother painted the scene outside their veranda doors onto a wide canvas while his father moved a cleric piece across a queen's board.*

*Through the window, the clear blue sky swirled, consumed by dark clouds and a flash of lightning. Roaring thunder followed. When the growling subsided, his mother lay slumped over her chair, green liquid dripping from her mouth. And his father had vanished. The cleric's piece fell to the floor and shattered.*

"Orin!" Sid's voice reverberated in his ear, pulling him from the nightmare.

Shadows still encased the room, but his golden-eyed guard towered over him, fully dressed, his pack strapped to his back. Venna sat on her bed, struggling to tie her boots.

"We're leaving." Sid poised his hand on the pistol at his belt. "Now."

Orin suppressed the urge to argue or ask questions. Sid was usually easygoing and a bit irreverent, but now he gazed warily around the room. Orin scrambled into his clothes while trying to shake off mere hours of sleep.

Sid led them out the door, down the steps, and through the empty parlor. Orin squinted at Sid's broad form in the dark. Having very little thurse blood, Orin lacked the ability to see clearly through darkness, unlike the guard before him or his cousin behind.

They exited the back door into the alley. A short, dark-skinned boy met them, clad in black shirt and trousers. With a silent nod, he and Sid greeted each other, and the boy led them down the narrow passage.

Every few seconds, a strange chill shook Orin, like someone had poured cold water down his back.

They passed a kobold man with pointed ears and a braided beard, leaning slack-jawed against a doorframe. Perhaps he was too drunk to notice, but it seemed he couldn't see them. The travelers moved swiftly but silently through the streets. Water lapping against the stone walls of the nearby canal accompanied the low timbre of a man singing:

*"Come ye Ruv o'r mount of flame,*
*lest we wear the ogre's chain.*
*Shed thy foul encrusted rag,*
*Take up thy long-forgotten flag."*

After they rounded the corner of row houses, the murky waters of the canal appeared. A pale man sat at the stern of a rowboat, pushing it along the canal with an oar while continuing his song.

Sid whistled, startling the man in the boat. The man ceased his singing and stilled his oar, resting it across his leggings. His sleeveless shirt, loosely fitting his thin frame, fluttered in a sudden breeze. The man's salt-and-pepper hair was bound in a topknot, facial hair hugging his jaw in a neat line. When he dipped his chin, he sported a flat-toothed grin on his narrow face.

Leading Orin and his companions, the boy signaled to the man. "Quaeo."

"Bren." The man waved. "This be the traveler?" He looked at Orin with wide, gray eyes. The man steered the boat along the edge of the canal, the moonlight glinting off the gold ring pierced through his lower lip.

Bren nodded, then motioned to Sid. "Quaeo will take us to the ship. It's at the mouth of the harbor."

Sid ushered Orin and Venna onto the rowboat. He still wore a serious, worried expression, and even Venna, who dreaded boats, jumped in quickly. She scrunched her face and clutched her stomach, scooting across the middle bench. Orin crowded next to her.

While jumping aboard, Bren shoved them off. Quaeo steered in silence and Sid perched across from him.

"I thought Rodden was guardian tonight," Sid said.

Quaeo pointed his thumb behind him. "He be 'round. I just be coming to stretch my legs, see what all the fuss be about."

As they approached a stone bridge, Bren jumped and swung himself over the bridge railing. When they glided under the structure, grunting noises echoed from above. Venna muffled a terrified squeal as Sid shoved her and Orin to the bottom of the dinghy. Orin's mouth filled with foul, salty water while he struggled to get his hands under him. When he righted himself and sputtered, a limp form splashed into the water behind them. The yellow-skinned face of a man floated, his eyes wide and his throat cut, bobbing in the opposite direction.

"Kumuni Cosazi," Sid whispered. "Assassins from Kumun."

Venna clung to Orin and buried her face into his coat. Her arm and shoulder felt soggy against him, and she muttered, "This isn't what I had in mind when you said 'adventure.'"

"Agreed," Orin said, patting her head.

When they passed from the bridge's shadow, Bren engaged two more Cosazi. It seemed the boy fought with many invisible hands against the masked, knife-wielding assassins. The streetlamp cast wild shadows on the nearby buildings, the smoky silhouettes of several shades whirling and striking at the boy's silent command.

Still, the Cosazi had earned their fearsome reputation. They moved like leaves on the wind, twirling and bending in deadly rhythm. One of them broke away, sprinting down the road along the canal. Sid readied a crossbow, firing a bolt. The Cosazi deflected the steel projectile with his curved knife and poised to throw a metal star, when a brown and black blur intercepted him.

"Oh, fires!" Venna shouted.

A great hellcat had emerged from an alley. He was the size of a horse, his hide stretched tightly across his muscular frame. His tail, thin and long, swished behind him, giving off a fiery glow in the light of the streetlamps. A cropped mane swirled in the breeze around his flat face, and tusks curved down over his lips. The Cosazi hung by the neck from the beast's jaw, and blood dripped from his chin onto the stone road. The throwing star dropped from the Cosazi's hand and plunked into the water.

With a shake of his head, the hellcat dropped the Cosazi onto the canal's ledge. The body draped for a moment, then rolled and slipped into the water. The hellcat prowled along the road, keeping parallel with the boat, its yellow eyes scanning the road and rooftops.

Just ahead, the canal expanded into the inky waters of the city harbor. The dinghy shook lightly, startling Orin and Venna. But it was only Bren, who had leapt onto the boat's bow.

Venna watched the prowling hellcat and gasped. "It's not seriously going to—"

The animal bounded toward the boat. Orin braced himself. The dinghy didn't have room for one more person, let alone a thousand-pound animal. Instead, a brown and black striped alley cat landed gracefully on the rear bench.

"A skin-changer." Venna let out a breath, putting a hand to her chest. "Two forms. Wow, that's—"

"Venna, shush." Sid sat and stowed his crossbow under the bench. "You can fawn over Rodden when we board the ship. I'm sure he'll love the attention. Captain might get jealous, though."

The cat licked his paws and rolled his eyes. They shone bright yellow, and eerily intelligent.

Quaeo placed his oar into its oiled crutch and muffled it with handkerchiefs. He dipped the other paddle into the water and sat down to row. The boat glided, its oars cutting softly into the water.

Orin slouched deep into the boat's hull, repelled by this strange new company.

The skin-changer didn't bother him as much as the human man. Quaeo kept glancing over his shoulder, smiling at Orin. When at last they passed the spindly watchtower at the edge of the harbor, a tall ship anchored just beyond came into view. The strange man continued glancing at him with a suspicious grin.

Finally, Orin's annoyance overtook him. He glared at Quaeo. "You smile a lot."

Quaeo smiled—again. "Look like your father. Brings back memories."

"I wasn't aware you knew my father."

"We share blood." Quaeo tapped his chest with his fist. "His mother be of my people."

"You're Sirahi?"

"That I be, Orin of the outlands. Welcome aboard the *Keol'ife*." He stopped rowing as the boat drifted alongside the broad hull of a two-masted schooner.

A rope ladder hung from the rail of the main deck. On Sid's order, Venna and Orin climbed first. As soon as Venna clambered over the rail, she dropped to the deck and cradled her head in the crook of her elbow. "Not another ship. I thought we were taking the road."

"Change of plans, bookworm," a voice behind them said.

When Venna lifted her head, her pale face turned a soft pink.

A burly, silver-haired Zereen stood in the middle of the deck, haloed in red and pearl moonlight. His olive skin and pale blue eyes typified a Zereen thurse. He ran a hand through his shoulder-length hair. It hung loosely rather than bound high or braided.

On his exposed arms, an unusual variety of tattoos—Ruvian and Karthan symbols—circled his biceps and elbows. And two horizontal scars marred each cheek—one still stitched and healing—the scars of a criminal marked for death. Overall, he appeared wholly unfriendly and dangerous, though he couldn't have been much older than Orin's own twenty-four years.

The Zereen winked at Venna, then locked eyes with Orin. "Do you know how many death marks were taken out on you in the last six months, Novelen? You'd think the king had already named you for the Yvean throne."

Sid leapt onto the ship with Rodden on his shoulder. "What in the fires happened to your face, zem'Arta?"

Rodden sprang from Sid's shoulder and landed onto the rail. He stretched while his long tail bobbed in rhythm with the sway of the ship.

"A parting gift from Henrick Lowe," zem'Arta growled.

Sid whistled, long and slow. "That's twisted."

A tall, dark human dropped to the deck from high in the rigging. Wearing an open coat, shirtless underneath, he cradled his head in his hands and batted his eyelashes at Venna. "I think it makes him look rather dashing, don't you?"

The Zereen flexed his clawed hand. "I could give you a few, Remm, if you like them so much."

A hand stroking his cheeks, Remm swayed. "And ruin this perfection?"

Venna and the Zereen responded with matching scowls. Usually, Venna rattled off a comeback. Instead, she gripped her stomach and groaned.

Orin narrowed his eyes, wondering what inspired this teasing.

Startling Orin, the skin-changer spoke in a smooth, deep voice. "It makes Shane a more tempting target for ambitious arbitrators." Rodden sat and curled his tail around himself. "As Henrick surely intended. It's fortunate we're crossing into the outlands."

Such a strange thing to hear a man's voice coming from a cat. But his words helped Orin understand. This was Shane zem'Arta, the infamous Red Watch captain, abhorred by the Zereens but protected by the First Lord.

Shane balked at the cat. "We? You part of this operation, too, Rodden? Or are you just out to see the sights?"

Rodden prowled along the rail toward the quarterdeck. "The last time I let you wander into the outlands, you left a trail of Drawlen corpses. What kind of fool do you take me for, pup?"

"Don't you give him all the credit!" Carris's gravelly voice echoed from the rigging. The spiky-haired kobold who had bested Sid in arm-wrestling the previous night hung leisurely from a rope halfway up the main mast.

With a clawed finger, Shane scratched at the stitches on his cheeks and narrowed his eyes at Rodden. "Fine, old man. You can come. But you'd better make yourself burning useful."

When Bren and Quaeo stepped aboard after tying off the dinghy, Remm saluted and whistled. "Captain on deck!" The other sailors snapped to attention before scurrying about the ship.

Bren slipped off to the forecastle deck while Remm offered Quaeo a deep blue justaucorps. Once he fastened the garment, he looked more like a sea captain and less like a crazed ferryman.

"Welcome aboard, Orin Novelen of Yvenea." Quaeo bowed politely, then faced Venna, who still squatted with her head in her hands. "Welcome aboard, Venna vel'Tamer of Thêen. Be at home in the captain's cabin. We've a long day of sailing ahead." Then he raised a hand and marched to the helm. "Raise anchor!"

The clinking of chains rumbled, sailors rushed across the deck, and the fore-and-aft sails dropped open.

Orin ducked under the boom and addressed Sid. "What about Lady Praya?"

Sid pointed to Shane.

"We'll talk in the cabin," Shane said and moved toward the door leading off the main deck. "Carris! Get this girl some sea legs."

Carris slid down the mast and lifted Venna to her feet. "Come on, lass. A nice, juicy orange and some ginger tea will get all that green off yer pretty face."

# 11

# CROSSING THE DOOR

*Palim, the Freelands*
*May 30, 1195 PT*

*Orin*

Orin followed Shane into the captain's cabin, with Sid and Rodden at his heels. The office housed a desk with an hourglass, a quill, and nautical essentials organized with military precision. Until now, Orin had only been on luxurious Yvean river yachts. The *Keol'ife* was a warship. If the rumors he'd heard at the Broken Spire were true, it had recently sunk *The Reaver*, the most notorious pirate ship on the Utheran Ocean.

Shane shut the cabin door behind them and stood at the desk.

Orin moved toward Shane and stuck out his hand. "We've not been properly introduced. Orin Novelen, seated Arist of the Yvean court, son of Leron Novelen, with whom I believe you're well acquainted."

Shane stiffened as he locked eyes with Orin. Letting out a slow breath, he shook Orin's wrist with an iron grip. "Shane zem'Arta. Captain of the Red Watch." He withdrew his hand and dropped into a chair. "I know Leron. In fact, finding out where he's stuffed himself and getting you on that pretty Yvean throne is my big pay day."

Chuckling, Orin shook his head. "Well, Captain zem'Arta, given all that's been happening here in the Freelands, I appreciate that you've decided to focus on finding my father."

Narrowing his eyes, Shane slapped a hand to his chest. "I didn't decide anything, prince. I have a debt to pay." He pointed a finger at Orin. "And don't call me Captain on this ship. You'll confuse the crew."

"Noted," Orin said.

Shane tapped his knuckles on a map spread on the desk. “Lady Praya and her escort will meet us at the embassy. Liiesh won’t risk her traveling with us now that we know Cosazi have accepted a death mark on you.”

Orin examined the map, freshly inked and charting the eastern shores of the Freelands. “Do we know who is so keen to see me floating face down in a Palim canal?”

Shane scratched at the tattoo on his forearm. “Take your pick. You’re the heir apparent. You have a lot of rich Yvean rivals and a church that wants to unravel any ties between Yvenea and the Freelands. Frankly, even the Greqs aren’t off the table.”

“Maybe we should invite the Thurans too. I’m sure they don’t want to miss the fun,” Orin said, earning a smirk from Shane.

Sid peered out the windows lining the back wall of the office. “Who’s escorting Lady Praya?”

A dark look passed over Shane’s face while he flipped the hourglass on the desk. “Tres.”

Sid blew out a long breath. “He must have really pissed off big brother this time. I sure hope Mona can keep you and Tres from stabbing each other.”

Covering his mouth, Orin yawned, the excitement of the night having worn off.

“Mona’s not coming,” Shane said.

While Rodden prowled along the windowsill, he snarled. “She’s aiding those injured at Highrock.”

Slapping his thigh, Sid grunted. “We’re going to sail a Ruvian ship into the Zereen harbor without Mona?” He pointed at Shane. “And with *you* onboard?”

Orin backed away and leaned on the windowsill. Rodden hissed when he leapt onto the floor.

Shane’s eyes reflected the red light of the Mortemus moon filtering through the windows. “We’re not going anywhere near Zeree, so keep your head on, Sid.” His gaze resumed its usual brightness. “We’ll land at the Bay of Storms.”

The effect disturbed Orin. Shaking off the eerie feeling, he rubbed his eyes. “Any sleep in this plan?”

Shane pushed the chair out from under himself. “I’ll show you to your rooms.” He opened the adjoining door to the captain’s quarters.

Sid entered the room while Orin paused at the threshold. “I’m grateful for your escort, zem‘Arta.”

Shane nodded. "Both of you get some rest. It looks like you've been dragged through the mud."

"A bed is a welcome sight," Orin said as he entered and shut the door. He set his pack on the double bed secured under the windows while Sid climbed to the top bunk built into the adjacent walls. As the horizon lightened, Venna entered the room, sipping a cup of tea.

Orin raised his head from the pillow. "You're looking better."

Plopping on the bottom bunk, Venna yawned while removing her boots. "Marginally."

When Orin woke, it was early evening. Sid's and Venna's beds lay empty, but voices drifted in from the office. He rolled out of bed and ambled to the closed door, listening to Shane and Sid's tense conversation.

"I had him, Sid," Shane growled. "I had Henrick Lowe by his burning neck, and now Liiesh is sending me in the opposite direction!"

"It was a dirty trick for Lowe to use your brother as a body shield," Sid said.

"I should have gutted that pirate."

"You'd be cleaning your brother's guts off the ground too. I get that you like to play the ruthless mercenary, but I know you're decent, and Lowe used that against you."

As soon as Orin touched the doorknob, a thump sounded on the other side of the door, followed by the creak of a chair. Shane rattled off an impressive string of Karthan curses.

"See, that's the way," Sid said. "I'm sure you'll have plenty of distractions in Setmal: assassins to run down, spies to catch . . . and you and Ven can ogle each other from opposite sides of the roo—"

*Smack.*

"All right, all right! I'll lay off," Sid said. He paused, then continued with a cautious tone. "So . . . what's your read on Novelen?"

Orin released his hand from the knob and pressed his ear against the door.

"He's a naïve young noble with no concept of the danger he's in or the fact Liiesh is using him to get his ancient hands on the Yvean throne. Not nearly as much of a dandy as the portraits I've seen though," Shane said.

Sid laughed. "Not Orin, idiot. I mean Leron. And by the way, Orin's a good deal less naïve than he seems. I'll tell him you said that."

"Don't bother. He's listening at the door."

Heat rushed to Orin's face, like a child caught stealing sweets. He fumbled with the knob and stepped into the office.

"Mornin' your majesty," Shane said as he lounged sideways in the captain's chair.

Orin placed his hands behind his back and rocked on his boots. "I rather thought my portraits were a good likeness." He seated himself across from Shane. "I am curious, however, what you might suspect about my father's untimely disappearance."

Shane straightened and placed his elbows on the desk. "It's unlikely he would have just vanished. If someone's gotten to him, he'd have gone down fighting, although this isn't the first time he's wandered off on his own." He leaned forward and clasped his hands, azure eyes fixed on Orin. "You have anything you want to tell me, prince?"

Orin recalled a year ago when he last saw his father in Setmal before leaving for the Freelands. "We were both deeply occupied, he with his work and I with my studies. He had seemed quite interested in what the university was teaching on Drawlen history. He borrowed a text from me before I'd left for Thêen: *The Blessing of the First Immortals*. Does it mean anything to you?"

Shane and Sid shared a knowing glance. As Orin's stomach rumbled, Sid slapped him on the back. "Better get to the galley, Novelen. Bren might have eaten everything on the ship by now."

Sid wasn't exaggerating. When Orin arrived in the galley, the gangly fifteen-year-old ralenta sat at the mess table with a loaf of bread and a slab of salt pork. He held a half-eaten apple and took a ravenous bite from the core. At the other end of the table sat a Greqi man.

Orin slid onto the bench next to him. "What do you recommend?"

The man pointed to the salt pork and snorted.

Carris laughed while squatting on the countertop, scooping stew into a wooden bowl. "Not much of a talker, that one. See, Morgel left his tongue in Kumun."

Morgel grinned and ran two fingers across his lips, mimicking a scissors.

Orin's stomach roiled. He grabbed an apple and excused himself.

"Squeamish, are we?" Carris cackled while she sat on the counter, digging into her stew.

Donning a fake smile, Orin paused at the door. "Just looking for some fresh air." The rest of his time aboard the Keol'ife, he longed for the refined company and comforts of Yvenea.

"Land ho!" a sailor called at sunrise, startling Orin from his musing on the main deck. Outlined in the pink glow of daybreak, the cliffs of the western shore grew larger as the ship sailed forward.

Venna jumped up from a corner of the deck, cradling her stomach. "Oh, thank Sovereign!" She leaned over the railing, letting her hair tangle in the wind.

Orin grasped the railing beside her. "Is this the adventure you had in mind?"

Venna glanced beyond Orin and smiled. "Other than the ship and the waves, there have been some agreeable moments."

Orin checked over his shoulder. Shane leaned against the open door to the captain's quarters, talking with Quaeo.

The land loomed larger as the minutes sped by until the ship dropped anchor a hundred yards offshore. After the traveling party loaded into the row boats, the crew lowered them to the water.

When they grounded at the beach, Venna leapt from the boat. She sloshed through the foaming water, spun, and collapsed on her back in the sand, arms spread wide.

Shane bent over her. "Worth having sand in your clothes all the way to the border, bookworm?"

"Oh yes," she said, tossing sand toward his face.

Orin expected men to fawn over his unusually attractive cousin. But Shane appeared more familiar than flattering, and Orin didn't like how Venna seemed to enjoy it.

"Let's go, *little cousin*." Orin stepped between them and leveled Shane with a glare. "All this standing around has made me want to stretch my legs."

When they reached the road, a spire watchman provided them with horses. They traveled several miles through fallen trees and washed-out portions of the path. Along the way, Orin learned Shane had not one, but three ralenta in his crew—Bren (who had accompanied Orin from the inn to the ship); Remm (the taller, older tSolani who had spent most of the sea voyage swinging merrily from the rigging); and Morgel (the Greqi man who apparently had no tongue). These three alternated scouting ahead and behind, disappearing for hours at a time. Even Rodden prowled in and out of the woods in his hellcat form. Despite the frequent rotations, Shane had no problem keeping tabs on everyone.

After a day of riding, Orin loathed traveling by horse back. He'd also had enough of his companions—even Venna.

That night, they camped off the road, gathering around a fire. Orin sat on his bedroll alone in the shadows.

The skin-changer lay purring, sprawled at the base of a tree, when Venna settled beside him.

"I was under the impression," she said, "that skin-changers could only hold their animal forms for a few hours."

"So I've heard," Rodden said while licking his paws.

"You have two forms, and I've seen you hold them each for several days. That must be some kind of record."

Rodden slunk away, looking over his shoulder. "Perhaps I should get a ribbon or be left alone by nosey young women." His yellow eyes gleamed in the firelight as he curled up beside Carris.

Remm walked over and sat beside Venna, leaning close. "Didn't you study in Yvenea?"

Tossing her hair off her shoulders, Venna edged away. "I did . . ."

"Did you cover Drawlen lore?"

"A bit."

"How about the World Burner?"

"Remm!" Shane growled. He stood at the edge of the firelight, having just returned from scouting.

"Killjoy," Remm mumbled, tossing sticks into the fire.

Venna smiled at Shane and sat taller. "The World Burner. He can't be that Rodden."

Shane shrugged. "He's an old geezer with no sense of humor. We know that much."

"Ask him how old he is," Carris said. "He *loves* that one." She swiped at Rodden as though to pet him.

Rodden leapt away and hissed. "All of you are *children*."

Carris scoffed and resumed burning a rabbit carcass over the fire.

Venna folded her arms. "You're all spinning a tale."

Huffing, Orin climbed into his bedroll. Rodden prowled past, glancing at him before disappearing into the woods. Something ancient lingered in the skin-changer's gaze. Orin dismissed the nagging feeling as he willed himself to sleep.

When the sun hung high the next day, the walls of the Door of Bamrian loomed into view over a jagged rise. As the company approached on horseback, the low clouds of a brewing storm darkened the eastern sky. Even so, the white stone rampart shone brightly, and the iron gate at its center glistened. The watchtowers emitted a great golden light on either side.

Four Zereen soldiers guarded the wicket entrance, the smaller door set in the corner of the massive gate. Two of the guards lounged under a canvas shelter, rolling dice on the ground and watching Orin's company with weary disinterest. Four rifles lay forgotten at the back of the shelter.

When Shane galloped ahead of the group, one guard grabbed his weapon and leapt to his feet, shouting, "The Vagabond approaches!" The others reached for their sabers.

Orin raised a hand and dismounted his horse. "There's no need for alarm, gentlemen. I have the proper documents if you'll allow me a moment."

A guard at the door stepped forward, pointing his sword at Shane. "There's no document that can let this one through." His knuckles turned white against his sword hilt.

The Red Watch crew casually halted their horses. Carris yawned and stretched her arms. Rodden lounged in front of Shane, licking his paw. Storm clouds rolled across the sky and the wind increased.

For a moment, Orin held the guard's cold stare, then pulled a black envelope from his vest. It bore a gold wax seal stamped with an ornate sun silhouetting a crescent moon—the First Lord's seal. "Let's make a deal, young lieutenant. Take this envelope and examine its contents. Then you will kindly allow my companions and me to pass through without trouble, and in turn, I won't tell the Palim Watch of your inattention to your sacred duty."

The guard frowned and turned to his companions before snatching the envelope, breaking the seal, and scanning the letter. Then he nodded to the other guard, who unlatched the door.

A heavy rainfall pelted Orin and his companions as they walked through the gate, leaving their horses behind. Ten Yvean soldiers dressed in pristine yellow uniforms stood at attention on the other side. They greeted Orin with heads bowed.

Two carriages—each with a team of four horses—along with the company of Yvean chevaliers, waited for them in the rain. Fredrick Divelos, Orin's head steward, attended the lead carriage with one hand on the door and the other holding the hood of his wool coat over his brow.

Sid greeted the steward first with a slap on the back. "Freddy. Been a while!"

Fredrick extended a foot to steady himself. "Hello, Master vel'Forr. It's . . . lovely to see you again."

When Orin approached, Fredrick replaced his frown with a smile and bowed low. "My lord," he said in his nasally voice.

"Fredrick." Orin handed his traveling pack to the steward. "I hope you've not been waiting long."

"Only the one day, my lord. As usual, you are very punctual. The weather has been enjoyable up until now. And who are your companions?" Fredrick wrinkled his nose at Shane and his crew. "I'm sure I would remember if we'd met before."

"This is Shane zem'Arta." Orin gestured to Shane, who stood beside him. "Captain of the Guard for the interim ambassador while my father is away on Freeland business. Captain, this is Fredrick Divelos, head steward of House Novelen."

Fredrick squinted. "Are you sure, my lord? They seem, well . . . not the type for a diplomat's guard." Fredrick glanced at Rodden, who was shaking himself out under the carriage. "And I don't believe their feline companion helps their case."

Orin smiled. "Oh, I'm sure with a little grooming and a uniform, they'll fit the part just fine." Then he whispered, "They're very good at their jobs." It was worth the scowl from Shane and the steward's slack-jawed expression. Orin stretched his back and stepped into the carriage, waving a hand. "As for the cat, he's merely along for the ride. You'll barely notice him."

After spending several days in the cramped carriage, Orin longed for the wind on his face and the sun at his back. He supposed he was more comfortable than his steward, however. Fredrick sat pressed against the opposite corner, Shane seated next to him, and Rodden lounging on the seat back, tail swaying in the steward's face. Venna and Sid slept soundly across from him, Sid's long legs covering the aisle.

Growing weary of the silence, Orin turned to Fredrick. "How fares our fine city?"

Fredrick scooted to the edge of his seat. Nothing motivated the steward more than gossip. "The Aristor houses continue to clamor for power. Your impending ascension has been met with an alarming amount of hostility since the news of your upcoming wedding, and your uncle's health has taken another turn." He patted his lips and sighed. "His mind is going now, I'm afraid. He has his moments of lucidity, but he often goes on endlessly about conspiracies and prophecies. He believes your homecoming will remediate these risks."

Orin put up a hand, and Fredrick promptly snapped his jaw shut. "Fredrick, not all conspiracies are the conjuring of an old man's mind. You wouldn't believe the trouble I had getting here from Palim. I have assured my uncle that I will address his concerns and put right the things that need correcting. It's high time the Court of Aristors had a good scrubbing, anyway."

Fredrick slapped his hands on his knees. "That is a splendid promise, my lord. I certainly hope you have a reliable way of following through with it." Fredrick gazed at Shane with wide eyes and an upturned nose. "I presume that's why you're here, Captain?"

Folding his arms, Shane leaned against the corner of the carriage. "What gives you that idea?"

Fredrick cupped his chin and squinted. "You have the look of someone who knows what others are about."

# 12

# MEETINGS AND MANNERS

*Setmal, Yvenea*
*June 7, 1195 PT*

*Orin*

The grinding of a great chain jolted Orin awake. Outside the carriage window, the western gatehouse of Setmal loomed overhead as the portcullis lifted. "But it's the middle of the day," Orin said, his brow furrowed.

Fredrick straightened. "Conspiracies and prophecies, my lord. The dynast has taken to closing the gates even during the day."

Rodden, still in feline form, arched his back and leapt out the window, paws landing on a passing wine cart.

While the carriage wound through the western district, Orin counted over two dozen yellow-clad guards on the city walls. They stood at regular intervals along the ramparts and manned the watchtowers.

Setmal remained one of the best fortified cities in Palimar—strategically positioned between two mountain rivers and only accessible by three drawbridges. Why the increase in guards? Orin's chest tightened when he realized the guards were facing the city instead of the surrounding country.

Patrolling the streets in twos, yellow-coated policemen received a wide berth from passersby. Pedestrians averted eye contact with each other as much as they avoided the police.

The carriage jostled Orin and the other passengers while making its way past a red-framed community board:

**NO LOITERING. VIOLATORS FINED AND ARRESTED.**

"Charming." Shane tapped the window.

Orin leaned forward and scowled.

They passed an adjoining alley, where a pile of rubbish blocked the entrance. A man in a tattered waistcoat dumped a wheelbarrow of broken baubles next to a large portrait with a gash down the middle—a damaged painting of Leron Novelen.

Orin shifted back and closed his eyes. He remembered attending the city theater during his childhood, watching dramas that romanticized his parents' meeting and his father saving the king from assassins.

When Orin opened his eyes, he met Venna's frown. He forced a smile. "How fickle a patriotic temperament can be," he said.

At the entrance to the Cilé Faíl, the palace complex, the carriage lurched to a stop. Guards in crisp yellow uniforms swarmed the two carriages and examined every detail. Only after Fredrick's loud protests did they cease their search and let the convoy onto the grounds. Inside the palace walls, a team of doormen bowed and opened the carriage doors. They escorted Orin and his companions, rushing them across the courtyard.

Orin's heart pulsated, his palms sweaty. At least one bodyguard accompanied every noble who passed them while they walked silently through the gardens. It appeared the loitering policy even applied here.

As Orin strode under the archway into the wider palace square, Sid and Shane pressed against his sides, tailed by the rest of his companions. In their traveling clothes and strapped with weapons, the two thurse stood out like razors in a jewelry box. They received wide-eyed glances while pedestrians skirted them.

Fredrick paraded ahead and flailed his arms. "Make way. Arist Novelen coming through."

Heads snapped and whispers followed.

Orin beamed. He had loved the attention since childhood, his mother from a prominent royal house and his father a heroic foreign ally. But his face fell when glares met his gaze. Across the courtyard, Orin spotted a welcomed face.

Garren Romell poised at practiced attention, the picture of a Yvean officer. The middle-aged captain of Orin's personal guard had a dignified bearing, kind brown eyes, and a lean build.

"Welcome back, Arist Novelen." Garren bowed.

Orin smiled. "It's good to be home, Captain Romell."

Sid slapped the man on his back. "Garren!"

The captain coughed and nodded. "Welcome, Mr. vel'Forr. How was the journey?"

Fredrick smoothed the ruffles of his collar. "Rather cramped."

"It was quiet," Sid said, glancing at Shane.

Garren followed his gaze, then raised a brow. "Captain zem'Arta. Welcome to you also. Lady Praya is waiting for you at the embassy."

Shane nodded, then led his crew toward the gate.

Turning to Fredrick, Garren motioned to the palace. "Master Divelos, make sure the suite is prepared. I can escort Arist Novelen and Miss vel'Tamer from here."

Fredrick bowed low and strutted off with his head held high.

Garren whispered to Sid, "Things can't be very quiet if zem'Arta's here."

Sid placed a finger across his lips. "Kumuni Cosazi are very quiet."

Letting out a breath, Garren shook his head. "Burning fires," he mumbled. Turning to Orin, he tilted his head. "This way, Arist." He led Orin and his remaining companions into the shadow of a vine-covered pergola.

The tension in Orin's shoulders diminished within the privacy of the garden.

Approaching a carved green door, Garren rested his hand on the gold handle. "My lord, I've a little surprise for you. It's not strictly allowed, but you'll thank me for it, I'm sure."

He cracked open the door and ushered Orin inside. For a second, Orin stood alone in darkness and his imagination jumped to the worst conclusions. Close calls with assassins were to blame. Outside the door, Venna and Sid's collective laughter calmed him. Once his eyes adjusted, he realized he was in a shuttered drawing room, staring at a dazzling young woman in a lavish gown.

"My darling," Leonora squealed and threw herself at him, arms locking around his neck.

Orin caught her clumsily. "Le-Leonora?"

She fixed him with her chestnut eyes and kissed him deeply. Orin rocked off balance, but he returned her gesture, pushing her up against the wall.

After a long, sweet moment, she giggled and pulled back. "Ah, Orin, look at you." She brushed his lapel and cupped his face. "You need a shave. You look so tired."

"I'm a mess, aren't I?"

Leonora beamed as she smoothed her hand across his chest. "You're gorgeous. So much better than those stuffy letters I've put up with all year."

"Stuffy? My dear, they were poetic, fit for an empress!"

Leonora slapped his shoulder playfully. "I prefer you in person."

"Hmm, in that case . . ." Orin nuzzled her neck. The smell of lavender and roses permeated his senses. "Marry me, Leonora Sesporan."

She giggled and tossed her curls across her shoulders. "Certainly."

Orin pulled back, gazing into her perfect face. "How about next month? Are you busy on July the 10th?"

She laughed again, smiling brightly.

Light streamed in when Garren opened the door. "Time's up, love birds."

Orin kissed Leonora's gloved hand and, slowly releasing his grip, slipped from the room.

Garren escorted them toward Orin's private suite. As Sid walked beside Orin, he chuckled and patted him on the back. "You sly dog. How do I get Venna to fall all over me like that?"

"Stop flirting with everyone who walks by," Orin said.

Venna rolled her eyes and scoffed. "Don't encourage him, cousin. It'll never happen." She stuck her little, pointed nose in the air. "I have refined taste."

Sid barked. "You call zem'Arta refined?"

Venna blushed furiously, turning from Orin's disapproving stare. "Wh—I—we're friends. Besides, at least he has decent manners."

*Shane*

The downstairs mantel clock chimed eight in the morning. Shane stood outside the master bedroom door of a stately house. With pistol drawn, he kicked the door. It burst open with a sharp crack, splinters flying.

Inside the room, a man in a fine, lavender waistcoat shrieked and jumped against the opposite wall, knocking his powdered wig askew.

"Hello, Hemley," Shane said through a fanged grin. He holstered his pistol and closed the door behind him.

The Freeland embassy doorman shook and stuttered. "Wh-what . . . oh, Ca-Captain. What a surprise."

"I'm sure it is, considering all the security you've hired." Shane tossed a cloth cap—which he had taken from the unconscious guard at the back door—

onto the bed. It landed next to an open trunk stuffed with expensive-looking clothes and a heavy coin purse. "Where's Leron?"

"Please, Captain. I swear, I don't know."

"Why did you start packing the second you found out I was coming to Setmal?"

While staring at Shane, Hemley opened and closed his mouth.

"Where is he?" Shane said.

Hemley straightened his wig. "Sir, I swear! I don't know anything. I'm simply going on holiday."

Shane cracked his knuckles and fully extended his claws. "It's a very bad idea to lie to me, Hemley."

With wide eyes fixed on Shane's claws, Hemley threw up his hands. "I swear on the Spire Lords, I don't know!"

"Is that what you're going to tell them?"

Hemley gasped and plopped on the bed. "Sir? You're . . . taking me to testify?"

Shane smirked, then opened the bedroom door. A tall, dark figure dressed in a black coat filled the doorway. At his belt, the man carried a long, ancient saber. Even without the Spire Watch armor, visible wings, or braided hair, the Second Lord of Palim loomed, as dangerous as a hungry drake. When he entered the room, Tres's black eyes caught the light from the tall window and glinted like polished obsidian.

Hemley shrieked, rolling off the bed and scampering toward the wall, probably wishing he could melt into the floral ribbons of the wallpaper. "M-my lord. This is—"

Tres grabbed the servant by the throat and glowered. "An honor, I'm sure," he said in a deep tenor.

When Tres's own eyes changed to white, Hemley's nervous twitching stopped, his face became blank, and the room turned frigid for a full minute. After releasing Hemley from the hindsight trance, Tres dropped him, and the man slid to the floor, whimpering.

"Indeed," Tres said. "He knows nothing of Leron Novelen's disappearance."

Shane wrenched Hemley off the floor by the back of his collar. "Who did he tell?"

Tres cocked his head, poised like a serpent about to strike. "He sold the knowledge of Leron Novelen's disappearance to a cleric in the central Drawlen temple for three thousand tallies."

Shane whistled, then glared at the man in his grasp. "You could hire your own fleet of river yachts for that, Hemley. Is that why you're packing all the leisure jackets?" He released his grip on the man's shirt and stepped back.

Scrambling, Hemley dropped to his knees in front of Tres. "Oh please, Lord Romanus. Please have mercy."

"Mercy for a traitor?" Tres spat. He turned to Shane. "Kill him."

Shane frowned and shook his head. "We can hold him at the embassy. The Spire Watch will send an escort."

"I don't believe he deserves the dignity of the Arbiter's circle."

"This is what got you stuck with me in the first place, Spire Lord. We're not Drawlen throat cutters. He gets a trial."

"They'll execute him anyway." Tres put his hand on his sword. "Am I not the Second Lord of Palim? Is this not a confessed traitor?"

Hovering on the ground between them, Hemley reached for his wig lying on the floor. Shane smashed his boot on the man's hand. "Right now, Tres, you're the ambassador's assistant. So for now, I outrank you. He goes to trial." Then he turned and shouted at the open door, "Morgel!"

The ralenta appeared in the hall, shades swirling around him and then evaporating. Shane pulled Hemley to his feet and shoved him at Morgel. "Show this fool to his new accommodations."

Morgel caught the man, and they both disappeared in a torrent of black vapor.

Tres frowned and locked his arms across his chest. "There was a time you would have jumped at the chance to snap a traitor's neck. Did you know he invested much of that money in Drawlen mining stocks?"

Shane's blood pounded in his ears, but he held his breath, resisting the bait. "We have a missing Red Watch agent. His son has nine death marks on his name, and half the countries on this burning peninsula are itching to start a war with each other."

"You left out the Drawlen agents slithering around looking for a godkiller."

Shane narrowed his eyes. "The point is, I have a lot on my plate. I don't need you picking fights with me on top of it."

Tres clenched his teeth and exhaled. "Why were you so sure the doorman sold the information?"

"He's been doing that for years," Shane said. "Harry's been using him to give our enemies bad intel."

Tres threw up his arms. "Now the Drawls know our agent is missing. What good does that do us?"

"Would you pay three hundred thousand marks for information you already know? The Drawls don't have Leron. Either he's gone off on his own, or someone else has entered the game."

Tres quirked his thick brow. "Greq? Perhaps the Thurans?"

"We'll see."

Remm swaggered into the room. "Gentlemen," he said, smiling and twirling his arms. "I hate to interrupt this . . . bonding moment, but you're both due to escort the lovely Lady Praya to an archery tournament in one hour."

Tres sighed. "Why, exactly, must we attend these frivolous social trials?"

"Try to enjoy yourself, Tres," Shane said as he examined the cracks he'd put in the door. "Otherwise, it's gonna be a long decade."

Two hours later, Shane had completed an inspection of the martial arena at Garren's order. After hearing of the assassins in Palim, Orin's captain of the guard took no chances.

A few bystanders and archers populated the arena. On the other side of a low, dividing wall, a group of engineers prepared an array of cannons for testing in an artillery field. Occasionally, a cannon fired, filling the south side of the arena with a loud crack, followed by powder smoke.

"You don't look anything like an officer," a voice said from behind Shane.

Shane pivoted.

Fredrick Divelos, Orin's chief steward, occupied a spot near him in the lower stands. His bell sleeves and layers of ruffles on his chest amplified his haughty appearance. He pursed his lips, scanning Shane's freshly pressed uniform. "But you do look a deal more civilized."

Although stiff and uncomfortable, Shane's gray coat covered his tattoos, which was prudent for the time being. He brushed some dust off his sleeve. "At least I look military."

Fredrick nodded. "There's no doubt you're a warrior, Captain. No doubt at all." He focused past Shane to a woman standing on the firing line. "Oh dear. Arista Yvette has wasted no time in stirring up a scandal."

She drew the bow and fired, hitting the center of the closest target, then fired at the next one twenty yards further. Even with five targets staggered down the field, she hit every one dead center.

Behind Fredrick, a small crowd of early comers congregated. They clapped and whistled, earning a scowl from the archer.

"Scandal?" Shane said.

"I don't know how things are done in the Freelands, Captain." Fredrick lifted his chin and glared at Yvette. "But in Yvenea, archery is not a proper pursuit for a woman. And her choice of dress is . . ." He bit his bottom lip and closed his eyes.

Leggings and a long, fitted green tunic adorned Yvette's slender body, her bright blonde hair pulled back in a tight braid. She looked perfectly practical.

"Ah, here is our prince." Fredrick bowed low as Orin stepped onto the risers, followed by Garren, Sid, Venna, and three members of his personal guard. The women in the crowd curtsied. Some teetered in their restricting corsets as they resumed a stiff posture. The men each dropped to one knee and removed their wide-brimmed, feathered hats in exaggerated reverence. Most dressed in richly colored coats with puffy sleeves over ruffled blouses.

Orin had donned similar garb to the noblemen, though he wore no hat. Indeed, he appeared every bit as self-important and fanciful as his portraits. He approached one of the women, who remained in her deep curtsy. "Here I came to find some entertainment after my long journey. It seems I've stumbled upon a delight far more worthy." He took the woman's hand and kissed it when she rose with a giggle. "I will count this a most glorious day, my dear lady, only because we have crossed paths."

The woman beamed. Her smile was genuine, unlike the overzealous grins of the other nobles clamoring for the favor of the heir apparent.

Fredrick covered his mouth with his fan and whispered to Shane. "Arsita Leonora Sesporan. The youngest daughter of the High Chamberlain, and sister to Arista Yvette. She is my lord's fiancé."

Shane folded his arms and darted his gaze between Fredrick and the noble woman.

Leonora straightened her necklace, brushing a long dark lock behind her ear. "Father will be cross that you have seen me already. It was his wish to present me himself."

"If I close my eyes, may I remain here, my lady?" Orin's comment brought spontaneous laughter and applause from his audience.

Venna rolled her eyes but blushed when she saw Shane. She startled, though, when one of the nearby noblemen took her hand. She feigned delight but extended her claws just as he brought her fingers to his mouth, causing him to leap back and yelp.

Shane snorted and stifled a laugh, as did the servant woman standing behind the archer. Arista Yvette proceeded with her practice, only acknowledging her fellow nobles with glares.

Sid stepped beside Shane. "Does the Arista not like an audience?"

Her servant regarded Sid and Shane with a wary glance. "The Arista came early to practice, not to put on a show." She surveyed the nobles in the stands, then the pair of them again, regarding each more carefully. "You're no Yvean gentleman, clearly. Where are you from?"

"Freelands," Sid said, his nose high. He jutted his chin at Orin. "Came with him."

The servant woman nodded. "With Arist Novelen? In what capacity?"

"Bodyguard. What's your name?" he said with a smirk.

She hesitated, but answered, "Darï. And you?"

"Sid vel'Forr."

Shane leaned toward Sid and mumbled in Karthan, "Stop flirting, moron."

"Sure, Captain," he whispered. Sid winked at Darï before returning to Orin's side on the stands.

Darï nodded at Shane. "You're the captain of the new Freeland ambassador's guard, aren't you?"

"I am."

A resounding boom drowned the thud of Yvette's arrow hitting the target. Garren flattened Orin and Leonora to the ground. The other nobles scrambled and shrieked.

A section of the low stone wall opposite the training field cracked and crumbled. Dust and debris settled to reveal a gap a few feet wide with the back end of a large cannon wedged through it.

The same nobleman who had attempted to kiss Venna's hand moaned, "Oh, my fires above. I am unharmed."

"Joy," Venna mumbled, though Shane doubted the man heard her in his self-absorbed inspection of his frills and feathers.

Yvette dropped her bow and ran to the wall, Darï following. A string of curses in a gravelly voice trickled in from the opening, a voice Shane recognized immediately. When he arrived at the wall, a bald old man stuck his head through the opening.

"I thought that might be you, Harris," Shane said. "No one cusses quite like you."

Leo Harris's eyes widened and twinkled as he brushed debris from his leather apron. Shane offered the short fellow a hand. When Leo hobbled out of the wreckage, he punched Shane in the arm. "Zem'Arta, you tramp! Look—look at you." He gasped between bouts of mocking laughter. "Must have been some bribe if it got you into a burning uniform."

"Watch the language, old man. There's ladies around." Shane rubbed Leo's bald head.

Leo turned and bowed to Yvette. "Arista Sesporan. Please excuse the mess—and the noise."

Yvette nodded as she picked up her bow. "It is no trouble, Sir Harris. You are hard at work, I see."

"Sir?" Shane said.

Leo rocked onto his heels and pulled at his leather suspenders. "Aye, *Sir* Harris. Got myself knighted last year for my innovations. Course you'd know that if you bothered to come around now and then, you scoundrel—er, Captain." As Orin approached, Leo fell to one knee and bowed his head. "Mother of Dryads."

"You must be Sir Harris, the chief engineer," Orin said.

Leo stood tall and straightened his leather apron. "Yes, my lord."

"I hear you have made some brilliant advances to our artillery."

"Well." Leo kicked at a small pile of broken bricks. "I'm working out a few—er—difficulties."

"I look forward to seeing your accomplishments." Orin nodded and headed back to the stands.

Shane noticed movement across the field. Rodden prowled in his alley cat form under the shadow of a vine-covered pergola near the martial hall.

"Better clean up this mess, old man. Your wife would disapprove." Shane smacked Leo on the back and took off. When he reached the pergola, Rodden lounged on the rim of a retaining wall, licking his paw.

"Harry is waiting for you, rather impatiently," he said.

Shane shook his head and cackled. "Harry's never impatient. The whole world would fall apart otherwise."

"Regardless," Rodden growled. "I was denied the chicken I caught fairly until I bring you to the safe house. These Red Watch folk are touchy, losing their heads over a measly bird."

Shane snickered, imagining Rodden, an immortal lord of shapeshifters, chasing after a fat hen in the yard of an urban row house. "Fine. I'll come as soon as I can."

Rodden arched his back, curling his long tail around his legs. "Bring the prince."

"Are you kidding?" Shane said.

Rodden stretched his paws. "I'm only the messenger."

Shane sported his fanged grin. "What's worse, your majesty? Being stuck as an alley cat or being a messenger boy for the First Lord?"

Rodden stalked away and purred. "I'll remember that comment, pup."

# 13

# CURFEW

*Setmal, Yvenea*
*June 8, 1195 PT*

*Orin*

A guard ushered Orin and his companions down the long corridor leading to the Celestial Hall. Their footsteps echoed in the bare space once warmed by rugs and tapestries. Sunlight no longer filled the room. Shutters hid the tall windows, and an armed guard stood in front of each one. A double iron door and ten more guardsmen lined the end of the hall.

Orin cocked his head. "What happened to the old door?"

"His Highest replaced the wooden door this past winter," Garren said.

The nearest guard stepped forward and saluted. "Weapons are not permitted in the throne room, my lord."

Shane crossed his arms, veins pulsing in his neck, then handed the guard his pistol and cutlass. Perhaps the Red Watch captain was just as deadly without them.

Tres, on the other hand, rested his hand firmly on the pommel of his saber, Stonebreaker. "This is a relic of my house. I will not part with it."

The guard blinked and stuttered. "There is—they're not allowed."

Tres locked his gaze on the guard, his brow creasing as he gritted his teeth. Even with his wings hidden, their shadows loomed. "I will not part with it."

A chill filled Orin's lungs, as if a winter wind whipped through the space. Shane stepped between Tres and the guard. "I'll hold it for you and wait here, if that is acceptable?" he said in a steady tone, extending a hand to Tres. Then he whispered in Karthan, "This is not the place for your mind craft, Spire Lord. Remember why you're here."

Nostrils flaring, Tres unfastened the curved blade from his belt. He relinquished it to Shane while speaking to the guard. "Very well. My retainer will hold this in trust for me."

Shane's eyes darkened, and he briefly turned his head.

Tres adjusted his belt and smirked. "Don't cut yourself, Captain. A scratch alone from that blade could kill you."

Shane muttered under his breath, "I'm sure you wouldn't mind." He leaned against a pillar with his arms folded, the sword's hilt clenched in his fist.

Orin addressed the guard. "May we enter now?"

The guard steadied himself, though his face remained ash white. "Yes . . . yes, Arist Novelen." He waved a hand, and another soldier pushed open the doors, ushering in Orin, Tres, Praya, and Venna.

A dome painted with scenes of Yvean lore overlooked the vast, circular throne room of the Celestial Hall. In the center, forty feet above the marble floor, stretched an image of a man holding a shield. In front of him, a dragon spitting fire poised as a multitude of people fled into a cave behind the man.

Windowless white walls with blue banners bearing a four-pointed star contrasted against multiple black pillars. Before each stood a member of the High Guard, the dynast's personal protectors. Once, portraits of past rulers had hung in place of the banners.

The Yvean Dynast, Aronos Hilmoran, lounged on his mahogany throne on the high dais at the opposite end of the room. For the last decade, he had seemed like a man ready to die. Now in his 112th year, however, he looked younger and healthier than Orin had ever seen him. Even his close-cropped hair appeared darker. He waved his hand and motioned for Orin and his companions. As they approached, Aronos rose.

He spread his arms and beamed. "At last, the return of the long-absent prince of the white halls. Glad am I that he comes, for all the while I feared he may follow his sire into silence. Come here, nephew, and let me know that you are real."

Orin embraced him. "My dear uncle, Your Highest. It's good to be home again. But I have not come alone, as you know." He nodded at his companions.

Stepping forward, Aronos bowed to Praya. "Of course. Lady Ambassador, I am blessed to meet you, but I am sorry it is under such an adverse circumstance."

Praya returned his gesture. "I am pleased to meet you, Your Highest. Unfortunate circumstances can still be turned to good tidings. I hope to Sovereign this is such a time."

"I as well," Aronos said. Then he thrust out a hand to Tres. "Ah, now here is a face I remember. Lord Romanus, Second of the Spire Lords. It has been decades since you walked these halls. I dare say you have changed little."

Tres bowed his head. "I remember, Your Highest. That was an unprecedented time. Peace was upon all of Palimar."

"Yes. A brief peace shattered by a hunter's stray round shot." A fit of deep coughs brought the dynast into a hunch while he clutched his chest. "Curse this mortal cage!" When he recovered, he straightened and grasped his nephew's shoulder. "A feast is ready for us, Orin, and strong wine will do me well. Come and sit."

Aronos led them to a marble dining table laden with a spread of meat, bread, and fruit.

After they sat, Orin lifted his glass. "To your health, Uncle. You look well, better than I remember."

"Ach." Aronos waved his hand dismissively and slurped his wine. "It is a superficial improvement. A draught of somulet in every bath does wonders for the skin but nothing for what lies beneath."

Orin suspected something more behind the dynast's improved form, but he changed the subject. "The city guard has increased. The palace guard as well."

When he lifted his goblet, Aronos scowled. "There is no measure too great to ensure the safety of our noble house." His tone sharpened and his aged soul broke through, as though a dark disease lay beneath his vibrant façade, revealed only by a turn of his temper. "There are many scheming minds bent against this crown." He pounded his fist on the table.

"I do not doubt it, Uncle." Orin shifted in his seat.

Praya distracted the dynast in small talk. The tension loomed, however. Even Venna, oblivious to the full gravity of the circumstances, studied the dynast when his attention wandered.

An hour later, when servants ushered them from the throne room, Shane waited outside the door. As he handed Tres his sword, he jutted his jaw at Orin. "How's our favorite monarch?"

Orin stroked his chin. "He's in remarkably good health."

Tres buckled Stonebreaker to his belt. "A most curious improvement."

"What happened?" Shane asked.

Orin motioned toward the end of the hall. "We'll talk in my suite."

Fredrick greeted them when they entered Orin's personal rooms. "Now do you understand what I've been saying, my lord? His mind has taken a turn."

"That was more than a failing mind," Praya said, smoothing her dress and relaxing on a settee by the hearth.

Tres nodded. "Agreed. The dynast is gripped with paranoia. Founded or unfounded, it's dangerous."

"It may be something else entirely," Orin said, unbuttoning his dinner jacket and draping it across a chair. "The dynast has always been cautious of his enemies. He seems to have stumbled upon a revived health, however. And that worries me."

Fredrick grabbed Orin's jacket and straightened it on a hanger. "I can't imagine why good skin products worry you more than an ailing wit, my lord."

Orin stared out the tall window overseeing the palace garden, now bathed in red and silver moonlight. "Because, Fredrick, when men believe they can cheat death, they are never far from madness. That has been the lesson of history, has it not?" He dropped onto the couch next to Rodden, who stretched across the back, still in his alley cat form. The feline fixed his yellow eyes on Orin and held his gaze.

Late that night, as the watchmen changed rounds, Orin and Shane slipped from the palace through a cellar. At the end of the passage, an iron door had replaced the wooden one, and the lock had been changed. The dynast's paranoia had reached this secret tunnel as well.

Orin dangled the silver key he'd been given as a boy after his mother's murder. "How are you at picking locks, Captain?"

"On a Yvean compound lock? Lousy." Shane pulled an iron key from his pocket and turned the lock. "Good thing I know the locksmith."

Orin heaved the door open and inspected the lock as Shane pocketed the key. Beneath the keyhole was an emblem of interlocking lines, the Vultan symbol of eternity. This same symbol matched one on the cannon that crashed through the firing yard wall the day before. "Sir Harris?"

Shane grinned wolfishly, then rushed up the mucky stairs out of the neglected cellar. Orin sprinted after him. The streets lay dark and quiet. A sign on a storefront read:

**CURFEW, 10 O'CLOCK. MERCHANT PERMITS REQUIRED BETWEEN 4 A.M. AND SUNRISE. DELINQUENCY FINE, 150 TALLIES.**

"The annual merchant tax is less than this fine," Orin whispered, tapping the sign.

Shane hesitated as he peered down the vacant streets. "I'm beginning to see why Liiesh gave me this assignment."

Orin hummed in agreement. "There seems to be something more foul brewing here than the usual squabbling of ambitious nobles."

"This place is a few steps from marshal law, or worse," Shane said.

They dodged in and out of alleys all the way to a residential district near the west gate. Here, cobblestone avenues weaved along a steady rise to the white city walls. Four-story brick row houses with brightly painted doors lined the streets. In this charming, middle-class neighborhood, lush flower boxes with climbing ivy decorated porches. During the light of day, it would surely be an enchanting borough. But like the rest of the city, night settled eerily upon it. Windows remained shuttered, gates locked, and lanterns dark.

From the avenue on the hill, Orin scanned the city. The domes of the Cilé Faíl glittered in the distance, and the many sunrock lampposts lined its gardens like stars upon the hill. To the south, the windows of Fort Roe stood alight, giving shape to its gray tower against the night sky.

But only a few lampposts glowed in the city outside the palace and the walls. Little blue dots—lanterns carried by night watchmen—bobbed in and out of his view. "This is not the noble city I remember."

"More like a prison." Shane led Orin into a small yard full of flowers and a chicken coop, then used his same key on the back door of the house.

Once inside, Orin blinked repeatedly, his eyes adjusting to the indoor darkness. Before he could identify anything, however, a metallic click cracked across the room.

"If you're here to rob me, you're wasting your time," a hoarse voice spoke. "I'm a member of the smith's guild, and they'll have you hung before sunrise."

"Since when do burglars get past your locks, you senile idiot?" Shane barked.

Blue light flooded the room, revealing a simple kitchen. Shane waved a glass cover, one that fit the housing of the sunrock lamp on the table. Sir Leo Harris stood in a wide doorway, aiming a pistol and sporting a pair of multi-lensed glasses high on his forehead. An oil-stained leather apron hugged his round belly.

"Ha." He slapped his sides. "I should have guessed. And who's yer friend here? Better not be dragging rogues into my house again, boy."

Shane scoffed and motioned to Orin. "Not a rogue, Leo. Though he sure moves like one."

Flashing his teeth, Orin dropped the hood of his gray cloak. "Stealth is handy when half the world wants you dead."

Leo stumbled into a bow. "My prince! An honor, an absolute honor, to have you in my home."

With a wave of his hands, Orin repaid the gesture. "It is my honor, sir, to be entrusted into a safe house of the Red Watch. And please, there is no need for such formalities here."

Behind the old man, a woman's call reached them from the hallway. "Leo, have you got company?"

Leo grumbled and set his pistol on the table. "No, Harriette. I'm talking to myself."

Shane smacked Leo on the side of the head. "Don't talk to the good woman like that, geezer."

"Who's with you, Leo?" Harriette popped around the corner and bumped into Leo. "Shane!" she called with delight as she bustled toward him.

Shane's shoulders tensed and he cleared his throat.

A smile dawned on the old woman's petite face. She matched Leo's short stature but had a thin, graceful figure. Her tidiness extended from head to toe, her hair in a neat bun and her white sleeping robe crisply ironed. "Oh, my boy, good to see you again!" She pulled Shane into a firm hug.

He received her with a hesitant pat on the back.

Harriette squeezed him tighter. "Shane, Shane." She released him and turned to her husband. "Oh, Leo, why didn't you tell me he was coming today?"

"It's damn near midnight, Harriette. It's not like he came by for afternoon tea." Leo grumbled under his breath as he set out plates and retrieved pies and cakes from the pantry at his wife's request. Harriette bowed gracefully to Orin and bade him to sit. The three men relaxed before a spread that easily could have fed ten.

"Eat your fill, please, both of you." Harriette pushed the apple pie near Orin and clasped her hands together. "And don't mind me. I've got to finish my cleaning." She shuffled out of the room, leaving the men to their feast.

"Cleaning?" Orin said. "At this hour?"

"Aye, cleaning," Leo said with a wink. "There's no end to it for that woman. Besides, with all this curfew nonsense, there's not time enough for that sort of thing while the sun is up."

Shane licked his fingers after consuming an entire plate of bacon. He had missed dinner, after all. "Does Harry have an ear about what's going on?"

"Don't ask me," Leo said. "I'm just a blacksmith. You'd better check in."

Shane nodded and disappeared through the doorway into the hall. Orin now sat alone with Leo Harris, who tipped a second helping of lemon cream pie onto his plate.

"Glad he didn't bring that little ralenta with him," Leo grumbled between mouthfuls.

"Bren?"

"Aye. Can't get hardly a crumb with that boy around."

Orin cleared his throat and straightened his back, glancing around the room. Above the counter, a pot of petunias with cascading blooms filled the sill of the shuttered window. Across from the pantry on a large hearth rested a tea kettle and stew pot, ready for the next day's work. The mantel displayed three clay urns, all bearing the image of an eight-pointed star—Sovereign's symbol.

"Do you not send your dead to the Harvest?" Orin asked.

"This is a Red Watch safe house, lad. Er—well . . ." Leo scratched the back of his neck.

Orin waved a hand. "Please, no ceremony needed."

"Aye. Well, my wife, Harriette, is a Freelander, and I have my own grudge against Drawlen. At any rate, the souls of my daughters and my son-in-law are not going to feed some fire demon in Drawl. They belong to Sovereign, and their urns belong to me." Leo's strange spectacles clinked as he set them on his plate.

For a moment, Orin held his breath. "Daughters—my dear man. I'm sorry. A father shouldn't have to bear the ashes of his children."

Leo glared. "They should not, especially for petty greed. My daughters died so Drawlen miners could dig earth where they had no business digging." He leaned forward, his burly forearm pressing into the table. "Do you know how much sunrock they got from that mine when they cleaned it out?" He slammed his fist on the table. The plates rattled. "Seven crates. Only seven. I have lost much to Drawlen's cruelty, Orin Novelen. I know you have as well. I, at least, have the comfort of knowing they paid dearly for my children's lives—very dearly."

Orin again studied the urns. They were similar designs with names painted on them: Gavin, Maier, and Nola. A small black wolf's head identical to one of the tattoos on Shane zem'Arta's back rested below Nola's name.

Orin's eyes darted to Leo. "Your daughter was . . ."

"Yes, ran off with that vagrant." Leo pointed to the hall where Shane had left moments ago. "They were eighteen and stupid. But all the same, I don't mind him as a son-in-law."

"And he repaid his wife's murder in blood?" Orin asked.

"With interest. Best if you don't bring that up with him though." Leo gulped the last of his tea. "Be careful with him, Orin Novelen. He has his reasons for helping you, and you couldn't find a man better for the work that needs doin'. But he's dangerous. Don't give him a reason to make an enemy out of you, not even a thought."

# 14

# HARRY

*Setmal, Yvenea*
*June 8, 1195 PT*

*Shane*

Shane approached the interrogation cellar in the safe house, a gnawing pain in his gut. Too much about the place remained the same since his last visit six years ago. He dismissed the vivid memories. That life had died with Nola, and he didn't need it haunting him when he had a job to do—a job far more complicated than Liiesh had revealed. It was just like him to pull these manipulative power plays.

Taking a deep breath, Shane opened the closet at the end of the hall and pulled the broken broom handle within it. A hidden door at the back swung open, revealing a downward stairwell. On the ceiling, a dim sunrock lantern lit the landing, and another door at the bottom of the stairs stood ajar. Through it, Tres's profile shuffled into view.

"Great," Shane muttered as he descended the steps and entered the room.

Harriette Harris, Shane's mother-in-law and commander of the Red Watch, fussed over a red-robed priest tied to a chair. She stood back and smoothed her apron before smiling at Shane. "Hello, Red Wolf," she said, patting his arm as he entered.

"Harry." Shane nodded and slowly circled the room. "More cleaning, huh?"

The old woman dabbed a rag on the priest's lips, cooing encouragingly. The priest, perhaps in his twenties, sported a bruised cheek and crusted blood in his blond hair. "Hospitality before hostility," she said. Then she set the rag on the table and pointed to Shane's cheek. "You look a bit rough yourself."

Shane plopped into a chair. "I'm sure I don't have to tell you."

Harry tucked a loose strand of hair under her bun and motioned to Tres. "Show your findings to Captain zem'Arta, my lord."

Tres turned, eyes white and gleaming, trapping Shane in his gaze. While locked in Tres's hindsight, Shane observed Rupert Hemley, the embassy doorman, through the eyes of the Drawlen priest:

*Hemley spoke in a whisper. "He kept a secret stash of Vultan artifacts in a trunk in his office. He stole them, I'm sure."*

*The priest's eyes widened. "Where are they now?"*

*Hemley scowled. "With him, I assume. He spent the last month cleaning out his office. Every speck of dust removed!"*

*"And you don't know where he's gone?"*

*"I told you already! He's disappeared. I've checked everywhere, like you asked. The man is a ghost. If he doesn't want to be found, he won't be."*

*The scene blurred, replaced with a hooded collector in a dark room. A shadow concealed the man's face, his body lean, his posture casual. He handed the priest a coin purse, bowed, and left.*

Unprepared for the sudden assault and release of mind craft, Shane doubled over, gripping the chair. He shook himself, head pounding. "Warn me next time, jackass."

Tres shrugged. "I was only following orders." He dragged the chair, the moaning priest still strapped tightly, into the adjoining room.

Dabbing her forehead and sighing, Harry sat across the table from Shane. "Now I'll have to find a new false informant. Such an inconvenience."

Shane contemplated Hemley's words. "Leron was stockpiling Vultan artifacts, burning packin' them. That little shit planned to disappear."

Straightening her apron, Harry nodded. "It seems so."

Shane scratched at the new scar on his cheek. "You keeping him around?" He pointed to the next room where mumbled prayers streamed from the priest, fading to silence.

"Too risky. As long as you throw this kind of work Tres's way, you two might actually get along."

"He does like being a bully," Shane said.

Harry pulled an envelope from her apron pocket. "Leron gave me a curious thing before he ran off." She removed two papers from the envelope. Placing them on the table, she pointed to a list. "These names he suspects are Drawlen sheep hiding in the noble Yvean flock." She flattened the other paper. "And then there's this." The torn paper contained a riddle in Leron's tidy handwriting:

> It's time for a hunt. But be cautious.
> The shepherd drinks from the cup of the western wolf.

Shane narrowed his eyes and crossed his arms. "The western wolf?"

Harry bent closer over the paper and rubbed her eyes. "I'm not sure of its meaning. I assume shepherd refers to the dynast. Drawlen seems like an obvious choice, though perhaps he meant Taval Sesporan, the High Chamberlain. His home district is on the western border. But he's not on the list." She slid back in her chair, shaking a finger in the air. "He's aware of us, though only in part. If we're very careful, he could become an ally. But that will be long in coming. I'm afraid Leron is referring to something more sinister than the classic court intrigue. The dynast has . . . changed."

Shane raised his eyebrows. "So I've heard."

Harry flipped the paper over, revealing one last word. "He left something for you too, didn't he?"

Placing his elbow on the table, Shane rested his forehead into his palm. With his other hand, he fingered a note in his pocket. Slowly, he removed it and laid it next to Harry's paper, matching the torn halves and completing an ancient Vultan phrase:

**FINIS ORIGINE PENDET**

"The end hangs on the beginning," Harry said.

Shane flipped over his note:

> The enemy is not who we think.
> The story we know is a lie.
> Go back to the place of our namesake.
> Remember the reason we spy.

Shane and Harry locked gazes. Sometimes, Shane saw her daughter looking back at him. He cleared his throat and fidgeted with the notes.

"Have you shown this to anyone?" Harry asked.

"No one. You?"

Harry patted her lips. "Not even Leo. Clearly, these were meant for you and me only. How did you get yours?"

"Vernon vel'Tamer. He knew nothing. Besides you, he's the only other person I can think of that Leron fully trusts. If he doesn't know anything—" Shane fluttered his lips and smacked the table. Leron had simply vanished four months ago, leaving only these cryptic farewells.

"What do you suppose he means by 'go back to the place of our namesake'?" Harry asked.

Shane scratched his chin. "The Red Watch, maybe?"

Harry frowned. "Named for the ancient guardians of the Devourer's Prison. The Mortari Order."

"Or," Shane said, "it could have something to do with Karthan or even Vultan history. I can't be sure."

From the clock on the wall, a somber tone chimed in the first hour of the night. Harry retrieved her note and stuffed it in her pocket. "Leaving us with cryptic riddles. I'll wring his neck when he shows up again."

"Right after you fill him with pie?"

Harry's frown cracked into a bemused smile. "No one wants to butcher a skinny hen. Now, we must get this Novelen boy through his wedding without having his own funeral along with it." She scurried to her feet and retied her apron strings. "Let's see what we can do about these Drawlen loyalists before then. We'll deal with the rest afterward. Send the boy down. I need to prepare him for his new life under the shadow of nine death marks." She put the list back in the envelope and slid it across the table. "Good hunting, wolf."

Shane peeked at the list, then whistled softly. It was going to be a busy month.

# 15

# A FAREWELL

*Lorinth, Taria*
*June 23, 1195 PT*

*Jeb*

Jeb slouched on a crate, cradling his chin in his hand while gazing at the market square. The table before him held baskets stuffed with early summer produce, stalks of rhubarb, bundled herbs, and hanks of spun qiviut. Although the morning waned, the market still bustled. Not that Lorinth was a big town, but it housed the only Drawlen temple within a hundred miles. Yet the temple was rather modest, or so Jeb had been told. On top of this, the Life Harvest had begun with the Lorinth caravan set to leave the next morning.

Jeb vividly remembered the last Life Harvest when he was eight—David had been taken. The old man's sallow face and kind smile played upon Jeb's memory. He clutched his chest and blinked away tears. Everyone, even the Drawlen clergymen, feared the rangers managing that caravan. In the town square, they had hung a dead man's body and ordered healthy citizens to join the journey.

This time, five years later, people implemented festival preparations with guarded enthusiasm. The night before, Father Ferren, the principal of the Lorinth Temple and a generally stern individual, had approved the fireworks at the Solstice Festival. Burn marks still marred the temple stage from the spectacular show.

Jeb startled when a sinister shadow fell over him.

"Hello, ginger whelp." Philip Creedle, a seventeen-year-old menace, hovered before him. Jeb imagined Philip bore the average persona of a slave driver's boy: cruel and slightly crosseyed.

Rattling off the prices, Jeb read the slate signs on the table.

"I can read," Philip said.

"Oh, well, I didn't want to assume." Jeb snickered. He dared to be so witty knowing his older brother stood inside the sick house next to his stall.

Sneering, Philip rested against the building, setting his cap on a window ledge. "I think you're trying to be clever, Therman." He ran his fingers through his hair and loomed closer.

Jeb feigned worry, widening his eyes.

The thick, pimply boy moved closer, gritting his teeth. With Philip's attention fixed on his target, he missed the hand snatching his hat through the window, and the other hand wielding a butter knife caked with bacon grease, lathering the top of the hat.

"I—my mother tells me I'm clever. All the time." Jeb leaned back.

"Does she tell you, you've a black eye?"

Jeb frowned. "No."

Philip reached across the table, grabbed Jeb by the collar, and formed a fist with his free hand. "She will today, you little—"

Jeb's sixteen-year-old brother, Nate, exited the sick house in time to grab Philip's wrist. "I wouldn't, Creedle-beetle. I really wouldn't."

Philip released Jeb and sprang away. Even though Philip was older and bigger, Nate had pummeled him many times in the last year. What Nate lacked in size, he compensated for in frightening determination.

Philip's upper lip twitched. He placed his grease-treated cap on his head and marched away.

"What was the point of that?" Jeb asked.

"Wait for the punch line." Nate blew on his polished bone whistle. No sound, but the result was instantaneous.

Ezron, their one-hundred-thirty-pound frost hound, sprang from the tavern steps and bounded toward Philip. The dog's tail wagging and his tongue lolling to the side, he tackled the unsuspecting boy and licked his head.

Philip screeched as two more dogs ran for him. He lay pinned beneath three beasts happily lapping at his head. A smaller dog darted from the smithy and ran off with the hat. After struggling a few minutes, Philip freed himself. No one helped.

Seething through gritted teeth, he glared at the brothers.

Jeb beamed, but Nate locked eyes with Philip, twirling the knife in his hand. Jeb expected Philip to stomp off pouting, so he yelped when Philip charged at them.

"Oh crap," Nate breathed.

Within arm's reach of Nate, Philip was blocked by the solid form of Will Loren. Adjusting the rifle slung across his back over his brown militia uniform, Will gazed woefully at Philip.

The boy returned an ugly scowl, then walked off, mumbling curses.

Nate applauded. "Nicely done, Sergeant. The good citizens of Lorinth thank you once again for fending off the dastardly menaces of the valley."

Will flashed Nate the same judgmental expression he'd given Philip. "Was that really necessary?"

Ezron trotted to Nate and sat, his gray muzzle level with the boy's waist. He panted and cocked his head. Nate scratched the dog's heavy brow. "Ata boy, Ez." He offered the butter knife, Ez lapping it eagerly. "You used to be so much fun, Willy. That uniform's got you all serious and boring."

Will cracked a smile, his deep blue eyes shining. "I get paid more if I'm boring." His smile fell when he looked beyond Nate.

Ella rounded the sick house, striding toward Donfree's Trading Post. A tall, handsome young man walked beside her. She smiled as he spoke, his copper-toned skin gleaming in the sun.

Will scowled. "Who's that with El?"

"Oh, you're behind on town gossip. That's Ari il'Dani," Jeb said.

"il'Dani?" Will asked.

Nate grabbed strawberries from Jeb's basket, stuffing them into his mouth and mumbling. "Yup. Abad's boy,"

Will swatted a fly with his tricorn hat. "I didn't know Abad had a son."

Jeb and Nate laughed while elbowing each other. "I don't think he did either," Jeb said, "at least until last summer."

Adjusting his belt, Will turned to Jeb with his brow raised.

"He's from southern Corigon, served in the martial ranks." Jeb tossed a piece of jerky at Ezron, who chomped on it. "He's our pa's apprentice. Helping with the business while Ella's assisting with the Life Harvest and . . . well, she's staying in Shevak again this winter."

Will glanced back at Ella and her companion. Ari bent closer and said something, causing Ella to snicker. They disappeared into the shop.

Nate patted Will on the back. "Don't you worry. Come tomorrow, you and El will be off on the Life Harvest, and you'll have her all to yourself."

Scraping his boot across the dirt, Will dropped his gaze. "Yeah. Not sure that'll matter much."

Jeb lifted a basket and offered Will its contents. "Oh, don't be so glum."

Will popped a strawberry into his mouth. "She just doesn't seem . . . interested. She's always running off on market trips with your pa or Cameron. Now she'll be spending the fall and winter in Shevak. Again."

"Of course she is!" Nate grabbed the nearby lamppost and swung around it. "Who'd want to stay in this dreary town if they could go off to Shevak? You want Ella Therman's attention, you're gonna have to offer more than those dreamy blues." Leaping from the pole, he flung his arms wide. "You need a grand gesture. You know, like rescuing her from the clutches of death or secretly being a prince and all that."

Jeb flung his head back and laughed.

Will smiled, but the expression faltered into a deep frown. "Neither of which will happen."

Grabbing the half-empty basket, Jeb consumed another strawberry. "With all the books you've read and those big muscles, I'm sure you'll come up with something." He gathered the baskets and arranged them in his crate. "Party's over, Nate. Mom wants us home for afternoon chores."

*Jon*

Jon took three puffs of his pipe, then dozed off while the sun climbed over the horizon. A moment later, he startled awake in time to catch his pipe before it hit the inky planks of the barn loft. Voices, youthful and chiding, echoed in the stone building. The angle of light streaming through the round window crowning the loft confirmed it was still early morning. Turning his attention to the conversation below him, he leaned forward.

"Let's have a real spar, Ari. Or is that sword of yours just for decoration?" Nate said.

It struck Jon how much older his son sounded. A boy of sixteen, Nate was eagerly approaching manhood—much too eagerly in Jon's opinion.

"It's for self-defense. You never know what you'll run into on the open road," Arimal said.

The Sidrian scout had practically been born to combat. It was ingrained into his posture; therefore, Jon instructed him to use a false backstory to explain his expertise to questioning locals and Jon's sons. Since he looked every bit a southerner, his story included being trained in the Corigish military. Honestly, the hardest part of the facade was remembering to call the young man "Ari" instead of "Arimal."

Everything else was legitimate—as much as a smuggler's apprentice could be legitimate. As a future leader of the Ruvian refugees, Arimal needed to learn as much as possible about the world outside his secluded city, especially since the Ruvians hoped to occupy their own recognized territory in Palimar within the next generation.

"Oh, come on," Nate argued.

Ah, still a bit of a rascally boy in that voice!

"Tell you what," Arimal said, "if you can pin your sister in a grappling match, we'll spar."

Nate scoffed. "You want me to pin a girl?"

A musical laugh trailed in from the open door. "Challenge accepted," Ella said. After a yelp, a series of grunts, and the grinding of gravel beneath booted feet, Ella gave a triumphant, "Aha!"

Nate moaned.

Arimal chuckled, sounding just like his father. "There's plenty of time for sparring after you do your chores."

Jon sat up. The back of Nate's head, a mess of brown waves, bobbed into view over the loft's edge. Arimal moved next to Nate, standing several inches taller with his hair newly cut in the chin-length southern style. He slapped a hand on Nate's back. "Time to get some work done."

Nate shrugged and followed Arimal out the door. A moment later, Jeb's rebuke echoed from the garden. "Hands out of my crop, you whelp!"

"Lighten up," Nate said. "It's just one tomato."

"Sure," the younger boy said, "every time you walk by."

Jon strode to the round window overlooking the garden between the barn and the house. Jeb, barefoot and donning a dirt-stained tunic, wielded a hand plow with ease. This thirteen-year-old could happily ignore the world in favor of a garden for the rest of his life.

Nate threw a small, green tomato in the air and caught it behind his back.

Tossing his hand plow, Jeb leapt over the low wall and lunged at Nate. The fluid motion stunned Nate, knocking the tomato out of his mouth. In a heap of limbs, the brothers tumbled to the ground. As the boys wrestled, the half-eaten tomato lay forgotten on the gravel.

Arms folded, Arimal propped himself against the rusty lamppost at the corner of the garden. He had just turned twenty-three and had all the grit of a young warrior, regardless of his farmer's guise. As he oversaw the match, he picked a yellow tomato and popped it into his mouth.

Clamping his pipe between his teeth, Jon chuffed. He descended the ladder, black chips of paint from the wood rungs falling into the pile on the ground. Nate still hadn't repainted the rungs.

"Spying, Papa? Or did you sneak off to have a smoke?"

At the sound of his daughter's voice, Jon spun around. She smiled at him from her perch on the partition between the empty stalls. On the bench at her feet sat neatly arranged clothes, tools, and a traveling pack. His heart leapt. Had the day come already? Of course, he came to the loft for this reason in the first place—to gather his thoughts and prepare to see his daughter off on another solo voyage.

He tapped his finger on the pipe, sending a small cloud of ash floating to the ground. "It's not spying if it's my property, but yes."

Ella landed on her feet, standing a head shorter than Jon. Layers of vest, tunic, and scarf protruded from her patchy traveling coat. A haphazard mass of dark curls framed her dirt-smeared face. As a woman of marrying age—and of beauty—Ella purposely presented herself in a homely manner without looking ridiculous. A tactic her mother taught her well.

This society viewed women as little more than breeding vessels. Yet, with her mother a slave and her father a convict, most of the bachelors in Lorinth remained cautious around her. She was the only daughter of Jon Therman, a shrewd merchant hardened by the Drawlen mines and a stay in Langry Prison. Once Ella left with the Life Harvest caravan, however, she would be outside the protection of Jon's reputation—twenty, unmarried, and alone.

"Papa?"

Jon sighed and pulled the pipe from his mouth. "It seems like you only just returned from spending the winter with Krishena."

Ella stared out the doorway, her face falling into a frown. "Perfect."

Jon followed her gaze. Will Loren approached on horseback, clad in a crisp temple guard uniform and black tricorn hat. Nate rushed him as he dismounted.

"Ready down, soldier," the boy yelled, putting Will into a sloppy headlock.

Will planted his foot and tripped Nate over his knee, freeing himself. "Been a while since you've been able to beat me, farmer." He pulled Nate up by the wrist, and they slapped one another on the back.

"What is he doing here?" Ella whispered. "He's supposed to be on leave. And he's in guard uniform! Oh, mother of dryads, is he—"

"Perhaps he's come to propose."

Ella glared at Jon. "Don't even joke about that."

Jon put a hand on her shoulder and laughed. "There was a call for militiamen to volunteer for the Life Harvest last week."

Ella sighed as she stuffed the last garment into her bag. "I don't suppose you discouraged him."

Jon smirked and placed his pipe into his pocket. "You'll be surrounded by young, undisciplined soldiers, Ella. He's the closest thing to protection I could secure."

Rolling her eyes, Ella cinched her bag. "He's been trying to court me all summer, Papa. He could end up being more trouble than help. How am I supposed to scope for Life Harvest deserters while he's following me around?"

"Don't worry. No one, especially the guards, will have time for things like romance. Once you join the caravan in Depbas, he'll hardly have time to sleep."

Ella huffed and slung the bag over her shoulder. "You'd control the weather if it were possible." She stomped out the barn door and marched down the drive.

Jeb smoothed his hair after Will muffed it. Arimal still leaned against the lamppost, a standoffish expression on his face.

In stiff motion, Will tipped his head to Arimal. "Mr. il'Dani."

Arimal nodded, acknowledging his alias, his eyes remaining cold. "Sergeant."

"William Loren," Ella said. "What in the fires are you doing?"

Will turned his sparkling eyes on Ella. "I'm your ride, m'lady."

As Jon caught up to Ella, he saw the defiance in her hazel eyes before she could hide it. She forced a smile and tilted her head. "That's awfully kind of you."

Jon gripped Will's wrist firmly. "Kind indeed, Master Loren. Join us for breakfast."

"Breakfast sounds grand, Mr. Therman."

Indeed, it was grand. Ruth had a feast ready in the kitchen. Clay platters of steaming eggs, hash, and vegetables covered the green, chipped surface of the table. Cameron Donfree, one of Jon's smuggling partners, was already seated, having arrived while Jon napped in the loft.

Around the modest table, they sat elbow to elbow, but the spread exceeded what most townsfolk could afford.

"Do you always eat like this?" Will asked between bites.

"Oh, fires, no." Ruth wiped her hands on her apron and passed a bowl of potatoes. "This is a sendoff. It's the last meal Ella will have at this table until next spring."

Setting down the potato bowl, Will frowned at Ella. She pursed her lips and stared into her coffee mug.

Near the end of breakfast, Jon intercepted Nate and Jeb throwing scraps of ham out the window for Ez. The dog shoved his gray head through the opening and drooled on the floor.

Jon pointed to the counter. "Dishes, boys. And clean the floor too."

Jeb's shoulders sagged. "Yes, sir."

A pile of plates in hand, Nate sauntered to the counter.

Arimal reached for Ella's plate. Will shot out his arm, and both men glared at one another with their hands on either end of the dish. Rolling her eyes, Ella snatched the plate from their collective grip. When she returned from handing the plate to Nate, Arimal hugged her. "See you next year, El."

Will folded his arms and glared at the other man.

"Let's go, Ari," Cameron said. "I want to make it to Hillarock before nightfall." After embracing Ella, Cameron left the house, Arimal following.

"Will, can you please tie up my pack while I say goodbye?" Ella asked.

He nodded and headed outside, leaving Jon and his family alone for the last time this year.

Nate sank into the nearest chair. "I sure hope I don't get drafted as a Life Harvest escort for my compulsory service." He slung a damp rag over his shoulder, his fingers wrinkled from dishwater.

"You'd rather serve a whole year in the militia? All they do is march around town and chase off teenage delinquents like you," Ella said. "I get to fry salt pork all summer."

Jon put up a hand. "We'll deal with that when the time comes. For now, focus on your burning chores, young man."

Nate sighed and went back to the sink.

Jon rose and brought Ella into a tight hug. Kissing her cheek, he whispered, "Be careful, precious one."

Ella gave her father a reassuring squeeze, then embraced her mother and brothers. Jon and Ruth followed Ella out front, where Will perched in his saddle. He grasped Ella's forearm as she slung herself behind him, and they trotted down the drive. When they disappeared around the hill, Jon let out a long breath.

Ruth snaked an arm around his waist. "She'll be fine. She's a very capable young woman."

Jon snorted and cocked his head at his wife. "The world is full of things foul and cunning. Capable or not, she's my daughter."

"Our daughter." Ruth patted his arm. "And we've prepared her the best we could. Now let's focus on preparing our sons for such a world."

Folding his arms, Jon pivoted toward her. Perhaps Ruth felt as world-weary as he did, though she hid it well. The gleam of mischief she always held in her hazel eyes grew especially present.

"Just last week, Nate got into a brawl over some nonsense in town." Jon brushed stray hairs away from her twinkling eyes. "Ferren dragged him here and gave me the longest lecture of my life. Can you imagine the trouble that boy would cause if we told him all we're involved in? Smuggling is one thing. Helping Ruvians build and arm a city? He'd burst out of his skin!"

Chuckling, Ruth kissed his cheek. "Well, Ferren's going to the festival in Drawl, so you needn't worry."

Jon scowled as he scratched his beard.

"Kidding," she chimed in, scurrying back into the house.

Jon pulled a crumpled letter from his pocket. It had arrived three weeks ago, the first his oldest son had sent in years. Written in messy, smudged script, it carried Remm's nonchalant humor.

Hey Pops,

I'm passing this through Auntie K's people, so I'm not going to say much. They're nosey. Remember when I used to pretend to be a pirate? I met a few lately. They're not very nice. Smelly too. They probably don't like sitting in a dungeon, but it sure was fun getting them there. Anyway, I'm going to be in Yvenea for a while. If you're heading east, let me know. Maybe we could catch up? Tell Mouse and Trickster thanks for the wanted posters again. Boy, was I a funny-looking kid.

All the best,

R

# 16

# THE COOK

*Lorinth, Taria*
*June 24, 1195 PT*

*Ella*

When Ella and Will arrived, an assembled caravan awaited them in the Lorinth town square. Three of the four wagons had canvas covers, open in the front and back, stretched over arched frames with the gray Tarish flag tied to either side. Only one caged wagon completed the lineup. Lorinth journeyers weren't known to be unruly, but the cold metal bars of this cage served as a reminder: the Festival of Souls ritual was compulsory.

"Oy, Sergeant!" someone called from the temple platform.

Ella spotted Edd Pran, one of her least favorite people, sauntering down the temple steps. He slung a flintlock rifle over his shoulder, his uniform wrinkled and dusty. The wanton look he flashed Ella turned her stomach. "Hello, dolly." As he came closer, his breath reeked of liquor.

"It's Miss Therman." Will straightened, stretching a few inches taller than the thin rifleman.

Ella grabbed her pack from Will, ignoring Pran and strolling up to Captain Arik Leir. The captain sat astride a stout horse at the head of the line of ox-drawn wagons. His uniform, yellowed with years, lay beneath a brown wool cloak.

"Ella Therman. Reporting for service, sir."

The captain nodded at the first wagon. "You'll ride there, Miss Therman." He bent forward in his saddle and whispered, "And if Edd gives you trouble, you give it right back, you hear? Boy could use a hard kick to the groin, if you ask me."

Ella smiled and headed to the wagon. Rose, Father Emrell Ferren's apprentice, blocked her way. Ella sidestepped the green-clad priestess, but the girl moved with her.

Arms crossed, Rose glowered, a contrast to her soft, chubby face. "I won't ride with a commoner."

Ella scowled as her hand went to her chest, subconsciously reaching for the stone pendant hanging from the leather band around her neck. Since Rose had arrived in Lorinth a year ago, she quickly gained the reputation as the snobbiest girl in town. She was a seventeen-year-old castoff of some noble family from Estbye—a common fate for girls of highborn families in debt. But Rose was just a girl, Ella reasoned, abandoned and afraid. Anger was the easiest armor to wear.

The incredulous scowl faded from Ella's face, and she set her pack on the ground. She stuck out her hand. "I'm the cook."

Hands on her hips, Rose scoffed and turned up her nose. "I don't care who you are, Therman. This is my wagon, and I'll decide who rides in it."

Dropping her arm, Ella sighed. "I mean no offense, but it's poor form to bite the hand that feeds you."

Pran trotted over and snaked a hand around Ella's waist.

She jerked away, glaring at him.

"You can ride with me, dolly," he said.

Rose groaned. "No one wants to ride with you, pervert."

Father Ferren burst from the doors of the temple in a flurry of green robes and swaying jowls, rattling the ornate glass doors against the marble wall. He grunted and laboriously descended the steps.

If anyone required a wagon to himself, it was this man. Other than being enormous and occasionally ill-tempered, however, Ella appreciated him. Ferren was, above all else, a fair man.

He dropped a heavy bag at Ella's feet. "Pack this up, girl. We're late."

Ella braced herself and heaved the bag into the cart.

Ferren placed a hand on Rose's shoulder. "Bellerose, make sure Miss Therman has everything she needs. If she's out of sorts, we don't eat. Understand?"

Scrunching her nose, Rose smiled with pursed lips at Ella, who shrugged.

Pran slunk away but continued to ogle Ella as the caravan readied to leave. Between Pran's persistence and Rose's complaints, Ella's mood soured. Seven hundred miles was a long way to travel even in good company. This journey would be a downright chore.

Four days later, Ella sat around a bright pile of sunrock with fifteen journeyers, seven soldiers, a cleric, and an apprentice. Ferren was concluding a boisterous retelling of one of Nate's latest delinquent escapades.

"I caught the Therman lad tying Philip Creedle to a post in the barley field!" Ferren choked out his words through bouts of laughter. "The poor boy was dressed up like a scarecrow. And I'm sure, had I not come, he'd have been there all night."

"I'd say that Therman boy's grown on you," Captain Leir said while turning the sunrocks.

Ferren balked, but Ella agreed with the captain. The priest often displayed a fatherly disapproval of Nate's antics but was never hostile.

"Well," Rose said, "I think he's a downright troll."

"That's because he keeps putting rosehip in your clothes," Will said.

"What? That was *him*?" Rose stomped off, fuming. "That whole burning family is a load of fiends," she hollered as she passed Ella, throwing up her hands.

That evening Will lingered after supper. He crated the sunrocks from the cook pile with an iron tong while Ella washed the pots.

"You should be sleeping, not doing my job." Ella wrung the water from her rag.

Will took the cloth and hung it on the line to dry. "Why would I sleep if I could be here with you?"

Ella blushed, but not from his flattery. Will was a kind man, so a part of her remained infatuated with him. But she didn't share his dream of a quiet life in Lorinth, raising a family, and taking over his father's inn. He knew nothing of the secret world where Ella belonged. She had no intention of giving up her mission to help the Ruvians in favor of a smalltown romance.

Will stared at her, lips pursed and eyes longing.

This was the only time Ella had ever been happy to see Edd Pran. He put an arm around Will's shoulder and shoved a flask into the younger man's hand. "C'mon, Loren. Let the shrew do her job. 'S not like she'll put out for ya. In a few days, we'll have to share this brew with those drunks from Depbas."

Ella scoffed as she heaved a cookpot into the back of a nearby wagon.

Will ducked away from Pran. "Must you be so vulgar, Lieutenant?"

Already intoxicated, Pran stuttered when Ella pushed him from the cook pile. "You make sure Mr. Loren has a jolly time. Don't drink too long though. We leave at sunrise." She gestured to the light pile across the camp. "Off with you both."

Pran smiled. "Maybe you're not a shrew after all."

Ella returned to the water barrel and her pile of dirty pots. As she finished her work, a tremor crawled down her back. She noticed Pran leering at her from the light pile. While tossing the dirty dish water, she rolled her eyes.

An hour later, she crawled into the tent with Rose. They tucked themselves in without a word, having silently agreed to ignore one another. Sleep came quickly and heavily.

Later in the night, a shuddering anxiety woke Ella so completely, she felt like she hadn't fallen asleep in the first place. The distant, diffused glow of the half-moons illuminated a form hovering over Rose's bedroll as the girl squirmed.

Ella sprang and kneed the figure in the ribs. A man's muffled grunt met her ears, and the pungency of liquor stung her nose. Ella pulled him to the ground, straddling his chest before he could move. When he squirmed, she punched him in the cheek.

He yelped, his voice unmistakable.

Ella gritted her teeth. "What the fires are you doing, Edd Pran?"

He growled and wrenched an arm free. Ella whipped out her dagger and pressed it to his throat before he acted on his advantage. "Careful, Lieutenant. I might slice your head off if I don't like your answer."

Moonlight glinted off a smear of blood on Pran's cheek. His eyes widened.

Rose whimpered and sat up, pulling her robe tightly around her chest. "He tried . . . he almost . . ."

Ella's mind blazed with a memory of bound wrists and a torn skirt. She seethed and grabbed Pran's free wrist, twisting until it popped. A sprain was far less than what she'd like to give him. He stifled a groan as Ella pressed her blade harder into his neck. Her eyes darted from the greasy pervert quivering in terror beneath her to Rose pressed into the corner of the tent. "I'll make sure he never touches you again."

Rose's breath hitched violently, and she sobbed into her gathered robe.

Ella pressed the knife tighter at Pran's neck. "You'll wish I had killed you, come morning."

A shriek interrupted the predawn quiet while Ella labored over the blazing cook pile. "Lieutenant!"

Others joined in the frenzy. Even the journeyers, who had watched Ella's handiwork, feigned shock. She had selected the location carefully.

In the middle of the camp, away from her tent and the cook pile, Edd Pran slumped against the caged wagon, tied to the wheel. Several guards gawked at his naked, unconscious body, blood on his face and a shallow cut on his groin.

Ferren lumbered toward Ella. "Did you do that?" he said, huffing.

She wondered if she had gone too far, if this act of vigilantism would cost her the opportunity to carry out her true mission. Controlling a nervous shudder, she widened her eyes. "Do what?"

Ferren plopped on the bench across the cook pile and clasped his hands. "What did he do, Miss Therman?"

Ella continued stirring the pot of oats. "Whatever he was going to do, sir, I assure you, he didn't get far, and he will not try it again." She held his gaze with all the tenacity she could muster.

After a moment, Ferren nodded. "That he won't."

Ella thrust a steaming bowl into the cleric's pudgy hands. "Why don't you have some oats?"

Ferren continued nodding. "Oats would be fine. Thank you."

"You're welcome, sir."

Captain Leir smirked upon seeing Pran strung to the wagon wheel. He took his time cutting the lieutenant loose. When he doused him with a bucket of cold water, Pran startled awake. The captain covered him with a blanket. "Who did this, Lieutenant?"

Turning his head, Pran remained silent.

Leir put his hands on his hips. "Well, nothing to be done about it, then."

From the serving line, Ella met the captain's eyes, handing out bowls of hot, mushy oats. She dipped her chin to the veteran soldier and promptly headed back to the cook pile to fill more bowls.

As she loaded the last of her supplies into the wagon, Will rounded the cart. Ella flinched when he wrapped her in a strong embrace. "I should have been there. I should have protected you."

In his arms, Ella froze. If he started hovering around her like a guard dog, it would make scoping for festival deserters impossible. She patted his arm and wiggled free. “Look. Nothing happened to me. I don’t need your protection.”

Will’s face contorted. “You know, just because you don’t need my protection, doesn’t mean I don’t want to give it. When did you become so cold, Ella Therman?” He trudged toward his horse, mounted, and rode away.

Ella sighed. Will’s anger meant he probably wouldn’t speak to her for a few days. That was good, right?

# 17

# RENDAL

*Depbas, Taria*
*July 1, 1195 PT*

*Ella*

During childhood, Ella considered Depbas a spectacular place. Now, having traveled the merchant routes of Corigon, she found this northern city underwhelming. Cradled before the confluence of the Vinn River and a smaller tributary, Depbas proved an aging husk of a bygone culture bathed in tar paint—the hallmark of Drawlen power.

At the crown of the hill overlooking the rivers sat the solitary Keep Moen, the ancestral home of Bruce Hayden, the outgoing High Lord Warden of Corigon and its commonwealth territories. The northern quarter of the city housed the largest Drawlen Temple in Taria. Like many of their temples, this one showcased a series of stacked squares and bronze embellishments, its marble walls and stained-glass windows glittering over the sloping edifice roofs. It remained the only thing in the city that could be called beautiful.

On the seventh day of their journey, the Lorinth caravan rolled into the fields surrounding the city wall with enough daylight left for Ella and Rose to restock in the market. As they entered the plaza, which buzzed with tension, Rose grew unusually quiet. The Festival of Souls always brought commercial opportunity and political unrest in equal measure. But with the approaching inauguration of Bruce Hayden's son, Gaylen, as the new High Lord Warden, people from every rung of society expressed their opinions. A few wealthy merchants pinned emblems of the Hayden family crest—a snake weaving through an apple tree—to their carts and stalls. The majority of citizens, however, wore white sashes to signify their disapproval of the High Lord Warden's choice of heir.

A group of men threw the Hayden family standard into the gutter and unbuttoned their trousers. Ella scoffed and pulled Rose through the gate as the men relieved themselves on the flag before street police tackled them. Still, Rose remained unusually quiet.

When they left, Ella and Rose passed an alley where a Hayden standard hung on a wall. Blood stained the sagging flag, slashed across the middle. Rose whimpered.

Grasping her hand gently, Ella pulled Rose from the scene. "Let's get back to the camp."

The next morning, Ella shielded her eyes against the bright sunrise as the caravan crossed the bridge—a tall row of stone arches spanning the Vinn River. The Lorinth caravan joined the twenty-one other Life Harvest wagons on the road to Pelton. Shaggy, long-horned wood oxen pulled rickety wagons of the living and the nearly dead, interrupted only by the occasional horse-mounted soldier. For every caged wagon, there were two covered ones, each displaying the Tarish standard, a yellow sun on a gray expanse.

Now cooking for one hundred and twenty-eight people instead of twenty-five, Ella had at least gained an assistant named Gwen. Having extra hands around the cook pile allowed her to pay more attention to the new journeyers. However, her heart sank when she found they were much the same as the journeyers from Lorinth: relieved to be on their way. Was it just Taria, or were all the people of Palimar this eager to die?

Five days later, the twenty-one-wagon caravan camped a half mile outside the Corigish capital. It was the closest they could get amid the other Life Harvest convoys and traveling merchants. The black towers of the city rose like iron needles seven stories over its ancient walls. At night, the towers blended with the dark sky, the blue light from their many windows twinkling beneath the stars.

Before sunrise, Ella awoke to Rose sobbing into a rolled-up blanket used as a pillow. She knelt next to Rose and put a hand on her shoulder.

"What if . . . what if he tries to hurt me after the Festival, El? You'll be gone. I'll be alone."

Ella pushed a wet clump of hair out of Rose's face. "Stay close to Ferren and Captain Leir. If you have to, put some of the tincture I gave you into Pran's drink. That's the best I can offer you."

Rose sniffled. "Can you . . . can you sing to me like you did the other night?"

"Sure." Ella smiled and crossed her legs. Taking a deep breath, she closed her eyes and sang:

*"Pay you no mind to the whispering wind;*
*hear not its cries on the reeds.*
*Listen instead to your mama's voice;*
*follow it true where it leads.*
*Though shadows may wander, you're safe under hill.*
*The sunstone shines bright in your eyes.*
*Though deadly shades hunt by the light of the moons,*
*They'll be gone when the sun comes to rise."*

When Rose's breathing slowed and steadied, Ella stepped out of the tent. One of the journeyers from Depbas scrambled to his feet. He rubbed his fingers under his large, sharp nose, then folded his thin arms over his chest and shivered. He looked about Rose's age.

"Sorry, m-m-miss. I was just walking by and—"

Ella shook her head. "It's fine."

The boy kicked at the dirt with a cracked boot. "My mother used to sing that."

"So did mine." Ella extended her arm. "Ella Therman."

The boy grasped her wrist. "Hale Trevon."

"You look . . . healthy for a journeyer, Hale."

His dark eyes darted to the left, then back to Ella. "I'm a—I've got red lung."

Prickles arose on the back of her neck. He was lying. Instead of pressing him, she patted him on the arm. "I'm sorry to hear that. You're pretty young for such an unlucky thing."

"Yeah." Hale hung his head.

From then on, Ella kept an eye on the young man.

When the caravan ascended the mountain pass to Shevak, the weather grew cool and damp. The air seemed to suck whatever life remained in many of the journeyers. At night, the cremation fires of those who had passed during the day's travel outshone the light circles in the camps.

At least one journeyer died each day: the strength of those remaining faded with each body lit. Except Hale's. On more than one occasion, Ella overheard him encouraging his fellow journeyers. He managed to talk one man, a miner with an amputated left arm, out of hysteria—until the man snapped.

Ella woke one cold morning to Captain Leir screaming for a rifleman. She sprang from the tent, Rose clinging to her side, as the injured miner ran for the trees. The early dawn illuminated his silhouette against the eastern run of the Modrian Mountains.

Pran slung a rifle on his back and climbed the caged wagon near Ella's tent. He aimed and pulled the trigger when the man neared a stand of trees. Though a far shot in dim light, it hit him square in the back.

The gawking journeyers retreated to their tents and carts as two soldiers dragged the miner's stone-gray body back to camp. Hale remained beside Ella and Rose, shaking his head.

"I don't understand," Rose said. "Why not go into the Garden where his soul can dwell forever? Now he'll just be a wandering shade." She marched toward the light circle, flinging a green shawl over her shoulders.

Hale watched Rose until she was out of earshot. "Fool should've waited 'til Drawl like I told him. It's more crowded."

Ella glanced around. "There are also Black Veil collectors in Drawl."

"You pity us, don't you Miss Therman?"

Ella tugged on the ratty fringes of her coat. "Why do you say that?"

He smiled. This was the first journeyer she had ever seen smile. "You not only stomach the dead being lit, you watch willingly. No one does that. The fire makes them nervous."

A familiar tremor ran through Ella. She spun to see Pran glaring at her from the other side of the caged wagon. Perhaps his wounds had healed, or perhaps shooting down the deserter boosted his confidence. Either way, he regarded Ella now with more malice than trepidation.

Ella turned back to Hale and smiled. "I have chores to do, sir."

Work filled her waking hours for the next few days. Now that two Black Veil collectors had joined the caravan on their way to Drawl, scoping for deserters proved impossible.

The collectors, lean and weathered men in their forties with hair slicked back and faces half covered by black scarves, emitted a spooky presence. They wore black tunics trimmed with silver. More heavily armed than any of the soldiers, each carried a pair of sabers, an array of knives, a rifle, and two pistols. They rode brenorix—majestic creatures with coats of pure white, cleft hooves, and short black tusks curling up at the corners of their mouths.

After dismissing Gwen, Ella crated the last of the sunrocks when one of the collectors approached her. She rose, fumbling the tongs. He put his left hand on his opposite shoulder and bowed his head, then pointed to the barrel in the open wagon behind Ella.

"You want some rations?" Ella asked.

"Please," he said in a familiar accent.

Ella quirked an eyebrow.

"Something wrong, miss?" the collector said.

"Sorry. You sound like you walked right out of Brill Town. I wasn't expecting that."

The collector's eyes crinkled with a smile, a gesture that appeared disingenuous. "I'm from Estbye. My partner, also. We stopped at the Tarish caravan to experience a little bit of home."

Ella forced a smile. *Emissaries walk a gray road*, Krishena had told her during her winter in Rotira. *We must be gracious enough to see our enemy as a fellow man, to walk beside him and see as he sees, and yet cold enough to recognize the threat he poses, to meet him with death when the time arises.*

Before Ella stood a mortal man with memories of a city by the sea, and perhaps of a family still living there. Regardless of how the Black Veil Order had twisted him, he possessed a heart and soul. Could she walk that gray road? Would she crush him if the need arose? She dismissed the thought and set aside the tongs. "I was born in Estbye. It's a beautiful town."

"I've always believed so. What's your name, miss?"

"Ella."

"I'm Rendal. I don't mean to impose, but Father Ferren insisted we could restock our rations here."

Ella gestured to the salt barrel. "Feel free, sir. There's jerky in the smaller barrel, if you prefer."

Rendal nodded. "That would be preferable. Thank you kindly, Miss Therman." He walked past her and opened the smaller barrel.

Ella's face flushed. He'd addressed her by her surname, which she had not given. She forced herself to walk casually toward the light pile. She wanted to run.

Rose stood amidst the crowd, holding her hands over the heat rocks. She jumped when Ella put a firm hand on her shoulder. "Don't *do* that!" Rose hollered.

"Sorry," Ella said. "I thought maybe you'd want to wash up at the river."

Rose wrinkled her forehead and glanced around. "Right now?"

Ella nodded. "Right now."

"No thanks." Rose rolled her eyes and rubbed her arms. "I just got warm."

Ella drew her hands into fists to still her shaking. "Fine. I'll go by myself." She scurried down a path to the stream obscured from the camp. She realized her mistake when Pran stepped from the brush as Ella unbuttoned her coat.

"Out here all alone, Therman?"

"I suppose you've been waiting for this." Ella noted the distance between them, and the sword on Pran's belt. She had two throwing knives in each boot and a utility blade in her vest. He'd be dead before he drew his sword, but she would need a clever explanation of how a merchant's daughter killed a trained temple guard before he could take up arms.

"I was looking for you in that tent, you know."

Ella's hand twitched, and Pran dove at her, reaching for his sword. She jumped back but kept her weapons concealed in favor of grabbing a fist-sized rock from the ground.

Before Pran could fully draw his weapon, a black knife struck him in the gut with such force, he doubled over in the air and fell on his neck, his hand still on the hilt of his sword.

Ella shrieked and ducked behind a tree, rock still in hand, listening for whomever had thrown the knife.

The crunch of boots on the rocky ground preceded the rolling thump of a body.

Peering around the tree, she met the dark eyes of Collector Rendal. He didn't break his stare, not even to blink. Ella took a deep breath and scrambled to her feet.

She was, of course, terrified, but not of what Pran might have done to her. It occurred to her that she would be in quite a deadly situation had she displayed any of her fighting prowess. She may be able to fool Leir or Ferren, but certainly not this man.

"He . . . um . . ."

Ella let the rock fall from her hand and hugged herself.

Rendal nodded as he pulled the bloody blade from Pran's stomach.

She gaped when smoke arose from the blade.

Rendal shoved the weapon into its sheath. "You're a lucky one, Miss Therman. He's been following you all day. You should watch out for yourself as much as you do your priestess friend."

Ella clasped her coat, pulling it tightly around her.

"Ferren told me about this one." Rendal kicked Pran's lifeless body with his steel-tipped boot. "The next time a soldier tries something like that, just kill him. The world will be better for it." He strode away, disappearing into the darkness.

Not lucky, Ella thought. Providence had caused her to pick up that rock, certainly. And she would take providence over all the luck in the world.

# 18

# THE STOLEN SISTER

*Temple Setvan, Shevak*
*July 8, 1195 PT*

*Mavell*

Dozens of skeletal gargoyles gazed hungrily at the approaching Black Veil collectors. Mavell and Detoa strode toward the Shadow Chapel carved into the granite cliff at the north end of the Setvan Temple. Like an ominous spotlight, the red light of the Mortemus moon shone through the breaking clouds.

Members of one order rarely entered the house of another. Tonight would be the exception. Pausing at the tall black doors, Mavell addressed his partner. "I've tried for six burning years to get the truth out of that witch." He gritted his teeth. "If the eternal ten-year-old has scrambled Tessa's mind, I'm going to give the godkiller a key to this place."

Detoa cleared her throat. "Has any guest ever come out alive?"

"Not yet." Mavell turned the long, curved handle of the door and pushed it open.

As they entered the chapel, moonlight illuminated a long, deserted hallway. Massive pillars lined the dark stone walls and arched overhead, following the shape of the cathedral ceiling. Between the pillars, long tapestries depicted a boy surrounded by silver smoke, hovering behind people who performed various malevolent acts. The one nearest the door portrayed a servant stabbing a king in the back, with the shadow-clad boy poised over his shoulder.

On the wall between each pillar and tapestry lay a frame of red-stained glass. Curious, given the entire structure was windowless. Past the fifth pillar, all the glass frames were shattered as though a storm had blown through the corridor, revealing dim sunrock crystals set in the walls.

When a shard crunched loudly under her boot, Detoa stilled. Broken glass covered the remaining floor. A tapestry lay heaped on the ground, revealing a narrow door on the wall.

The hall reverberated with the crunch of glass. A man emerged from the doorway and marched toward them. Detoa's knife slipped from her sleeve into her hand, and Mavell readied his invisible shades. The two collectors froze, perfectly silent, perfectly still.

The man approached, wearing a black robe with a wide, bloodred hem—the uniform of a Shadow Chapel apostle. Deep wrinkles lined his sallow face, his long gray curls combed over one shoulder. His eyes—one of which appeared cloudy and milky white—darted between the pair of collectors. "What business do collectors of the Black Veil have in the house of the Eternal Child of Shadow?" he asked in a raspy voice.

Meeting the apostle's gaze, Mavell answered, "We are here on Lady Mylis's behalf to retrieve the oracle and her child."

A piercing screech erupted farther down the corridor, echoing in the vast space.

The apostle remained stoic. "You should come another time, Collector. Our master is . . . occupied."

"That is precisely why the Mistress of Prophecy sent us and not another oracle," Mavell said.

The apostle straightened and folded his hands, steepling his fingers. "Since when does the Black Veil Order do the bidding of lesser immortals?"

"Since when does a high immortal kidnap and torture the property of his fellows?"

"You are not welcome here."

Mavell narrowed his eyes, smirking behind his black scarf. "I'm not looking for an invitation."

The apostle opened his mouth, but his retort died on his tongue when the hall shook with a metallic boom. Fifty feet behind him, huge bronze doors exploded, snapping off their hinges. The flickering orange light of a fire beyond the doors filled the space. Silhouetted in the doorway stood Selvator Kane, robed in red and wreathed in dark shadows.

Appearing as a child, he was thin and scowling. His flat soot-colored hair clung to his head and covered one misty eye. In truth, he was one of the oldest immortals, and among the most feared next to the Veiled Man and Refsul himself.

"Who dares—" he screamed. When his eyes fell on Mavell, his brow rose, and he smiled. "Collector. What a fortuitous visit."

Mavell and Detoa exchanged a glance. Then Mavell bowed with his fist on his chest. "An honor to be welcomed into the Chapel of Shadows."

Sel dipped his chin. "I presume Lady Mylis has sent you after her oracle."

Mavell nodded stiffly. "It seems her staff is rather busy, so we . . . obliged her."

"Of course, of course." Sel clasped his hands behind his back, and the shadows around him slowed their quivering. "Right this way. Larabelum"—he faced the apostle, then waved his hands—"clean this mess."

When he passed Mavell, Larabelum stuck up his nose and shook out the fallen tapestry. The collectors followed Sel across the threshold into a massive parlor. Mavell instinctively scanned both corners behind him.

Haana, clothed in white, her hair matted and sweaty, quivered in the corner. She pressed herself between the wall and a pedestal. Before her lay a vase in pieces on the floor. She lifted her head when Sel entered with his new guests.

A fire blazed in a hearth spanning the wall across from the door. The orange and yellow flames danced six feet high, fueled by logs and a charred sapien skeleton. The reek of burnt flesh lingered, despite the choking thickness of incense wafting from ceramic trays mounted every few feet along the walls.

Above the lavish furnishings arranged on richly patterned rugs, a woman dangled, suspended in the middle of the room. Her head hung forward with her waist-length red hair covering her face. Soot stained her shimmering, singed robes.

Shades held her a few feet off the floor, their smoky tendrils wrapping around her wrists like ropes. Her head lolled to the side, revealing the ashen face of Tessa the Oracle.

Mavell clenched his teeth and sucked in a breath. Tessa was useless to him now. Her eyes wide and vacant, a glossy line of drool oozed from her mouth.

On the low marble table in front of the fire rested a golden amulet. It bore the impression of a single eye, the pupil set with a gleaming onyx stone. Sel's high apostle had worn this token. Between the skeleton, the furnishings, and the floating woman, this place held the morbid appeal of a finely decorated dungeon.

"My deepest condolences to you, Master of Secrets," Mavell said, "for the passing of your high apostle." He choked on the pungent air as he motioned at the skeleton. "It's fortunate you have a harem child already selected to replace her."

Sel whirled around, his face twitching. "I very much doubt that you, Collector Mavell, would be foolish enough to insult me."

"Oh, no, my lord!" Mavell put a hand on his heart with an exaggerated flourish. "I meant only to be polite. Please excuse my presumption." He glanced at the whimpering girl. "I'd only heard that you had selected a harem child."

Sel tilted his head, growling at Haana.

"Her?" Mavell said, feigning surprise. "She seems a bit . . . young to have command of her power."

"You were younger still when you were given your first shade." Sel circled Tessa's body, which slowly revolved and bobbed as the shades holding her shivered in malicious excitement. "It is not her age, Collector. I have been—lied to." Sel twitched his fingers. The shades shook Tessa's body violently, screeching in delight. He flung his hands toward Haana. "That girl is no ralenta. She hasn't a shred of shade craft."

Haana whimpered and ducked behind the pedestal.

Mavell crossed his arms. "Odd. Did the girl not pass the crafting trial? Did her mother not have exceptional power before she was . . . recruited?"

Sel cackled. "Did she!" His eyes darkened, matching the high apostle's amulet. He whipped his hand to the side. The shades shrieked and flew across the room, slamming Tessa's limp body into a tapestry. Both the woman and the tapestry slid to the floor. "Did she?" Sel's voice boomed as if several voices spoke in unison.

He screamed at the woman and ripped fistfuls of hair out of her head. "Fraud. Liar. Traitor. Imposter!" He spun around, throwing locks of red curls at Mavell and Detoa. "I looked. I saw her mind."

Detoa shuddered next to Mavell.

"How far did you see?" Mavell said in a warning tone.

"Every corner." Sel's eyes faded to his flat, gray gaze. "She's been spying. She's been passing information to the Freelander dragon spawn. She isn't a real foreseer. They helped her manufacture prophecies, including her prediction about this godkiller you've been searching for these past six years." He smiled toothily at Mavell. "Oh, yes. I know about your little side mission. Not even the Veiled Man can fool the Master of Secrets."

Mavell sneered beneath his scarf. And yet, this mortal woman had fooled Sel for a decade.

Sel continued. "This godkiller—he was part of that little charade. He was sent to kill Hoven by the First Lord's pet, the Red Wolf. And this . . . whore—she's not even the one my agents selected in Oberan. She has a twin! She traded places because her dear, beloved sister was pregnant." He approached the vacant-eyed woman and kicked at her shoulder, causing her to topple. "I'm sure if she had the capacity for thought now, she would regret that little act of charity. It will cost her the life of her own child."

"No!" Haana wailed.

Sel strode closer to her, and Mavell sensed the boy-monster's fury. Mavell didn't personally care for the girl's wellbeing. But if Tessa really was working with Freelander spies, Haana might yet be useful. After already losing one lead, he deliberately stepped between Sel and the girl. "This is a most startling revelation," Mavell said.

Sel shifted murderous eyes on him.

Detoa's hand twitched near her dagger.

Grabbing her wrist, Mavell cleared his throat. "We can certainly send collectors to search after Tessa's sister. If she has children, it is likely at least one may have what you need."

Sel's eyes softened. "That won't be necessary. I know exactly where she is." He waved his hand toward the doorway. "Fetch Fenris and Gorova. We're going to test Arch Purifier Gorova's new invention."

Mavell curled his fists, considering how to turn down being made yet another immortal's errand runner without getting murdered. "Lord Sel, given the information you've provided, it's clear I should be investigating the Freelander presence in Setmal."

The shadows, which hovered around Sel like bodiless spider legs, leapt back and crushed a nearby armchair into a pile of splinters. When the last bit of fabric and wool stuffing settled on the floor, Sel spoke slowly. "Deliver the message."

Mavell hesitated, tempted to rebuff Sel's request. Valuing his life more than his pride, he bowed his head. "Certainly." He walked to the door, Detoa matching his every step.

"Oh, Collector," Sel said. "Once you've delivered the message to Fenris and Gorova, find a temple watchman and bring him to the Wraith Cellar."

Mavell let out a long breath and addressed the Master of Secrets. "Any watchman in particular?"

"A former member of Odysa's rangers. His name is Joran Wilde. Tessa's Red Watch contact. I very much want to chat with him."

Mavell bowed. He couldn't go to the Fire Master with such a vague order. Fenris had a worse temper than this immortal brat. "My lord, I'm sure Fenris will need to know your intended destination to prepare his convoy."

"Lorinth, Taria," Sel said. "We leave tomorrow."

The first bands of morning glow crested the mountainous horizon beyond Shevak as Mavell and Detoa rummaged through Captain Joran Wilde's private quarters in the temple guard dormitory. The mission ended fruitlessly, as Mavell had suspected from the start.

The Master of Secrets was usually cunning and thorough, fully deserving of his name. But the death of his high apostle—as well as Tessa fabricating her own and her daughter's talents—had made him desperate and stupid.

Undoubtedly, the rumor of Haana's abduction and Tessa's cruel fate had reached Joran Wilde hours ago, while Mavell was summoning Fenris and Gorovah. But the collectors couldn't return to the Shadow Chapel empty-handed. So they examined every shred of paper and dismantled the captain's entire wooden wardrobe.

Joran proved a shrewd spy. He was well regarded by his peers and lauded by his superiors. Missing his eleven o'clock shift, his comrades had reported his disappearance by the time Mavell and Detoa arrived.

Detoa emptied the straw mattress onto the floor. "He can't be far. Shall we search the city?"

"No," Mavell said as he unrolled a crisp pair of socks. "He had an exit plan. This was a courtesy visit. Now we are done doing favors for the Child Immortal."

Detoa dipped her head in agreement, then ran her hand along the windowsill. Mavell peered over her shoulder out the east-facing window, gazing down over the main gate of the temple complex. The centuries-old portcullis drew up like the open maw of some sharp-toothed beast.

A train of five black wagons waited to roll through the stone archway. Tattered canvas bonnets covered the wagons, pulled by wood oxen and driven by men dressed in traveling clothes. They looked like rangers disguised as merchants. Into one wagon climbed three of the most notorious members of the Drawlen regime—Selvator Kane, the Master of Secrets; Berneas Gorova, the Arch Purifier; and Fenris, the Fire Master.

"I don't understand what Sel needed with Tessa's child." Detoa wiped the filthy window glass with her sleeve. "If he needs more shade craft—"

"Sevlator Kane doesn't need craft," Mavell said.

"How else does he bond with his shades?"

"He bonds with a ralenta."

Detoa's eyes widened. "*What* is he?"

"I'm not entirely sure, but I believe he's something between a shade and a ralenta."

Detoa picked straw from her boot cuff and tossed it on the floor. "There are things like that?"

In the last wagon of the caravan, Sel sat at the back rail, the bonnet shadowing half his face. He glared at the window where the collectors stood.

"The world is full of monsters," Mavell said. "And Selvator Kane is one of the foulest."

"Why doesn't he just pick another ralenta from the harem, or have one scouted? Why is he so bent on going after this other woman's children?"

Mavell waited until the wagon train rolled out of sight through the gate. "That is the question, isn't it? Perhaps bloodlines are still important for some things. The Yveans certainly believe it." He kicked aside some straw with his boot. "There's a royal wedding taking place in Setmal in a few days. Apparently, our godkiller may be acquainted with the spies who've escorted the heir apparent from his holiday in the Freelands."

He plucked a formal officer's cap from the floor and placed it on Detoa's head. It fell to the side, covering one of her eyes. "Why don't we acquire an invitation and attire suited for a formal celebration?"

# 19

# THE HUNT

*Setmal, Yvenea*
*July 10, 1195 PT*

*Venna*

Royal weddings tested Venna's patience. She shifted her weight discreetly from one tired leg to the other. After all, she stood in plain view of the entire city and thousands of Yvean and foreign visitors. She could also do without Yvean fashion. Before first coming to Setmal five years ago, she had never worn a corset. She still dearly wished she hadn't. Breathe from the shoulders—that's what Leonora had advised.

From across the stage, Leonora smiled at her. Venna smiled back, energized by her friend's encouragement. Even as a bride, Leonora's mind was ever on the wellbeing of others. She would make an excellent queen. When they'd first met at the Royal University, Leonora treated Venna as a friend, instead of a foreign curiosity.

Venna fanned herself more vigorously. Filled with people, the whole garden buzzed with the fluttering of fans. When an occasional cloud rolled over the sun, the noise ceased. However, there hadn't been such relief for nearly an hour. The flitting of fans accompanied Dynast Aronos's rambling speech.

Venna coveted the vacant seat next to her. What she wouldn't give to plop down and fall asleep under the shade of the climbing roses . . .

She straightened and scolded herself. What a selfish thought. This was her Uncle Leron's chair, placed in his absence to signify Orin's faith that he still lived. Venna doubted, but she would never say so to her tireless cousin.

She struggled to smile but remembered Fredrick's insistence about this posture. So, she employed her imagination, picturing the fine outfits of the crowd turning to snow and melting in the sun. She averted her eyes to keep from laughing, only to meet Sid's bright gaze. Standing guard a few feet from Orin, he winked. That cured her phantom laughter.

Roaring applause startled her. After catching her breath, she clapped along. The dynast bowed and smiled at his cheering audience, oblivious to the true nature of their gladness. The rest of the ceremony progressed swiftly: a quick vow, exchange of rings, the kiss, and off to a feast without a whisper of an assassin afoot.

Alongside the rest of the wedding party, Venna bustled into the banquet hall. As hungry as she felt, she was far more grateful to sit down. She nearly jumped out of her chair, however, when Shane—wearing the guise of a wedding guest—appeared behind her. He was like a ghost, the way he moved. "Don't *do* that!"

"Dance with me," he said.

Her pulse quickened. Venna hoped she heard correctly, but she'd been imagining silly romantic things all day.

"Venna." He sounded irritated.

"Wait. What?"

Shane closed his pale eyes and took a deep breath, putting a hand on the hilt of his sword. "Just humor me. I need to eavesdrop."

"Oh." Venna's shoulders sagged. "I thought you were really asking."

Shane smirked. The scars on his face had faded considerably since they'd arrived in Setmal. She wondered if it was because of the elixirs mixed into the bathhouse waters. All the same, she found him incredibly dashing when he smirked.

"I can always get Sid to do it instead," he said.

Venna huffed and offered her hand. "No, thank you. Shall I lead or do you actually know what you're doing?"

Shane laughed as he led her into the crowd of women in swirling gowns and men in silly, wide hats. "You're never short on wit, Ven."

"Well, it's what I have going for me." She placed a hand on his shoulder and tried not to blush. "I'm a simple merchant's daughter, after all."

"That's more than I have going for me." Shane scanned the throng of dancers.

"Aren't you a Freelander hero or something, Mr. Red Wolf?"

"The Red Wolf is an ugly beast who eats greedy children in Palish folk tales. I don't think the spire brats who came up with that meant it as a compliment."

Shane's gaze darted everywhere except on Venna, yet he had not missed a single step of the dance.

"You're awfully agreeable right now, Captain."

"It's part of the hunt." He met her eyes for a split second and winked. His usually pale-blue irises were dark, reflecting the ruby-studded chandeliers above them.

Venna's heart fluttered. "Oh, so you're annoyed with me right now?"

"A little."

"Who are you spying on?" Venna suppressed a giggle. Sometimes her humor took a dangerous turn.

Shane growled. "Venna."

"Sorry. I'm just trying to entertain myself. By the way, where did you learn to dance?"

"Also part of the hunt."

Venna beamed at him. "I bet you learned it in some far-off land while you were a pirate."

Shaking his head, Shane furrowed his brow. "You've still got your head stuck in all those books, don't you?"

"It's a hobby."

"Take up fencing." Shane's eyes narrowed, focusing on something behind Venna. He steered them in that direction.

"Why? That's not a *lady's* hobby." She snickered.

"You're not a lady. You're a Red Watch commander's daughter. Besides, dancing and fencing are basically the same. You'll do fine." In the middle of a twirl, Shane abruptly let her go and dashed off between the massive pillars partitioning the grand hall.

"Wh—okay, rude! See you later, I suppose." Venna caught her balance and mumbled to herself. "At least he didn't run off during a dip."

She smoothed her hair and shifted in her heels until an Arist of one of the lesser houses stepped next to her and held out his hand. "Dear lady, may I?"

Venna studied him. He looked unremarkable, except for the enormous feather protruding from his hat. "Oh, why not," she said. "But if you call me an exotic flower, I'm going to trip you."

*Shane*

Shane tracked his quarry—a slender woman with black hair and a fitted orange gown. During the ceremony, he had observed her at the back of the crowd, using her shades to avoid notice of the palace guard. At one point, she had taken out a dart gun, but after the guards changed position, she stowed her weapon in her dress. Her flashy appearance meant she was probably a rogue.

Shane's chief concern was protecting Orin, but there were any number of important names running the assassin circuits. A royal wedding presented opportunity to catch them in the open. As he neared the rogue, Shane navigated undetected among the twirling dancers and bystanders. When he came within reach, the woman held his gaze before disappearing in a swirl of shadow. Shane stilled and clenched his fist.

*'Behind you,'* Tres's voice rang in Shane's mind.

Spinning around, Shane flicked a paralytic-coated dart into his hand from his armguard. He stuck the dart into the woman's hip and grabbed her wrist with his other hand. Too late, though. The string of her necklace fell from her mouth, revealing a broken glass vial. The poison did its malicious work instantly. A small dagger fell from her fingers as her eyes dulled. Shane supported her dead weight with an arm around her back and put his boot on the dagger to stop its clanging and hide it from view.

He lifted the dead ralenta and kicked the knife across the floor. Sid caught the blade underfoot. Dropping the assassin into Sid's arms, Shane hurried to dispose of the ralenta's unbound shades. Holding the body close, Sid used the folds of the woman's dress to cover her as she petrified.

Four shades hung in the air above Shane, becoming more and more opaque. They were invisible phantoms to most of the people present, but an eerie hiss issued from their shapeless forms as they awoke. Soon they would grow agitated, being severed from their master's control, and prey upon the crowd.

An obese Corigish woman in a ruffled dress stared at Sid. He shrugged with the stiff corpse in his arms. "Too much wine."

"Where's Bren?" Shane whispered. "She was a ralenta."

Sid's golden eyes flashed with horror. He nodded to the side. "By the casks, last I saw. How many shades?"

"Four." Shane spotted Bren among the row of wine barrels lining the adjacent wall. The teenage sentry dashed toward them, using his own shade to invisibly dodge the crowd.

The unbound shades' moaning grew loud enough for human ears, so a few nearby wedding guests turned in their direction. Bren appeared in front of Shane. The fat woman next to Sid fainted when the boy emerged from nowhere. Her companion caught her, fumbling his wineglass.

"I only have enough craft to take two of them. Morgel's on his way," Bren said.

"Do it," Shane said. "We'll draw the others to the courtyard."

Bren navigated directly under two of the shades. Reaching over his head, he touched their shadowy tendrils and pulled on the dark wisps. The shades shivered before fading like steam from a mirror.

Shane and Bren exited the open doors lining the east wall of the ballroom. The lawn beyond had been cleared of chairs and litter from the afternoon ceremony. With the sun setting, the domed building cast a long shadow over the gardens.

"Sunlight would've been nice to kill the rest of them," Bren said in his usual passionless voice.

"Yeah," Shane mumbled as they entered the terrace. "We're doing things the hard way again."

In his alley cat form, Rodden jumped onto the half wall of the terrace outside the ballroom.

"Get them into the open," Shane said as he ran past.

Rodden called to the shades with a strange purr too low for the party guests to hear. The shades, bending and twisting in agitation, stretched their shadowy arms toward the doors. They darted in front of the fae skin-changer, causing him to spring from the ledge.

At Shane's signal, the guards closed the glass doors of the ballroom. Glass wasn't an obstacle to shades, but the doors hindered any guests from wandering outside.

Rodden ran into the middle of the lawn, one of the shades flying after him. While Shane and Bren manned the terrace, the remaining shade floated near them. Bren used two of his own to block it, the ghostly forms wrestling in the air like miniature tornados.

Finally, Morgel arrived, slipping silently from a side door. The Greqi ralenta grabbed one of the shade's dark limbs, and the menace disappeared. One more shade remained.

An unearthly shriek sounded from the lawn. The final shade dissipated in the breeze. Tres stood in front of Rodden with his sword drawn. In the moonlight, the metal of his saber shone bloodred. Stonebreaker, the ancient mortari sword, sung eerily as the terrion lord shoved it back into its scabbard.

Shane wiped the sweat from his brow, but his relief was short-lived.

"Captain." Bren pointed to the ballroom. A fifth unbound shade hovered above the crowd.

*Mavell*

Mavell watched impassively, sipping a glass of wine and glancing occasionally through the glass doors as the Freelanders fought their phantom quarry. He hated to admit it, but the Red Wolf impressed him. Mavell had always believed trolls to be a little slow. His experience was limited, however.

A drunken pair of noblewomen passed by, jostling Mavell's wineglass against his chest. He sneered, and they shuffled out of the way.

"At least pretend to enjoy yourself," Detoa said, twirling in her deep-blue gown. The ruffled bodice bobbed, and she flattened the white-lace trim along the high collar when she settled next to him.

Mavell straightened his formal blue justaucorps and matching waistcoat. While his partner flaunted her long black hair, curled and pinned like the other women in the room, his own hair lay hidden beneath a wig of ridiculous white curls, as highborn fashion dictated.

Without his scarf covering his face, he felt chilled, exposed. One of the inebriated women still stared at him, her cheeks reddening under her rouge. Like a wounded sheep lusting after a prowling lion. Fool.

Behind the woman, a dark shape drifted through the tall archway from the adjoining corridor—an unbound shade, rippling like blood through water. Mavell leered. The woman before him backed away, then stomped into the crowd.

When Mavell returned his attention on the doors, the teenage sentry peered into the ballroom with a panicked expression. Dashing ahead of the boy, the Greqi ralenta threw open the door, rattling the panes. He sprinted into the crowd with the Red Wolf behind him. Trumpets sounded from the balcony at the south end of the room, announcing the official arrival of the bride and groom. Roused by the noise, the shade sped toward the wide staircase as the guests of honor stepped onto the top landing.

"I don't have to pretend," Mavell said, smiling at Detoa. "I'm having a marvelous time." He studied the Greqi ralenta, who grimaced in concentration about thirty feet from him. The troll, partially obscured, stood beside the ralenta.

Detoa raised her glass. Mavell clinked his own glass against hers and took a sip of wine but instantly spit it out. A glowing red blade flashed between the ralenta and troll, catching Mavell's attention. His breath caught. Now he could see the resemblance in size and posture of this ralenta and the hooded godkiller from the harem child's memory six years ago.

Mavell's mouth curled into a sinister grin. He'd found the godkiller. And here he'd thought this little venture was a waste of time. What fortune!

"Mavell," Detoa whispered.

Mavell snapped his head to where she pointed.

The shade hovered fifty feet from the couple descending the stairs. If the godkiller was going to act, his opportunity proved fleeting. However, another dark form then rushed past the shade—no, through it—like wind through a lazy cloud of smoke. The joyful sound of trumpets drowned out the shade's death cry. After obliterating the shade, the form settled in the far corner of the room and shifted into a pale man in a purple coat. Immediately, he ducked into the front corridor.

"Morgel, party's moving," Shane said as he and the ralenta dashed after the man in purple.

Detoa stepped forward, but Mavell put out a hand.

"No, Coll—dear," he corrected himself as guests pressed in on both sides, shouldering their way to the banquet tables. "We have what we came for—a face and a name. The Red Wolf and his pack will certainly follow this intruder. We mustn't get involved . . . it's time for us to leave."

*Shane*

At Shane's signal, Bren and Morgel traced after the man in purple. When Shane and Sid finally struggled through the crowd to exit the ballroom, the two ralenta were already at the heels of the retreating man.

Halfway down the corridor, a burning pain ripped through Shane's head and chest. He stumbled to the wall and collapsed, gritting his sharp teeth.

"You okay?" Sid stood over him, staring down his big, hooked nose.

"It's nothing." Shane leaned against the wall.

Sid offered a gloved hand. "Better get you up, then. Don't want anyone to see the Red Wolf lying down."

Shane chuckled between haggard breaths, grasping Sid's hand. When they reached the front gate, Bren and Morgel waited by the ramparts away from the palace guards.

"He got in a carriage," Bren said. "Rodden slipped onto it before he took off. That's better than following him ourselves."

"Ralenta are especially wary of each other," Sid said.

Morgel and Bren exchanged a curious glance. "I'm not so sure he was a ralenta," Bren said. Morgel nodded.

"Why?" Shane asked.

"Have you ever seen a ralenta kill a shade, Captain?"

"No," Shane admitted. "But what else could he be?"

"Do we at least know who he is?" Sid asked.

Bren pointed at the gate. "Gatemaster says he's Farr Grallen, a warden lord of Rotira. And guess who's putting him up: the High Chamberlain."

"So this fellow is a Corigish lord, probably a ralenta, and he's a house guest to the father of the bride?" Sid shook his head. "Make sense of that."

Shane growled quietly and put his hands on his belt, trying to quell the shaking of his arm that always came after the pain. "We did what we could. But this party isn't over. Back to it."

Just after midnight, Shane collapsed into a plush velvet couch next to Venna in one of the alcoves along the banquet hall. The nobleman on Venna's other side startled with a shriek.

He scrambled to his feet, backing away from Shane. "Oh . . . my! The time. It's been a most memorable evening my dear, eh . . ."

"Venna," she said with a frown.

"Yes, Lady Venna. May I, perhaps, call on you some time?"

Venna flashed the man a dazzling, sharp-toothed smile. "You may not."

Shane muffled a laugh. Over the last few years, he'd spent weeks at a time in Thêen working out of the Red Watch safe house, Venna's family home. Watching her verbally emasculate many unwanted admirers developed into his hobby. He leaned forward and stared at the man, who promptly bowed and left.

Venna exhaled and plopped back against the couch. "Why couldn't you have done that an hour ago?"

"I got distracted by all the assassins running around."

Venna surveyed the room with raised brows. "Where? I didn't see any."

Shane grinned. "I know." He downed the remaining contents of the nobleman's abandoned cocktail and puckered at the overbearing sweetness. "Besides, you usually do a fine job chasing these fools off yourself."

Venna plucked at a loose pin in her elaborate hairdo. Altogether, she was beyond radiant. "I got tired of scaring them off after the fifth one," she said with a sigh. "Besides, it's much more fun watching them run from you."

Shane smiled. "The dress doesn't help." Immediately, he regretted his words. He was too exhausted to sensor himself.

Venna blushed and turned aside. When she met his gaze again, she scowled. "Would it kill you to just tell me I look nice? It's the least you could do after ditching me on the dance floor."

Shane considered a careful reply, one that would appease her but not encourage her ill-placed affection. Rodden's sudden arrival solved his predicament. The alley cat slunk next to a side door, silhouetted by the lanterns in the adjoining corridor. Shane cocked his head at Venna and shrugged. "Probably another assassin."

As he left the room, she called after him, "You owe me a dance, zem'Arta."

Shane followed Rodden to an empty room off the main corridor. "Anything?"

Rodden's eyes crinkled in amusement. "I didn't mean to interrupt your quality time."

Shane scoffed. "It's not what—it was small talk."

"Does she know that?"

Shane huffed and changed the subject. "What did you find?"

"Harry was right to be cautious of the High Chamberlain. That fellow I followed is a rogue. His name is Calla. Farr Grallen is an alias. He mentioned his master to the servant who met him in the drive. Dantiego was the name."

Shane paced, if only to keep himself awake. "That would be Krishena Dantiego, the rogue master out of Rotira. She runs the biggest ring in Palimar. Remm used to run with them—claims they're related. Not sure I buy it."

"I've heard of her," Rodden said.

"She's a godkiller. Supposedly did in one of the Beast Barons. Drawlen has a bounty on her for thirty thousand tallies. The only one worth more is the Arch Traitor, Alistar Soral. He killed the other one."

"Arch Traitor?" Rodden stretched his neck. "I didn't realize my precious title had been usurped."

"I'm sure you're still Refsul's favorite." Shane patted Rodden on the head, snapping his hand away when the cat sliced at it with his claws. Shane laughed. "Who was the servant who met the rogue at the manor?"

"The red-headed one that often accompanies Arista Yvette. The one Sid's always trying to chase after."

"Darï?" Shane said.

"Yes, that's the one." Rodden scratched his ear with his hind leg. "But we probably won't see that rogue fellow again. He's left the city already. Darï mentioned going to the Festival of Souls though."

"Did she?"

"They didn't say why, but it's not for love of the festival. Perhaps Remm could ask—"

Shane shook his head and leaned on the back of a long wooden bench. "He left their rogue ring on bad terms. We have to be careful about approaching Dantiego and her people. Keep an eye on Darï for now. The festival is still a week out. I'm heading to the embassy before I pass out."

Rodden leapt onto a windowsill and fixed him with a yellow stare. "She's a lovely young woman, and it wouldn't kill you to be happy."

Shane looked away, his gaze falling on a portrait of a finely dressed man and woman—dancing.

"You did well today, pup," Rodden said.

"Not well enough for you to stop calling me *pup*."

# 20

# A PROSPECT

*Pilgrim's Road, Yvenea*
*July 16, 1195 PT*

*Ella*

The road from the Modrian Mountains to Drawl bustled with wagons, oxen, horses, and pedestrians. Stone pillars set with bright sunrock lanterns lined the highway. Once lit with solarite to ward off wild shades roaming the river valley centuries ago, the lanterns now served as a monument to the struggles of history.

As the road curved around a hill, the caravan halted behind carts from Agenom. At mid-morning, a dung shoveler bumped into the side of Ella's wagon bench. "Pardon me, miss," the woman said.

Ella recognized Darï, a fellow Ruvian emissary, and nodded. "No harm done. Carry on."

The Tarish caravan resumed their slow pace. It was like a city on the move. When they reached the Syres River, the Tarish group camped amid a mass of wagons, tents, and animal corrals. While unpacking the cookware, Ella found a note from Darï stuck to the underside of the wagon bench. Ducking behind the wagon, Ella read the message. She shredded it in her hand and mixed it into the slop bucket. After finishing breakfast prep, she washed up for bed.

Merchants who peddled their wares by day had erected tent markets that night. One such market next to the Tarish camp boomed with boisterous noise past midnight. The traders sang and drank by the light piles long after Ella and Rose settled inside their tent.

Rose grunted and covered her head with her scarf. "You're from a merchant family. Tell them to shut up," she whined.

At first, Ella ignored her, easily able to sleep through the noise. She had spent a winter living with rogues and Ruvian scouts in Rotira. *They* were rowdy. But she used this as an excuse to leave camp and check in with Darï.

"Fine." Ella scooted out of her bedroll and slipped on her boots and coat. She reached the edge of the camp when Will rounded a wagon in front of her. Ella had only seen him twice since Pelton. Their brief conversations had been cordial.

"Going somewhere?" He spoke in a polite tone, but there was a coldness to him ever since the collectors had left.

Ella pointed to the merchant tents. "Shutting up the neighbors."

Will stepped aside and motioned for her to pass, then continued his patrol.

She strolled into the merchant camp and spotted Darï sitting by a crowded light pile. They made brief eye contact. Ella sat on the bench next to her and accepted a mug of ale from a bearded fellow who told her repeatedly she looked like his sister. After an hour, the crowd thinned.

"Prospects?" Darï asked.

"One," Ella answered, sipping from her mug.

"Condition?"

"He's able." Ella kept her eyes on the light pile.

"Does he know?"

"No. Still just a prospect."

"If it's too slim, you can help with the ones from Shevak. There are thirty."

"No," Ella said in a firm tone. "This one is worth it."

"How do you know?"

"Healthy."

Darï stood. "We do as we do, then."

"We do as we do," Ella repeated. After Darï left, Ella waited a few minutes to head back to the Tarish camp. Along the way, she tossed a coin to one of the vendors and told him to quiet the crowds.

The next morning, they completed their journey. Since leaving Lorinth, thirty-six days of slow, relentless travel, the Tarish caravan finally settled on the sandy shore of the Syres River, in view of the glittering walls of Drawl. They could get no closer among the throngs of soggy wagons and tents. Rain had been their constant companion the last three days and only dwindled when they completed pitching the tents.

As Ella served soup around the cook pile, she spotted Hale sitting alone beside a wagon. She took two bowls of soup and told Gwen, her assistant, to finish serving the line.

Ella approached Hale and handed him a bowl. "Not feeling well?"

He smiled and patted the grass next to him. "Feeling fine, Miss Therman. Care to join me? It'd be nice to have my last meal in beautiful company."

Ella blushed and glanced from side to side. No one paid them any mind. She squatted next to Hale and rested her back on the wagon wheel. "I suppose I can't blame you for being so bold in your last days."

They made small talk as they ate until the others had gone to the light pile or their tents. Hale knew more jokes than Carl Loren, so he had Ella's side aching from laughter.

A silence settled between them. "I don't have red lung," he said, slurping the last of his soup.

Ella checked around to assure no one was within earshot. "I know."

Hale studied her. "I'm not sick at all, actually. Just born to the wrong woman. I'm the bastard son of Bruce Hayden, and now my brother, Gaylen, is cleaning up after our father. He's afraid one of us might challenge his inheritance."

Ella tightened her coat, shivering in the cool night air. "I thought it might be something like that."

"You're different from the others," he said. "It's like you're the only one who's alive, who actually sees what's happening. I hope you mourn for me like you did the others, Miss Therman."

Ella held his gaze and took a deep breath, softening her voice. "Hale, if you had the chance to get out of the Festival, would you take it?"

His lips fell into a frown. "It's more complicated than just wanting to live. I'm going to tell you a secret. I have a twin sister. My brother doesn't know about her, but if I had put up a fight, he might have found out. I'm doing this for her. If I die quietly, he'll never even know she exists."

Ella jostled the empty bowl resting between her feet. "I have a secret too. I can get you out of this, and I know people who can protect your sister. Both of you could disappear if you want."

Hale's lips quivered. "You a rogue?"

"No. I'm a smuggler, and not the petty, rum-running kind."

"Sounds expensive."

Ella shook her head. "No money involved. But you and your sister will have to leave your old life behind. That's the price."

Hale stared at his feet and twitched. "I guess I've nothing to lose. But you . . . how do you know I'm not a spy?"

"I have a talent for knowing when people are lying to me."

"What do I need to do?"

"Just wait. Once you've been counted by the clerics in Drawl, my people will come for you. If you run before that, guards will chase you down. And Hale"—she got to her feet and peered into his eyes—"when I give my word, I keep it."

Hale rested his head against the wagon wheel and handed Ella his empty bowl. "I trust you."

Ella walked to the cook pile and handed the bowls to Gwen.

"Take the night off, Miss Therman. I've got this," the girl said.

Ella sighed. A night off would do her well. She needed to find Darï again. After thanking Gwen, she hurried along the shore of the river. Within moments, Will caught up with her. She suppressed her irritation and smiled at him.

"I wish you wouldn't wander off by yourself," he said. Ella opened her mouth to protest, but he put a firm hand on her shoulder. "I know. You can take care of yourself. You've proven that quite plainly, El. I just—" His eyes softened, and he moved closer.

Oh fires, he was trying to kiss her. Ella deliberately stepped back. A sharp feline hiss startled them. Ella jerked when something furry tugged at her boot and then darted between her feet.

Will jumped, regaining his balance by grabbing Ella's arm. The brightness of the moons illuminated a shaggy brown cat, who scrambled onto a rock beside them. Its yellow eyes fell on her, and it meowed. She wanted to hug the creature, as much as she didn't care for cats.

"There you are, you monster!" A boy of perhaps fifteen and wearing a fitted traveling coat snatched the cat by the neck. The animal hissed, curling its tail and twitching its hind legs. The boy turned his eyes on Ella. His hood obscured most of his dark face, and something about him made Ella wary.

Will threw his arm around Ella, pulling her closer.

The boy stared, stone-faced. He matched Will's height, but probably weighed fifty pounds less. By his tattered but smartly designed outfit, knives at his belt, and casual stance, Ella guessed he was either a rogue or a street thief.

"Sorry about that," he said.

"Is that thing yours?" Will released his grip as Ella stiffened. He put his hand on the hilt of his sword.

The boy's eyes flashed to the weapon and back to Will's face. Otherwise, he remained still. He wasn't afraid, just calculating.

Ella inhaled through her nose and spoke with exaggeration. "I'm so sorry, mister."

"No need, miss," the boy said as the cat dangled from his hand.

Ella smiled. "Oh, I was talking to this handsome fellow." She cupped her hands around the cat's face and scratched behind his ears. He was the size of a small dog, much too big for a normal alley cat.

The boy's brow rose in guarded amusement. "Apologies if this brute scared you, miss. He has no manners." He studied her like a thief surveilling a potential score.

Will—not accustomed to the habits of thieves—seemed annoyed. He stepped in front of her, nose to nose with the boy. "You should keep that thing on a rope."

The boy smirked awkwardly, as though willing himself to do so. But the dangerous glint in his eyes appeared genuine. "I meant no offense. Carry on, soldier." The boy dropped the cat and strode down the beach, the animal slinking after him.

Will tugged at Ella's coat and led her in the other direction. She glanced over her shoulder. The cat was out of sight, but two men joined the boy. They stared after her, then continued along the shore.

"I've been offered a place in the Southern Infantry, Second Division," Will said.

His comment drove the encounter with the strange boy right out of Ella's mind. She snapped her head toward him. "What?"

Will faced the river, staring with a pained expression. "If I had a reason to stay in Lorinth, I would turn down the army. I can afford the fee. But it would have to be a reason, not a fancy, not a hope."

Ella bent her head and fidgeted with her pockets. She could not give him such a reason. But to see him march under a Drawlen flag . . .

"I don't have one, do I?" Will lifted Ella's chin. "Look at me, Ella Therman."

Reluctantly, she met his gaze. Her heart pounded. A tear trickled down her cheek.

"I would have quit the militia if that's what made you happy." Will's eyes grew moist, and his voice cracked. "I would marry you tomorrow. I spent all summer trying to make you see that. I thought you were just trying to hang onto your last threads of youth. But now I see that's not the case." He lifted her chin and wiped away the tear. "Something's changed you, El, something I can't reach. Look me in the eyes and tell me once and for all that I'm chasing a lost dream."

Ella held his gaze and blinked away more tears. It had been several years since she withdrew from him and all her childhood friends. Most of them had married or moved to other towns to find work. "Will, I care a great deal for you. But you're right, something has changed me. I can't—"

Will shook his head and placed a finger on her lips. "I just needed to hear it from you."

# 21

# THE HARVEST TEMPLE

*Drawl, Independent Drawlen City-State*
*July 18, 1195 PT*

*Shane*

Shane crept through the streets of Drawl, trailing Ella. He followed the alleycat form of Rodden, who prowled in and out of sight. Nearing the second hour of night, most of the drunks had found their beds, so the city remained quiet and dark.

He'd hoped Bren was wrong about Ella meeting with Darï. Jon Therman and his smugglers were bold, to be sure, but whatever they were doing at the festival exceeded their style and territory. Moreover, Jon didn't get involved in politics or religion, but spiriting people away from the Festival of Souls was wholly both.

Tracking Ella proved to be a chore. Even with Rodden using the scent from her shoelace, a piece he had procured the previous day, they lost her twice. She stalked the streets like a coin thief, slipping past the pedestrians and guards without garnering attention. Several times, Shane and his feline companion had dashed behind obstacles as Ella stopped and gazed in their direction.

When Rodden squatted in a shuttered doorway, Shane stopped behind him, peering around the doorframe.

Ella flattened against a wall in the alley, hands in the deep pockets of her oversized coat, and hood drawn around her face. The outfit, along with her small stature, resembled a street urchin. A moment later, footsteps resonated from farther down the alley.

"Spare a quarter mark, ma'am?" Ella said.

"Got no purse." Darï's voice chimed, followed by feet shuffling. "What are you doing here?" Darï sounded annoyed. More importantly, though, she spoke Ruvish, not Palish. Shane held his breath.

"My prospect didn't get intercepted," Ella answered in fluent Ruvish, as if she had spoken it her whole life.

Darï huffed. "He was counted by the clerics later than we liked. It wasn't worth the risk." Heavy footsteps drummed on stone. "Ella." Darï scolded.

"I gave him my word." More footsteps—Ella came closer to the opening of the alley.

"Don't run off to do something foolish, El."

The footsteps ceased. Ella now stood around the corner from Shane, so close, he could hear her breathing. "Of course not," she said and headed into the streets away from Shane's hiding place.

He knew Ella would sooner throw herself into a pit of fire than leave behind someone who needed help. After Darï left, Shane exited the alcove.

Rodden slunk around Shane's legs. "This has become something far bigger than trailing a few rogues. These are outlander ashers."

Shane raised a brow at the slur. "I'm going to tell your wife you said that."

Rodden hissed. "These people aren't like the Sirahi. They are the scattered Ruvian tribes who abandoned their homeland to live in slums and take scraps from Drawls. Don't you understand what they're doing? They're snatching journeyers, probably for their own profit."

"Snatchers?" Shane rolled his eyes. "I thought you'd gotten over your bad blood with Ruvians when you married one. Or is Mona an exception?"

"Leave her out of this, pup."

"If it weren't for her, you'd probably call me ogre instead of pup." Shane growled as he followed Ella's path toward the temple.

Rodden sprang after him. "Where are you going?"

"That asher," Shane said, "is Remm's little sister. And she's about to do something stupid."

Rodden twitched his ears. "A family trait, I assume."

Shane jogged along the road. "Feel free to explain to him why you chose your ancient ego over keeping her out of a Drawlen prison—or an urn. And while you're doing that, tell him she's going to break into the Harvest Temple." When Shane crossed the street, Rodden darted behind a building and vanished. Shane shook his head and gritted his teeth.

Weaving along the alleys, he neared the outer wall of the Harvest Temple, hoping to find Ella. After passing a deserted market corridor, he entered the center of the city beside the inner walls.

Before him stood one of the three Great Temples of Drawlen, accounting for a third of the city's total size. Only one gate interrupted the smooth surface of the circular wall, now closed and patrolled by Black Veil guards.

Shane followed the wall east along the road. A quarter mile from the gate, he spotted Ella climbing a tower of black crates set against the wall. As he neared her, Ella swung from a horizontal flagpole and grabbed the ledge. She hung for a moment as a guard strolled along the battlement. When he passed, she lifted herself onto the ramparts and slipped over the other side.

Shane scaled the crates and leapt onto the ledge.

Many buildings—shrines, green houses, and dormitories—filled the space between the wall and the Harvest Tower, providing ample places to hide. Behind a green, marble house dedicated to the Eternal Oracle, Shane lost his quarry. He scanned the empty avenues.

The song of a blade being drawn from its sheath jolted him as he looked up. Cold hazel eyes met his gaze, and sharp steel chilled his throat. Ella Therman hung upside down by her knees from a support beam, a knife in each hand, crossing the blades in front of Shane's throat like scissors. One of the more humbling moments in his life: Shane zem'Arta, veteran of the Red Watch, caught at knifepoint by a reckless young smuggler.

"Can I at least explain myself before you cut my throat, Little Mouse?"

Recognition dawned on Ella's face. "Shane?"

She scrambled to stow her knives and flipped down from her perch. For a few seconds, they stared at one another. No longer wearing her patchy coat, she now sported a sleeveless, knee-length tunic, fitted leggings, and soft-soled wool boots. Fingerless gloves hid her palms, and dark strips of cotton covered her forearms—the ensemble of an experienced thief.

Pulling back his hood, Shane chuckled.

Ella raised a brow, studying the new mark on his right cheek. "What happened to your face?"

"Ran into an old friend."

She glowered and punched him in the arm. "What in the fires are you doing here?"

"Following your red-headed friend."

Ella squared her shoulders. She barely reached Shane's chest at her full height. She'd clearly grown a few inches since their last meeting but still looked younger than her age. "So? You just decided to follow me instead?"

"I thought you'd be easier to catch."

"Sorry to disappoint you," Ella said.

Shane glanced behind him. "Your big brother would be proud."

"Remm? Is he with you?" Ella's eyes brightened, and Shane saw the hopeful girl beneath.

"He's around," he said with a sigh. "I'll set up a family reunion—if you'll do something for me."

"What? Are you keeping him in a box?"

Shane chuffed. "No, but I'll keep that in mind for the future. He's a pain in the ass sometimes."

Ella shifted to the side, regarding him with a scowl. "What do you want, zem'Arta?"

"I want to have a chat with your boss."

"You don't need me if you just want to talk to my father."

"Your other boss," Shane said. "Dantiego."

Ella's expression faltered, and she pursed her lips. Shane placed a hand on the wall next to her, blocking her between himself and the corner of the alcove. "Do your parents know you're running with rogues, Little Mouse?"

She ducked and rolled out from beneath his arm, surprising him. "Well, look at you," she drawled, "having me all figured out. Okay, Freelander." Crouched on the other side of the alcove, her muscled body and lithe posture mimicked that of a ring fighter.

"Where can I find Dantiego?" Shane asked.

Ella stood, crossing her arms. "That's a big ask. I'll need a little more from you to even things out."

"Like what?"

"Help me get my friend out of the temple, and I'll get you an audience with the top brass *after* you let me see my brother."

Shane rubbed his chin, then offered his arm, which Ella accepted with a firm shake. "Deal." He had at least a hundred questions, the foremost being how she came to learn a language he *thought* was only spoken in the Freelands. But no time to ponder that mystery.

He grabbed Ella around the waist and pushed her under the shadow of the overhang, slapping a hand over her mouth when she protested.

A guard rounded the corner, holding a pistol in one hand and a sunrock lantern in the other. Ella gripped her daggers. Whether luck or Sovereign's favor, the weapons proved unnecessary.

The guard paced at the mouth of the alley, his lantern light falling short of where Shane and Ella hid. He moved his head from side to side and shrugged. Then he resumed his patrol, mumbling about ghosts and pigeons.

A minute passed before either of the intruders moved. Ella peeled Shane's hand from her mouth and stepped into the alley. Surveying the area, she whispered, "I have some ground rules."

Shane recalled saying the same thing on their joint venture five years prior, right before their job turned unexpectedly violent. "I'm listening."

"First, no killing. I don't want this to be Estbye all over again—there's no river to dump bodies."

"Sewers work fine."

Ella put her hands on her hips just like her mother. "Second, I'll take you to my contact, but whether you get to meet with Krishena in person isn't up to me. It would help if you told me why."

Shane shrugged. "My people and her people are getting in each other's way. We could help each other instead."

"Help me first and I'll see what I can do." She dodged across the street with Shane at her heels.

They traversed the temple grounds—like shadows chased by moonlight. Only once did they break their soundless progress when they encountered a guard relieving himself in an alley. After Ella struck a drugged dart into the guard's neck, he toppled into his own puddle, unconscious.

# 22

# ENCOUNTERS

*Drawl, Independent Drawlen City-State*
*July 18, 1195 PT*

*Rose*

Rose shivered as she lay alone in the tent. Ella still hadn't returned. The murmur of activity in the camps had quieted over an hour ago, and Rose fretted.

Unable to still the tremors in her limbs, Rose crawled out of her sleep sack, her wool blanket wrapped tightly around her shoulders. She struggled to shove her feet into her boots and groaned when her sock bunched. "Great."

The memory of a warm manor and sheepskin slippers tormented her. She even preferred the cellar dormitory of the Lorinth temple over these miserable accommodations.

Scampering under the canvas flap, she wandered toward the edge of the Tarish camp. The tightness in her chest grew. Ella was somewhere in the city, and Rose couldn't shake the feeling her friend wasn't safe. She glanced at the sleeping camp and staggered toward the latrine. Near the canvas-curtained outhouse, a dark mass blocked the path.

"Probably one of those moronic temple guards passed out drunk," Rose mumbled.

She skirted the body and paused when her foot squelched on wet ground. She lifted her boot, the glint of moonlight exposing blood dripping from her sole. Stumbling back, she gasped. Not a soldier. It was Gwen, the camp cook. Blood covered her head, and she stared with frightened, dead eyes.

Rose scrambled backward and fell. A figure emerged from her tent and vanished behind the rows of carts. Rose hustled to her feet, shaking so much she lost her balance. An iron grip snatched her, pressing her back into a warm body. A hand clamped over her mouth.

"Not a sound, or they'll hear you," Captain Arik Leir whispered hoarsely in her ear.

She nodded and obeyed, despite her terror. The brief, startled cries of death in the camp filled the sky.

"Run, Bellerose. Get into the city and do not come back. Ever." Leir pushed her forward.

She slipped on her hands and knees across the wet grass. Straining to stand, she fell over the edge of a ditch, suppressing a screech. Landing on a patch of moss, she cowered within the shadow of a willow tree.

From her hiding place, she recognized Leir's frustrated grunt and the sound of a blade clattering on the gravel. "Where is she?" a woman's voice demanded. Rose bolted.

*Ella*

Ella eyed Hale, who rested on the stone floor with his back against a clay pot of tall, exotic greenery. A hundred other journeyers surrounded him. The guards had counted and marched them into the temple grounds too late, preventing them from making it inside the tower.

The Harvest Tower doors closed promptly at sunset, supposedly to prevent the spirits of journeyers from haunting the city. Drawlen superstitions typically annoyed Ella. Now, however, they provided a chance to rescue her friend. A difficult promise she was determined to keep. Twenty guards watched over the crowd of sleeping, coughing, and dying journeyers.

"Now's your chance, mouse," Shane whispered.

Ella fingered the smooth pebble she'd plucked from a nearby flower bed.

"Sure you don't want me to do it?" Shane muttered in a condescending tone.

She glared. Even with his hood shadowing his face, his smirk was obvious. She tossed the pebble. It clinked at Hale's feet.

Hale snapped his head up and met Ella's gaze from across the room. She nodded and sank behind the barrier. Wringing her hands, she quelled their shaking and dried the sweat.

"Ever done this before?" Shane squatted directly across from her. He hadn't changed much in the last five years, other than the new scar on his face. She was sure the mark had something to do with the Freeland justice system. Ella had witnessed him steal, lie, and kill before, so no surprise. Still, during their time together in Estbye, he seemed haunted. Now he acted more like he was winning a few hands of marauders.

"No—yes. I mean, I've never done this with half the Black Veil Order in town."

"Just take care of your friend," Shane said. "If we run into trouble, leave the Drawls to me." He turned to check on the guards. The moonlight hitting his face highlighted the two horizontal scars on his cheek.

Hale's voice carried over the buzz of coughs and groaning. "I need to piss."

"Make it quick," a guard said.

As soon as Hale rounded the corner, Shane grabbed him and put his rough hand over the younger man's mouth. Hale startled.

Ella punched Shane lightly on his shoulder. "You didn't have to do that."

Shane let go and shrugged. "Would you rather I said 'hello' and served him tea?"

Once outside the greenhouse, they hid behind a statue of Rodden the World Burner while a pair of temple guards strolled by.

Hale grasped Ella's hand. "Thank you," he whispered.

Shane shushed him, giving the boy a full view of his strange eyes and scarred face. Hale blanched. Perhaps he'd never seen a troll up close.

Minutes later, Shane crept from their hiding place and led them along a walkway. They weaved quietly between buildings, rounding corners just in time to evade the night patrols. It was uncanny. Ella wondered if Shane's people were somehow looking out for him.

They paused in a dark alley at the border of the open grounds surrounding the Harvest Tower. Before them, the windowless, octagonal structure loomed. Surrounding the tower stood eight octagonal pyramids. Three bronze rings lay on each flat top.

With no guards in sight, not even at the tower's stone door, Shane backed further into the alley and hunched down. Pulling Hale with her, Ella crept closely behind Shane.. His gaze shifted all around, only meeting hers for a second. "Ella." His tone was quiet and serious. "Take your friend over the wall. Don't stop, and don't look back."

"What about—"

"Just run." He spun and darted into the temple square.

Ella's mouth went dry. Her hands shook. She led Hale through the grounds and over the wall. As they lowered themselves onto the crates, a sharp chill filled Ella's gut. She scanned their surroundings.

Over the low buildings of the temple grounds, the tower and the platforms surrounding it remained unlit and vacant. However, while she couldn't see any shades, by Sovereign, she could feel them. Cold and hostile, they concentrated near where she and Shane had separated. Ella squeezed the flame stone at her chest, a comforting habit she'd developed over the years.

"Hale, go to the north market. Find the door marked with three scythes. Ask for Calla. Tell him I sent you. Oh!" She pointed to the ground below them. "Bring my coat. It's behind the bottom crate."

Hale jumped to the ground. "Got it." He sprinted into the darkness.

Ella leapt onto the ledge and ran down the parapet stairs. A clash of blades rang in the air as she neared the tower. At the edge of the alley, she halted. Three temple guards lay on the ground, their heads twisted at horrifying angles. On the steps of one platform, Shane dueled with a collector. It was Rendal, the one who had killed Edd Pran.

Shane and Rendal fought with fury, sabers clashing. They wielded knives in their opposite hands. When a guard rounded the corner, Shane threw his knife, hitting him in the chest.

Rendal thrust his blade toward Shane. He parried and threw Rendal to the ground. Sword in one hand and claws extending from the other, Shane pounced. His feral growl rang over the twang of steel when the collector blocked his blow. Too late, though, for Shane's free hand swiped his face.

Beyond them, a monstrous hellcat prowled along the edge of the platform, shoulders hunched and hackles raised while it growled—no, *spoke*. It spoke to a tall, sinister-looking man in a long black coat. The man paced on the other side of the octagonal stage.

"I see you're enjoying godhood, Refsul," the hellcat said.

Refsul laughed.

Ella shuddered. Krishena had told her the Drawlen immortals were very real and very dangerous. The cardinal rule for any rogue or smuggler: Stay out of their way.

Fires. She was really in it now.

The talking hellcat and the Drawlen High Immortal circled each other. Absorbed in watching them, Ella failed to react when a gloved hand grabbed her wrist and a black blade flashed in her face.

"Best you just cooperate, lass," a man said. He pushed her into the light of the square and yelled, "Mind your claws, troll, if you don't want a knife in your lady's throat!"

Shane growled as he met Ella's terrified gaze. With a frustrated grunt, he leapt away and threw his sword aside. He put his hands on his head, exposing his subtly pointed ears. How had Ella never noticed them?

"A half-breed ogre," Rendal spat at Shane. He pulled a pair of metal shackles from his belt pouch and held them in the air.

A thump sounded and Ella's captor cried in pain, loosening his grip on her hands. When Rendal paused to glance toward her, Shane spun with claws extended and broke the collector's arm, ripping open his throat.

Ella twisted free and reached for her captor's hand. Instead, she grabbed his blade, which bit into her palm with a freezing sting. Pulling away, she stumbled forward.

The man lunged at her, a small knife protruding from his back. He grabbed Ella's necklace, ripping the oval pendant from her neck.

"No!" Ella cried.

The man's black scarf came loose. He smiled at her with crooked teeth. As another blade penetrated his throat, he fell to the ground.

Ella scrambled to recover the necklace, her most cherished possession. Hissing as blood dripped from her hand, she lifted her gaze and met a pair of hauntingly familiar hazel eyes. "Remm!"

"Better scramble, Little Mouse. This catfight isn't for you." Remm danced around her and unsheathed a coordinating set of blades—a Kumuni-style short sword and a dagger. Two guards approached.

Shane snatched both his and Rendal's swords and joined Ella's half brother. Remm twirled his blades and cackled.

An eerie shrill came from the platform. The temperature in the square plummeted. Refsul shifted into a black mass like an opaque shade and dove at the hellcat. The two forms smashed into one another in midair. The hellcat thudded, falling next to a bronze scepter lying between them. Ella recognized the scepter, for its likeness was in the hand of every statue of Refsul she'd seen. The hellcat howled and lunged for it.

The mass transformed into Refsul. "No!" he shrieked.

The hellcat stomped his front paw on the staff. The moment he touched it, a tremor shook the campus. Ella toppled to her knees. Everyone around her fell too—except for the skin-changer who had just a second ago been a hellcat.

Broad shouldered and dressed in buckskin pants, he looked more like a wild animal than a man. A tapestry of colorful tattoos covered his back, partially obscured by russet locks of hair.

The skin-changer faced Refsul, exposing his profile. He was horrifyingly recognizable. There was not a living person in all the Drawlen territories who hadn't seen his likeness. The villain in every story, the nightmare of every childhood, the phantom of every pious Drawl's fear. He was the First Arch Traitor, the World Burner, Rodden the Fiend. He twirled the scepter in his hand, studying it with a smug expression.

He glared at Refsul. "Shall we end this the way it began, your majesty?" He slid his thumb along one of the jewels encased in the staff. From the end shot a long steel spike.

Refsul growled. Inky tendrils of smoke erupted around him and whipped at Rodden, who parried every attack. One of the tendrils smashed into the stairs near Ella, sending chunks of stone everywhere and causing her to roll to the side.

A guard sprang for her but met her knife as Ella struggled to her feet.

Like a maniac, Remm laughed at the two men on the platform, and Shane cussed in Karthan. More Drawls poured into the square—collectors, purifiers, soldiers—a deadly crowd. Shane and Remm cut through them like a pair of scythes.

The air grew cold. Ella wondered why she couldn't see her breath.

Rodden and Refsul continued their destructive spar. Finally, Rodden knocked Refsul to the ground and pressed his ornamental weapon to the high immortal's throat.

Refsul laughed. "What will you do after you kill me, Rodden?"

"Kill you again." Rodden shoved the spear into Refsul's neck and pulled it out. The shades surrounding the high immortal writhed for a moment. They stilled, hovering like fog. Slowly, the bronze rings on each platform around the Harvest Temple spun.

"Shit!" Shane screamed. "Rodden, get out of there!"

Rodden's yellow eyes widened. He moved away, but the shades hovering over Refsul wrapped around him like ropes.

His wound now fully healed, Refsul rose. A malicious grin spread across his face. Some of the shades whipped out to either side, crashing into the seven other platforms. They formed a trembling, shadowy circle around the Harvest Tower.

The scene blurred and swayed as Ella's hand throbbed. It wasn't the cold . . . it was her. With a resounding crack, Refsul and Rodden disappeared. Ella's vision clouded.

*Rose*

Rose squinted through her fog of tears. She sprinted past the silent encampments and the outermost streets of Drawl. She pushed through the burning pain in her side and ignored the urge to vomit.

Stumbling, she collapsed to her hands and knees in a stinking puddle. Her shoulders shook, and she sobbed. A lifetime passed until boots clicking on cobblestone startled her. Slowly, she raised her head.

A figure approached, silhouetted red and silver by the moons. "There you are," the man said.

Rose gasped and looked on with wide eyes at the finely dressed man.

He raised his hand, the pistol in his grip gleaming as he pulled back the hammer. The echo of a shot sung in the street.

Rose closed her eyes. No pain. No blinding light. Only flesh thudding against the ground.

When she opened her eyes, the man lay in a heap before her. His left hand clutched his chest, and the pistol hung loose in his right. Footsteps from behind paralyzed her.

"Rose," came Will Loren's voice.

She whimpered and trembled. He dropped to his knees, landing in the puddle, and wrapped her in his arms. "It's okay. We're going to be o—"

Rose shuddered when Will stared with glassy eyes. His grip slackened. He slumped over, revealing three black darts protruding from his shoulder.

In a strange fit of bravery, Rose wrapped her hand in her sleeve and pulled the darts from Will's back.

More footsteps. Rose lay still as a corpse, holding her breath. She felt Will's body roll away, felt the breath of his killer on her arm. She sprang forward, driving the triad of darts into the killer's thigh.

A woman screeched. Rose scrambled through the puddle. She jumped to her feet. The woman, a black scarf over her nose and mouth, convulsed on the ground. Her blonde braid writhed in the shallow puddle like a snake.

*Run and don't come back*, Captain Leir had pleaded. Rose grabbed the abandoned pistol. She took one last look at the second soldier who had saved her life that night, then ran.

Turn after turn, she weaved through the streets of Drawl until she came upon another horrifying scene. Hale, the journeyer always trying to chat up Ella, pressed himself against a wall. A short, lean woman wearing a ratty bandanna on her head cornered him. She held a thick knife to his neck. A malevolent glint in her eyes told Rose she knew how to hurt people.

With trembling hands, Rose lifted the pistol. Her finger twitched at the trigger. Warm gusts whirled around her, followed by the scent of apple blossoms. A strong hand rested over hers. It belonged to a man whose dark, narrow eyes flashed dangerously. He cupped the gun in her hand, lowering it. Rose felt weightless. As she drifted out of consciousness, a great shadow emerged over the stranger's shoulders. She thought of a dragon.

# 23

# THE ROGUE MASTER

*Drawl, Independent Drawlen City-State*
*1:00 a.m., July 19, 1195 PT*

*Shane*

Shane stumbled out of Remm's trace onto a rickety balcony. Remm carried Ella's unconscious body. Behind them, four collectors appeared from a swath of shadow. The closest managed one step before Shane's knife sliced his chest. With a swift kick, Shane lobbed the petrifying corpse, knocking down the others as it sailed over the railing, where it splashed into the canal and sank.

In the opposite corner, another shadow formed and receded, revealing a dark-skinned woman. A white scar ran from her left brow to her jaw. She wielded two long, thin blades and barreled over Remm as she attacked the oncoming collectors. Remm rolled to the floor, curling Ella closer to his chest.

The woman's dreadlocks, heavy with beads matching the rings on her coat, twirled as she stabbed her blade into a collector's stomach. When her other sword slashed his throat, the metal cuffs on her neck clanged.

The remaining two collectors fled toward the railing, only to come face-to-face with Calla, the rogue who had obliterated the shade at Orin's wedding. He now wore rags, but he sported the same prim face and neat black hair as when Shane had spied him in Setmal.

Smoky tendrils erupted around him, obscuring his form and swallowing the collectors in inky vapor. When the shadow dissipated, the two collectors lay in a heap on the balcony, bleeding from their eyes, noses, and mouths.

"Above you," Bren's voice called.

Shane jumped back as a collector crashed from the roof. The railing buckled under his stony form, and he, too, toppled into the canal. Several pieces of the painted railing tumbled after him and bobbed in the water.

The woman with the scarred face surveyed the balcony and roof. Shane readied his dagger, looking warily at her and Calla.

Bren leapt from the roof, landing alongside Shane. "I met them at the Tarish journey camp." He nodded to Calla and the woman. "They came to rescue Ella. But collectors and apostles cleared the place. No one's left alive."

Shane stowed his dagger. "Krishena Dantiego."

She, too, sheathed her blades. "And you are the Red Wolf. We seem to have aligning interests," she said in a rolling tSolani accent.

The whine of a door interrupted the tension. Remm strode over the threshold into the musty apartment with Ella cradled in his arms. Krishena and Calla followed Shane into the room while Bren scouted outside, watching for more Drawls.

Placing his sister on the moldy mattress beneath a boarded-up window, Remm knelt before her. He cradled her hand and examined it. Faint black veins snaked from a shallow cut on Ella's palm.

"What have you done to her?" Krishena asked.

"Nice to see you too, Auntie K," Remm said through gritted teeth.

"What happened, Remm?" the rogue master demanded.

Shane paced the room. "Collectors. She got cut by a wraith blade."

Krishena startled, drawing her hand to her belt. "When?"

"Half an hour ago," Shane said.

From the pouch at her waist, Krishena pulled a vial of silver liquid.

Shane shook his head. "It's too late for antivenom."

The woman brushed past him and knelt next to Remm, taking Ella's hand into hers. "I'll take the chance." She uncorked the vial and spread open the cut on Ella's palm, trickling several drops of silver liquid into the wound. "Foolish girl," she muttered, then addressed Shane. "What are you doing in Drawl?"

"Tracking him." Shane pointed to Calla.

Krishena smoothed Ella's hair off her face and shot Calla a hard look. "I see."

"I don't remember ever getting in your way, Mr. Wolf," Calla said, a wispy shade swirling around him. "In fact, I thought I'd been rather helpful."

"You were supposed to be discreet in Setmal," Krishena said.

Calla raised his hands, an impish grin growing on his face. "What was I to do? The bride and groom were seconds from death or madness. I had to intervene."

The rogue master lunged at Calla and pressed her index finger into his lapel. "And now you've gained the attention of the Red Watch and Sovereign knows who else."

Remm sighed. "I see you two are still as adorable as ever."

Glaring at Calla, Shane growled under his breath and clenched his fists. "You're not the only one who's gained Drawlen's attention." Running a hand over his face, he kicked the broken remains of a sunrock lantern across the room. "Fires! Damn! That selfish fiend." He sank to the floor and pressed against the wall. The whine of the wraith gate rang in his memory. "This is a mess."

Remm caressed Ella's sweaty forehead. "If Mona were here . . ."

Shane straightened, the impact of Remm's words giving him renewed hope. "We need Tres. Where the fires is he?"

Remm shook his head. "Mona can't make a mind calling this far. You know that."

"It's worth a try," Shane said.

Krishena leaned against the window. "Why are you so interested in my people?"

Shane rose and folded his arms. "We're getting in each other's way. For starters, what's your connection with Taval Sesporan?"

Krishena lifted her chin. "I owe you no explanations, Mr. zem'Arta. I'm certainly not endeared to your cause since you absconded with one of my agents." She narrowed her eyes at Remm.

Remm scowled. "I left your merry band on my own, thank you."

The deck boards creaked, and Shane spun around.

Carris burst through the door, dragging Hale behind her. The boy stumbled out of her grasp, knocking into Calla and dropping Ella's lumpy coat on the floor.

"What the hell?" Carris growled. "Getting a little crowded in here."

Hale gasped as his eyes fell on Ella, then shifted to Shane. "Is she dead?"

"What'd you bring him here for, Carris?" Shane demanded.

Carris rolled her shoulders and plucked the ratty bandana from her head. "This damn city's crawling with collectors and apostles"—she flashed her sharp teeth at Krishena—"and rogues. They're looking for something, for someone. Didn't want this kid to go blabbing."

Tres loomed in the doorway, a blank-eyed girl in his grip. She blinked slowly, entranced by the spire lord's mind craft.

"Who—" Shane began.

"A survivor," Tres said, "from the Tarish journey camp." He shot a hard look at Morgel, who stepped in after him. "This charity was not my idea."

Morgel shook his head and patted Tres on the cheek. Tres gritted his teeth, letting go of the girl. Morgel took her hand and led her to a chair in the corner.

Tres surveyed the room, his gaze lingering on Krishena and Calla. "Where is Rodden?"

Shane drew in a deep breath and squatted next to Ella. Sweat drops dotted her forehead, and her skin had become pallid. "He picked a fight with Refsul."

Tres blanched. "What?"

Krishena cocked her head and set a hand on one of her daggers. "You speak of Rodden Morrien?"

The crackling of mind craft dominated the room.

Shane pointed to Tres. "Cut that out!"

Tres pursed his lips, but the power subsided.

"Mr. zem'Arta," Krishena said. "I saw the wraith gate activate from afar. Am I to assume the World Burner was involved? There are rumors he's allied with your master."

Shane quivered at the word *master*. "Somehow, Refsul knew we were coming."

Krishena reached into her pocket. She pulled out a crumpled piece of paper and held it up to Shane.

Remm peered over Shane's shoulder and growled. "What the fires! Why does my sister have a Drawlen death mark?"

Krishena turned the paper around, studying Ella's likeness. "I don't know. But it seems we've stumbled upon a conspiracy the Drawls have gone to great lengths to enact. They culled the entire Tarish journey camp."

"For one person?" Carris asked.

Krishena pulled another death mark from her pocket. "Not just one."

"That's Will," Hale said. "Where's Will?"

The girl in the corner sniffled. As she regained her senses, she scanned the room with wide, fearful eyes. "Will," she muttered. "He—"

"Rose!" Hale ran and knelt beside the girl.

She wiped her nose with the back of her hands and wailed, falling into Hale's embrace. "They killed him, Hale. They murdered Will. They murdered everyone!"

Hale gripped Rose's hand, then addressed Shane. "What's going to happen to Ella?"

Calla scoffed. "It's wraith poison, boy. She has hours to live."

"Maybe not," Shane said, eyeing Tres.

The terrion grimaced, then approached Hale and Rose. "I require the chair."

Rose shuddered into Hale's shoulder as he glared at Tres.

"Move," the spire lord ordered.

Stumbling to his feet, Hale lifted Rose and helped her to the opposite corner.

Tres collapsed into the chair and pulled his sun-shaped limiter from under his shirt. He laid it on the floor at his feet and closed his eyes.

"A mind calling cannot possibly help," Krishena said.

"It can if we reach the right person," Shane argued.

The room quieted, except for Rose's shaky breaths.

After a few minutes, Tres opened his eyes. "Mona cannot make the connection. That leaves us with only one option." He gestured to Ella's unconscious form. "Are you sure we should bother?"

Shane seethed through gritted teeth and punched the wall, sending plaster chips flying to the floor. He pressed his palm against the cracked surface and closed his eyes. Scratching his forehead with his other hand, he contemplated. Everyone waited silently. Shane opened his eyes, addressing Tres. "We're going to bother. And Liiesh will help."

Tres folded his arms. "How can you be sure?"

Shane pushed away from the wall and smirked. "I have leverage."

# 24

# LAIR OF IMMORTALS

*Harvest Temple, Drawl*
*2:00 a.m., July 19, 1195 PT*

*Mavell*

Mavell stepped from his cloak of shades before the Harvest Tower. Waiting on the wraith gate, Detoa eyed the body slung over Mavell's shoulder. He dropped the body next to an unconscious priest lying on the platform.

As Detoa rolled the man faceup, she examined his stained temple guard uniform. "Who is he?"

"Another survivor," Mavell said.

"I doubt he will be for long." Detoa pressed her boot against the black veins of wraith poison on his face.

"Orders are orders," Mavell said. "I found him next to a dead collector in the city streets."

Beside the man, the Tarish priest moaned. Detoa stared at the priest's swollen eye. It oozed onto his fat, sallow face.

"Shall we?" Mavell asked.

His partner nodded.

The Harvest Temple's circle of wraith gates still hummed from the earlier encounter between Refsul and Rodden. Mavell had witnessed the fight from a rooftop blocks away. Immortals had their own agendas, which Mavell deliberately avoided. Lately, he found himself involuntarily ensnared in their machinations.

Holding his breath, he nodded to the guard at the control wheel near the tower and called up a shade. He begrudgingly sacrificed it to the ancient contraption, feeling the temporary drain. The air chilled. In the span of a breath, the scene changed. He and Detoa now stood one hundred and sixty miles away in the heart of the Temple Setvan overlooking the mountain city of Shevak.

"I hate using those things." Detoa doubled over with nausea.

As a ralenta, using the wraith gate caused Mavell no such side effects, so he ignored her and descended the steps.

Below the gate platform, the Veiled Man waited on the landing. His silver robe sparkled in the red moonlight. Two masked guards flanked him while he glided into the square.

In matching silence, Mavell and Detoa followed him as the guards collected the two limp bodies. The onyx, featureless edifice of the Temple of the Veil loomed before them. The castiron door opened, and they stepped into the dim interior after their master. When two disfigured goblins shut the door, the Veiled Man spoke.

"This has been an eventful evening. Has it not, Collector?"

Mavell inclined his head, his eyes still adjusting to the blue lanterns illuminating the hallway. "It would seem so," he said.

"We have a very honored guest in our midst," his master said. "We shall visit him shortly, but first, your report."

Mavell bowed. "The Freelander and his companions had an unplanned encounter with our revered lord. It did not go well for the Red Watch. They appear to be partnering with the Rogue Master of Rotira. They were quite adept at evading our pursuit. Wherever they went, we could not follow. I suspect they are returning to Setmal."

The shimmering shroud covering the Veiled Man's face swayed. "I think not, Collector. They will come here. We have something they want—desperately."

"The Fiend?" Mavell said. "They seemed acquainted. But it would be rather foolish of them to attempt a rescue."

The Veiled Man made an eerie noise that could have been a laugh. "Rodden is one of the First Lord's greatest assets. He will surely want his lone immortal returned. I've no doubt he would sacrifice the entire Red Watch to retrieve him. Rodden has been a thorn in our side far longer than the entire Romanus line has reigned in Palim."

Mavell raised a brow. "I thought Romanus killed any immortal that crossed his border."

The Veiled Man motioned toward the goblins, and they opened the door. "The First Lord is, like any mortal, a man of contradiction." He entered the corridor, Mavell and Detoa trailing. "Come, we have been summoned to Refsul's hall."

Many times, Mavell had walked from the Temple of the Veil to the belly of Refsul's cathedral. Twelve minutes if one kept a good pace. Following the ethereal Man of the Veil, however, the journey took twice as long. Mavell's legs grew twitchy. When they crossed the threshold, deep in the bowels of the mountain forming the rear of the temple complex, the scent of woodsmoke filled his nostrils.

At the far end, swelling piles of embers in two hearths lit the cavernous room. Between the hearths, backlit by the red light, stood a towering bronze statue of a man with wild hair and a crown of flames—Refsul, the High Immortal. His eyes glowed with rubies, and he gripped a bronze staff. Shallow grooves filled with burning oil crisscrossed the edges of the room, casting a sinister glow.

Along the hall's length, three levels of ledges housed the statues of all sixty-six Drawlen immortals. Square pillars separated the statues set under triangular gables. One sculpture on the lowest level lay scattered across the floor. This stony debris once depicted Rodden the Fiend.

A crowd of immortals gathered the smaller pieces and hurled them at a man suspended in the middle of the room—Rodden himself.

Groaning and drooling, he hung by his wrists on a chain dangling from the high ceiling. One small stone hit the suspended man on his head, causing him to bobble.

If there was a place on Ethar closest to hell, it was this room. Unlike the other statues, Rodden's had depicted an accurate likeness. The others were idealized—and rather inaccurate—portrayals of the immortals in the room. Perhaps due to hubris, or else so the whole of Palimar would not recognize them.

Despite this portrayal, Mavell understood the truth. He relished knowing all their filthiest secrets—how many centuries they'd endured past their natural lives; how many harem concubines they visited each week; who had real power and who didn't. It allowed him the best sense of control in this brutal world of immortality and corruption.

Refsul paced around Rodden's twitching, bleeding body. Unlike his chiseled statue, Refsul wore no crown of flames, his eyes steel gray instead of red, his body thinner and softer. Even so, his proud posture and long black coat cast a menacing presence.

"The World Burner," he said. "The wayward warrior come home to face his long overdue justice." He thrust the spike of his scepter into Rodden's ribs, deep enough to cause the man to cry out, shallow enough not to puncture his lung. A dozen more wounds peppered his body, oozing blood onto the floor.

"We've missed you, my dear battle brother." Refsul pulled out the spike. "Your lovely wife has been positively *petrified* at your absence."

The gathered immortals cackled.

"Would you like to see her?" Refsul flashed a wicked grin and gestured toward the door. "Take him to the tree of Eruna! Let them spend some quality time together before you throw him in the Wraith Cellar."

Two slouching trolls unchained Rodden from the ceiling. He crashed to the floor. As they dragged him from the hall, Refsul addressed the crowd.

"Sovereign has blessed us this day, brothers and sisters. We have perfected our tool of travel." He paused, enjoying the delighted roar from his audience, then lifted his hands. "Even now, we advance in the north. I am confident that, seeing as we have been graced with the return of this wayward brother, Sovereign has also ordained the return of another immortal. Then the Deep Wood shall be ours."

He pointed to one of the few mortals in the room. The man stepped forward, dressed in layered red robes that swished heavily over the floor. His gray hair lay combed away from a gold plate fastened in place of his left ear. The scars around it spread onto his fleshy neck. Mavell knew him well: Calron Maltez, the High Cleric of Refsul's order and head of the Drawlen priesthood.

"High Cleric," Refsul said. "Ready any aid Fenris requires. We shall feast and honor our advancing forces with prayer and celebration."

Maltez bowed and swaggered from the room. Rangers clad in pristine gray uniforms flanked him. As he passed, he spared a sharp glance at Mavell. Once he crossed the threshold, goblins in red tunics swarmed in, carrying banquet tables, chairs, barrels of wine, and all manner of savory, steaming platters.

Standing apart from the crowd, the Veiled Man spoke in Mavell's mind, *'Prepare to greet the mortari upon his arrival. Zem'Arta will lead his force, including Morgel, here to the temple. Make sure he is successful. I would very much like to introduce myself.'*

Mavell nodded, then spirited himself from the hall on the tendrils of a shade, pulling Detoa with him.

Hours later, as the sun rose, he and his partner walked the dark hall of the Temple of the Veil. Ascending the curved staircase, they arrived at the inner chamber. Despite the great door to the balcony being ajar and a fire burning in the hearth on the opposite wall, the room remained eerily still. Like the rest of the temple, the obsidian walls shimmered, decorated only by blue sunrock lanterns.

The Veiled Man waited in his oversized chair. His elbows rested on the blocky armrests. The high-backed throne, wrought from the same stone as the floor, served as the room's only furnishing. After an excruciatingly long moment, he inclined his head, sending a ripple down his face covering.

"Our agents are in place, my lord," Mavell said.

His master nodded. "And you went unnoticed?"

"Yes, my lord."

"Oh, I doubt that," came an amused drone from above. The Veiled Man sprang from his throne and turned his back to Mavell. Detoa startled, bumping into Mavell. He gripped her arm and steadied her.

High on the wall behind the throne, Refsul lounged on a windowsill. He examined his fingernails, then regarded the Veiled Man with amused gray eyes. "You've been scheming again, F—"

"No!" the Veiled Man screamed. "Do not speak it. Do not break the vow!"

Refsul cackled. "Must I keep promises to a wayward servant who seeks to usurp me?" His form shifted from a man to a quivering mass of smoke. The mass enveloped the Veiled Man and disappeared as if sucked into the inky wrinkles of the immortal's robe. Writhing like a dying animal, the Veiled Man fell to the floor.

Detoa stepped forward, but Mavell shot out his arm. He remained still, masking his malevolent satisfaction with a stony expression. For his entire forty years, this moment had been building. He did not resent his position as a subject of the Drawlen order, but there was nothing quite as fascinating as watching powerful men destroy each other.

The shadowy mass emerged from the silver fabric of the Veiled Man's robe and solidified into Refsul's black-haired form. "Did you truly believe you could fool me, old man? I've known for six years what you've been hiding. And now you've brought it to my doorstep. Don't you know? Everything you covet, everything you possess, even your very breath belongs to me. The mortari who is coming to the temple, he is mine as well." Refsul lifted his foot and slammed it into the Veiled Man's neck on the floor. The Veiled Man gurgled.

Finally, Refsul stepped away, turned to smoke, and vanished. After a long moment, the Veiled Man twitched and straightened his neck. He rose, steady and mechanical, as though no injury had occurred. "Collector," he said. "Bring the mortari to me. I don't care if you have to tear through a squadron of purifiers or the High Cleric himself. I want him."

"Understood, my lord." Mavell left the room, descending the wide stairs with Detoa at his side.

When they veered into a claustrophobic hallway leading to the collectors' quarters, Detoa whispered, "What should we do, Collector Mavell?" Head and shoulders shorter than he, and paired with her childish questions, she often seemed comically naïve.

"We follow orders, Collector Detoa. The quarrels of immortals are not our business."

# 25

# BEHIND THE CURTAIN

*Lorinth, Taria*
*July 22, 1195 PT*

*Nate*

Most days, Nate found life in Lorinth rather dull. Today marked a spectacular exception. A circus packed the square with the weirdest, most wonderful street performances.

Outside Donfree's Trading Post, a tiny woman wearing a headscarf walked on her hands while balancing a barrel twice her size with her feet. In the middle of the square stood a toothless, flat-faced bear doing tricks at the whistling command of the circus master, who wore a bearskin cloak. Other performers goaded pedestrians into playing impossible-to-win carnival games. Vendors crowded the outskirts of the square, touting their wares.

Best of all was the carnie right in front of Nate. Wearing baggy trousers and an open leather vest, he juggled his assortment of shiny, curved swords and red sticks. The flames at the end of each stick illuminated his yellow skin and the red and gold feathers in his hair.

"They must have paid a fortune for a pyro permit," Nate said to himself.

The man winked at him and bounced a sword by its pommel off his knee.

"Mother of dryads," said a voice behind him.

Nate jerked to see his brother Jeb standing next to him. While Jeb gawked at the juggler, Nate elbowed him. "It's something, isn't it?"

Jeb gaped. In his hands, a burlap sack dangled. He yanked out a leafy stalk of chamomile that poked through a small hole. Mesmerized, he chomped on the leaves and handed some to Nate.

"Jeb Therman!" Ruth hollered from the sick house door, a hand propped on her hip.

"Better go. No fun for you today," Nate teased.

"There'll be no fun for you the rest of the summer once she finds out you still haven't painted the barn ladder." Jeb stuck out his tongue and sprang from Nate's reach, bouncing and laughing all the way to the sick house.

For the past three days, Nate hadn't done much of anything. How could he bother to do chores with a circus in town?

When a strong hand squeezed his shoulder, he spun and peered at the smiling, russet face of Ari il'Dani. "If you stare too long at fire, your eyeballs will melt right out of your head."

Nate punched him in the arm. "Sorry, il'Dani. I'm not as gullible as Jeb."

"Not as diligent, either. Your old man'll have your head when he finds out you've been slacking."

"Okay, Mother," Nate said. "Where is my old man, anyway?"

Ari cocked his head at the brownstone building beside them. "In the tavern." Ari braced against a lamppost, watching workers carry hammers and chisels to the temple. The men hurried in and out behind a long canvas curtain obscuring the temple stage. "What are they doing up there?"

"Dunno," Nate said. "Maintenance? They've been at it since I got here this morning. Maybe a set for the closing performance tonight."

"Hope it's worth the wait. Let's get something to eat." Ari steered him toward the tavern. "And not this carnie food. It tastes like that stuff your sister makes."

Nate laughed. "Nah, can't be that bad. At least it smells good."

They entered Loren's Inn and Tavern, surprised to see only a few patrons. Jon waved them to the booth along the back wall near the bar. After returning from an overnight trip to Hillarock, he still wore his traveling coat, and his brown beard had grown scraggly.

He smiled as they sat, then put a finger to his lips and pointed behind them. Nate and Ari exchanged a curious glance as they listened to guttural voices from the nearby booth.

"What'll we do 'bout it, Rowley?"

"What ya mean what'll we do 'bout it? Nothin'. They's burnin' Drawls. They's can do a lot worse than usurping our act. We's lucky, Benny. They's still letting us put on a bit o' the show. And we's got that bloke Sir Doniva in town.

Ya know why he's here, dontcha? He's come round to scope our act. He's looking for talent to round up for the coronation of the new High Lord Warden."

"Coronation?" Benny squeaked. "Dontcha mean inauguration? He ain't no king, Rowley. Thought you knew that, being all smart on politics."

A bang, like a fist slamming a table, sounded. Rowley grumbled. "Ain't no burning difference. So, he's got a gavel 'stead of a crown? Still stomps on all us little uns. Still names his own heir. Ya know what this new one's in for, dontcha? Gaylen's fixing ta name his own son as heir after he's confirmed. They's saying back at the port, he's got men goin' round pickin' off his old man's other bastards. Ya know, Gaylen was a bastard. Got his pop Bruce to declare him legit 'fore he went senile. Now this bloke's scared ta ashes some other un's gonna put him out."

"Well, maybe that's why Sir Donny is here," Benny reasoned. "Sniffing out Bruce's other bastards."

"Sure hope not. I heard they cleared a whole slum down in Depbas looking for one of 'em. Bodies everywhere. Nothin' no un could do 'bout it. That's how it is, ya know."

"Ah," Benny cried. "Here you go then. Another pauper's speech."

"It's just the truth," Rowley said. "You'll see. This Hayden fool'll name his highborn brat heir, and all these start-up aristocrats and all those old king's men'll be calling for his head. But he won't give it to 'em. He's got the whole burnin' temple backin' him. Then ya know what'll happen?"

"What?" Benny said in a disinterested tone.

"They'll have 'emselves another civil war. An' the first blood spilled'll be us little folk, common, lowborn. There'll be rivers of our blood 'fore any'n gives a burnin' shit what's goin' on. That's always how it's done. Even when they chased the ol' king outta Corigon and put up their 'warden for the people,' they killed half the common folk in Pelton to do it. And in the end, it dun' make no burnin' difference. Only thing really changed is these temple snobs gets to go 'round doin' as they's please."

When the argument died off, the men paid their tab and exited. Nate surveyed the few remaining customers, then studied his father's face. Jon stared with furrowed brows, as though the carnies' conversation contained more than gossip.

Jon blinked hard and smiled at Nate. "How's my boy?"

"Swell. There's a circus in town."

Jon laughed. "I noticed. Say, I've got to visit the outhouse. Why don't you get us some food?" He slid two coins across the table and forced a tight-lipped smile.

After his father ducked out the back door, Nate plopped onto a barstool.

Plump and rosy-cheeked as usual, Carl wiped the counter. "Well, hello there, Master Therman. What'll you have?"

Nate tossed the coins in the air. "I'd like some—"

The tavern door banged open when another man entered. Nate swirled in his stool and his eyes bulged. Dressed from head to toe in velvet, ruffles, and embroidery, the stranger sported the fanciest attire Nate had ever seen.

The man slicked back his neatly combed hair, which matched his curled mustache and groomed eyebrows, giving him the appearance of perpetual surprise. His hand moved to his hip, where a long rapier hung. The two bodyguards who flanked him wore red uniforms matching the man's outfit, minus the ruffle and gold trim.

The few remaining patrons scurried out the door.

The trio approached the bar, one guard within arm's reach of Nate.

"Mr. Loren." The fancy man eyed Carl and smirked while tipping his hat. "It has been some time, hasn't it?"

"S-Sir Doniva." Carl's cheeks grew red all the way to his ears.

Raising his brows higher, Sir Doniva licked his teeth. "I hear your son has become quite the strapping young man. Where might I find him?"

Carl whipped the towel from his shoulder and clenched it in his hand. "He's grown and gone. Left town."

"How nice." Sir Doniva twirled one of his mustache curls, and Nate felt an intense urge to pluck it off his pointy face. "And to what grand horizon has he gone?"

Jon returned, slipping between Nate and the guard. Ari filled the space alongside the other guard at the end of the bar.

Glancing at Jon and Ari, Carl's face shed its redness. "Ain't none of your business what a free man does with himself."

"Oh, come now. Let's not be *unfriendly*."

Carl shook a stubby finger at the man. "If I were being unfriendly, I'd just plain toss you out."

The guards reached for their pistols. Jon and Ari did the same. Shuffling closer to their master, the guards removed their hands from their guns.

Sir Doniva pressed his elbow on the counter and leaned forward. "And if I were being unfriendly, I'd say something unfortunate may befall your lovely wife if you don't tell me where her bastard has gone."

A long, tense silence followed. Jon and Ari shifted closer and stared, unblinking, at the trio.

Bastard? Nate's blood boiled, his fists twitching to put a good bruise on Sir Doniva's grinning face. But this wasn't an alley brawl with Philip Creedle. This rich man had an armed escort.

"He's on the Life Harvest," Carl said through clenched teeth.

Sir Doniva clicked his tongue. "Pity. Got himself sick?"

The corner of Carl's mouth turned up, and he whipped the damp towel onto the counter with a soft smack. "Got himself a Drawlen uniform. And if you go after him or come slithering 'round here again, I'll sic the whole burning temple on you. Now get the hell out of my town!"

Nate had never heard Carl mutter a curse, not when dropping a glass or even touching a hot kettle. He always acted like the gentlest of giants. But in this moment, he resembled the flat-faced bear outside, only with teeth.

Sir Doniva rocked back and steepled his fingers. "Now, now. I'm simply here for a courtesy call. And I'd be quite remiss to skip this evening's festivities. After all, I hear the performance is going to be—a burning sensation."

He clapped his hands and left the tavern with his guards in tow. Nate buried his face in his hands, resting his elbows on the counter. Ari fumed through deep breaths.

When the door closed, Carl bent over the bar, clutching his chest. "Oh fires, Jonny."

Watching the three men through the little front window, Jon spoke calmly. "Carl, get Margaret. Pack your things."

"Look, we don't need to—"

"Carl." Jon's voice escalated. "You're leaving. Now."

"Wh—what about my business?"

"What about your life? We've talked about this. We've planned for this. You're leaving. Ari, tell Cameron to get a cart ready."

"Yes, sir."

Jon grabbed Ari's arm. "How quickly can you get a message to your father?"

Ari's eyes flickered for a second. "I'll see what I can do." He ran out the back door.

Jon put his hand on Nate's shoulder. "Son, we're working the inn today. We can't have Sir Doniva getting suspicious."

It took Nate a second to register his father's words. "Okay. W-what's going on?"

"Remember what those carnies were saying? Sir Doniva isn't here to watch the show."

For a moment, Nate wondered if he'd fallen asleep in the barn and slipped into a weird dream. It seemed too sensational to be real, but the horrible fluttering in his gut told him he was indeed awake. "Burning fires," he muttered. "Carl isn't his father? What's gonna happen to Will?"

"Will is in Drawl by now," Jon said. "Far from the reach of Gaylen Hayden or his agents. We'll intercept him when the Tarish caravan passes back through Shevak."

"Seriously—a burning prince," Nate mumbled. He picked up the rag from the bar and threw it over his shoulder, mimicking Carl. Jon plucked the towel away and pointed him toward the kitchen. Nate saluted and grabbed a tray of dirty dishes.

A few hours later, Nate remained frying sausages and scrubbing pots in the tavern kitchen.

The dinner rush had come and gone, but Nate peered longingly at the circus crowd visible through the passthrough and front window. He had never been so jealous of the backs of people's heads. Probably his father's idea of a suitable punishment for neglecting his chores at home.

He rotated the hearth stones with tongs when a chill like a frigid winter wind filled the room. He fumbled the tongs and stood, but the chill vanished as quickly as it'd come. Perhaps he'd imagined it.

Jeb burst through the back door, wide-eyed and panting. Nate jumped and dropped the tongs, which clattered loudly on the ground. Both boys stared at one another until the ringing ceased.

"Burning fires!" Nate said. "Don't startle me like that. I might have fallen into the cook pot. What's with you?"

"Did you see a boy run in here?"

"No . . ."

Jeb balanced on a crate and peaked through the passthrough. "I saw a boy cutting purses in the crowd. He had black hair and blisters on his face. I thought I saw him run in here."

"Well, I've been here for hours. But I promise, if I see a pimply pickpocket, I'll stick him in a sack for you, sheriff." Nate patted an imaginary pistol at his hip.

His brother smiled. "Ha. Thanks."

Flirtatious laughter from the empty tavern drew their attention. Jeb ducked below the passthrough, groaned, then hid behind Nate as they entered the dining area. Their mother sat on the counter, facing their father, who had his nose buried in her neck.

Nate tossed a damp towel over the back of his father's head. "There's a room upstairs, love birds," he teased.

Jeb scrubbed at his eyes. "I think I've gone blind."

Ruth laughed, and Jon mumbled about the shoddy accommodations. Mercifully, Ari appeared at the front door. He was out of breath but smiling.

Jon detached himself from Ruth's embrace. "All set?" he asked Ari.

The young man nodded. "They're well out of town. Once they pass Hillarock, they'll head to the checkpoint."

Ruth wiped a tear off her cheek. Jon pulled her hand to his mouth and kissed it. "This was inevitable, love."

"I know," she muttered. "Just one more reason that lecherous fiend deserves the deepest bowels of hell."

Jeb raised an eyebrow at his parents. "Has somebody taken sick?"

"More unexpected business, son," Jon replied. "If anyone asks about Carl or Margaret, you know what to say."

The boys nodded. Though they'd always known their father was a smuggler, he'd only recently introduced them to the more secretive nature of his trade.

Nate recalled Remm "taking sick" ten years previous. The memories of his elder half brother were vague but wonderful, and he often imagined the reckless ralenta going off on grand adventures while he was trapped in this mundane northern village.

"Nate." His mother's voice roused him.

"Huh?"

"Sweetheart, I've called your name twice now."

"Sorry."

Ruth put her arm around his shoulder and steered him to the front door, where Jeb waited. "Come on, boys. We've all worked hard today. Let's not have all this commotion dampen our spirits. There's a circus in town!"

Jon held the door open as they all left, then locked it behind them. The four of them worked their way to the front porch of Donfree's, where Leena, Cameron's shop manager, rested against a post with Ezron the dog panting happily at her side.

"Nice to see you taking a break for once, Ruthie," Leena said, smiling.

"You as well, Leena."

Whoops and applause from the crowd drowned out their collective laughter as the curtains along the temple stage drew back.

The spectacular street performances and evening dramas of the past few days were rubbish compared to what unfolded onstage. Pyrotechnics erupted along the apron, shooting out red, blue, and green sparks. They sputtered and parted to reveal a shirtless man in shaggy fur pants who wore a hellcat hide, complete with top jaw and fangs, like a hood. Nate recognized the performer as the juggler he'd seen earlier.

A narrator's feminine voice boomed from backstage: "Once, the world burned. The Fiend, the First Arch Traitor, and his hordes of demons sought to bring an end to all. What they could not rule, they wished to destroy."

The juggler in the hellcat headdress whirled and danced across the stage, flames shooting around him as if he willed them. Costumed performers swarmed onto the stage behind him. Wearing every variety of horrific masks and accessories, they cackled and tossed the skulls of various creatures between them.

"For six years," the narrator continued, "they terrorized the world, unchallenged. The Blessed Immortals had been imprisoned by the Fiend, and none could stand against his horde."

The curtain rolled further back to reveal a crude cage containing four figures: a pale man with red hair; a dark woman in a white dress; a tall, broad person obscured by black robes and a hood; and a masked boy in a black and red coat.

"That's him," Jeb whispered, pointing to the masked boy. "He's the cutpurse."

"No surprise there," Nate said. "Everyone knows half their profits come from pickpocketing."

Smoke billowed from the middle of the stage, swirling like a miniature tornado toward the cage. The demon performers threw themselves theatrically out of its way.

The narrator continued. "Angered by the sins of the Arch Traitor, and trapped between heaven and hell because of his treachery, the souls of the fallen rose from their own ashes, tearing into the Immortals' prison and freeing them to seek vengeance on their behalf." The sooty whirlwind slammed into the cage, sending splinters of wood in every direction.

"By the moons," Ruth gasped.

Jon squinted at the stage and scowled.

Jeb quivered. "Was that . . . was that a real shade?"

"Maybe that's what those guys in the tavern meant by Drawls usurping their show," Nate said. "It seems overly religious."

The players engaged in a mock battle, twirling and flipping over each other. When slain, they fell dramatically into the crowd, who cheered gleefully. Clearly, cutting purses was one of the masked boy's minor talents. He emerged the star of the battle, backflipping out of reach of his adversaries, disarming them with deft turns of his hands, and throwing grown men over his shoulder into the crowd. It was all choreographed, obviously, but his movements thrilled the audience.

Ezron's growl drew Nate's attention. The dog stood at the edge of the porch and faced the alley, hackles raised, head low. Nate kicked him lightly in the rear, assuming he saw a cat or a squirrel. Instead of whimpering and complying, the frost hound continued to growl and crept into the alley, stalking out of view.

With an impatient huff, Nate trotted after him. He caught up to the hound at the door to the back of Powet's shop. Ez hunched, growling fiercely. Nothing appeared out of place, but Nate trusted his dog's instincts.

He reached for the door latch, when a hand clamped over his mouth like a hot vise and another grabbed his wrist. Nate squirmed, but Ari's voice in his ear stilled him.

"Shut it, Therman," he whispered, then backed himself and Nate into a shadowed space hidden among stacks of crates alongside the building. He lifted the bone whistle hanging at Nate's neck and blew twice. Ez ceased his growling and trotted around another corner. The door creaked open. As Nate peered through gaps in the crates, two figures emerged.

Nate's heart pounded as he held his breath.

The sinister men sported shaved heads and wore fitted, dark-silver robes. One held a long, bloodied knife. After peering down both sides of the alley, the man stowed the weapon at his belt. Then the two parted in opposite directions. As one passed where Nate and Ari hid, Ari's steady gust of breath reached Nate's cheek, signaling Ez with the whistle. A call Nate didn't recognize.

In the span of a few heartbeats, Ari sprang from behind Nate, lunging at the nearest man with his own dagger. Nate stood frozen and wide-eyed. Simultaneously, Ez streaked out of the alley, teeth bared and claws stretching before him. He tackled the other man to the ground and bit into his jugular at the same moment Ari drove his dagger hilt deep into the first man's back. This victim died quickly and quietly, while the man at Ez's mercy gasped and reached for the knife at his belt. He convulsed, then stilled before he could grab it. Ez backed away and sat, shaking his jowls and looking to Ari for approval.

The sight of human blood on the muzzle of Nate's beloved pet conflicted with the exuberant innocence in the dog's eyes. He panted, his tail thumping rhythmically on the gravel.

Ari hunched over the dead man, searching his clothes and stuffing items into his own pockets. He met Nate's gaze.

As he struggled to recognize his friend before him, Nate's breathing hitched. Ari had always seemed streetwise but still cheerful and eager for whatever tasks Nate's father gave him. Now, he seemed older, sharper, and infinitely dangerous.

"Therman, get your father," Ari commanded. "We need to leave. Now!"

# 26

# THE BRONZE RING

*Lorinth, Taria*
*July 22, 1195 PT*

*Jeb*

"What's taking Nate so long? He's missing the best part," Jeb muttered to his parents.

The battle performance onstage rushed toward its epic conclusion. When Rodden the Fiend stood alone against the High Immortals, he struck the woman in white with a metal rod, and she mock-froze. Stagehands dressed in black velvet scurried in and surrounded her in gold branches. The masked boy kicked the metal rod from the Fiend's hand.

In a booming tenor, the man with red hair playing Refsul issued the famous curse, "For the land you have ravaged and the blood you have spilled, you shall be shut out of the afterlife, cursed to spend eternity in the form of the beast you truly are. You shall wander Ethar forever, loathed by all, never allowed rest or redemption."

The Rodden performer thudded to his knees and roared. The curtain fell. Cheers rippled throughout the square. Hats sailed in the air and flowers hurled haphazardly at the stage. A minute later, the curtain reopened. The cast locked arms across the stage, bowing and smiling. All stepped back except for the man representing Rodden in the hellcat headdress. With another bow, he removed the headdress, revealing thick black hair adorned with red and gold feathers.

"My beloved ladies and gentlemen," he bellowed. "You are a most gracious and delightful audience. No doubt, you've heard that story before." He gestured to his fellow cast members. "Well, perhaps never like this."

Cheers and chuckles erupted from the crowd.

"It is as sacred and important as it is ancient," the Rodden performer continued. "Our land still bears the scars of that treachery. Our nights are still haunted by the ghosts of both past and present. But thanks to our beloved Immortals, these shades remain at bay. This story is, of course, a good reminder of the evil that still prowls this world. It lurks in shadows, settles around us, even sometimes blends in." His eyes scanned the crowd and lingered on Jeb.

"Jon," Ruth whispered nervously.

His father's strong hand gripped Jeb's shoulder. "Let's get out ahead of the crowd, son. Otherwise, we could be here all night." His voice mimicked cheerfulness, but his smile didn't reach his eyes.

Jeb nodded and headed to the far end of Donfree's porch while his parents said a polite farewell to Leena.

The cutpurse suddenly appeared in front of them. He ripped the mask off his face and flashed a sinister smirk. His dark eyes held no reflection. His thin lips curled into a smile that seemed more at home on a wolf than a boy.

"Hello, girl," the boy said.

Jeb whirled around.

His mother froze behind him, eyes wide. "You!" She clutched the porch pillar and gritted her teeth.

Jon drew his pistol and blocked Ruth with his arm.

The boy chuckled. "You really did have me fooled." His smile fell. "But the game is done."

Behind the boy, Ari moved silently into Jeb's view, knife in hand with a finger to his lips.

"You've taken enough from me, Kane," Ruth said in a biting tone.

"Ha!" the boy barked. "I see there is even more to take—much more." He lunged at Jeb, who stepped back, but the cutpurse matched his stride. Just as his hand brushed Jeb's collar, Ari drove his knife into the boy's neck.

Kane paused and grunted, blinking slowly. Then he cackled, grabbed Jeb by the collar, and pushed forward.

Jeb felt as if someone had slung him down a waterfall. Once he could breathe again, he opened his eyes. Kane's clammy hand remained locked on his throat. But instead of peering down the alley, Jeb looked out at the crowd—from onstage.

His mother's scream rose above the chaos of the square. Ari and Jon pulled her into the alley.

"Turn it on," Kane commanded. "I have what I came for."

Jeb stared at the sinister boy. He saw no knife in his neck, nor evidence there ever had been. To the side of the stage, a man dressed in silver robes cranked a lever. Eight men in leather uniforms carried bronze pillars onto the stage and placed them at equal intervals in a circle around them.

Beneath Jeb, inlaid bronze rings covered the stage floor. Prior to the circus arriving a week ago, the floor had been bare stone.

With the pillars in place, the bronze rings spun, shaking the entire platform. A buzzing noise filled Jeb's ears, and a dark mist formed around them. Once again, he felt like something had dragged him through frigid water.

*Find your courage*, David had said. *Courage.*

Jeb took a deep, shaking breath. Then he flung his arm out and knocked Kane's hand away. Before Kane could react, Jeb leapt from the stage and into the audience. As he weaved desperately through the crowd, the boy screamed, "Get him! Turn it off!"

*Jon*

Jon and Arimal each held Ruth by an arm and charged through the side door of Donfree's.

Nate paced inside, panic lighting his eyes. "Why are they doing this?"

Jon slammed his hands on the boy's shoulders more forcefully than he intended. "Nathaniel. You need to look after your mother. Ari—Arimal will get you out of town. Follow him. Do whatever he tells you. Do you understand?"

Nate stared, slack-jawed, at his father.

"Jon, we can't let Kane take him." Ruth's voice quivered.

Jon's eyes brimming with moisture, he ran his rough hand along her damp cheek. "He won't, Ruth, not as long as I breathe." He pulled her to him and crushed his lips against hers.

He wanted to disappear into her embrace, to wake up in her arms yesterday and start the last day and a half over again. He would have accepted her request to stay in bed and hold her close instead of rushing to get on the road. He would have taken his family with him, headed east, and just kept going until the road met the Utheran Ocean.

With a sigh, he let her go and turned to Nate.

His son's eyes gleamed with quiet determination. "I understand, father," he said.

Jon nodded, then dove out the door and into the crowd. As Jeb tore through the throng of frantic townsfolk, Jon caught his arm and met his terrified gaze. He rushed Jeb toward the porch when hell itself erupted.

A wall of flames blocked their path, and tortured screams filled his ears. All around, fire swallowed the crowd. Over the screams, the voice of the Rodden performer resounded. "It's terribly rude to leave before the final act, gentlemen. Especially when you're part of it."

The man sauntered through the crowd—through the very flames. He remained untouched by the heat, and with a flick of his wrist, a flameless avenue opened between Jon, Jeb, and the stage. "Come along, now. Or more of these dear citizens will get caught up in this charade." He pushed a hand to the side, sending more fire rocketing into the crowd.

"I don't have time for your dramatics, Fenris," roared a voice. An icy hand gripped Jon's back. A shadow obscured his vision. When it lifted, Jon and Jeb appeared onstage, Jeb still clutched in his father's arms.

Selvator Kane stepped around them, his black and red coat swirling. Jon had seen him briefly, long ago. He hadn't believed it then, but it was obvious now. This was the Master of Secrets, second in command of the Drawlen regime.

Kane's eyes pierced them with palpable malice. "What a nuisance," he spat.

"You won't have him," Jon said, tightening his grip on Jeb. His words felt futile.

Kane laughed, then snapped his fingers. Three Black Veil guards grabbed Jeb like living vises and lifted him from the circle of bronze. Two others flanked Jon, securing him with iron fists. Again, Kane snapped his fingers, and the rings whirled. It grew cold, and Jon's vision faded. His son's screams grew faint.

*Nate*

Nate rushed after Ari and Ruth to the second-floor window of the Loren Inn and Tavern. He arrived in time to see his father disappear from the stage in a cloud of smoke.

He turned to Ari. Or was it Arimal? He felt torn between horror and confusion. He cursed every moment of his life he'd ever longed for anything besides a boring day in his quiet town.

"Burning fires in hell," Arimal whispered, shaking his head. "They were building a wraith gate. They can *do* that?"

Ruth dashed into the hall. Nate darted after his mother with Arimal close behind. As they followed, Arimal pleaded for her to stop. She grabbed a rope dangling from the ceiling and pulled down the hatch. Dull evening light flooded the hall, shadowed by their forms as they climbed the steps onto the roof.

"Don't wait for me," she whispered, then leapt over the roof's ledge and landed on the neighboring building.

Nate lunged, but Arimal's firm grip on his arm halted him.

"No. She's doing what must be done. So must we." He crouched. Hesitantly, Nate mimicked him. Hidden behind the ridge of the tavern roof, Nate watched his mother scurry across the buildings bordering the square. As graceful and soundless as a cat, she slipped from one building to the next until she reached the temple.

Below them on the stage, men in silver robes fiddled with levers and pillars at the increasingly impatient orders of the boy called Kane. Arimal pulled a pistol from his belt. It would be a miracle shot. But what else could they do? Nate held his breath.

A shot rang, and the priest at the controls of the wraith gate collapsed onto the lever, activating the gate. Nate faced Arimal, whose gun had not fired. Across the square, Ruth stalked into view from the back of the stage, bayoneted rifle in hand and the pan smoking.

As the metal rings on the floor spun, Kane laughed. Jeb squirmed and kicked at the two guards who secured him. Ruth howled and leapt at Kane, brandishing the rifle. Instead of shoving the bayonet into her adversary, however, she lodged the blade between two of the spinning rings on the stage.

The reaction was instant. The rifle ripped from her hand, the rings squealing and rattling against each other while two of the rods sprang from their housings like arrows off a bow. In a whirlwind of smoke, everyone in the circle vanished.

Arimal exhaled a shaky breath. "Damn!"

"What happened?" Nate demanded. "Did they go through?"

"I don't know. I don't think these Drawls do either."

Priests and guards scrambled to reset the gate. The Rodden performer screamed orders, the red and gold feathers in his hair flailing with each command. People who could still move scrambled to drag their fellow citizens as far from the stage as they could. The Drawls ignored them, fully occupied with the mystery of the gate. Painful moans sounded from those who could not help themselves.

Once the guards reset the poles, a lone priest stood in the middle of the gate. A guard pulled the lever, and the rings reactivated. A moment later, the priest within the rings erupted into a shower of blood and bone.

Arimal pulled Nate back through the hatch. "We're out of time," he said as he led Nate into the cellar.

"What about the others? There's dozens of people out there," Nate said.

When they entered the smuggling tunnel, Arimal turned to him. "You can't do anything for them right now. Do you know who these Drawls are, Nathaniel?"

"N-no."

"The masked boy, that's Selvator Kane, the Immortal Heir. And the man burning everyone is—"

"Fenris the Fire Master," Nate offered grimly.

"Exactly. They're Refsul's immortal thugs, and they'll kill you as fast as an ant under a boot. I don't know why they're here. I don't know where they took Jon. I don't know what happened to Ruth or Jeb. But you're here, and I'm keeping you alive. Let's go."

"Go where?"

"To my father."

"In Shevak?"

"No," Arimal barked. "Abad is not my father."

"So who are you?"

"I'll explain when we get into the woods. I don't know these tunnels well, but Jon said there's one that goes east. Do you know it?"

"We're going into the woods? Aren't there forest demons in there?" It seemed childish once Nate said it, but after today, dragons living in thunder clouds wouldn't have surprised him.

"Surely, there are many terrors in the woods," Arimal said. "Only those aren't trying to kill us. Can you get us to the east tunnel?"

Wiping his forehead, Nate motioned for Arimal to follow along the passage to where a stack of crates hid a low, narrow opening. They made the two-mile length of the eastbound tunnel at a hard run. When Nate led Arimal out the hidden access in the side of a rocky hill, the night sky loomed.

A small rise hid the tunnel door from the road, but they could hear horses cantering along the gravel. To the west, Lorinth burned an angry orange against the fleeting gray band of twilight on the horizon. The breeze carried a revolting mixture of woodsmoke, wheat fields, and burnt flesh.

"This way," Arimal ordered, trudging through the long grass toward the tree line.

Nate quivered. "I can't. They're all dying. How can I run?" He paused his lament when Arimal laid a gentle hand on his shoulder.

"You're not abandoning them, Nathaniel. You're one boy. You alone can do nothing but die with them."

"What do I do, then?"

Arimal smiled coldly. "If it's monsters you face, get some of your own. The Deep Wood is the best place to look."

*Jon*

The smell of pines and incense hit Jon like a hurricane. He fell on his face and found himself prone atop the mount in the center of the Setvan Temple, almost six hundred miles from where he had been a moment ago.

No chance to marvel at—or fret about—this new predicament. A guard jolted him to his feet and dragged him halfway down the steps.

At the bottom, a tall woman in forest-green robes waited. She raised her tired, green eyes and pursed her lips. "Is this all? Lord Sel made a rather grand promise of replacing what he took from me."

The guard scowled but stood at silent attention. Ignoring Jon, the woman stroked her long, black hair to a silky shine while staring at the platform.

Jon shifted his weight to balance on the steps, but at his slight movement, the guard slammed Jon's shoulder into the ground. Minutes passed. Jon lay quiet and frozen under the guard's grip. His mind swirled, trying desperately to formulate an escape plan. But he was alone and out of options. The sky darkened quickly. A clocktower chimed in the ninth hour.

"Where is he?" The woman paced.

The frantic drum of boots on stone sounded behind Jon, but he didn't dare move his head. A purifier came into view. She sported a series of scars across her head as though a beast had once ripped apart her skull.

"Lady Mylis," the purifier began, "we request you wait in your temple. We must ensure your security—"

The woman named Mylis raised her hand. "What is there to threaten the safety of an immortal? Or is there something your master wishes me not to see?"

The purifier bowed her head. "As you desire, my lady." She ascended the stairs and stood in the center of the platform.

With gut-wrenching horror, Jon recognized the contraption before him and the one in Lorinth—wraith gates. Many of the world's modern powers had figured out how to use some of these ancient gates, despite their limited range. However, the idea that the Drawls knew how to build one horrified him.

The purifier signaled to someone out of Jon's sight. With the scrape of metal on stone and a static buzz, the gate rings moved anew. Something seemed amiss though. The buzzing morphed into a loud hiss, like a torch being doused in water, and the whole mount shook. A high-pitched scream reverberated for a second, followed by a grotesque squelch, like mud sucking at a stuck foot.

Mylis screeched while a wet and warm goo splashed across Jon's face. He dared to touch his cheek. His fingers came away wet with blood and bits of white, like sand. The guard lifted him, allowing a brief view of the platform. The wraith gate was splattered in gore, and the purifier nowhere in sight.

Jon's stomach lurched, accompanied by a morbid relief. The gate no longer worked. For the time being, Selvator Kane would have to find another way to get Jeb to Shevak. Arimal would know how to protect Ruth and Nate, and Sidrian scouts were a horn's call away. Perhaps Jeb, too, could manage an escape.

Mylis surveyed Jon. Her eyes seemed old and weary, at odds with her otherworldly beauty. Like Richard's eyes.

"Clean this up," she said to the guard, waving a hand at the platform. "My men will bring the prisoner to the dungeon."

Two hulking trolls lumbered up the steps. The guard shoved Jon at one of them who caught him with a clawed grip. Mylis led the trolls, dragging Jon across the temple grounds. They led him next to a brick wall. She wrung her hands while she glanced side to side, then paused in front of Jon.

"What is your name?"

Jon remained silent.

The woman huffed. "I could help you."

"I bet you could," Jon muttered.

Mylis lifted Jon's left hand and peeled back his fingerless glove. She ran a cool thumb over the Drawlen brand marring the back of his hand. "Tessa spoke of you. She never gave anyone's true name. She called you 'Sun Thief'."

Jon ripped his hand from her grip, earning a grunt from his trollish captor.

Mylis stretched her neck and smoothed her hair. "Her secrets are no longer safe. The boy-rat has taken them all. If you want any chance to save the people you love, then you will listen to me."

Jon narrowed his eyes. "I don't know what you're talking about," he lied.

"The child would be about twenty by now, yes? Tessa believed it would be a girl. Was she right? Or was it a boy? Is this the child Selvator seeks?"

Blood pounded in Jon's ear. Mylis tore open old wounds. "What do you want from me?" he said.

"There is something beyond this door that is important to me. I want you to protect it until I can secure a . . . release."

Jon cocked his head and studied the wall. It shuddered the longer he stared at it. A shade door—a tricky, costly thing—used on high security vaults and, of course, dungeons. "You lose your jewelry in the dungeon?"

"Ha!" Mylis smiled briefly. "A treasure to be sure. There is a child of my concern. She has managed to avoid the riffraff, but it is not enough. If you promise to protect her, I will get you out."

"When?" Jon asked.

"I can't say," Mylis whispered. "But you'll not find a better offer, or any."

"I have a lot of friends," Jon said.

"Not here. Besides, if you are so determined to protect your family, you can start with your niece. Her name is Haana. Give her this pendant, and she will know to trust you." Mylis stuffed a cool round object into Jon's hand and shoved him into the shade door.

Instead of meeting the bricks, he tumbled into a murky space and broke his fall with his forearms, landing on a rough stone floor. One of the trolls stalked after him and pushed him down the narrow corridor. Within the darkness, only the ground directly at his feet remained visible. The drip and stench of filthy water and the far-off shrieks of anguished prisoners welcomed Jon.

# 27

# GHOSTS OF THE DEEP WOOD

*The Deep Wood Northeast of Lorinth, Taria*
*July 22, 1195 PT*

*Nate*

Nate stared into the Deep Wood. He shifted his weight from foot to foot at the edge of the forest. The shadows obscured Arimal's profile as he ventured ahead between the trees.

Nate faltered as he recalled five years prior when his Lorinth friends had hovered at the threshold of this very forest.

They had goaded Nate, watching as he crossed the forbidden boundary and crept through the undergrowth.

*With each step, Nate's heart had pounded. Lost in wonderment, he hadn't noticed how far he'd gone. The babbling of a stream caught his ear, and he followed it until he came to the water's edge. On the opposite bank, a yellow lady slipper wavered in a thin band of sunlight.*

*Nate snatched the flower and turned. An endless expanse of forest greeted him. Huffing, he tracked his same path through the undergrowth—or so he thought. After a half hour had passed, adrenaline coursed through him, and sweat dotted his forehead.*

*A tree rustled behind him. He whirled around. No sign of life, but the stirring had shifted everywhere, like the ground itself writhed. He swallowed hard and bolted. His foot caught on a thick vine, knocking him headfirst to the ground.*

*His vision blurred, and he lay with his eyes closed for what felt like an hour. A cool breeze tickled his face.*

*He blinked away dust and tears. On his ankle, a bruise had bloomed. A wad of poison ivy lay smashed in his fist, instead of the lady slipper prize. He jumped to his feet and shook the leaves from his hand.*

*The edge of the woods spanned before him, overlooking the sleepy town of Lorinth. His gaze darted from the forest to the village. The burning rash along his arm had convinced him to never step into the Deep Wood again.*

Until now. He shook himself and caught up with Arimal. The man led him along a narrow path, spotted with ferns, and winding around mighty oak trees. In the darkness, Nate stumbled on roots and rocks cluttering their way. Red and blue bands of moonlight cast shadows through the canopy. Owls hooted. The wind whispered. Crickets stilled momentarily, then resumed their music after Arimal and Nate had passed.

The path weaved between towering pines, the ground becoming rockier as they descended a treacherous slope ending in a gully. Arimal rested against the rock wall. Nate panted, his legs limp as he collapsed on a bed of leaves.

"I'm sorry, Nate," Arimal said through deep, ragged breaths as he sank to the ground.

Hugging his chest, Nate closed his eyes. "Were those men collectors?"

"No. Purifiers." Arimal clasped his knees and hung his head.

"They came for Jeb. I think he's a ralenta."

Arimal's eyes widened. "Seriously? Fires, Nate."

"Why else would they come?"

Arimal shook his head. "Purifiers are assassins. The Drawls don't bring immortals and assassins to nab one ralenta. They certainly don't turn a whole town into a mass grave to do it. This was something more. I heard—it seemed like Kane knew your mother. It sounded personal."

"My mother?" Nate laughed morbidly. "What business would she have with a Drawlen immortal?"

"Who can say?"

Nate stood and arched his back. "So, where are we going? We can't just hide in the woods forever. Do you suppose the roads will be safe any time soon?"

"We don't need roads. We're going further into the Wood, where we can get help."

"What? You know your way around here?"

"Better than most."

Nate narrowed his eyes. "What do you mean?"

"I'm from here." Arimal rose and felt along the craggy rocks, stopping when he reached a deep, narrow crevice. He retrieved a wool blanket. Placing it on the ground, he unrolled it, revealing a bow, a quiver of arrows, two long daggers, and a copper whistle.

"What is—who are you, really?"

Arimal picked up the bow. "Well, I'm not Ari il'Dani."

"I figured that much."

Arimal extended his hand. "I am Arimal Soral, emissary of the hidden Ruvian city of Sidras. Pleased to honestly meet you, Nathaniel Riley."

Nate shook the man's wrist and furrowed his brow. "Riley? How do you know that name?"

Arimal nodded. "I met your father several years ago. You know, you have Ruvian blood yourself. Your father's family name was Riley before David took him in."

"Yeah. But that's—what do you mean *hidden* city? The only Ruvians I've heard of live in the slums of Pelton or wander in caravans around tSolan."

Arimal ran his hand along the length of the bow. "Well, it wouldn't be very hidden if people knew about it."

"But my father knows?"

"What's he told you about your heritage?"

Nate shrugged. "Next to nothing. I learned most of it from David."

"Has Jon ever mentioned where he came from?"

"He said he grew up in the North. I always assumed he meant Lorinth or somewhere nearby."

"It's near enough." Arimal slung the quiver over his shoulder. Stringing the whistle around his neck, he handed two daggers to Nate. "Your Ruvish is pretty good, so this shouldn't go too badly," he said—in Ruvish.

Nate blushed. "You—you speak Ruvish? You've known what I've been saying the whole time?"

Arimal smirked. "Yeah. It was pretty funny, you and Jeb having your secret little conversations."

"You burning—" Nate chuckled, but the mention of his brother brought him back to reality. Jeb was gone. There would be no more mumbled jokes between them. No more pranks played on Philip Creedle. No more quiet evenings on the hillside, watching the sunset and talking about the adventures they would have when they got older.

He wiped his eyes, the forest adopting a solemn mood, as though it were a living thing holding its breath. The shivering branches overhead stilled, and the night creatures quieted.

Arimal crouched, his attention steady. "Keep low," he whispered. He descended the narrow path between the two sloping walls.

Nate followed closely, feeling the heat off Arimal's back. He rested one hand on the hilt of the dagger in his belt and balanced with the other.

They continued through the dark terrain. From time to time, Arimal stopped and listened. Nate mimicked him, holding his breath until they resumed walking.

When a breeze cut through the thinning trees, Arimal froze again.

Nate huddled behind him, scanning the forest. The trees seemed to thrash at one another.

Arimal squinted into the canopy and nocked an arrow. The red light of the Mortemus moon filtered through the branches. Suddenly, its crimson form blinked out of view. The creak of leather sounded overhead.

"Shit!" Arimal fired the arrow into the sky. "Run!" he yelled as he yanked Nate alongside him and sprinted forward.

Nate stumbled trying to keep his pace. Behind them, something heavy thudded on the ground.

A shrill staccato rang in Nate's ear when Arimal blew the copper whistle. As they ran, the noise of their pursuer grew louder—the crunch of leaves, the squawk like a choked bird. Nate turned but dearly wished he hadn't.

Red moonlight broke through the canopy, lighting a monstrous figure. Maybe it had been a man once. Its limbs were gangly, its face sharp with obsidian eyes. Its great black wings spanned double its height while its sickly gray skin stretched over bone and muscle.

Arimal pulled Nate behind a pine tree, where they panted and pressed their backs against the bark.

The creature would certainly have overtaken them, but a maze of vines entangled it.

At Arimal's next whistle, the vines snapped tightly and drew the creature into the shadows.

Nate struggled to form words between breaths. "What—was—*that*?"

"Banshee."

Nate's eyes widened. His throat constricted. His hands shook.

Arimal urged him forward, so they continued, weary and frightened, tripping and flinching at the slightest rustle of leaves or the hoot of an owl. The ghastly silhouettes of banshees crossed their path periodically, but they stayed hidden from the creatures for a time. Their luck soon ran out.

The trees ended at a sharp ravine. Arimal grabbed Nate's shirt, pulling him from the edge. A hiss from above caught Nate's attention. When he lifted his head, he stared right into the inky gaze of a banshee hovering overhead. Its too-wide mouth keened. It swooped down with clawed hands outstretched. Arimal shoved Nate to the ground. The flying fiend swiftly snatched Arimal into the sky.

Nate grabbed for him, but he was carried to the other side of the ravine in seconds. When Arimal slashed the creature's forearm with a knife, Nate sighed in relief. Arimal dropped into the brambles on the other side of the raging river dividing the landscape.

A shrill cry startled Nate. He ducked, but the banshee overhead knocked him off the cliff into the jagged rocks below. He plunged into the frigid water, his back crushing against something hard while the cold pierced him like a knife to his lungs. Silent . . . dark . . . empty. He remained suspended in that abyss—unseeing, unhearing, unfeeling.

Then warmth flooded him to his bones, and images filled his mind. They felt like memories—but memories of things he'd never known.

*Fire surrounded him, burning hot and red, only to be replaced with blue-green flames. He stood on a hill, a field of grass in front of him. The sun rose, sending warm, orange light across the expanse and haloing an ancient, walled city. The scene shifted to a raven-haired girl twirling across a lawn, laughing and admiring the stars. Blurred images swirled before Nate. The emptiness returned, warmth fading.*

Slowly, consciousness replaced the void, and Nate awoke, sore and damp. A wet, scratchy tongue lapped his chin, and a familiar whine startled him. He sat up. The swift river pulled at his feet. Shore pebbles stuck to his backside and hands. Nothing around him looked familiar, except for Ezron.

The frost hound perched next to him, tail thumping against the rocks while he basked in morning sunlight. The blood from Lorinth no longer sullied his gray muzzle.

Nate flung his arms around the dog. "Ez!"

Shaking and panting, the hound licked Nate's cheek. Nate pulled back, glancing around the ravine. He remembered falling into the twisting river, but the water before him flowed slowly, the river wider, and the craggy slopes lower than from where he'd fallen. He searched his body. He remained unscathed, save for a small cut on his leg and a bruise on his forearm.

"Sovereign's grace," he mumbled. He stood, finding his legs as strong as any morning after a good rest. He patted his waist. One of Arimal's knives dangled precariously from his belt, the other lost. Nate removed his boots and searched them, pulling out his throwing knife, lock picks, and stash of coins. Tipping one boot, he shook it. A pile of pebbles tumbled to the ground, followed by a stream of brown water. He blanched at the smell.

Removing his shirt, he wrung it before wrestling back into it. His stomach growled. Ez lay on the ground, legs splayed and big gray eyes on him.

"Well, Ezron, I don't suppose you have directions to a hidden Ruvian city?"

His dog whined and tilted his head.

"I thought so. We should head north."

Nate walked to the edge of the trees along the shore and crouched, searching the sky and listening. The previous night, the whole forest had frozen upon the banshee's approach. But now, the woods stirred with sound and movement. Nate surveyed every branch, rock, and bramble in sight.

Ez paced along the shore. Then he turned and barked.

Nate scrambled after him, shushing the hound.

Together, they wandered. Nate focused on the path before him, if only to fend off his growing despair and hunger. Ez walked beside him, nose to the ground. Nate cautiously tasted some blue fruit growing along the path. It was sweet, but cloyingly so, unlike the tart-sweet of a blueberry. Spitting it out, he dropped the rest. "Burning nightshade."

Ez wandered into a thicket of huckleberries, not yet in season, and Nate lost sight of him. A moment later, the lanky silver dog appeared on the narrow game trail, hopping in place silently. When Nate reached him, Ez trotted ahead and veered to the right, into a grove of cherry trees sagging with ripe fruit.

"Oh, Ez, you genius!" Nate cupped the dog's face and kissed his wet nose, then scratched his chin and ears. He grabbed a handful of cherries and devoured them, spitting the pits onto the ground. The fruit tasted bitter, but Nate would have eaten a raw turnip if he'd found one. Ez loped around the grove, then pressed his nose to the ground and wandered into the bushes again.

Nate spat another trio of cherry pits but was promptly nailed in the head when a shivering vine batted them back at him.

He jumped away. The vine moved like a snake along the trunk of the cherry tree. Taking in the grove with renewed caution, Nate witnessed dozens of vines curling among the trees and twisting toward him.

Another pit struck him in the ear. Something brushed past his ankle. He flinched. A vine snaked around his leg and, with a painful jolt, lifted him into the air. He hung upside down, yelling and groping his belt for the knife. As soon as he reached for it, the knife fell. He kicked the vine with his free leg, attracting another to bind that leg as well.

"Burning fires in hell!"

Childish laughter sounded behind him. The vines pulled him higher and swung him around. He came face-to-face with a green-eyed boy squatting in the branch of another cherry tree.

He looked to be eight or nine, barefooted and wearing only cotton trousers. Although thin and dirty, he stood confidently, legs apart and arms crossed. The sun shone on his ivory cheeks, and his skin shimmered. He narrowed his eyes, and Nate wondered if he was trying to be intimidating. The effect disappeared in the boy's innocent features and the pointed ears protruding from his wild hair.

"What you doin' in my Wood, round ear?"

Nate held out his hands. "I'm lost. I didn't mean to trespass."

The boy tilted his head, quick like a bird, and blinked at Nate. "Too far in, Drawly."

"I'm—I'm not a Drawl."

"Ya came from that way." The boy lifted a hand, and the vines tightened painfully around Nate's legs.

"Ruvian," Nate yelled, then said in Ruvish, "I'm Ruvian. I was heading to Sidras. There are Drawls in the wood. Come on, kid, put me down."

The boy jerked his head back. "I don't know your funny southern language, Ruvy."

Nate huffed and repeated himself in Palish.

The boy laughed. "Drawls in my wood?"

The vines shivered, causing Nate to sway.

A round shot whizzed by and shattered a mature branch near the fae boy. The vines loosened, sending Nate to the ground. He cushioned his fall with crossed arms and rolled to his feet.

The boy landed next to Nate, twitching his head about.

Nate grabbed the boy's arm and ran. Two more shots blasted into nearby trees. Nate skidded along a leaf-covered path with the boy at his side. Picking up a thick branch, Nate hurled it down the hill before them. It tumbled and slid, disturbing the leafy path and breaking branches along the underbrush. He yanked the boy to the side and burrowed with him under the protruding roots of a great oak tree.

The boy grunted but stilled when Nate clamped a hand over his mouth. Leaves crunched under booted feet, and the sharp stench of red powder filled the air. The boy waved a hand across his lap. Nate heard the slithering of vines and the grunts of men. One more shot fired, followed by the splintering of wood and a deep voice shouting, "Hold!"

The boy repeated his gesture, and more grunts sounded from above, along with another gunshot. The boy recoiled and grimaced. He waved his hand, but no vines moved.

Nate listened for Ezron, hoping the dog would not come loping back curiously. When only gunfire reverberated, he grabbed the whistle at his neck and instinctively mimicked the long, pulsing command Arimal used for Ez in Lorinth.

A growl followed, along with a terrified shriek, then gurgled cries and the tearing of flesh. A happy bark echoed above, and Nate peeked at the grove.

Two uniformed rangers hung by their necks from vines, fifty feet off the ground. Ez loomed over his kill, a priest wearing a bloodred robe and a heavy iron chain around his neck.

The boy, who clung to Nate's waist, gasped at the man on the ground. "Chain master," he whispered in a shaking voice. "That means banshees." He tugged at Nate's pants.

A keening wail sounded from far away. The boy hurried down the hill. Nate and Ezron followed. As the trees thinned, the wails grew closer.

Nate and the boy sped up, but the banshees flew faster. Circling the canopy like vultures, the creatures took turns diving into the trees. Each time, the boys dodged their attacks, but one banshee eventually grazed Nate's arm.

A spiked whip erupted from the ground, wrapping around the creature's wing and pulling it down. It crashed through the forest floor into a deep trench.

Out from the trench jumped three men carrying weapons. They wore green vests over tan tunics and studied the canopy with fearless fury.

Another banshee dove and received two crossbow bolts in the chest. The third, seeing its comrades felled, ascended toward the treetops. A vine rocketed from the trees and yanked it into the forest. One of the men fired another bolt, hitting the banshee in the forehead.

The man regarded the boy with relieved, pale-blue eyes. They were simultaneously kind and fierce.

"Are you all right, Fergus?" he asked.

Fergus squeezed Nate's hand. "I'm well, sir."

"The Wood is not safe today. Full of strangers." The man cast his eyes on Nate. His hardened face held features that bore years of toil and heartache. His cropped blond hair and lean build would have put him right at home as a Drawlen ranger.

"Your fellow here kept me safe," Fergus said.

The man looked to his comrades, who shook their heads. He pointed his crossbow at Nate. "He's not one of ours."

Fergus flinched and jumped away from Nate, who threw up his hands and yelled in Ruvish, "Wait. I was with Ari—Arimal Soral. We got separated. He was taking me to Sidras."

"Clever," the man said. "But he's not in the Wood presently. He's on assignment elsewhere."

"I know. He's working with Jon Therman in Lorinth."

"Don't know him," the man said casually.

"Jonathan Riley." At Nate's declaration, the blond man withdrew his crossbow. "I'm his son, Nathaniel Riley."

The men exchanged glances before returning their attention to Nate, holding their weapons ready.

"There are Drawls in Lorinth," Nate said. "Purifiers, chain masters—and immortals. Fenris the Fire Master and Selvator Kane."

"Kane?" cried a squat, balding man in his fifties. "Burn me alive. Colas, we need to tell Alistar."

"Just wait, Paul." Colas waved his hand and moved toward Nate.

Out of the underbrush behind them, Ezron prowled, haunches quivering and hackles raised, growling. Colas stood still.

Nate put out a hand, and immediately Ez quieted and sat next to him.

"That your dog, boy?" Colas asked.

"He is."

"All right, then. We are sentinels from Sidras. We've come to see what's got all the locals so spooked." Colas patted Fergus's head. Then he pointed to the young man on his left who sported a red beard down to his chest and carried two rifles. "Rolan, get two more scouts and search for Arimal."

"On it," Rolan said as he sprinted into the forest.

"Paul, we're taking these boys to Sidras," Colas said, grasping Fergus's hand.

Securing his rifles, Paul pressed a hand to his chest. "I'll take up the rear."

Colas slung his crossbow over his shoulder. "Nathaniel Riley, follow me."

# 28

# SIDRAS

*Sidras, the Deep Wood*
*July 23, 1195 PT*

*Nate*

Nate trudged behind Colas with Ezron at his side. The Ruvian pushed the group at a grueling pace while Nate recited for them the horrors of the previous evening.

The mid-afternoon sun peeked through the leaves, and Fergus stayed close to Colas's side. Paul brought up the rear, scanning the woods and sky with his rifle ready. When Colas reached the threshold of dense underbrush, he paused and put a hand on his leather baldric. At his shoulder, the brass emblem stamped with a seven-tongued flame shimmered in the sunlight.

Before them, thickets with long thorns blocked their way, spreading beyond their sight in either direction.

"Fergus," Colas said. "We'd appreciate a shortcut, if you don't mind."

With a nod and a smile, the boy put his hands together as if in prayer, then slowly separated them. The earth rumbled, the creak of heavy branches answered, and the forest before them moved. Like a heavy curtain being opened by invisible hands, the great, twisting oak trees and thorny underbrush drew themselves aside. The rumbling stilled, revealing a tunnel of brambles and oak boughs leading to a bright point of light.

Colas patted the boy on the head and led them forward on the cleared path. Nate froze, consumed with the sensation of falling into another dream. The surreal moment was spectacular, but it came at the cost of everything that had happened in the preceding twenty-four hours.

Part of him hoped the light would wake him, illuminating his straw mattress, where he would be lying tucked into an earthen nook inside his farmhouse. Jeb would be outside working the soil. The dog would be waiting at a rabbit hole, downwind and patient. Ella would be sitting on the rock, sharpening knives and organizing her smuggler's tools. Their parents would be in the kitchen, pretending to make bread while secretly flirting. They would be happy. They would be together.

As Nate trailed behind Colas, his tears fell silently, jaw quivering, hands fisted. Whatever awaited him at the end of the tunnel, he vowed to take no comfort, no awe in it, save that it gave him the power to return to his decimated town and channel vengeance itself against those who had torn his world to pieces.

As he and his strange companions emerged from the forest, the thicket creaked and rumbled as it closed in behind them. Nate dried his eyes and gaped at the scene before him.

The sun tilted to the west. Cicadas and dragonflies buzzed among enormous trees. Their ribbed trunks and branches jutted high like outstretched arms turned up at the elbows. The trees' broad leaves resembled a great green umbrella. Little stone huts and larger wooden lodges dotted the edge of a shimmering lake. People milled about along the shore and further into the valley. They traipsed across arching wooden bridges that connected the main shore and surrounding islands. Secured with beams and hemp cord, several wooden cabins rested on high branches or hugged the circumference of wide trunks.

Colas descended the switchback path leading into the valley, Fergus on his heels. Ez bounded after them and rolled in the grass near the lake. A gentle hand rested on Nate's shoulder. He met Paul's bright green eyes.

"You're safe in Sidras, Master Riley."

Nate stared. "I don't want to be safe. I want to find my family, save my friends."

Paul nodded. "You can't do that on your own with wet boots and a rusty knife, lad. Follow me. Watch yourself, though. Colas and I'll vouch for you, but that doesn't mean you won't get asked a lot of questions. Drawls in the wood make everyone a little skittish."

Paul headed toward the lake, and Nate marched alongside. He didn't have time for skittish woodsmen, and he would let them know it.

As they arrived at the shore, armed men flocked around them. One of them drew a knife and babbled in Ruvish. Another scowled at Nate and said to Colas, "You've brought an infiltrator through our front door, Warden!"

Several others hooted their agreement. Colas raised a hand, quieting the crowd. He turned to Nate and spoke in Ruvish, "You've made friends here already, Master Riley."

"I didn't come here to make friends," Nate spat in Ruvish. A murmur passed through the crowd.

"Silence!" commanded a voice from the back. The crowd parted for a bald man with a liver-spotted face. "What is this, Warden? You've made no request for admittance of this stranger." He hobbled to Nate and assessed him with a glower.

"There was no time, Councilor Burnan," Colas said. "Drawlen chain masters have invaded the Deep Wood. Purifiers have culled the nearby village. This boy has witnessed it. And"—he placed a hand on Nate's shoulder—"he's also witnessed the presence of two Drawlen immortals."

Murmurs erupted from the men. Burnan stomped his foot. "Here in the North?" His tone was scornful. "The truce holds them back. They wouldn't—"

"They have." Fergus jumped and tugged on Burnan's coat. "I saw them. A chain master, rangers, banshees . . . all with my own eyes."

Thumping his cane, Burnan scoffed.

"Doubt the child if you want," Paul said. "We took down three banshees just hours ago. You can see their corpses if you're brave enough to venture to the scouting lines."

Burnan wagged a finger at Colas and Paul, then glared at Nate. "And who is this? An emissary of Aplada? One of Halas's?"

"I'm from Lorinth," Nate said.

"Ah, an outsider! Warden, he could well be a spy. Cage him, and we shall deal with this matter in good order."

Men grabbed at Nate. Ezron raised his hackles and snarled, his lips quivering. The men sprang back. A shrill whistle blew, stilling the crowd.

"He's no spy," came a voice so wonderfully familiar, Nate's heart swelled. Arimal limped through the crowd. Torn fabric of his coat hung from the left shoulder. Blood matted his hair, neck, and ear. His disheveled appearance and flushed face displayed his exhaustion.

A short woman with delicately pointed ears and yellowish complexion flanked him. Her gray hair, white dress, and carved walking stick only added to her ethereal presence. At Arimal's other side stood a tall man in a buckskin tunic, his own pointed ears framed by red hair brushed over one eye.

"We have a protocol," Burnan insisted. "He must be caged."

When the woman tapped her stick on the ground, a line of blue-green flames erupted, snaking along the grass like a lit fuse.

Nate flinched, fighting the urge to scream and run. In the Lorinth square, Fenris had commanded flames, consuming anyone he pleased. These flames, however, flickered benignly. They fluttered through the crowd, causing the men to step away. They shot between Burnan's feet, and he yelped while stumbling to the side. Finally, the flames encircled Nate. They faded as soon as his accusers retreated.

He met the woman's eyes. Green and blue lights danced within them as she smiled. "He is no intruder." She spoke with a gentle authority, a voice that could lull children to sleep and command armies at the same time. "He is Nathaniel Riley, son of Jonathan Riley, heir of Ruvia."

Her declaration fell upon the crowd like a hammer. They gasped and grew silent.

Overwhelmed with disbelief, Nate made no protest.

Arimal nodded with a slow exhale, slapping Nate on the back and muffing his hair. "I'm glad you made it all right. I was sure you'd hit the rocks when you fell."

Nate huffed and playfully punched him in the arm. "So was I, honestly. I'm glad you're all right too."

"Pleasantries aside," began the red-haired fae, "there are a plethora of trespassers in my Wood, and I'd like to see them put out. Warden, until the protector arrives, the call to arms is yours."

Colas nodded. "Indeed, Lord of the Wood. The protector should arrive shortly. We will not abandon the terms of our alliance now. We remain your grateful tenants. Ask what you will, Halas."

"As many armed men as you can spare."

Colas snapped his fingers. Immediately, the crowd dispersed.

Halas addressed Fergus. "Take the northern path, little one. Your parents are worried for you."

"Yes, my lord." The boy scurried off.

Arimal gestured to the two fae. "Nate, this is Sadiona. She's a deacon of the Serenity Creed, our city's spiritual advisor, and a member of the High Council of the Scattered Tribes. And this is Halas, Lord of the Deep Wood, in whose domain we've enjoyed nearly three generations of peace and secrecy."

Nate gazed at Halas, remembering the strange stories Ella had told when the three siblings would lie in bed, restless but weary. She had once spun an enchanting tale of a great fae king and his secret country, where no human dared venture, lest they be ensnared by the magic of the forest. He wondered if perhaps his sister had been telling more truth than fiction.

"The spitting image of his father, don't you think, Halas?" Sadiona said.

The man scoffed. "Perhaps just as much trouble, too, if he's at all like his brat of a sister."

"My sister? You know Ella?"

"Only by accident."

Arimal chuckled. "All in time, Nate. But at the moment, we need to tell the council what we saw in Lorinth. They're gathering now. Come."

Ezron whined at Nate's side, waiting with open-mouthed expectance.

"Go lie down," Nate said as he followed Arimal.

The dog scampered to a lush patch of grass under the shadow of a maple tree, where he rolled gleefully, belly in the air.

Arimal and Nate headed toward the largest lodge among the scattered buildings. The grain on its wide logs shone beautifully, unmarred by tar paint. The carved doors, a contrast to the light walls, stood open, and Arimal ushered Nate down a hallway through another set of doors leading to a wide atrium.

Steps descended from the corridor into the arched space. Standing open, the louvered cathedral doors lined the opposite wall. Light flooded the space, revealing an inlet to the lake brimming with cattails and lily pads.

Men and women populated the rows of benches skirting the oval-shaped room on either side of the stairs. The steps landed at a flagstone stage, furnished with a long walnut table. Four elderly men and women occupied chairs along the table, facing the crowd. Burnan sat among them, scowling and whispering to the dark-skinned woman next to him. Sadiona's flowing garment brushed past Nate as she descended the steps. She nodded to those at the table, then took her place at the center seat.

"All rise for the warden and protector," shouted a voice from the balcony. The crowd rose in murmuring unison. Colas entered and gave Nate an encouraging nod as he seated himself at the front end of the table. From a side door, a man wearing a green uniform emerged. His resemblance to Arimal struck Nate, causing him to realize what he'd missed in Arimal's introduction. Alistar Soral, Arch Traitor of the Drawlen Empire, took the last remaining seat at the opposite end of the table.

Nate turned wide eyes on Arimal and whispered, "Your old man is the Arch Traitor?"

Arimal smirked. "Why do you think I needed an alias?"

At the pounding of Sadiona's cane on the stone floor, the crowd sat, the mumblings ceased, and the woman rose. "As this is an emergency gathering, we will dismiss the formalities." She pursed her lips at Burnan, who glared at her. Then she continued. "Hostile forces have crossed the border of the Deep Wood. We have news from reliable witnesses that a party of Drawlen rangers, commanded by immortals of significant rank, gather in the village of Lorinth."

"Reliable?" Burnan barked.

Alistar shot him a piercing stare. "Do you find my son *unreliable*, councilman?"

"N-no. I only meant—" Burnan stuttered.

"We've had no reports of military movements on any of the roads," said the councilwoman next to Burnan. "It must be a small number. Perhaps they hunt a quarry that has sought refuge in the woods. In which case, we should give them over. It is not our business."

Colas tilted forward, glancing from Nate to Arimal. "And what do the witnesses say?"

Nate avoided eye contact, hoping the warden spoke of someone else. To Nate's right, Halas leaned on the doorframe, head resting on his hand. He gestured with a nod for Nate to speak.

Thankfully, Arimal stepped around him and spoke first. "They didn't take the roads. They didn't have to." He drew in a deep breath. "Lorinth has a wraith gate."

The hall exploded in cries of disbelief, outrage, and panic. Burnan and two other council members sprang to their feet.

"This is impossible!" one woman shouted. "Just because a few soldiers pop out from behind a circus stage doesn't mean one of those cursed things is—is—"

Sadiona banged her cane on the ground, but Halas swaggered down the stairs and pounced onto the table. The crowd recoiled and hushed at his disapproving gaze.

"Quiet, all of you!" he said. "It's my domain they've invaded. You are guests here, and I am a gracious host so long as you don't lose your heads."

People shrank into their seats with silence descending on the sunlit space.

Halas paced across the table. "This is no stage trick. Three days ago, what appeared to be a circus caravan arrived in Lorinth. They were given use of the temple stage, and now we know why. There is a wraith gate in that village. Somehow or another, the Drawls built it, moved it, whatever. Regardless, it works, and Drawlen filth is pouring into the valley like rats spilling from a hole in the ground.

"My scouts have spotted chain masters and banshees in the forest and a company of rangers camped at the edge. Hardly a soul remains alive in that town. This isn't some random culling. They are testing their innovation, and they are using it to assess the strength of my border. I'm gathering my people as we speak."

The crowd bristled.

Halas's eyes shone cold and fierce, like an ancient force long dormant rose within him. "This threat will not go unanswered. If you have the will, then face them with me. If you are content to cower and complain in your ignorance, then get the hell out of my country."

Murmurs erupted around the room.

"Are there truly immortals among them?" someone yelled from the crowd.

Halas's gaze bore into the man. "Yes." He glanced at Sadiona, who nodded. "My scouts confirm that Fenris the Firemaster leads this invasion."

Agitation flowed through the audience. "What about the Master of Secrets? Is he among them?" yelled another.

Halas faced Nate. "Tell them what you saw, boy."

All eyes landed on Nate. He had once loved attention, but in this moment, he'd rather be invisible. "I s-saw . . ." he said. Arimal's hand on his arm steadied him. Nate cleared his throat. "Selvator Kane used the wraith gate to kidnap my family. My father was taken through first. My brother and mother . . . she tried to stop Kane. She—" Nate's hands trembled.

A sour taste of vomit burned in his mouth. The crack of the wraith gate as Ruth drove a bayonet between the rings rang in his mind. His mother and brother disappearing replayed over and over. The sight of his father vanishing peppered his memory. The room spun.

"They're gone," he muttered, sinking to the floor. His stomach clenched.

As he lifted his head, his eyes locked onto Halas's dark stare. The man's eyes narrowed, then his gaze fell. Clearly, he was no stranger to this pain.

Arimal spoke, but it sounded distorted and distant. Someone lifted Nate to his feet. He closed his eyes, blocking the burning sunlight. The floor jostled underfoot. He reached out, grasping a broad, strong shoulder. The light dimmed.

When he opened his eyes, he found himself seated in a wooden chair in a small cottage. Shuttered windows covered the curved outer walls. Two interior walls ran from the corners of the room and met at a wide angle in the center, where a tall hearth stood. Curtains of vertical reeds closed off the doorways on each wall. With a woody rattle, one curtain drew aside, and a girl emerged.

Nate choked and shook himself out of his daze. The girl appeared about his age, and her radiance enthralled him. Complementing her soft, long face, her skin reminded him of sunshine on dark sand.

"Excuse me." Her brown eyes glinted. "I didn't mean to startle you."

"Oh, I wasn't—" Nate tried to say something intelligent, but his parched mouth constricted his speech.

She drew closer, carrying a tray laden with bread and hot tea. Her weathered boots thumped softly upon the rug, kicking up dust particles lit by filtered light from the windows. She set the tray on a table in the middle of the room, her dark hair falling forward as she bent. She stepped back and brushed her hands on her blue dress.

After setting out a plate, she cut a generous piece of bread. It steamed as she separated it from the loaf. "Here. You should really eat something."

Nate leaned forward. He felt as close to starving as he could ever remember, but he fixated on her. She smiled and handed him the plate. He took it with limp hands, mouthing his thanks. After a few bites, he recovered his senses and ravaged everything on the plate.

The girl laughed as he licked the crumbs. "You can have more."

"Yes, please. I'm Nate, by the way."

"Amara."

Even her name was pretty. He took the slice she offered and ran it through the wad of butter.

"I have cherries too. Fresh yesterday."

Nate froze mid-bite, the feel of sinister vines ghosting along his ankles. "No, I'm good with the bread."

"Oh, okay."

A whimper came from the third room, then quickly became a wail. A baby's cry.

Amara placed her hands on her hips with a huff. "Oh, fires, he's supposed to be asleep." She disappeared through the curtain and returned with a chubby infant on her hip. The baby's dark eyes matched hers; a swath of black hair crowned his round head.

"You're a mother." Nate wanted to put the words back in his mouth when he saw her frown.

"Fires, no. He's my nephew. My brother is with the scouts, and his wife is delivering a baby."

"She's having another baby?" Nate looked surprised since the child seemed about six months old.

"No, she's a doctor."

"Oh. My mother's a doctor." The words soured as soon as he said them. "Well . . ."

Amara placed the infant on the floor, then seated herself beside Nate. "Arimal told me a bit of what happened. It's horrifying."

"Is Arimal your brother?"

She nodded.

"Seriously? A husband and a father. What else don't I know? What about your mother?" Nate asked.

At this, she stilled, then slowly spoke. "She died. I was little. There was a fever that came through Sidras. A lot of people died."

"Forgive me. I didn't mean to—that was stupid of me."

Amara smiled and patted Nate's hand. He thought about how shaky and sweaty his hand was, but at the same time how much he wanted her not to let go. "I understand," she said. "I know what it's like to lose everything. A lot of people here do too."

Her words filled him with more nervousness and more courage than he'd had in the last day. A day that would be ending soon. The sun shone at a hard angle, golden and drowsy, through the gaps in the blinds. He jumped up, startling the girl, who let go of his hand.

"The scouts," he said. "Have they left yet?"

Amara shook her head. "Some have, but they go out in squads of four or six. They're gathering intel."

"I need to go."

"Nate, no." She grabbed his arm and pulled him back to the chair. "You need rest and food. You nearly passed out at the council meeting."

Nate tugged free and stepped toward the door. "I know everyone in that town, and I want to find out who's left, who needs help. I want to find my parents and my brother. I want to know if my sister is safe, if Will is safe. They were after him, that Sir Donny guy." He slowed his breathing and bit his lip.

The baby rolled onto his back, clutching his feet and giggling. How could anyone be joyful in this moment when the world was falling apart?

"I have to go." He reached for the door but sprang back when it opened.

A tall, thin woman stood before him. She carried an open satchel laden with all manner of supplies Nate would have found in the Lorinth sick house.

"Oh, you're on your feet!" she said as she stepped into the cottage. "I'm Cory." Her expression turned somber as she added, "Arimal told me what happened in Lorinth."

Behind Nate, the baby shrieked and giggled. His chubby arms extended as he beamed at Cory. When she did not immediately go to him, he squawked.

"Are you Arimal's wife?" Nate asked.

"Yes," Cory said. She scooped up the child. "Roan gets pretty fussy this time of day. I truly am sorry for what you've been through the last two days, Nathaniel. But my husband might not have gotten out of that town without you. I thank you for that."

Nate watched the baby, who pulled at his mother's smock and buried his nose into her shoulder. "I don't know that I did much, ma'am. Arimal saved my life at least three times since yesterday. He almost died pushing me away from a banshee."

Cory shifted Roan onto her hip and grasped Nate's shoulder. Her smile rivaled the sadness in her eyes. "You're safe here."

Heat rose in Nate's chest at the thought of comfort in his own safety. But the deep light in Cory's eyes held patience and compassion, causing Nate to temper his sharp rebuttal. "Thanks," he said. "But I left a lot of people behind who aren't safe." He stepped around the woman but paused when he faced another person in the doorway.

Alistar Soral, the most wanted man in Drawlen-controlled Palimar, blocked the threshold. Long ago, Jon had taught Nate to distrust depictions on wanted posters since they often portrayed inaccuracies. Alistar Soral's wanted posters, however, were an exact likeness. He was an older, harder version of his son, and Arimal's humor wasn't present as Alistar looked down at Nate. "Going somewhere?"

On a normal day, Nate might have feared this man. But he'd left his caution in the wooded tunnel that led to Sidras. "I'm going to find my friends, whoever is left. I'm going to find my family."

Alistar folded his muscled arms over his broad chest. "And how do you plan to do all that?"

"I don't know yet. Help if you want, but I'm not hiding out in here."

"And what use are you?"

"What use? You got anyone in your woodland gang that knows every road and rock and burrow between here and Depbas? Anyone besides your boy speak Palish without sounding like a Shardling runaway? You got anyone who knows the smuggling tunnels better than I do?" He scowled as Alistar's expression remained impassive. "Believe me, even Arimal doesn't know all of them."

"You're no Ruvian scout, child," Alistar said.

Nate fought the urge to roll his eyes. "You don't need a Ruvian scout. You need a Tarishman. You need a smuggler. That is, if you don't plan on condemning to death everyone who remains in Lorinth. And if you do, then I don't think we can help each other."

Alistar turned to Cory and Amara. "Remind you of someone, ladies?"

They both beamed, and Amara giggled. "You sound like your sister."

Alistar chuckled, proving he did, in fact, have some humor. "About five years ago, she ended up here by a happy accident. Do you know your father is smuggling rock and raw material for a large client?"

Nate hesitated but nodded despite himself.

"I'm the client."

# 29

# FOREST DEMONS

*Sidras, the Deep Wood*
*July 24, 1195 PT*

*Nate*

The city of Sidras was charming during the day. But at night, it became a mythical wonder. Golden sunrock lanterns hung in the trees and on lampposts, lighting the windows of sleepy cottages. Made of solarite, this kind of sunrock brought in taxes five times its value by Drawlen trade guilds and fetched a high price on the black market. Nate wondered if his father had smuggled them here.

The lake, though, proved the real marvel. Glowing koi fish swarmed around docks and under bridges, giving the water a blue-green glow. Nate rested at the end of a dock, too disturbed for sleep, twitching his toes in the water.

Outside the wisdom house, a mechanical hammer struck a wind chime four times. The plunking melody lingered as Sadiona stepped onto the dock. She squatted, joints popping, and sat next to Nate. Her beige nightdress and open robe waved in the breeze, her hair wrapped in a white scarf.

"Have you slept at all, child?" she asked.

Nate shrugged. "A few hours. I'm heading out with a scouting party at sunrise, so it didn't seem worth trying again."

Sadiona hummed and nodded. "Alistar has told you of your father's history with this place, I hear. And his dealings with us these past few years? And your sister's involvement?"

Nate nodded along with her words. At the mention of Ella, he chuckled. "Fires, I imagined she had a secret lover. Actually, when Ari—I mean when Arimal moved in with us, I assumed it was him because she stopped disappearing so much. I guess I was pretty off the mark."

"Oh. I don't know. For a little spot of time, they were quite sweet on each other. Young love is fickle though. Yet it builds character and thicker skin."

Nate thought of Adeline Davis, the curly haired daughter of the town smith. In the last year, she had enticed him and scorned him at least three times. Only recently had he given up on her. His gut churned when he wondered if she was still alive.

He shook away the idea and splashed his feet in the water. "I used to pretend. I mean, I always dreamt of leaving home to chase impossible odds and great rewards. I guess I never really considered what gets those kinds of adventures started."

"And what is that?"

"Tragedy." He watched a fish leap from the water. "I regret every minute I spent wishing to do something grand, to live anything but the life I had."

Sadiona took Nate's hands in her warm, calloused grip. "Nathaniel, you did nothing to bring this fate upon yourself. Regret festers when you linger on it. Learn from it, but never live in it. You know Sovereign's grace is sufficient for your sins?"

"Yes."

She patted his hand. "It is also sufficient for your suffering. This is a beginning. A dark, dangerous beginning, but nonetheless, you must go forward." She stretched her cane into the water and dragged a lily pad toward her, then snapped off the flower. Plucking the petals, she chuckled. "I taught your father to swim in this lake. We'd gather the children and float on wooden rafts on warm nights."

Nate stretched back against the dock and watched the stars. "Remind me again why he left."

"Oh. The people," Sadiona answered with a sigh. "It's always *people* who drive others from something good. But it's also people who can make that thing good again. New Donness, the city we're building, is on the ruins of Mercena, the ancient seat of the Gravosian empire, the realm over which Refsul ruled when he was still mortal. At first, he was a good and fair king. But the temptation of immortality corrupted him, so Sovereign cursed his throne. The Dying had once claimed that land. But now, it seems, even dead things can live again. Old things can be made new. Tragedies can become treasures. It's not easy to see amidst the darkness, but when you look back . . ." She smiled and brought a petal to her nose while breathing in deeply. Then she broke her reverie with a startling declaration. "Fenris is my brother. We were Drawlen harem children, only a year apart."

Covering his mouth, Nate shot up and snorted. "Don't take this the wrong way, Sadiona, but you look at least a decade or two older than he does."

They laughed together, and Sadiona smacked his thigh. "Oh, you're a gentleman, aren't you, Riley?" She tossed the lily petals into the water. "Refsul made him immortal, but that was after—well, I dare you to imagine a worse way to be brought up in the world. We were trained to command fire, to consume life with it. We were the first fire wielders born in almost three hundred years. Refsul used us to cement his authority on the northern and western territories. His ambition was halted at the Deep Wood, Halas's territory."

"You mean Halas's ancestors?"

Sadiona shook her head. "No. Halas is one of the seven original Blessed Immortals, whom Refsul betrayed. He has been the guardian of the North ever since. His way of preserving his decimated homeland. When Refsul ordered us to burn the wood, I was about your age." She picked up her walking stick and twirled it in her tiny hands. "Halas kidnapped us. He intended to use us against Refsul."

"What happened?"

"Oh, he fell in love with me."

Nate laughed, but quieted when she placed a finger across her mouth.

"Ah, but that flame burned out long ago. The fickleness of young love. Still, I'd tasted freedom, and I would never go back. I thought it was the same for Fenris, but I was so very wrong."

Drumming his fingers on the dock, Nate watched moonlight shimmer across the water. "Was Sidras here back then?"

"Two hundred years ago, it was only an encampment, and farther southeast of where we are now. My birth mother was stolen from there . . . I met my grandparents, learned about my people. It was a wonderous time."

Nate scrunched his face. "Is that why Halas allows the Ruvians to live here, because of you?"

Sadiona tightened her robe around her. "It certainly was at the beginning. If you ask me, I think he's grown quite fond of them."

Nate recalled Halas's blunt and frustrated speech in the wisdom hall. "It didn't seem like it."

"He's a curious man. The more he seems to dislike someone, the more he truly cares."

"He must be fond of my sister."

Sadiona laughed. "Oh, he's got quite the soft spot for Ella. Almost everyone here does. She's a charmer."

"You're telling me. She once talked her way into the royal kitchens in Pelton! We were moving rock, and one of the crates got put on a dry goods cart headed to the Tower of Theron by mistake. She got herself an apron and a handkerchief, waltzed right in with a crate of eggs and then right out an hour later with the rocks."

Sadiona ran her hands along her cane. "I hear you're quite the little trickster yourself, and not too bad in a brawl either."

Lifting his feet from the water, Nate pulled up his legs and rested his chin on his knees. "Nothing too impressive—just street fights. I've never so much as broken a man's arm. I've certainly never killed anyone."

Sadiona put a hand on Nate's shoulder. "Taking life is no virtue, Nathaniel. A necessity sometimes, perhaps. But it's what you fight for, not against, that matters. When you go with our scouts, you may very well find blood on your hands. It will haunt you, as it should. So, consider whether you want to live with that burden or have others carry it for you."

The lake rippled under the warm breeze. Increasing to a strong gust, the wind blew Nate's sweat-crusted locks from his face. Dirt caked his fingernails. Soon they could be stained with more than that. His pining for glorious adventure had dissipated, but he resolved not to hide in safety while others fought. Breathing in the fresh air, he waited with Sadiona until the sun rose.

Two hours later, golden light spilled across the rough wooden table where Nate stood, along with Halas, Alistar, and several others. Upon the table lay a map of the Deep Wood.

Halas addressed a thin fae man. "What do you have for us, Orego?"

The man spoke in a nasally voice. "Drawlen engineers have been working without pause to repair the wraith gate. We should assume they will succeed. Despite that, a company of the Third North is on its way from Depbas."

Alistar scratched the gray scruff on his chin. "We could lift the control rings from the pedestal easily enough."

With sharp, brown eyes, Orego regarded the Sidrian protector. "There aren't any. This gate works differently. There is a lever mechanism that moves the rings of the actual gate, but it is only for convenience. The pillars also seem inconsequential. They can dial the rings manually. I've never seen a gate like it, not even in Gravos before the Dying."

Halas adjusted the pistol on his belt and folded his arms across his armored, leather vest. "So, it won't be easy to disable permanently. That doesn't mean we can't do it damage, right Nate? Your mother stopped it with a bayonet?"

Everyone turned to Nate, who blinked. "Yes." He cleared his throat. "But now she's gone to who knows where."

"And Selvator Kane with her," Halas added. "It's a twisted blessing. We don't have to deal with him in this fight, which makes us much better off, but we are still outgunned. I pray your mother and brother are in Sovereign's grace, wherever they are."

"Thank you," Nate said, casting his eyes to the ground.

Hovering over the map, Colas drew an imaginary line with his finger from Sidras to the southeastern edge. "We don't have many men to spare, but perhaps we should consider getting a message to Mumagra. Jonathan Riley is very likely locked up in Shevak, and his knowledge of our operations is extensive. We may have more than one front to worry about."

Sadiona clicked her tongue and leaned on her staff. "I feel for his predicament, and I certainly believe Dontel would hold nothing back from his aide. But I don't think Jon's connection with us has crossed Refsul's mind. It's possible that Selvator Kane is the sole sponsor of this operation since he personally came to Lorinth. With him out of the way, however temporary, Jon would merely be the Wraith Cellar's newest resident." She shifted her weight to the other side, adjusting her grip on her staff. "Don't forget, while we are painfully aware of Drawlen's threat to our cause, they are not aware of us at all. Secrecy may save us still. We'll not enter this fight under a Ruvian flag, but as warriors of the Deep Wood, as forest demons."

His countenance softening, Halas faced Sadiona. "That is prudent. But still, you should consider moving your more vulnerable citizens elsewhere, perhaps to Apleda. This assault is personal for Fenris. I'm his chief target."

His forearm pressed to the table, Alistar hunched forward. "We've started a count of who will go and who can stay to contribute to the defense of your land." With his finger, he drew a line on the map. "Rolan will lead the exodus. We appreciate your appointment of a fae escort as well, Halas."

"It's wise to be cautious," Halas said. "I won't abide innocent blood being spilled in my Wood."

Alistar nodded. "All the same, we're grateful. They'll be ready to depart within the hour."

Halas took both of Sadiona's hands in his. "For as much as I have failed you, my lady, let me keep this promise: You will never have to face your brother on the battlefield. Go with Rolan."

Sadiona smiled and patted his cheek. "Old fool. It's been a hundred years since I was afraid of that boy. I've been *waiting* for this moment."

A scout arrived. He handed an envelope to Halas, who tore through the Drawlen seal.

He read the opening line and addressed the group. "Fenris sends a formal declaration to annex the Deep Wood. How quaint."

"What does that mean?" Nate asked.

"It means, Master Riley, that he is posturing like an overzealous peacock and will soon find himself without a tail." He slammed the letter on the table and put a firm hand on the messenger's shoulder. "Get word to Silas. If the Drawls want to let fliers loose in my skies, I'll bring some of my own."

"I request permission to go instead, Halas," Orego offered, stepping forward. "I'll be much faster than riders."

"Very well," Halas said. He nodded to the messenger who bowed his head and sped away.

A smile spread across Orego's thin lips. "See you soon, brother." Then he extended his arms out from his sides and leapt into the air, transforming into a brown hawk while soaring into the sky.

Halas raised his hand and declared, "Ladies and gentlemen, there is Drawlen game in my forest. Let's go hunting."

After Nate received a scout's green uniform, a crossbow, and rations, he departed with Arimal, Colas, and Paul. He had hunted dozens of deer and elk, but always in the wide-open hills of the Lorinth countryside.

Everything felt different in the timber. The limited visibility and dappling sunlight proved utterly deceiving. Creaking trees and squawking birds occasionally interrupted the intense silence. Nate spent the next hours sitting with Arimal in blinds built high in the trees. Dense vegetation camouflaged the blinds, equipped with additional weapons and supplies. Nate preferred stalking in the fields, of course, but those held wild game, not hostile Drawlen rangers and flying monsters.

He ran his fingers along the smooth stock of a rifle hanging on a rack against the tree trunk. The far-off cry of a banshee punctuated the silence.

"The only way I want to see one of those things again is over a rifle barrel," he mumbled.

"I'm with you on that," Arimal said. "They're terrion, you know—or they used to be. Drawls breed them, torture them. They do the same to trolls. Their way of insulting the Freelands without risking a war. Just another way they enslave."

Nate rested against the tree trunk. "My mother is still a slave, technically. When my—when we had to leave Estbye, the Drawls gave my parents a choice between imprisonment or a fifteen-year indenture. My father took prison time while my mother got assigned to the sick house in Lorinth. She's not allowed to go more than five miles from town."

Arimal's jaw dropped. "I had no idea. I knew Jon did time in Langry, but I'd never heard why."

"I have an older brother—well, half brother. Remm discovered a nobleman was snatching girls for himself and that he had his eye on Ella. He sent men. Remm killed them. I was seven, but I remember him coming home, covered in blood and carrying my sister. I don't know what happened after that. My parents never talked about it."

"Fires, Nate. I thought *my* life was one tragedy after another."

"Not looking to win a competition."

Arimal scratched his shoulders against the tree trunk. "Still—"

A chipper whistling cut him off. A signal from Colas, stationed with Paul to the south. The sound blended with the woodland chattering of birds and squirrels. The animals soon quieted, however. Someone was moving through the woods. Three short chirps: three walkers. One long and two short chirps: The first target belonged to Nate and Arimal.

Arimal tapped Nate's crossbow and whispered, "You're a better shot."

Nate gaped at his friend. True, of course, but this wasn't wild game; it was a man. Nate had never taken a sapien life. With a shaky hand, he picked up the weapon and checked that the bolt was secure and the string was taut. Then he ran his fingers along the foregrip.

"I'd rather you hesitate now and get it over with than if we get into a melee later." Arimal picked up his own crossbow. "I'll cover you, so don't worry."

Nate nodded, then searched the forest. He watched the crisscrossing game trails, imagining he was waiting for a buck. A gray mass emerged slowly from a tangle of poplar trees—a Drawlen ranger. Dressed in a scouting uniform, he carried a rifle, finger poised straight along the trigger guard. Step, pause, step, pause.

Nate lined up his shot, his finger caressing the trigger of his crossbow. He cleared his mind and waited. Chirp-chirp came the signal. Without delay, his finger pulsed on the trigger. The twang and kickback of the weapon felt natural. He watched the bolt bury into the man's chest, watched him crumple to the ground, and then reloaded his weapon with detached automation. When Nate turned, he met Arimal's stare.

"It was a good shot. How do you feel?"

Nate glanced at the body, twisted vines dragging it into the underbrush. He felt nothing. It was a target, and shooting it served a higher purpose than not shooting it, just like game. "Fine."

"Sometimes it's numbing, the first one," Arimal said. "It will hit you later when you're not expecting it. Just know, you did well."

In truth, the numbness terrified Nate. He wanted to feel the weight of what he'd just done, but there was nothing. He needed a distraction. "Who is Silas?"

"I'm not really sure. I've heard he's a terrion who rules the Drakelands, the country between Palimar and the Devourer's Waste. He has some kind of alliance with Halas. Supposedly, he's been around since the Terrion Wars."

"Immortal?"

"I don't think so. Terrion live about three or four hundred years."

As night emerged, they ate their rations, rotating between watching and sleeping. While Nate took the fourth watch, the moist air cooled. A thin fog rolled in, which made spotting from the platform difficult in the half-light.

But a growing pressure in his ears startled him. He shook Arimal's shoulder. The young man opened his eyes and jerked forward.

"Do you feel that?" Nate asked. He focused on the buzzing in his bones, the cold, quivering in the air. "There's a ralenta in the woods, somewhere close by."

Arimal blinked. "How can you tell?"

"You can't?"

"Yes, but I've been trained."

"We're not the best smuggling family in Palimar for nothing. The signal?"

Arimal lifted the copper whistle to his lips and blew four short and three long pulses. It echoed around them.

Vines lying dormant on the ground shot up, weaving together to form a crisscrossing maze of vegetation three feet high. A startled cry sounded below them, and a woman in black materialized. The net of vines clotheslined her, causing her to momentarily lose control of her shades. Nate aimed and fired a dart into her chest with the same dead-eyed efficiency he'd used to dispatch the ranger the day before.

The woman fell forward, dangling over the vines. It hit Nate that he'd just killed a ralenta. "Fires. What about the shades?"

"If you could feel her that clearly, you're in no danger."

"Others might be."

Arimal put up a hand and smiled. "One of the requirements for being a Ruvian scout is shade immunity. It's the first thing we learn. Did David teach you?"

Nate nodded.

"He taught most of the older scouts here too. We'll lure these specters to their old masters, where they can pay a surprise visit. Again, you did well."

A chirp sounded farther south, and the quivering pressure of nearby shades faded. Reverberations of the signal dwindled. "That's amazing," Nate said. "Creepy, but amazing."

"When we're done with Fenris, we'll teach you to see shades—and manipulate them a little."

"Like a ralenta?"

"No. A ralenta uses shades like an extension of the mind. What we do is more like herding cattle."

"Well, that's not as good, but I'll take it."

As the sun rose, the fog thickened. While Arimal slept, Nate kept watch. Breathing deeply, he welcomed the warm, acrid aroma of woodsmoke. Arimal jumped to his feet. Frantic signals came from the south, different than those sounds Nate had learned in his brief training.

"What do they mean?" Nate asked.

"They're advancing . . ." Arimal said. "Fire. He's burning the woods. The watch is over. The real fight is coming." He pulled two bent metal bars from the supply rack and moved aside one of the nets camouflaging the platform. Above it hung a thick, taut rope extending into the forest. He handed one of the bars to Nate, straddled the rope with his own, and pushed off. Nate slung his crossbow on his back and imitated him. They glided across the forest canopy before landing on another platform.

The retreating forms of other sentinels disappeared as they, too, glided along another cable extension. For about an hour, Nate and Arimal zipped along until the rope angled low and they landed on the ground.

A group of scouts gathered in a clearing, young men and women pacing and watching the sky. Colas and Paul arrived a moment later, followed by ten others.

"Where are Garret and May?" Colas asked.

The last man to descend the zip line hung his head. "A purifier snuck up on them, sir. I'm sorry."

Colas closed his eyes. "Sovereign, protect us." He placed his hand on his heart and inhaled deeply before opening his eyes. "All right, listen. This is no skirmish. The Drawls have been planning this. They won't be deterred by the usual tricks."

A shrill cry sounded overhead. Soaring above the canopy, a banshee dove at the group. As it descended, a shot rang out, and the creature fell, wings curling in like the legs of a dead spider. Nate spun around.

On a shallow ledge of rock stood Amara, rifle still pressed to her shoulder, hair bound in a thick bun behind her head. Seeing her poised in her scout's uniform, Nate's throat constricted. Her eyes met his, and his cheeks burned.

"Let's move back, everyone," Colas said. "It's not safe to linger."

Nate reverted his gaze to the main group and followed the scouts with Colas leading them through the forest.

The landscape grew steadily rugged as they traveled farther north than Nate had ever been. Elms, oaks, and poplars transitioned to great, towering pines.

The paths ran steadily uphill, and soon changed to switchbacks. Through the rare gaps in tree cover, Nate spied jutting cliffs ahead.

"Hi there," an unfamiliar voice said. A young boy, perhaps about fourteen, with long limbs and a round, pimply face caught up to Nate and walked alongside him. "I'm Aaron."

"Nate."

"I heard."

"Heard what?"

"That you're Nate—Nate Riley."

"Yeah, I guess."

"Heard you took out a ralenta last night."

Nate huffed and stepped around a protruding root. "Didn't have many options."

Aaron fiddled with the strap of his rifle. "Were you scared?"

Nate scratched his head. "Probably should have been. I just don't have much left to lose."

When they came, at last, to a break in the trees, Aaron joined his company. They gathered on a ridge teeming with Ruvians and fae, all dressed and equipped for war. Colas signaled to the group of scouts. "Stand with your combat squads. Arimal, Paul, Nathaniel, you're with me."

Nate followed Colas through the crowd, which parted hurriedly for them. Observing the faces as he passed, he distinguished fae from human by their ears. But their attitudes also differed. The fae fidgeted, staring wide-eyed, some in tears. The Ruvians remained stoic, eyeing Nate as if saying, *We expected this. We're ready.*

At the crown of the ridge, Sadiona, Halas, and Alistar waited. Two fae women stood beside Halas as well, one with a graying braid and a fur vest, the other sporting golden locks and knives at her belt. They regarded the approaching Ruvians with cold blue eyes and matching scowls.

"They've reached the scouting lines," Colas said. "He's burning a path for them. If we let them get far enough, we could block them in."

Halas consulted the two women, who both shook their heads.

"They've taken measures against such actions, I'm afraid," he relayed. "They're driving spikes of wraith poison into the soil as they go. We won't be able to move anything onto that ground for years."

Past the ridge, a pillar of smoke bent across the landscape. Nate watched from the edge of the cliff. A vast expanse of forest lay before him. A line of black and gray plumes billowed from the ground far ahead. The base of flames flickered beneath it. And beyond, the smoldering remains of Lorinth, separated from the wood by a thin, brown band of grassland. A sudden burst of gloom fell over the town, like a shadow settling over it, before lifting. The wraith gate was working again.

"We've got to break that gate," Alistar said from behind him. "We need to gather a team of infiltrators."

"I'll go," Nate said.

"No, lad," Alistar said. "This is not a mission we expect many to return from."

Nate approached the man. "I'm not afraid to die."

Alistar held his gaze and breathed slowly. "No doubt, but it's still not a mission for you. When we've driven them out, you can look for survivors. But you're not properly trained for this mission. I'm sorry." He faced Halas. "Arimal will lead a team into Lorinth. Can you spare any skin-changers? The more subtle, the better."

Halas nodded to the fae women next to him. "Sephora and Nyla are well suited. You could use their muscle."

"Agreed," Alistar said. "Arimal, take Paul and a few others with you."

Moving near his father, Arimal nodded. "Yes, Protector. We'll have that gate broken before the next sun rises."

Alistar put a hand on his son's shoulder. They shared a tense, tender moment before he dropped his arm. "Sovereign watch over you, son."

"You also, father." Arimal descended the hill.

Nate ran after him. "Wait. I *need* to be there!"

Arimal halted and bit his bottom lip. "Sorry, Nate. This one's not for you."

"Why not?" Nate demanded, arms crossed.

Arimal put a hand on Nate's shoulder like his father had just done for him. "I'll see you when I get back. You're needed here, Nate."

Nate's shoulders sagged. He looked down when he heard a familiar whine. Ezron, whom he'd left in Sidras before going with the scouts, sat dutifully next to him. Nate glanced from his dog to his friend. Removing the bone whistle from his neck, he held it out to Arimal. "At least take Ez with you."

Arimal nodded and grasped the tool. As he continued down the path, Ezron trotted after him. The two fae women followed, along with Paul and a few other Ruvians. The crowd clapped them on their backs as they departed.

Returning to the hilltop, Nate watched the smoke of Fenris's fire. His chest tightened.

"This battle will start and finish long before Orego returns with Silas's fighters," Alistar said.

Using her staff for support, Sadiona squinted at the distant flames. "We've faced worse odds." She turned to the fae. "Halas."

"Yes, Ona?"

"Are there still some drakes wandering around in the Crags?"

A sinister smirk grew on Halas's sharp face. "Why, yes, my lady, there *are*."

# 30

# DEBT

*Palim, the Freelands*
*July 19, 1195 PT*

*Liiesh*

If he could earn a five mark for each hour of his life lost to the drivel of court gossip, Liiesh Romanus would be an even richer man. He stood in the grand hall of his family spire, surrounded by a throng of overdressed, chatty people. This assembly banquet might be more tolerable if Tres were here to suffer with him. It made him miss his insubordinate younger brother . . . almost.

His Aunt Braella ambled toward him through the crowd. He prayed to Sovereign for an excuse to avoid her lecture about property taxes. Not a sincere prayer, but it was promptly answered, nonetheless. The pull of a mind calling caused him to stumble. He braced himself against the back of a mahogany chair, startling the Kumuni diplomat across from him.

*'A moment,'* Liiesh pleaded in his mind.

*'There is no time,'* came his brother's faint answer.

Liiesh righted himself and backed into the hallway. Mel, his Thêeni bodyguard, followed silently, and they slipped into a vacant parlor. Dust danced in the light streaming through the west-facing windows. Canvas sheets covered the furniture, including a grand piano in the middle of the room.

Mel locked the door and rested against its frame. Resting a hand on the pistol at his belt, he bowed his head and remained still. He was Liiesh's favorite groundling—quiet, not so twitchy.

Liiesh lifted the chain of his limiter over his head and set the talisman on the piano's lid. Closing his eyes, he focused on the pull of Tres's mind calling.

When he opened his eyes, a familiar, hollow expanse of glittering fog surrounded him. His brother stood before him.

Tres's outlander clothing disguised him as a common merchant, although the sword he carried—Stonebreaker—emitted a foreboding presence. His hair lay unbraided and tied at the nape of his neck. A gash marred his cheek. Next to him, Shane zem'Arta glared. Being covered in blood and open wounds was nothing remarkable for the Red Watch captain, but his distraught expression alarmed Liiesh. He glanced back and forth from his brother to the captain. "What happened?"

Both men talked at once, stopped, and sneered at one another. Finally, Shane spoke. "Rodden went after Refsul and got himself a free ride through a wraith gate."

As he processed this, Liiesh blinked. Time moved strangely inside a mind calling. "Damn."

"He went rogue," Tres said. "Captain zem'Arta gave appropriate orders. The skin-changer disregarded them."

Liiesh raised a brow. He'd never heard his brother speak to or about the Zereen without insult. Maybe this subjugation served well for Tres after all. "Where is he?" Liiesh asked.

"Shevak, we think," Shane said.

"I'll inform Raza. He happens to be on standby for another operation. Consider yourselves fortunate, gentlemen." He closed his eyes, intending to dissolve the mind calling.

"Wait!" Shane said. "That's not why we brought you here."

"Oh?" Liiesh opened his eyes.

Tres and Shane parted from one another, revealing a figure on the ground.

Liiesh stared at a young woman, her pale skin glistening with fever. A tangled mass of brown curls clung to her forehead and cheeks. "Who is this?" he asked.

"She is our only link to a very important contact," Tres said.

"Who?"

"Krishena Dantiego," Tres answered.

"Look," Shane growled before kneeling beside the woman. "Mona can heal her easily. We only need your help summoning her."

Liiesh put up a hand and shook his head. "No. I have other ways to contact the Rogue Master if need be. Performing a healing over a mind calling is no simple feat."

"So, Mona will get a headache for a couple of weeks. This woman is going to die!"

"What is it to me?" Liiesh asked.

Shane scowled, then hung his head.

Liiesh studied the woman. A smattering of deep brown freckles peppered her nose and cheeks. Dark circles framed her eyes, and her face appeared swollen. Wearing a ragged coat, she looked like a member of Shane's crew. Perhaps she was Shane's lover. Liiesh dearly hoped not. The last time Shane lost a woman, he'd nearly exposed the Red Watch exacting revenge.

Shane rose and locked eyes with him. "That night in the archives twelve years ago—I hesitated."

Staring into the Zereen's eyes, Liiesh remembered the desperate boy who once held a knife ready to slit his throat in the dark.

"I would have killed you," Shane whispered and gestured to the woman. "You have her to thank. It's time to pay your debt, Liiesh."

The First Lord let out a long breath. A life debt was nothing to shrug off. Straightening, he clenched his fists. "Very well." He placed his hands on his temple and called mentally to Mona.

*'I'm ready. I've been waiting,'* she spoke in his mind.

At his summons, his half sister materialized within the wintery mind calling, directing a sorrowful smile at Shane.

"Mona, I tried to—" Shane said.

"I know. He picked a fight."

"I'm . . . sorry." Shane's words held such sincerity, Liiesh thought he misheard.

Mona nodded and stepped around him, her long hair and green dress swaying in harmony. She knelt and put her hand over the unconscious woman's forehead. "Wraith poison. I may only be able to give her days, but I will try. Pray for Sovereign's grace." Hovering her hands over the woman's chest, she closed her eyes and twitched her fingers.

"Who is she?" Liiesh asked.

Shane scratched his chin with his claws and exhaled. "Before I met you, Henrick Lowe wanted me to snatch her in Estbye. Her parents interfered. I swore they were going to kill me." He shook his head. "Instead, they showed mercy. They fed me. Gave me a bed. Told me I could stay."

Liiesh pressed his lips into a thin line. He believed he'd wrung every detail from Shane about his time as the Shardling pirate's snatcher, but surely more secrets remained. "You didn't stay though. Why?"

Shane rubbed his brow, gazing at the woman's still form. "I knew what Henrick would do if I stayed. Make me repay her family's kindness with blood and shackles. They couldn't help me. I needed someone stronger." He crossed his arms, staring at Liiesh. "Freedom didn't enter my mind until I met them. Otherwise, it wouldn't have occurred to me when I was sent to kill you."

Liiesh smiled. He would accept this as the closest "thank you" he'd ever get from Shane.

Mona drummed her hands in the air over the woman's chest while whispering. Several minutes later, she rose and addressed the men. "My work is done. Time will tell. It's in Sovereign's hands, my brothers."

Liiesh nodded to each of them and ended the mind calling. When he resumed his presence in the parlor, twilight filled the Romanus tower. Mel acknowledged the return of his lord's consciousness with a glance.

Liiesh slipped his limiter around his neck and sat on the piano's bench. He threw off the canvas, rolled back the key cover, and played "The Winds of Vulta." Despite the instrument's need for a tuning, he preferred playing over returning to the banquet.

*Ella*

A beautiful woman with a long, narrow face bent over Ella, her silky black hair surrounding them like a curtain. Her hands hovered above Ella's chest, and a warm light emitted from them. Perhaps she was Aginoman, but her eyes and face appeared too angular, too ethereal.

Beyond her, in a surreal field of snow, waited three men. Two of them bore the woman's dark-honey skin and sharp face. One in a rich red justaucorps reminded her of a king. The third man seemed familiar, but her memory proved elusive in this strange reverie. His tawny complexion accentuated his rough, broad build while his silver-blond hair fell loose around his shoulders.

Ella closed her eyes and drifted between near-waking and a snowy dreamland. Hours—or maybe days—passed. She heard voices occasionally: Rose.

Hale. Shane. The cut burned in her hand, the sensation spreading slowly up her arm. Her body jostled.

During one of Ella's wakeful moments, she heard Calla's snide voice. "Are we bargaining with trolls now?"

"It's a fair offer," came Krishena's steady reply.

"They turned your nephew into a monster," Calla said.

"Some would say you did the same to me, *Wraith King*."

"Only because you asked me, dear wife."

"Save your flattery."

*Again Ella slipped away. She dreamed of hovering deep in the ocean, swaying with the currents of dark waters. A flame flickered in her hand. It grew and solidified into a blade of red steel. A cove emerged, filled with water still as glass. She appeared on the crest of a bluff next to someone she recognized but couldn't identify. Longing to remain, she felt at home, but the scene dissolved into disappointment when she woke.*

"Come on, Little Mouse." A firm, sweaty grip squeezed her hand. "Wake up."

*Remm? Remm!* She struggled to open her eyes. But darkness chased her relentlessly, and she floated in the sea.

After time tumbled through her unconsciousness, Ella's eyes flitted open. She breathed crisp air laced with the fragrance of pine, nothing like the stale, city flavor of Drawl. She lay alone in a room of crumbling plaster walls and sun-pocked, shuttered windows. Rolling to her side and pushing off the bed, she sat up—surprised at her strength but otherwise feeling normal. A clear memory entered her mind: a wraith knife slicing her palm, the poison crawling through her body like boiling molasses. She traced the scar across her hand.

"Has anyone checked on her?" Rose's voice came from the other side of a rotting black door. "She was worse than I've seen her since Drawl."

A gruff female voice replied, "Go be a mother hen if it pleases you, girly. Don't know why we're bothering with all this."

"You've a heart of gold, Carris," Rose snapped. The door opened, and the girl who had once scorned Ella now gasped, her eyes wide and face beaming. "Ella!"

"Hi," Ella spoke in a hoarse voice. "Is there food? I'm really hungry."

Rose ran and threw her arms around Ella, sobbing into her shoulder. Ella squeezed her back.

Krishena appeared in the doorway, a somber smile on her face. "Rose, please get her something to eat."

The girl jumped and flitted out of the room. Krishena sat next to Ella and hugged her while drawing in a deep breath. "El—"

"I know I was foolish," Ella said.

"No—well, yes. But you did right by Hale. I'm afraid there are more sinister forces at work apart from your own recklessness."

"I saw Refsul, I think, and—"

"That was merely an unhappy coincidence for you. There is something else." Krishena lifted Ella's hand and cupped it between her warm, quivering palms. "My agents watch for death marks commissioned out of the Temple Setvan."

"I know."

"Your name came up. Your friend Will Loren's as well. Collectors were searching for you in Drawl."

"Will? Will . . ." Ella shook her head. "He's okay, right? You came for me. You must have—"

"We tried." Krishena's dark eyes grew glassy, her usually proud face drooping. "Collectors were already in the Tarish camp when I got word from Shevak. They left no survivors, save one. William Loren died saving the life of your priestess friend. And if Remm and his Freelander acquaintances had not arrived, Rose, too, would be dead."

Ella's whole body shook.

Krishena patted her hand. "There is . . . more. Other names. Your mother and your younger brothers."

Ella stared at Krishena, wide-eyed. "Why? When?"

"My rogues found out about their death marks four days ago. They went immediately to Lorinth. Word came to me the day you rescued Hale."

"How long was I—"

"Three days. We've been riding nonstop, trading our horses or stealing them. It's a miracle you didn't die on the journey."

"My family?"

"I sent more agents, people to help. Calla returned a few hours ago with word from Shevak. Yesterday, your father was sent through the wraith gate and thrown in the Temple Setvan. But he was alone. We don't know where he was sent from. There are no wraith gates in Taria. Perhaps he was in Pelton on business?"

Ella shook her head. "He was staying in Lorinth until September. Maybe something came up?"

"Perhaps. However he got there, Jon is in the Cellar."

"You can get to him, right? There isn't a prison in Palimar you can't get into."

The woman put up a hand and smiled. "Getting into the Cellar is easy. Getting out—no one has ever succeeded." She rested her hand on her thigh and inclined her head. "However, that will change tomorrow. I was very offended eight years ago when your brother chose to run with Freelanders over me. Now, I see it was Sovereign's will. This troll friend of yours, zem'Arta, do you trust him?"

Ella nodded without hesitation. "Yes. He's like a brother to me. Is he here?"

"He's scouting. We expect his return within the hour."

# 31

# THE CELLAR

*The Wraith Cellar: Prison Complex Below the Temple Setvan*
*July 22, 1195 PT*

*Jon*

Jon Therman was no stranger to prisons. Several month-long stints in the Estbye workhouse peppered his youth, and the scars of four years in the notorious Langry Prison remained etched into his body and soul. A dangerous penitentiary in western Palimar, Langry seemed a seaside holiday compared to the Wraith Cellar. The Cellar earned its reputation as a cesspool from its violent criminals and jailers' habits of neglecting the dead.

As Jon stumbled into the stinking vestibule, a petrified corpse at arm's length quivered. A thin fog rolled off the body. Like a cold draft in a hot room, Jon felt the shade. He stiffened, aware he was the closest living thing before this freshly hatched menace. Further into the room, a prisoner screamed. The frigid presence of the shade drifted toward the sound.

With shaky breath, Jon rose to his feet. A vast room of stone surrounded him, interrupted only by the heavy metal door behind him. He squinted in the dim light of sunrock lamps hanging from the ceiling.

A sunken expanse traversed the middle of the room, where tables and benches lay scattered like the aftermath of a memorable bar fight. To Jon's left, a dry water trough with a stone spigot jutted from the wall. On the right hung a similar basin crusted with mold and crowned by a pass-through window, barred with steel shutters.

At the far end of the prison lay a rusted row of stocks with missing shackles. Disheveled men played cards and rolled dice upon the benches. Cells lined the sidewalls. Some units sat empty, but most housed about ten prisoners pressed against the back walls, eyes bulging and heads quivering.

Jon's heart quickened when every conscious person stared at him. He donned his best cold-blooded stare and stepped forward. Clutching Mylis's pendant, he scanned the cages. Men populated most of the Wraith Cellar. The few women who had the misfortune of calling this place home huddled together, locked in their cages.

When he spotted a girl alone in a cell halfway down the right-hand wall, Jon's eyes widened. Appearing about eleven years old, she hovered in the corner. Her dirty-blonde hair hung down her stained white robe while she stared with haunting hazel eyes—Tessa's eyes. Ruth's eyes. Ella's eyes. Jon studied the room, contemplating how to reach Haana without becoming prison amusement.

Two men on the far side flashed a wicked grin as they sauntered nearer. The muscular, gray-skinned troll glared with bright eyes. Jon figured he could take the skinny Yvean man, but the troll sported a sharp set of claws and teeth.

Water gushed from the spigot above the trough. Like a stampede of pigs for the slop buckets, prisoners flung open cell doors and scrambled over one another. Jon Therman, the newest guest of the Wraith Cellar, stood forgotten. A perfect position for a smuggler who relished hiding in plain sight.

He scurried by Haana's cage, slipping into the adjacent cell. Using the modified lock that latched from the inside by a pull bar, he secured his door and sat against the wall.

Nodding to Haana, he tossed her the pendant while the other inmates gathered their water rations. As the necklace sailed through the cell bars, Haana caught it, her face brightening. She hunched and turned her back.

"Mylis asked me to look out for you," Jon whispered.

Haana glanced over her shoulder and scowled at Jon. As he moved slowly toward the bars, she slipped the necklace over her head and huddled in the opposite corner.

Jon clasped the bars and leaned his forehead against them. "I won't hurt you. Perhaps we can help each other."

Stroking the pendant, Haana pursed her lips. Jon stared, but she remained silent. He wondered about the grit needed for a child to survive in the cruelty of the Drawlen harem. Haana's countenance reminded him of Ruth when they'd first met, when she was a pirate's jaded ex-lover, scorned and pregnant.

Jon waited until exhaustion consumed him. Short of ideas and miracles, he collapsed on the floor. With a deep breath, he closed his eyes and dismissed his thoughts, especially how he'd gotten here in the first place. He drifted to sleep.

Hours later, he awoke to the scrape of metal against metal. Beams of sunlight filtered into the dungeon through the air shafts along the ceiling. The redheaded Yvean man stalked outside Haana's cage and clanked a metal bolt against the bars.

"Hey, missy, missy. We wanna *play*."

Below the cell platform, the troll sat on a wide step near the pit. He licked his lips and chomped his sharp yellow teeth. Haana glared and stiffened with crossed arms.

Jon stood, stretching his stiff legs. He hung his arms over the crossrail of the cell door. "Yo. I got a stash of coca if you'll tell me who's who in this place."

The two men slithered closer to Jon, panting like ravenous dogs. "How much you got, old man?" the redhead said, twitching his fingers. "Got me a high tolerance."

Jon removed his boot and reached inside, feeling for the pocket along the heel. Pulling his hand free, he held up a wax packet of white powder between his middle and index fingers. He raised an eyebrow and surveyed the room with an elbow on the crossbar. "Who's the big bad in here, friend?"

Thumping his chest, the redhead pressed against the bar. "That'd be me."

Jon sneered. "Not your troll friend, there?"

The troll jeered and licked his teeth.

The redhead smirked and twirled the bolt. "Bert's my number two. I'm Kit."

Jon nodded. "When does the food come? What's the routine?"

"Water's been finicky these days." Kit pointed to the trough. "Seems to come whenever someone new walks in. Food comes at sunrise. You missed today. If you run with us, no one'll touch ya, and you'll get a go at the, ah"—he glanced at Haana—"entertainment."

Jon suppressed the urge to grab him by the neck and drive the bolt Kit was holding through his skull. Instead, he waved the package. "My gift to you, Master Kit, with the understanding I'll be left to do as I please. And just in case you get ambitious, this is all I have. I might get more if the right people show up."

"At's a good man." Kit snickered and grabbed the packet.

"Not more than a finger's worth." Jon placed his index finger across his mouth. "This is drake dust from Agenom. You'll kill yourself if you get carried away. Maybe share it with your crew. They look a little bored." Jon inclined his head toward the group at the back wall, all staring with hungry eyes.

"Ha! Will do, eh. What's yer name?"

"Jon."

"'Ey!" Kit yelled, addressing his men. "Boys, this here's Jonny. No one touches him. He's done us a good un." He waved the packet and promenaded to his crew.

Within minutes after inhaling the full contents of Jon's gift, Kit and his eighteen men passed out. This reprieve would be brief though. The packet was meant for only five or six. Jon quickly left his own cell and fiddled with the lock on a neighboring cell so that it latched from the outside. One by one, he dragged the unconscious men inside, tipping them into a pile of comatose thugs. Each time he deposited a new body, he secured the lock. Twenty minutes later, Jon trudged into the pit where Kit and several more thugs remained. Scratching his dark beard, Jon turned Kit's drooling face to one side with his boot.

From a nearby cell, an elderly woman watched. "That weren't no drake dust. What you give 'em?"

"Essence of Alunen."

"Praise the mother o' dryads."

Jon huffed and wiped the sweat off his forehead. "No offense, woman, but a dead immortal had nothing to do with this."

"Sovereign, then."

Jon dried his hands on his sleeves and sighed. "Maybe." If the last forty-eight hours had convinced him of anything, no god particularly cared for his fate.

The exterior metal door burst open, and two new prisoners stumbled through. The first man appeared middle-aged, bare chested and covered in dried blood, wearing a torn pair of trousers. His russet hair hung to the middle of his tattooed back, and he looked like he could put any of Kit's thugs in their urns if he wasn't already wounded. The second man, fat and balding, wore a green priest's robe. He teetered and landed on his face. With Kit's gang unconscious, the newcomers received only blank stares from everyone except Jon, who ran to the priest.

"Father Ferren." Jon fell to his knees before the still form of the Lorinth temple's principal priest. He shook the man's shoulder. Blood soaked through his filthy robe. "Wake up, Ferren."

The priest groaned and opened his eyes, swollen and bruised. "Not telling you a damn thing, you soulless . . ." he trailed off and blinked rapidly. "Fires and moons! That you, Therman?"

"Unfortunately."

A stirring from the pit alerted Jon. Kit and two of his thugs fell over a bench. Jon jumped and dragged Ferren in front of his own cell. Kit, Bert, and a tSolani man with sores covering his mouth stumbled to their feet.

"Hey, Jonny," Kit sang, stretching his arms overhead. "That weren't no coca, friend. You done us a *bad* turn." He lumbered over the bodies of his still-unconscious comrades and staggered toward Jon. Reaching into his trousers, Kit pulled out a crude knife.

Jon heaved Ferren behind him and held up his fists.

Kit lunged at Jon. Still under the drowsy spell, Kit slashed into the air as he stumbled. Jon knocked the blade from his hand, tripped him, and slammed his head into the ground. He lay unconscious and bleeding from the temple.

With chipped claws, the troll grabbed Jon's throat. In mid squeeze, the troll released him and slumped to the ground. The wounded man who'd come through the door with Ferren now stood over the troll, wielding a bolt the size of his forearm. Blood mingled with the orange rust on the head of the bolt. With bright yellow eyes, the man glared.

"Behind you!" Jon cried. The yellow-eyed man spun right into a knife held in the remaining thug's hand. It sank to the hilt into his stomach, blood oozing from the wound. Without pause, the yellow-eyed man ripped the knife from his own stomach and shoved it into his assailant's throat. The thug toppled over, and the yellow-eyed man collapsed to his knees. He pressed his hands over his wound and grinned. "Finally," he wheezed, then slumped forward.

Jon gasped and rushed to Ferren, dragging him the rest of the way into the cell. As the other drugged men twitched and moaned, he propped Ferren against the wall. When the clanging of a cage door and patter of quick feet sounded behind him, Jon turned. Hanna ran to the dry water trough with a tin bowl in hand. As she held up the bowl, not a breath passed before water gushed from the spout. At the sound of running water, all cell doors creaked open and prisoners emerged.

Haana scampered away, avoiding the desperate prisoners as they, too, produced vessels for their own water rations. Jon expected the girl to hide in her cell, but instead, she stood outside of his, extending the bowl with trembling hands. He let her in and quickly re-locked the door. Haana knelt before Ferren and used the fringe of her robe to dab fresh water over his face.

Ferren mumbled his thanks to the girl, who nodded and smiled. The priest's wounds revealed a severe whipping, front and back, and a deep cut to his ribs, likely puncturing his lung. With clammy fingers, he grabbed Jon's hand.

"She's alive, Jon," Ferren said. "Ella. They didn't get her. That's why—why they tortured me. They want your children. I don't—don't know why. I'm sorry. I wish I could tell you more. Ah—that old heathen, David. He was right. Drawls—these immortals—they've made themselves gods. I'm sorry—I'm sorry I helped spread their lies. May Sovereign have mercy on me." He grunted when Haana peeled back his robe at the shoulder. "May my shade haunt these heretics until the next moon breaks!"

Jon clutched the man's hand. "Ferren. Hey. Listen to me. You're the best burning priest I've ever known. You've brought something to the Lorinth temple that's never been there: kindness. You've looked after my family, helped raise my children. Nate got away too. They'll never find him. Too clever because you always pushed him, always showed him up when he got cocky. He was careful this time, and because of that, he lives. I can think of no one more suited for Sovereign's mercy than you, Emrell Ferren."

The priest spit blood. "Get out of here, Jon. Find a way. If anyone can, it's you. Get out. Go show the world the festering beast Drawlen has become." He gurgled, then tilted his head back and took his final, labored breaths.

Jon held his hand until his body stiffened and grayed with petrification.

Haana screeched, her gaze fixed on three of Kit's men outside the cage. Maneuvering a bolt and a block of wood, they worked to force the hinge pins from their housings.

Jon's mouth felt dry and sour. He reached into his boot, pulling out a steel dart. Haana plucked a sharp rock from the ground and stepped alongside him.

Behind the men, the yellow-eyed prisoner rose, his wounds no longer present.

Jon's arms fell to his side while he gaped, but he welcomed the miracle. Taking a deep breath, he pushed Haana into the corner of the cell. "Stay here," he ordered.

"Won't matter," one man said, holding the wooden plank. He cackled, and his comrades joined him. His laughter turned to a strangled cry when the yellow-eyed man fell upon him, stabbing him with the knife and tossing him in the air.

Jon grabbed the nearest man and yanked him face-first into the cell bars, knocking him unconscious. Then Jon shoved the drugged dart into the side of another man's neck, causing him to pass out. Two more men scrambled forward from the stocks, but the yellow-eyed man stood ready.

Unlocking the cell door, Jon strained to open it against the weight of the maimed men. Seeing the pile of bodies at this new resident's feet, the remaining thugs retreated.

Jon's accomplice threw out his hands in challenge. The crusted blood and chaotic back tattoo made him look like he belonged on a battlefield in another era. "Anyone else?" the man bellowed. "If it's hell you wish to enter, Rodden the World Burner is here to send you!"

At the stocks, the men gathered before scrambling into an empty cell, locking it, and cowering on the ground. The other thugs Jon had locked up struggled to secure their cell from the inside.

Rodden paced—no—he *prowled* before the cell block, his eerie stare causing the other inmates to huddle in their cages. Jon gawked. Where was the gash in his stomach? Or the many stab wounds that had covered him moments ago? He held an uncanny resemblance to a certain villain made so popular by the Drawlen church. But it couldn't be.

When Jon emerged from the cell, the man's stare caused him to hesitate.

But he peered past Jon. Smiling, he extended a hand to the girl. "It's going to be okay, Haana."

Her face brightened and she nodded before moving slowly toward the door.

Water dripped from the spout above the trough. The World Burner—Rodden the Fiend—fixated on the trickling fount. Then he pivoted to Jon and Haana. "I'm not overly fond of dungeons. Mylis tells me you two aren't either."

Jon shifted in front of Haana. "You're an immortal?"

Rodden dipped his chin in confirmation.

"How do we know we can trust you?" Jon asked.

"Your options aren't great," Rodden said. "Mylis spoke to me in secret. Told me to find the smuggler and Haana. Shared her plan to get us out. How about we go on our way?"

"And what way is that?" Jon asked.

Rodden pointed to the rusted door. "Raza is at work." A stream of water leaked under it, and liquid spurted from the door jam. The whine of metal under pressure echoed before the door burst open. From the hallway, a wall of water gushed, carrying along the bodies of four troll guards, all blue-faced and bloated.

Rodden sloshed through the brown-gray flow and pulled a pistol from the holster of a dead guard. He examined it. "Black powder. Cheap scoundrels." With a huff, he discarded the pistol and stepped over the threshold.

Wading through the water, Haana splashed down the hall after Rodden. Jon followed his new companions into the dark, latching the metal door behind him.

At the far end of the dim corridor rippled the shade door Jon had come through the day before. Rodden led them into an adjacent hall. They passed several chambers adorned with chains and stained with dried blood.

Searching the rooms, they scavenged an array of accessories. Jon found each of them a pistol, powder horns, and extra round shots. Rodden grabbed two sunrock lanterns, and Haana slipped on a pair of boots.

After a short trek, they came to a set of ascending stairs that, in the dim light, appeared endless. Water wept down the steps, twisting and dripping.

Rodden handed Haana one of the lanterns, and she marched up the steps.

Jon pressed against the wall of the staircase next to him. "How do you know this way will get us out?"

Rodden examined the water creeping along the floor away from the stairs. "Well, it's not the first time I've been here. Fortunately for you, my friends have made . . . arrangements. Consider yourself invited."

"Awfully kind of you," Jon said as they pursued Haana, side by side. No more deals with immortals after this was over, he thought.

"Don't thank me now," Rodden said. "I'm very expensive, and we're not out of this yet."

Jon peered into the gloom of the stairwell. "Well, I'm not exactly a rich man. But I'm a decent smuggler. Would you take a barter?"

Rodden chuckled. "That why you're in here?"

"Not exactly."

They climbed in silence. Just when Jon wished the stairs would end, they turned and continued. By the next level, his legs ached, but he rallied himself when Haana grunted at him.

At yet another landing, with his lungs burning, Jon slid down the wall and slumped to the ground. They halted at a steel door.

Rodden examined its lock and growled. "Fires."

Jon chuckled. "That curse takes on a little irony, coming from you."

Rodden fixed him with a narrow, yellow gaze. Jon hoped he hadn't angered the fae, but the man smirked. "It does, doesn't it? Not all legends are true though." He tapped the lock. "I don't suppose either of you found the key on any of the bodies?"

Reaching into the lining of his boot, Jon smiled at Rodden and held up a pair of lock picks.

Rodden scratched his brow. "This is a Yvean compound lock, you know. They're nearly impossible to pick."

As he struggled to his feet, Jon groaned, twirling one of the picks on his finger. "Well, that's just advertising."

After three tense minutes, the lock popped, and Jon pushed the door slowly. It opened with a low whine. Across the threshold water rolled, thick with dirt and fouler things, splashing past their feet and down the stairs. The dim light of their lanterns shone into a narrow, low corridor beyond.

Rodden grinned and tapped the open door. "Not bad for a smuggler."

Jon tucked the picks into his boot. "I do my best not to disappoint other high-profile criminals when I meet them."

Rodden chuckled and placed a hand on Haana's shoulder, stopping her at the door. The girl flinched, scowling at him. "It's a long way through here, little lady. Let us old men catch our breaths for a second." With a huff, he sat down in a dry spot and closed his eyes.

Jon rolled his head from side to side, his neck cracking. "So, you're really him, Rodden the Fiend?"

The immortal's eyes popped open. "Would you like an autograph? Maybe a lock of hair? I hear they're lucky."

"I'll pass." Jon waved his hand.

"What's your name, smuggler?" Rodden asked.

"Jon Therman."

Rodden bent forward and tilted his head, reminding Jon of a cat. "You wouldn't happen to be a rock smuggler from Taria, would you?"

Jon choked on his breath. "I must not be that good if I'm famous."

Rodden slapped his thighs and laughed. "I think Sovereign has a taste for irony. I'm an, eh, associate of your son, Remm."

Jon narrowed his eyes. "Remm."

Nodding, Rodden twirled his finger in the air. "Interesting lad. A little crazy. Takes a lot of risks. But he's good at what he does."

Jon was hesitant to believe his son—who had a violent hatred toward Drawlen—partnered with immortals. "And what exactly does he do?"

"He brings Drawlen heads to the First Lord of the Freelands."

Jon hummed in agreement. "With Shane zem'Arta?"

Rodden smiled broadly. "Those two are making a name for themselves. They're probably halfway here by now."

Jon snickered at the thought of Remm and Shane terrorizing Drawls at the behest of a mysterious, winged monarch.

"And Jon"—Rodden paused, frowning—"your daughter is likely with them."

The blood drained from Jon's face. "Why would she be with them?"

"We ran into her in Drawl. She and zem'Arta worked out a deal. We help her get some poor kid out of the Life Harvest, and she gets us a handshake with Krishena Dantiego. It started out well, but then—we ran into trouble."

Jon's mind swirled, picturing Ella dragging Shane into some hopeless cause. Ferren said the Drawls were looking for her. And now she was coming to them. He imagined her being tossed into the Wraith Cellar, clothes torn, blood on her face.

His head throbbed. His hands trembled. "No, no!" He punched the wall, bruising his knuckles. "I can't. I can't lose all of them."

A light pressure stilled one of his arms. Haana rested her hands over his shaking fist, gazing at him with a soft smile.

Rodden sighed. "You paid a heavy price for coming here, didn't you?"

Jon shook his head. "They came to my village. Tried to take my little boy. I came through the wraith gate first. I don't know what happened, but it didn't work after that. I have no idea where they are."

With fierce but weary eyes, Rodden regarded Jon. Like Richard and Halas, the man bore the weight of immortality on his soul. "You won't be stuck here for long, Therman. We're getting out. We're going to tear a hole in Refsul's gut, one he can't come back from. And if the rest of your family are as clever and stubborn as Remm and Ella, they may yet live."

# 32

# BRIMHOLT

*Smuggler's Cabin East of Shevak*
*July 24, 1195 PT*

*Shane*

The moons hung low when Shane and Morgel reached the remote smuggler's cabin. Morgel elbowed Shane and pointed past the building. Ella sat upon a wide tree stump, her back facing them. Shane nodded, parting from the voiceless ralenta, and headed along the grassy path.

He slid onto the stump next to Ella and fidgeted.

Tears staining her cheeks, she hugged her legs to her chest. "What could the Drawls want with my family?" she whispered.

"We don't know," Shane said. "But we'll find out and return the favor."

She sniffled and rubbed her nose. "I don't want payback, Shane. I want my family." Her eyes filled with tears, and she leaned into him.

Shane cringed, then lifted his arm and awkwardly placed it around her shoulder. Each time she showed up in his life, Ella had challenged his belief about himself. Now this girl mourned the good things torn from her life. And all Shane did with his blessings was hold them at arm's length. Maybe when he returned to Setmal, he would give Venna the dance he owed her.

After a long silence, Ella cleared her throat and wiped her cheeks with her sleeve. "I hardly recognized Remm."

Shane blew out a long breath. "It's been ten years."

"No, I mean, his eyes. I don't see my brother in them. It's like he's hiding."

Perhaps Shane's brothers felt the same the few times they'd seen him since they were children. He knew why. He squeezed Ella's shoulder. "When you're the one that had to leave, it's hard to face the ones you left. Brings back all the pain."

"Is that why you write Nate and me, because it's easier than trying to go back to your own family?"

"Yeah," Shane said, lifting his arm off her shoulder and cracking his knuckles. "Plus, that midget brother of yours needed some pointers. He's bound for trouble."

Ella chuckled, her frame shaking against his side. "If anything, you encouraged him."

"That's what I said. Pointers."

She threw her head back and laughed.

A banging door drowned out their conversation. Tres burst from the cabin. Rose followed, red in the face.

"*Groundling*?" she spat. "Would you like it if I called you a pixie?"

Ella and Shane spun around.

Tres whirled on the human girl, shifted his form, and unfurled his wings.

"Woah," Ella said.

"Do I look like a pixie to you, fool?" Tres said.

Battle-hardened men had cowered before the Second Lord. But not Rose. The Drawlen brat—as Carris had dubbed her—folded her arms and rolled her eyes.

Rose huffed. "Sorry. Oversized bat."

Tres growled and soared into the sky. Rose threw up her hands and stomped into the cabin. Ella gazed at Tres's fading silhouette in the night sky. "I've never seen a terrion before."

"I've never seen anyone talk back to him like that." Shane smiled at Ella. "Don't get me wrong, she's a major pain. But I like her."

Ella grinned. "Me too."

An hour later, Shane's company tacked up their horses. A faint gray light stained the eastern sky. Krishena mounted her steed and addressed the group.

The Rogue Master had initially been suspicious of Shane but warmed up to him over the past few days, or at least to the idea of their partnership. She seemed eager at the prospect of breaking into the Drawlen temple and making off with Refsul's most-wanted enemy. If they succeeded, this would be the crown jewel for Krishena's reputation.

"We'll reach Shevak by midafternoon if we keep a good pace," she said. "If we work quickly, we'll have the upper hand. My people are prepared, and we've contacted your Red Watch agent." She raised a brow at Shane. "Curious that you should have acquired Jon Therman's brother-in-law as your insider."

Joran was merely a go-between for Tessa and the rest of the Red Watch network, but Shane had kept that to himself. He shrugged. "I like to keep things tidy."

"Shall we get on?" Tres said. "Or is this a social hour?"

"Let's move," Shane said, mounting his horse. "We've got a damsel in distress to rescue."

Krishena slapped the reins on the side of her horse and led the group. Calla flitted ahead in a shadowy ribbon to scout the road. He still had not given Shane an answer about how he'd disposed of the unbound shade in Setmal.

Ella, Hale, and Rose trotted after Carris, Morgel, and Remm. Shane and Tres rode at the rear.

Rose's hushed voice carried in the morning breeze. "These people can't be trusted, Ella," she said. "They're everything you think of when you hear about murderous rogues and pirates."

"Those are my favorite kinds of people. They're never boring," Ella's humor masked her grief. It seemed to be a Therman thing.

Hale glanced over his shoulder. "Rose is right. The troll fellow isn't so bad, though."

Rose scoffed. "Not so bad? He's a *troll*!"

"I'm just saying, he probably won't stab me at a moment's notice." Hale rubbed his neck. "Unlike the others. Especially the flyer."

"Oof! Don't even get me started," Rose said. "The goblin woman gives me the creeps. And honestly, I never thought I'd miss your cooking, El."

Ella rose in her stirrups and glared at the mousy-haired girl. "What's wrong with my cooking?"

Hale and Rose glanced at each other. Then Hale said, "You do tend to overcook things a bit."

"Oh, burn you both." Ella huffed. She hung back, steering her horse between Shane and Tres.

"Miss me?" Shane asked.

"Is my cooking that bad?"

Shane scratched the back of his head. "I mean, it's been a few years for me. I'm sure it's . . . improved."

Ella rolled her eyes and shifted her attention to Tres. "So, you're popular."

As he sat erect in his saddle, Tres glared straight ahead. The horses trotted along the grassy path.

Ella turned to Shane. "Where'd you find him?"

"I work for his brother. Neither of us really had a choice."

Tres rolled his eyes at Ella, then fixed his gaze on the path. "Certainly not zem'Arta's usual crowd. Not among your favorite kinds of people either, I hear."

Ella forced a laugh. "Well, I don't really rub shoulders with noblemen in my line of work."

"One would hope not." Tres ducked under a pine branch as their horses jostled up a hill. When they descended the small rise, he said, "You seem recovered."

"Oh, yeah. I feel pretty good, actually."

"I hope it was worth it." Tres glowered at Shane.

"Of course it was!" Shane flicked his reins. "No one in Palimar picks locks faster than this kid. And no one knows better how to slip past a street full of police while dragging an unconscious body."

Tres shook his head. "I'll not bother asking."

"Please don't," Ella said with a frown. "Thanks, though, for bringing Mona to heal me."

Tres locked eyes on Ella and furrowed his brow. "We will soon learn if your gratitude is worth anything, groundling. I trust you won't make a habit of disregarding orders and trying to play hero when my life is in the balance."

Ella gaped, her eyes wide.

"Hey!" Shane pulled on the reins and maneuvered his horse between the two. "Rodden picked that fight. It had nothing to do with her. You're a real asshole, Romanus."

Tres snorted. Kicking his horse into a canter, he rode ahead by himself.

All chatter amongst the riders ceased. The clip-clop of hooves filled the woods. Ella hung in Remm's shadow, but he flinched every time she came near.

As the sun dipped to the west, they crested the overlook of Shevak, the cliffside home of the Drawlen Immortal Order. Two raging mountain rivers split the city into thirds. Arched bridges connected the various boroughs. The Temple Setvan loomed at the crown of the city, tucked against a seventy-foot cliff of smooth granite. The many shrines within its walls sparkled like an open box of jewels set atop a busy ant hill.

The clock towers rang in the sixth hour when Shane's group traversed the heart of the city. They passed their horses to a stableman before gathering in the parlor of a stately manor within the wealthy Goldway borough.

"What's this place called?" Carris asked.

"Brimholt," Ella said. "It's how rich people do things. They're too good for addresses."

Carris cackled. "Oh, I like you so much better than your foul-mouthed brother."

Remm smirked and pretended to drop a throwing knife, landing it between Carris's feet. She plucked it from the floor and flicked her wrist, sticking it deep into the ceiling. Ella covered her mouth to keep from laughing.

Two men entered the room. The first, tall with dark skin and black hair bound at his neck, closed the door behind them. His tailored maroon suit hugged his frame perfectly. His companion, a shorter muscular man with a plain shirt and tired green eyes, stepped forward, his eyes widening at the sight of them.

"Joran!" Ella said. She ran to the second man, who enveloped her in his thick arms. He closed his eyes and breathed a long sigh.

Then his gaze fell on Shane. He let go of Ella as his expression contorted into a scowl. He sprang toward the Freelander, fists balled and spitting as he yelled, "You murderer! You made her—you promised!"

To Shane's—and everyone else's—surprise, Tres pulled Joran away. He backed Joran against the wall and held him firmly by the collar. A faint buzz hummed in the air as he employed mind craft to supplant the man's rage. "If you must vent your anger, outlander, the closest you'll get to the responsible party is me."

Joran's breathing slowed. "All of you. All of you got Tessa killed! You promised to protect—" He sank to the floor and buried his head in his hands.

Shane hated himself for the things he'd done in the name of the Red Watch. Joran had every right to his anger. Liiesh and his agents had used Tessa like a mouse in a snake pit. But he couldn't say such out loud, so instead, he grimaced and offered platitudes. "We can still protect Haana," he said. "The Drawls made a move we didn't expect. I'm sorry for what happened to your sister. But we'll tear that temple apart to get her daughter out. That's why we're here."

"I'm not an idiot, troll," Joran spat. "I know who you really came for. I know they have Rodden Morien in the temple."

Shane crouched to Joran's eye level. "Hate me if it suits you. Tessa chose to stay in Setvan six years ago. She chose to do as much damage to them as she could while she drew breath. Your sister died for Drawlen greed. Be angry, but not at us. We won't leave without Haana. Do you want a part in this or not?" He held out his hand.

Joran stared for a long moment before grunting and taking it.

"Well," said the man in the maroon suit. "Now dat we're all getting along, welcome to Brimholt. I am Abad il'Dani. Calla has told me why you've come. But even before dat, I've been hearing a lot of chatter from all around de city." He pivoted toward Tres. "You have a problem, master terrion. Your enemy knows you're coming. And while I am very good at sneaking around, I can't make you invisible."

Folding his arms, Tres nodded. "We expected a welcome gift."

Abad swept a hand across the room. "At every door and window out of dis place? Dey've blocked you in, Freelander. De sewers, de caves below the city, de cliffs above it."

Tres looked at Shane. "Check for a weak point. We need to exit this city by daybreak."

Shane nodded and snapped his fingers. Remm, Bren, and Morgel vanished in ribbons of black. "The rest of you get some sleep," he said, falling into the couch before the hearth. The door clicked shut, and Shane closed his eyes.

Allowing his vision to settle in the darkness, Shane rubbed his eyes. Ella and Remm spoke quietly, out of his line of sight.

"They miss you, Remm," Ella said. "We all miss you. I don't care what you've had to do. I can't imagine—"

"No, and I hope you never have to. I'm a killer, Ella. Don't you know that by now?" Remm spoke with more sincerity than Shane had ever heard.

"My hands aren't exactly clean," Ella replied.

"Can you count the number of people you've turned to ash?"

"Yes—"

"Well, I can't."

Ella sighed. "The world has been cruel to you, Remm. It doesn't change the fact that you're my brother."

Remm clicked his tongue. "You sweet, innocent little mouse. Don't you get it? Some killers are made. Others are born. I'm the latter. You don't belong in my world, sister, and I don't belong in yours. When this is over, you'll go back with our father to your smuggling and dreaming, and I'll go back to decorating Palimar with Drawlen blood."

Shane glimpsed the top of Remm's head, bobbing as he walked out of the room. Then Ella slammed her fist onto the table.

She met Shane's gaze, startled, with crimson cheeks and stormy eyes. This wasn't a child barely avoiding a slaver's brig, or a girl thrilled at the chance to pick a few locks for a foreign mercenary. This was a woman embittered. Shane would have to remember to beat the lungs out of Remm when this mad hunt was over. The man was an insufferable ass, but he could at least be grateful for his family's unconditional devotion.

"Sorry," Ella said, massaging her knuckles.

"Want me to break his arm for you? He deserves it."

Ella smiled, but immediately faltered. "Is he?"

"Is he what?"

"A born killer."

*Yes,* Shane thought, but he stayed quiet for a long moment. "The first time I met him, he tried to drown me. He saw me talking to you, tracked me to my ship, saw me with Henrick. He was only eleven, but he knew exactly what he was doing, like he'd done it before. He told me once he *needed* to purge the wicked from the world. If he must kill, he's found the best way to do it. We don't deal with the innocent, El."

Ella pursed her lips and stared at him. "Thank you, Shane."

"I'm not sure I deserve gratitude for that."

Ella rubbed her arms. "You always tell me the truth."

"Well, I don't have much else going for me." He spotted Bren down the hall. The boy nodded to him and disappeared through a doorway.

"Time to move." Shane rose and steered Ella toward the corridor. "We're probably gonna have a fight on our hands tonight. You can show that idiot you're not the innocent little mouse he thinks you are."

"So, what am I, a tiger?"

Shane laughed. "Maybe a viper."

They entered the dimly lit back room. It was set up as a servant's quarters but operated more as the meeting space of Jon and Abad's smuggling network. Abad stood at one end of a tall square table, Krishena and Calla flanking him. No longer wearing her many tSolani bracelets, Krishena had donned the more practical wrist guards. Her dreadlocks were tied back, and she carried a pistol at her belt.

Calla, on the other hand, took a different approach. When Shane had faced him in Drawl, he wore rags, disguised as a street beggar. Now, clad in fitted black pants and a padded shirt, he took his spot at the table with knives protruding from every place possible. Coils of red-powder fuses hung on his belt. His face was clean-shaven, and he'd combed his hair straight back.

Although the two rogues were married, the way they glared at each other suggested a mere business arrangement.

Hale and Rose hovered off to the side, looking respectively determined and nervous. Joran and the rest of Shane's crew waited around the table. Their attention shifted when Shane and Ella approached. Tres stepped to the side, making room for them.

Shane planted his hands on the flaking surface while he pored over a map of the city. The ink of his left forearm tattoo had faded considerably. Or maybe it was dirt. He scratched at it.

"It's like a clogged sieve out there," Remm said. "Not a damn window shutter left open."

Morgel shook his head and held out his open palms, showing he'd not found anything either.

Shane crossed his arms and nodded at Bren. "Anything?"

The boy, gangly and growing by the day, bit into the rye roll in his hand. He shrugged. "There's a few caves, but you'd have to risk the river. I struggled to get there."

"That might be our only option," Shane said with a sigh.

Abad shook his head. "Dat's probably where dey want you to go. My people are setting up false trails. De Drawls assume you have arrived unprepared and without aid. We will keep dem believing dat. But we still need to find a way to get you out dat doesn't involve starting a war in de streets. My people are smugglers, not fighters."

"What about a distraction?" Hale asked.

"You're staying here," Ella said. "You too, Rose."

Hale moved closer to the table. "But Ella, we—"

"Can you pick a lock?" Shane interrupted.

Hale shook his head.

"Can you shoot? Can you throw a knife? Do you know any stealth protocol? Have you ever killed anyone?"

Hale shook his head and mumbled "no" to all of Shane's questions.

Shane gestured around the room. "Everyone at this table has at least ten jobs like this under their belt. I get that you want to help your friend. So help her by staying safe and alive."

Hale regarded Shane and Ella with wide eyes. Ella responded with pursed lips. Remm, too, regarded Ella with slack-jawed surprise.

"They know I'm involved with the Red Watch," Joran said. "Wherever I show up, Drawls will come swarming. Perhaps we should use that to our advantage."

Shane nodded. "We'll use that for keeping the rats away while we're in the temple. Once we get our people out of the Cellar, though, I don't think any distraction will do the trick."

"There must be another way out," Tres said. "Something they haven't accounted for."

All eyes turned to the map, and for a long moment, no one spoke.

"So," Carris said, leaning forward, "they've corked the bottle. All Refsul's best throat-cutters are at the gates, on the walls, in the sewers."

"He's thorough," Calla said. "He must know there's something worth catching if he's gone to the trouble of setting such a fine trap."

Carris and Morgel exchanged a glance and smiled wickedly. Carris jammed a clawed finger onto the southeast gate. "So, if he's prowling all the doors and windows, who's watching the throne room?" She moved her finger to the drawing of an octagon in the middle of the Temple Setvan. "Isn't there a nice, big trap door in the middle of this dung pile?"

She looked at Shane with a sharp-toothed grin. Shane mimicked her smile. "Carris, you burning little elf genius."

"Don't call me *elf*!"

# 33

# THE WELL

*The Wraith Cellar*
*July 24, 1195 PT*

*Jon*

As Jon, Rodden, and Haana trudged through the musty corridors of the Wraith Cellar labyrinth, hours crept by. Jon felt claustrophobic within the low ceiling, walls, and floor, all made from smooth stone. The stink of sewage hung around them. Periodically, a warm current wafted from a side passage, and Rodden urged them forward. Sweat dripped into Jon's eyes. The lantern in Rodden's hand grew dim. Perhaps only a few hours of light remained between his and the one Haana carried. Jon watched his feet, avoiding the pockmarks and uneven edges of the path. Haana's boots thudded on the hard surface ahead of him.

Bumping against the wall, Jon felt water trickle down a crack in the mortar. He wiped the slime from his hand onto his pant leg. "I thought we might run into a guard or two by now."

Rodden glanced over his shoulder. "They've abandoned the labyrinth. Doesn't mean this place is unoccupied."

When a yowl reverberated behind them, Haana stuffed her hand into her pocket, where she had stowed a pistol. Rodden skittered forward, ducking under a low beam. Jon jogged alongside Haana, searching periodically above and behind.

Another hour passed. Rodden stopped at an intersection and checked each passage. He handed his lantern to Jon and pointed down the right tunnel. "Keep going. Don't turn until you come to the end of this path. Then go right.

I should catch up by then, but if not, don't take any turns after that. Go straight until it dead-ends." He stepped to his left and transformed into a brown alley cat.

Haana craned her neck as the cat padded into the darkness.

"It's pretty amazing, isn't it?" Jon said.

Haana shrugged. "I—thought he'd be bigger."

Jon smiled, relieved his patience had begun to thaw her frigid demeanor. "You're right. When I heard as a boy that Rodden the Fiend prowls the world in the form of a *great cat*, this isn't what I expected." He winked, earning the closest thing to a smile he'd seen from her.

They continued down the passage. By the time they reached the next intersection, Jon's lantern had fizzled, and he discarded it next to the wall. They veered right but stopped as the light from Haana's lantern exposed a gray, panting form.

Jon and Haana stared into the pointed, slate-eyed face of a dire rat. About the size of a wolf, it sat still for a moment and hissed. Then it squealed and hurtled at them. Jon reached for his pistol and aimed. When he pulled the trigger, only a hollow click followed.

With the rodent inches away, Jon grabbed his dagger, pushing the girl behind him. Haana screeched, and a wind cut through the tunnel, toppling the rat. Jon lunged at it and jabbed his blade into its armpit, puncturing the heart in a single thrust.

Haana yanked Jon by the collar. As he fell, a second dire rat emerged and climbed upon the corpse. Jon scrambled backward as Haana fumbled with her pistol. The rodent hobbled over its fallen nestmate, one of its forelegs tucked against its belly.

Another growl, even more predatory, came from the adjoining corridor. A brown and black hellcat the size of a horse streaked toward the rat, tackled it, and disappeared down another hall. Squeals and growls echoed, then stilled. A second later, the hellcat pounced into the lamplight and shifted into Rodden's sapien form. His pants were torn, and long, shallow scratches covered his back. Blood splattered his face.

Jon closed his eyes and dropped his shoulders. "You're a welcome sight."

Haana mumbled, "Still smaller than I thought."

Rodden huffed. "Burning things got away from me."

"Just the two?" Jon said.

"There's a nest. We've gone wide around it. That's why it's taking so burning long. But don't worry, we're nearly—"

A rumbling erupted. All three pivoted, fixated on the passage now filling with rats. The darkness writhed and squealed.

"Fires! Run!" Jon grabbed Haana's arm and sprinted through the tunnel, keeping himself between her and the stampede of vermin. He steered them around corner after corner, Rodden at his heels. The farther they ran, the more the labyrinth transitioned from cut stone and mortar to hewn granite. With each turn, the arched hallways grew more dilapidated.

Several feet behind them, rats swarmed along the ground and scampered across the walls, howling and hissing. Jon sprang and stumbled over rubble from a rusted track. He snatched a loose rail lying on the ground and hammered at the rotting trusses that framed the crumbling rock in the ceiling.

Rodden too seized a bar and battered above them. In the middle of the corridor, Haana pointed her pistol into the darkness. As the ceiling frame creaked and bowed, the rats arrived.

*Bang!* The first rat met with Haana's round shot and skidded along the ground. The beams and rock plummeted. Jon grabbed Haana, spilling half the sunrock dust from her lantern. All three lunged from the onslaught of falling rock, instantly separating them from the teeming rodents. As the dust settled, the three fugitives stood gasping in the dim passage.

Jon hunched over, hands on his knees, panting next to Rodden. "Please tell me you know another detour."

"We'll mark our way just to be sure." Rodden followed the mining tracks until the metal disappeared under another pile of rubble. He stepped around the heap, scratching a line on the wall.

Haana ran ahead, splashing through puddles, then stopped, mesmerized by the water. From her pocket, she pulled Mylis's necklace. Kissing the locket, she dangled it above the liquid before dipping it in. At once, the water crawled along the floor as though the labyrinth had been tipped to one side.

She followed the flow while Jon and Rodden jogged to keep pace. "Friend of yours?" Jon asked.

Sloshing through the water, Rodden nodded. "Seems so."

The light from Haana's sunrock lantern dimmed while they pursued her. The drum of a waterfall overtook the sound of trickling water below their feet.

Haana halted as Jon stepped forward, but she pulled him back, smiling. Before him lay a drop into an abyss.

Haana opened the lantern and shook some powder over the ledge, illuminating a five-foot descent into a black pool. The water swirled angrily. After setting down the lantern, Haana bent her knees and pushed off the ledge.

"No!" Jon reached for her but missed. The water splashed his face as she disappeared.

Rodden placed a hand on Jon's shoulder. "Just hold your breath." He, too, leapt into the water.

Jon gulped and grabbed the lantern. "Mother of dryads." With legs shaking and heart pounding, he plunged into the well.

The cold water stung. It dragged him deep, the pressure bearing down like hammers in his ears. His hand scraped the bottom, and the water's tide thrust him forward.

Just when he ran out of breath, the current spat him onto the frigid ground. In his arms, he cradled the lantern with a smidge of powder remaining. Rolling to his side, he jumped to his feet and held out the light. It seemed as if an invisible wall held back the water, partitioning the aqueduct.

Jon joined his two companions, equally wet and shivering. "Drowning would have been a poetic end to this crucible." He cast the light on Rodden's face. "Not that it matters much for you."

Rodden shook himself, draining water from his ears. "Immortality does have its perks." He led them down the cramped aqueduct as their only remaining lantern extinguished. "Just around this corner."

When they turned, a yellow light blinded them. Jon shielded his eyes, but Haana shrieked and bolted ahead.

"Haana!" a woman's voice cried.

As Jon exited the aqueduct and lowered his hand, Mylis, the Eternal Oracle, came into view. Though she wore the same flowing green gown, her intricately pinned hair and delicately painted face befitted a queen.

Beside her stood a most otherworldly person. More like a painting than a man, he reached Mylis's shoulders, sporting a bald head and a braided white beard that draped down his bare chest. Wearing only shimmering pants, he regarded Jon with eyes of wavering colors.

Bending down, Mylis embraced the girl, and they cried quietly together.

Jon rubbed the back of his neck, prying away from the intimate moment. His boots crunched on a pile of coins that littered the well's floor. Above them, the water hung suspended, distorting the view of a room beyond, lit with sunrock lanterns.

The stranger next to Mylis bowed and cast his twinkling eyes on Rodden. "Hello, old friend."

Stepping toward the man, Rodden smirked. "Good to see you, Raza."

The water above Raza shimmered as he spoke. "It's good to see you on two legs. I'm sure your lady will be quite pleased."

Rodden patted his thighs. "Hopefully it will make up for all the trouble I've caused. But her brother might not be as easily swayed."

Raza folded his arms across his chest and nodded.

"Gentlemen." Mylis rose to her feet.

Haana pressed herself into Mylis's skirt, the green and ivory layers folding around her.

"Lady Mylis." Rodden inclined his head. "We are grateful for your help."

"I do not seek gratitude, my Lord Rodden, only that my wish be fulfilled."

"I don't know the terms of your deal with Romanus," Rodden said. "But the First Lord is good for his word. I wouldn't suffer his lordship over me otherwise."

"We shall see." Mylis faced Jon. "I thank you, mortal, for what you have done for my Haana. She is . . . she is the one precious thing to me that remains in this world."

"Tessa—what happened to her?" Jon asked.

Mylis's lips quivered. "Selvator Kane's anger. I will speak no more of it." She pulled the girl forward and cupped her cheeks. "My sweet one. You have endured so much. Today, you begin a new life. This man," she pointed to Jon. "He is your uncle—the husband of your mother's sister."

The girl's eyes widened, and she furrowed her brow.

Mylis lifted Haana's chin. "I'd hoped you and I would have more time, truly. But Lord Selvator acted out of turn, and now we must flee. The world outside these walls is nothing like the one you know, Haana. It is both better and worse. I am entrusting you to these men."

Haana shook her head and leaned toward Mylis, who stroked the girl's hair.

"Listen. I will come with you, but I cannot remain by your side." She peeled back the green silk sleeve from her arm to reveal inky blotches on her skin. Above her elbow, the skin looked like unlit charcoal, wafting with the faint smell of rotting fruit.

"Oh, my lady." Raza placed his hand on her arm.

"I thought you were immortal," Jon said.

Mylis lowered her sleeve. "Your people call us blessed. But it is a lie. Refsul uses the Life Harvest to purge our bodies of Corruption. Yet it spreads the more we . . . return. When we disobey him, he makes sure we remember our place. I was slain twelve times in the last week and denied the Cleansing."

"Because you're helping the Red Watch?" Jon asked.

"Because I was party to Tessa's deception. She tricked Selvator Kane into believing she was a foreseer and that Haana possessed shade craft. I believe you played a part in helping Tessa take your wife's place originally. Deception has been her only means of survival these past twenty years."

"And you helped her?" Rodden asked.

Mylis shook her head. "I didn't know the nature of her schemes until Raza came to me three days ago. Selvator has left Shevak, and Refsul does not suspect my involvement with the Red Watch yet." She raised her chin, the fluttering light of the water reflecting on her face. "I'm sure that will change shortly, so we have little time."

"Selvator is in Taria," Jon said. "That's how I got here. That little demon came to my town, looking for my wife and my children. Have they . . . did anyone else come through the gate after me?"

"It stopped working for a whole day," Mylis said. "Now they are sending soldiers and purifiers through. Tell me, are any of your children ralenta?"

"The youngest might be. But he's only thirteen."

Rodden growled. "Sel will certainly be after him."

"Don't they have a horde of their own already?" Jon asked.

"I don't understand it fully," Rodden said. "Only that Refsul and his children need ralenta of a certain bloodline. Something to do with Corruption. A closely kept secret between Refsul and his son."

Raza stroked his beard. "He had other children that he made immortal. Their fates were not kind."

Jon studied the water suspended above Raza. "So you're immortal too."

Raza bowed, and his body quivered. "One of the Seven Immortals. I hid from Refsul when I learned the disturbing nature of our blessing. Now, however, it seems Sovereign's hand is against him, and I've lost my taste for being a coward. I'm an elemental of water, the last of my kin. There are none like me born today. The power of the fae is fading." He drew a hand to his chest. "Our punishment for what we have wrought on the world."

"What have you wrought, exactly?"

"The Dying. It fuels our immortality. We corrupted Sovereign's gift, the Everstone, and now the whole world pays the price."

Jon gestured to Mylis's arm. "The price? Being used like cheap game pieces on a board where you immortals bicker between yourselves over a disaster of your own making?"

A coin dropped from the water above and clattered on the floor. A Freeland five mark. A shadowy figure, distorted by the rippling water, leaned over the ledge of the well, peering down at them.

# 34

# THE HALL OF PROPHECY

*Temple Setvan, Shevak*
*July 24, 1195 PT*

*Jon*

Jon squinted at the figure hovering over the rim of the well. His pulse thrummed.

"Your escort is waiting," Mylis said.

With a curl of Raza's wrist, the water bent and pressed to one side from below, exposing a stone ladder built into the wall. "Go. I must continue to play my part here."

Haana drew Mylis to the ladder, and they climbed into the room. Jon and Rodden followed. They emerged from the well into the center of a wide, domed room decorated with glittering gold accents. Pilastered windows and doors lined the circular space.

"Papa," Ella cried as she flung herself at Jon in a bone-crushing embrace. His legs buckled, and the two clung together on the marble floor. Ella sobbed into his shoulder.

"My little girl," Jon whispered, pressing against her messy curls.

He drew back and cupped the sides of her face. A haunted light shone in her puffy eyes. Kissing her forehead, he lifted her to stand next to him.

When Rodden came over the rim of the well, a hush settled in the space. Leaning against an idealized statue of Mylis, Shane zem'Arta folded his arms over his chest and glared. "You're in one piece."

A harsh light flashed in Rodden's eyes before he schooled himself. "I'm sure I don't deserve it."

Jon approached Shane who flashed a crooked, sharp-toothed grin, his blue eyes clashing with the warm light of the room. Another scar decorated his face. Jagged and deeper than the other three, perhaps he'd earned this one in a fight instead of a court room.

"We need to stop meeting like this, Jon," he said. "People are going to start rumors."

Gripping Shane's wrist, Jon patted him on the back. "It'll spoil both our reputations."

"Welcome to the show," Shane said, clutching Jon's wrist.

"The invitation was hard to turn down."

"Meet my crew." Shane gestured to a short woman with sharply pointed ears who sat on a bench pressed against the wall. "This is Carris."

Nodding to Jon, she balanced a curved knife on her outstretched finger. Beside her, a Greqi man perched on the back of the bench, retying his black topknot.

"And the silent one here is Morgel." Shane pointed to a cove behind them where Remm stood, partially obscured by a statue. "And this scoundrel needs no introduction."

Remm stared with the same look he used to give Jon as a boy whenever his father caught him snatching cakes or sneaking out at night. He was lanky, much taller than Jon expected—a bittersweet reminder of the ten years since Jon had last seen him.

Jon strode toward him. "Seems you've found your way into trouble again, boy."

Remm's lips twitched into a smirk. "I blame my parents."

They remained a few steps apart, the weight of the past decade holding them back. Jon nodded at the deep gash on Remm's cheek. "Still don't watch your left side."

Remm chuffed. "Gotta have *some* flaws."

Chuckling, Jon pulled his eldest son into a fatherly embrace, slapping him gently on the back. When he moved away, Remm tugged at a curl of Jon's hair along his ear. "You got some gray, Pops."

"I blame my children."

Ella crouched, eye level with Haana, who ducked behind Mylis. "Hey there." She extended a hand toward the girl.

The girl poked her face out and fidgeted with her necklace.

Mylis put a hand on Haana's shoulder and stepped back. "It's all right. These are the people who have come to take us from this prison. This woman"—she motioned to Ella—"is your cousin, Ella. She is Jon's daughter. And this is his son, Remm." She waved a delicate hand at Remm, who turned away from the child's hard gaze.

Ella smiled. "It's nice to meet you, Haana."

Carris poked Rodden in the arm. "Been a while since you stood up straight, eh? Might wanna consider a haircut too, pussy cat."

Rodden muffed her hair. "I always think of you, Carris, whenever I want to get my life in order."

Hinges creaked as a tSolani boy entered the room. Around Nate's age, he reminded Jon of a tall and gangly Remm in his early teen years.

"How do we stand, Bren?" Shane asked.

Without blinking, Bren replied in monotone, "Dantiego's rogues have started their distraction. We should move now. The gate is empty."

Removing a boot, Jon shook out some water. "What kind of party are you guys planning this time?"

Remm flipped a coin into the air and caught it. "It's a page right out of your book, Pops. We're going through the cellar door while their backs are turned."

Jon's stomach dropped. He wished to never see or think about a wraith gate again. "You . . . know how to work it?"

"Mr. Chatty does." Remm pointed his thumb at Morgel.

The Greqi man inclined his head at Jon with a grunt and a wink.

"Bren," Shane addressed the boy. "You're Morgel's backup if he can't work the gate."

Nodding, Bren moved behind Morgel.

Shane snapped a finger at Carris. "You're the vanguard. Keep our way clear."

"I'll slice up whatever's in front of us." Carris gave a sharp-toothed grin, and flexed her thick, chipped claws.

"Rodden." Shane's voice dropped as he ran a hand over his face. "If you pick another fight, I swear to Sovereign, I'll hand you back to Liiesh in pieces."

When Rodden locked eyes with Shane, Jon wondered who was more dangerous.

"Understood. Captain." Rodden saluted by pressing his left fist to his chest.

Shane put a hand on Ella's shoulder. "We need to get through fast and quiet, El. We're taking a cellar tunnel from here to the greenhouse. There are two locked doors. How long do you need for a compound lock?"

"Twenty seconds, maybe thirty."

"Fires," Rodden said under his breath.

"That's our little mouse," Remm sang, draping his arm around Ella's other shoulder. He wagged an eyebrow at Shane. "Am I allowed to take souvenirs?"

"No," a voice boomed as the heavy curtains drew aside, revealing a lean, stoic man with honey-colored skin. His long hair, bound atop his head by a leather cord, framed his sharp face. At his hip hung an ancient sword.

"All set?" Shane asked.

The terrion nodded, then fixed his obsidian eyes on Jon, who felt pulled into his gaze, like the man could perceive his every thought.

"Tres Romanus," Ella whispered in a bitter tone. "Second Lord of the Freelands."

Tres narrowed his eyes, and Jon assumed he heard Ella from across the room. "You are responsible for these two delinquents?" Tres nodded at Ella and Remm.

Crossing his arms, Jon glowered. Here stood one of the most powerful and feared men in Palimar, attempting a daring escape with Jon's help and his children's. Yet he had the audacity to insult them.

"Be *grateful*, spire lord," Jon retorted, keeping his tone level. "Rodden might still be locked in the Cellar if it wasn't for me. And I'm guessing you wouldn't have made it into this city alive if it weren't for these two." He gestured to Ella and Remm, who both straightened.

Shane gave Jon a sinister smirk, then regarded the terrion behind him. "This is Jon Therman, Master Smuggler of Corigon."

"You intend to take us through the wraith gate, Lord Romanus?" Every head turned as Mylis spoke with an air of doubt. Beside her, Haana stared at Tres with pursed lips. She stepped in front of Mylis, lifting her head high and crossing her arms.

"We have made the appropriate arrangements," Tres said.

"Meaning?" Mylis placed her hands on Haana's shoulders.

"You shall see."

"Where will the gate take us?" Jon asked. "I'm not going through that thing again unless I know the destination."

“Zeree,” Shane answered.

Tres shot the troll a displeased glance.

Jon threw up his hands. “I need to get back to Lorinth.”

Shane drew in a long breath. “Dantiego sent people there already. This is the only way out of Shevak, Jon. Refsul knows we're here. He's locked every gate, gutter, cellar, cave, even every burning mousehole that leads out of this city. And he'll keep it that way for a while. So, the fastest way for you to get home is—”

“To go hundreds of miles in the other direction?” Jon clenched his fists.

“Yes,” Shane said. “It's not my favorite place either.”

Remm and Carris snickered.

Jon ran a hand through his hair. He frowned, swiping his greasy fingers down his pants.

Shane waved to Rodden and Morgel. “You two make sure Mylis and the girl get through, no matter what.” Then he turned to Tres. “Keep a look out for company, but stay clear of any ralenta.”

Tres tilted his head. “Naturally.”

“Jon,” Shane said, “back up Ella with the locks and keep an eye out for shooters when we get to the platform. Remm will get you a crossbow. Guns are too loud.”

“I agree.” Jon removed his other boot and shook out the water.

“Ok,” Shane said, circling a hand above his head. “Let's get out of this snake pit.”

One by one, his crew members followed through the doorway. As Jon neared the curtain, Tres placed a hand on his shoulder.

“Groundling, a word.”

Jon studied Tres. His smooth face and tight skin gave the appearance of someone in his mid-twenties, if he were human. But being terrion, he likely neared a century old. He addressed Jon like an adult to a disobedient child.

“Mylis told me of the wraith gate in your village. How was it built?”

“Are you serious?” Jon asked.

“About knowing how the mortal enemy of my country managed to resurrect a technology that's been lost for two millennia? Of course. You stood on it, went through it. My brother has made learning how they did this our chief priority.”

Jon peeled Tres's hand from his shoulder and seethed. Demanding and haughty, just like any young man. "I don't give a burning pile of ash about your priorities. My only concern is finding and protecting my family. If Liiesh wants that wraith gate, he can get it himself."

# 35

# MANHUNT

*Shevak, an Independent Drawlen City-State*
*July 24, 1195 PT*

*Mavell*

Mavell waited next to Detoa in the back of the room—if it could be called one. The stench of gray water permeated the air, despite his tight scarf. Lighting the underground space, rust-colored sunrocks filled crevasses in the crumbling brick walls, casting odd shadows across the low, moldy ceiling.

Splinters from a shredded barrel flew in Mavell's direction. He and his partner dodged the spray. As if a pack of blood-mad wolves had been let loose, Refsul overturned this tidy but abandoned smuggler's hideout. He threw himself at a moldy straw mattress, becoming a storm of shadow. Out of that screaming darkness, pieces of straw sailed like darts through the air.

The shadow became a man again, and he paced, his black, drakeskin coat flapping wildly behind him. When anger consumed the Chief Immortal, no one was safe. Mavell and his partner stayed as still as statues, behavior befitting their order. On the floor before Refsul lay a quivering purifier, taking the full force of the demigod's wrath.

"How many times have you failed me tonight, Vice Purifier?" Refsul growled at the silver-clad man.

The man whimpered, struggling to form words through the gashes and oozing wounds on his face. Some cuts smoked from sunrock powder wedged into his skin.

"How many?" Refsul screamed.

"Fi—" the purifier sputtered.

"And how many times is it *acceptable* to fail me?"

The purifier shook his head.

"How many!"

"N—"

"Yes. None." Smoky tendrils snaked around Refsul.

Mavell relished the immortal's murderous intent.

The purifier groveled incoherently. Shifting into his phantom form, Refsul disappeared into the man's chest. For a moment, the man stared blankly at the wall.

With an otherworldly voice, the purifier shrieked and ran around the room on his broken leg. After a few hobbles, he picked up a splintered chair leg and impaled himself. Just before his head hit the floor, Refsul extracted himself from the purifier and stood in his corporeal body once more.

Detoa groaned and turned her head aside. Mavell remained stoic. His partner was young and had never witnessed Refsul's discipline. Mavell, however, had endured these episodes countless times.

The three other purifiers in the room shrank back. But with their gaudy outfits, they glittered like towers of sun crystals in the dingy room, impossible to overlook. And Refsul had just killed the second in command of their order.

"Find the Red Wolf. Find him tonight. And do not summon me until you have him in chains!" With this declaration, Refsul resumed his shadow form once more and sped from the room.

Mavell let out a slow breath, facing the purifiers cowering along the opposite wall. He usually liked his scarf, but this once, he would love for these cowards to see the smile cemented on his face. "Gentlemen," he said, "perhaps it is time for us to split up, cover more ground. Seeing that this is the eighth dead end and night wanes, it would be prudent."

The more senior of the purifiers stepped forward. They had both grown up in the harem, but the man was utterly unremarkable, so Mavell couldn't remember his name. "This is not a game, Collector Mavell. Our spies witnessed the Red Wolf and the traitor guardsman in this room not twenty minutes ago. We shall all have our guts spilled on the floor by sunrise if we do not find this heathen."

"Precisely my point, purifier. However, this is the third room in which the Red Wolf has supposedly been seen within the last hour." Mavell pointed at the message on the wall adjacent to him, written in the same block letters as the bloody message in Hoven's temple six years prior:

**DEORUM FALSUM IN INFERNIS ARDERET**

"Clearly, someone believes this to be a game. And if we keep chasing the pawns, I doubt we shall survive to face the queen."

The purifier narrowed his eyes, then whispered to his companions. Mavell thought about sending a shade to listen but decided it wasn't worth the effort.

Beside him, Detoa's fingers twitched. "What will become of us if Refsul does find the mortari?"

"Do not worry, Collector Detoa. Arrogance is *always* rewarded."

She tilted her head, then faced the lettering on the wall. "What does it mean?"

"False gods burn in hell." Mavell smirked behind his scarf. He was developing a morbid respect for the Red Wolf.

# 36

# THE GODKILLER

*Temple Setvan, Shevak*
*July 25, 1195 PT*

*Ella*

Ella ignored her surroundings, concentrating only on her lock picks and the mechanical puzzle in front of her. After a few seconds, the pop of the lock broke her concentration. As she pivoted, the dim hallway came back into focus, packed with the escaping crew.

She nodded at Bren, who slid through the open door to scout the next passage.

"Fires, girl," Rodden said, scratching his back against a protruding stone. "You're a burning wizard."

Jon adjusted the crossbow on his shoulder and held up the sunrock lantern. "She's taken all the fun out of family game nights."

"Ah, the Sunday night lock picking races," Remm said. "I do miss those."

Ella twirled the picks in her hand before placing them in her pocket. She remembered sitting next to Remm at the kitchen table as a young girl, lacking the focus and dexterity to match his accomplishments with curtain picks and bump keys, but trying, nonetheless. They were robbed of those happy days when Remm had to run for his life. Now, Ella was running for hers.

Shane handed Ella and Carris sacks of jerky. "See who's hungry. We need to keep our strength. We're not in the clear yet."

Ella tore off pieces for Mylis and Haana, then gave some to her father. "What happened in Lorinth?"

Jon chewed on the jerky and sighed. "Selvator Kane came looking for your mother. He needs a ralenta of a certain bloodline—your mother's bloodline. He got hold of Jeb and me. I was sent through first. After that, the gate stopped working."

"I burning hope she broke it." Remm pounded his fist on the wall across from Ella.

"She was heading to the smuggling tunnels when I went through the gate," Jon said.

Remm cocked his head. "You seriously think she would run off if her little boy was anywhere near that gate?"

Jon's face soured. "No, I suppose not."

Pulling out a twisted, three-sided knife, Remm picked at his fingernails. "Mylis told us the purifier who tried to come through exploded. That can only happen if a gate connection is interrupted, which isn't easy to do. And I doubt anyone in that dead-end town knows better than Ruth Therman how those things work."

Jon bit off another hunk of jerky and shook his head. "If Ruth did as you suspect, then she trapped herself and your brothers with the two most dangerous immortals in Palimar. Fenris the Fire Master was there too. And apparently, they've been sending purifiers through since."

"Fenris," Ella whispered. "He must be going after Halas."

Rodden's bright-yellow eyes narrowed. "What makes you think that?"

"Our town borders the Deep Wood," Ella said. "The Drawls wouldn't build a wraith gate to go after one woman and her child unless it served a bigger purpose."

Rodden raised a brow. "I didn't realize Halas was so widely known by the Tarish locals."

"He isn't," Jon said. "Ella's favorite hobby is making friends with dangerous people."

"Must be a family thing," Carris mumbled as she passed the sack of rations to Tres and Morgel.

"Halas isn't in the habit of being anyone's friend, especially a human," Rodden said.

Ella laughed. "Oh no. He likes trolls *much* less."

"Hey," Shane barked. "Save the history debate for after we don't die getting out of here."

"Yeah," Remm pointed his knife at Shane. "Save it for when we're watching Zereen arbitrators trying to lasso a noose around our dear captain's neck."

Shane smacked the back of Remm's head when Bren appeared out of a trace at the door.

"Clear," Bren said.

Shane clutched his crossbow and snapped his fingers. "Let's move." He hurried them along the cellar passage, taking up the rear. They ascended a staircase and halted at another door. After Ella picked the lock, Remm and Bren scouted ahead.

*Tap, tap,* pause, *tap, tap* on the door signaled their return. Shane ushered the group into a gigantic glass atrium—the Temple of the Tree.

An array of exotic plants filled the room, creating avenues and alcoves bordered by lush greenery. The Tree of Eruna dominated the space. Its trunk was the width of a wagon, and its petrified branches, strung with cords of glittering sun crystals, webbed along the ceiling. Rodden stepped into a band of Mortemus's moonlight that rimmed his profile in red.

Ella's throat constricted as she watched Rodden, knowing what this place meant. His life had fallen apart here where his first wife was ripped from him. And now he stood, centuries later, gazing at the symbol of that loss.

Shane placed a hand on his shoulder. "We can't stay here, Rodden. Mona's waiting for you."

Rodden moved near the glass doors. At the threshold, Bren and Remm watched the open square and the wraith gate in its midst. It sat atop a platform bordered by eight bronze pillars and encircled by steps.

The heavy twang of a crossbow bolt broke the somber moment.

Shane knocked Tres to the ground. The bolt grazed Shane's shoulder and sank into the trunk of the petrified tree. Ella dove to the floor while Jon fired his crossbow, hitting a black figure who fell from the vines.

Another bolt twanged from within the labyrinth of palms.

Jon ducked beside Ella. The bolt sailed high, shattering a ceiling panel.

Carris rolled out of the brush, dragging a bloodied collector. With the collector's finger still hugging the trigger of his weapon, his body petrified at Ella's feet.

Remm and Morgel appeared in a swath of shadows with two dead collectors in their arms.

"I hate these kinds of surprise parties," Remm muttered as he dropped a body.

Morgel grunted, dropped the other body, then disappeared in a trace.

Tres drew Stonebreaker and pointed the ancient sword at Mylis. "We appear to be expected, oracle."

The woman shrank under Tres's stare. With his eyes fully darkened, Ella felt the power of his gaze burning like knives shoved behind her eyes.

"Please, my lord. I have not betrayed you!" Mylis clutched her chest with one hand and shielded her eyes with the other.

Haana scurried away from Mylis. Ella whirled to catch her, but the girl sprang toward a bubbling fountain. From her pocket, she pulled her silver locket and dipped it into the water.

"Stop her!" Tres demanded. Now his gaze turned on Ella, and she felt the full force of his mind craft.

Ella recoiled from the blinding pain of his stare. A thought invaded her mind: *Give this man everything he demands, and the pain will end.*

Ella shook her head and shoved Haana behind her, pulling a knife from her belt. "Back off." Instantly, Tres's spell broke.

"Move!" Shane yelled. His voice was drowned out as water jetted from every fountain, pool, and nozzle.

A few feet from Ella, a floor tile dislodged. A woman in a black coat and scarf scrambled out of the hole. Screeching after her, a dire rat lunged forward and snapped her leg between its pointed jaws with a fleshy crunch.

All around the atrium, collectors sprang from trap doors and hidden cupboards, stabbing at the rats spilling from the earth.

Ella grabbed Haana's wrist and ran. Tight behind Shane and Carris, they sprinted across the square and up the steps of the mount that encircled the wraith gate. Mylis remained an arm's reach behind, her layers of clothing flowing freely.

Carris whirled around once she reached the top of the mount. "This plan is *mental*."

"It was your idea, Carris," Shane spat. He loaded a crossbow as Tres and Morgel brushed by to position the controls on the pedestal at the outer edge of the mount.

Jon, Remm, and Rodden ascended the steps when Tres hollered, "Zem'Arta! This is not right."

As Shane studied the controls, the color drained from his face.

"Where's Bren?" Ella called out, spinning around. "Bren?" She halted and held her breath.

Upon one of the eight bronze pillars surrounding the gate mount, a collector lowered his hood, exposing blond hair slicked over his forehead and savage green eyes. His scarf hid the rest of his face. He cocked a bent elbow on one hip. On his outstretched finger, he twirled a flat bronze ring.

Shane shifted, exposing the controls: Two bronze rings of descending size, the third missing—the one in the collector's hand.

"A shame, truly," said the collector in a nasally voice. "You were doing so well."

From behind Ella, Jon fired his crossbow. In a streak of smoke, the collector dodged and appeared on the next pillar. Jon's bolt clattered to the ground.

Remm and Morgel employed their own shades to lunge at the man, but he traced away.

"Can we turn the gate ring ourselves?" Jon asked. "The one in Lorinth had no control rings, just a lever."

Shane moved around the pedestal and shoved a loaded crossbow into Tres's arms. "Shoot them." He pointed to the other collectors spilling into the square from the atrium. Then he jumped onto the inner gate rings and attempted to move them with Rodden and Carris pushing against their housing.

As the blond collector reappeared near Tres, he sent a shadowy mass at the back of the spire lord's head. The terrion collapsed, clutching his face and screaming.

Shane sprang to his feet. "Get it out! Remm!"

Jon reloaded his crossbow, and Mylis retrieved the one abandoned by Tres. They both fired. Jon's bolt cut through a collector's neck. Mylis sank hers into another collector's hip.

Morgel and the blond collector flitted around one another.

"Stop holding back," the collector said as they crossed blades. "Show me your true power, Freelander."

Remm bent over Tres, holding out his hands in an attempt to free him from the shade's attack.

Ella dove beside her brother and assessed the sweating, writhing terrion in his grip. Tres looked like a madman ready to tear himself apart.

"It's an unbound shade," Remm said through gritted teeth. "Bren could get it out. Where is that brat?"

"I can help." Ella reached into her belt pouch, pulling out an empty shade box, a wooden contraption with a silver-plated interior.

"I don't have enough craft, El. It won't answer to me."

"We don't need it." Ella tipped open the box so Remm could see the uncut onyx diamond affixed to the bottom. "Just watch my back."

Remm gaped and nodded.

Like a storm advancing from nowhere, the pressure in the square dropped. It built until the air felt as if it weighed a thousand pounds.

Everyone halted. The dire rats, which had been roving violently around the temple grounds, screeched and dove into the shadows. The few remaining collectors stiffened, including the blond ralenta, arms clasped behind their backs.

An unnaturally tall sapien figure, covered head to toe in dark silver fabric, appeared in the square.

Rodden stood between this terrifying creature and his companions on the platform. "All this trouble for me, Man of the Veil?" His voice held steady, but his hands and legs shook.

In fact, the rest of their company lay hunched near the ground. Ella's head pounded as it had when Tres turned his obsidian eyes on her, although the pain seemed distant, like a lingering headache.

Mind craft, she realized. The Veiled Man was terrion. Even Shane knelt, head bent low. But the heaviness rolled off Ella. So, she picked up the shade box and held it above Tres.

The Veiled Man answered Rodden's challenge in a breathy voice. "For you, World Burner?" He lifted a sickeningly long hand from the folds of his robe, pointing to the blond collector dragging Morgel by the hair. "You were only the bait."

Morgel's face contorted for a second before his mouth settled in a grim line. He looked to his comrades crumpled atop the wraith gate.

The Veiled Man tilted his head at Morgel, his silver robes rippling. "Show me, mortari. Show me your power by dispatching this heathen." He pointed to Rodden. "End his cursed existence, and your friends may go."

Shane lifted his head a fraction and signaled to Morgel, who nodded at the Veiled Man.

Ella moved the box near Tres's head, working to extract the shade from his mind. For a ralenta, manipulating a shade was like drinking water. But for Ella, who had no shade craft, it was like siphoning an oil vat. The pressure of the Veiled Man's mind craft added difficulty. But now, a new energy built around her, slowly diminishing the Veiled Man's power.

"Show me," he demanded again in a drawn-out voice.

The collector released Morgel but stayed inches behind him as the Freelander approached Rodden. The fae's hateful yellow gaze fixed on the Veiled Man.

"Yes!" the Veiled Man pointed his long fingers at Morgel. "Yes, I can *feel* it. Use it. Kill the World Burner."

Ella focused on her work, holding the shade box open over Tres's body. Shadowy wisps crawled along Tres's shoulders and chest, reaching for the irresistible pull of the shade box.

"That's not possible," Remm whispered, his jaw slack.

"Amazing what a little mouse gets up to when no one's looking," Ella said, smirking. She glanced around, wondering why the Veiled Man's mind craft weakened.

On the other side of the platform, Jon lay prone, using his coat to hide his loaded crossbow.

A warm breeze reeking of sulfur meandered across the square. Shane flicked his wrist at Remm.

"Give me the box, El," Remm held out his hand. "Then get this fly boy onto the gate."

Once the twitching shadows filled the box, Ella snapped the lid and shoved it into her brother's hand. "A gift for the Veiled Man."

In that instant, the roof of the Temple of the Tree shattered. Glass shot out in every direction, pushed by flames and a cloud of black smoke. Glass fragments pelted the collectors nearest the temple.

Morgel lunged at the blond ralenta who held the control ring. The collector flitted away using a shade, avoiding Morgel's attack. But Bren appeared behind the collector, plucked the ring from the man's hand, and vanished.

The collector pivoted and parried Morgel's assault. Using a hooked blade, Morgel ripped the dagger out of his opponent's grip.

Jon fired his crossbow, felling another collector, and rolled out of the way of a round shot fired from further in the complex.

Bren arrived at the command pedestal, and Remm disappeared into his own shadow.

Ella dragged Tres's body across the platform. He was lighter than she'd expected. Hollow bones.

The Veiled Man's mind craft had dissolved completely, and he screamed.

Carris growled, throwing her hands over her ears. The Veiled Man's scream brought her to her knees halfway down the steps.

Ella heaved Tres into the middle of the gate next to Shane, expecting to see him in the same state as Carris. Instead, he rose to his feet. The air around him rippled like invisible fire. His eyes shone bloodred, glowing like embers. In his hand, he gripped a long, curved knife matching the red of his eyes. The power was coming from him.

"You wanted the godkiller, you wingless worm," Rodden bellowed a few yards ahead of them. He straightened and pointed behind him. "Come and meet him." He stepped aside, and the Veiled Man received an unobstructed view of the real mortari.

The immortal flinched and staggered back. "No! An ogre? It isn't possible!"

Shane lunged and threw the glowing red knife.

When the Veiled Man attempted to dodge it, Remm appeared and ripped open the shade box in the immortal's face. The unbound shade flew, shivering and shrieking, into the folds of the Veiled Man's face covering.

As the immortal crumpled to his knees, the red blade sank deep into his upper arm.

A collector thrust a wraith knife at Remm's back. Remm turned, caught the man's wrist and shoved the knife into his assailant's stomach. The collector convulsed and doubled over as Remm traced away.

Morgel still dueled with the other ralenta, who had recovered his knife and overtook the Freelander again. Just as the collector went in for a critical stab, Remm grabbed Morgel, and they materialized in the center of the wraith gate.

Carris threw herself into Morgel's arms. "You reckless idiot!"

"Captain!" Bren called after replacing the third control ring on the pedestal. "It doesn't have the right symbols for Zeree."

Shane glared with red eyes at the Veiled Man and the blond collector, the last of the immortal's servants left standing.

The Veiled Man ripped the smoking red blade from his arm and cackled. "Whatever kind of monster you may be, godkiller, you are mine. You and your—"

*Bang!* A choked breath left the Veiled Man's mouth as a round shot rocketed through his forehead. Haana stood beside Mylis, holding a smoking pistol. The Veiled Man toppled over. For a moment, all grew still and silent.

The lone collector sighed and crossed his arms. "You're still stuck here, you know."

"We will be gone before he awakens," Mylis replied, motioning at the Veiled Man. "I have foreseen it. This day I will be free. It could be your freedom, too, Mavell. You don't have to be their slave."

Mavell snorted. "Freedom? Every mortal has a master, Mylis. And fate is the cruelest master of all. I'd rather answer to a more"—his gaze flitted downward to the Veiled Man, who began to stir—"corporeal overlord."

"So be it," Mylis whispered.

"Turn it on!" Jon ordered.

Ella whirled toward her father, who spun the control rings to a new destination.

"Where are you sending us?" Shane asked.

"Your First Lord is going to get his new toy, after all," Jon said. "Turn it on."

Shane took a deep breath. "Bren, do it."

Bren leapt with Jon onto the gate. He released a shade that swirled overhead, bouncing from one bronze pillar to the next until a curtain of shadow obscured the world around the gate.

Ella and Carris screamed as a wraith blade twirled through the black mist, aimed at Shane. Simultaneously, the world disappeared, enveloping Ella in empty darkness. A second later, a moonlit scene appeared, more wonderful and horrible than the one she had just left.

# 37

# THE SPECTER

*Temple Setvan, Shevak*
*July 25, 1195 PT*

*Mavell*

In the aftermath of discovering the true godkiller and battling his companions, Mavell stood amid a crowd of corpses. Nine collectors lay petrified in the square. With most of the temple agents scouring the city for the godkiller who had vanished in the chaos, only a few guardsmen and servants bustled about the grounds. Flames flickered in the Temple of the Tree as the fountains and pipes flooded the space.

The Veiled Man screamed at the black-clad guards, who ushered him toward the Temple of the Veil. "Quickly, fools! The arm must be removed. This is no ordinary wound."

Mavell shuddered. He assumed, come sunrise, he would meet his master's wrath, both for misidentifying the godkiller and for failing to protect the Veiled Man from zem'Arta's attack. Regardless of the improbability of an ogre wielding a shard of Agroth, the Veiled Man had little tolerance for failure.

Dismissing the inevitable, Mavell called his shade and traced to the empty wraith gate. He appeared at the command pedestal next to Detoa. She studied the symbols on the controls.

"They've gone to Lorinth, to the Arch Purifier's gate," Detoa said as she tore off her sleeve and wrapped her burned arm.

"It seems so," Mavell said. He froze for a split second when he noticed the inner ring missing. "Detoa, go to the Arch Purifier's laboratory. We must use the old ring."

Detoa bowed and ran toward Refsul's temple. Mavell watched her disappear through the great bronze door, contemplating what he should do once she returned. They could gather a company of guards and go to Pelton, the closest gate to Lorinth. It had the advantage of delaying whatever punishment his master would concoct for him.

Interrupting his musing, a silver knife glinted in the corner of his eye, sailing toward him. He traced out of its path and emerged face-to-face with a thin, pale man in a gray coat.

Mavell recognized him immediately—the man who had obliterated an unbound shade in Setmal during Orin Novelen's wedding. Vanishing in shadow, Mavell appeared atop one of the eight pillars surrounding the wraith gate. "I'm afraid your friends have long since parted from the temple."

The man bent one arm across his back and the other in front, bowing low to Mavell. "I've not come for them, Collector. I've come to make sure my companions aren't followed. But of course, it would be rude not to introduce myself." He waved his hand with a flourish. "Calla Dantiego, Deputy Rogue Master to the honorable godkiller, Krishena of Rotira."

While Calla blabbered, Mavell readied a wraith blade. He snapped his arm back. In a heartbeat, Calla appeared before him, and the sting of a knife pierced Mavell's gut.

Calla shoved him over the ledge of the platform, causing Mavell to drop his own knife and roll down the steps. He sprawled on the ground, blood spilling from his wound like oil from punctured earth.

Mavell stumbled to his feet in time to witness Calla cloak himself in a cloud and lunge at the control pedestal. The sound of grinding rock accompanied debris flying out of the shadowy mass. Calla reappeared in the middle of the wraith gate, leaving the pedestal a pile of rubble.

He was like Refsul—like Selvator. Mavell was outmatched. His shade pulled him into a trace, but a frigid hand dragged Mavell back. He landed on his hip, and mind-numbing pain shot through his abdomen.

Calla bent over him, knife poised to stab again. From behind, a silver chain shot at the rogue and wrapped tightly around his wrist—a wraith chain. Calla lunged away, but the silver chain rendered his power unusable.

Detoa held firm to the other end of the chain.

Calla yanked his wrist forward and flipped over Mavell, landing gracefully on his feet and pulling Detoa off hers. Snapping the chain to his side, Calla cackled when Mavell reached for it but missed.

As Mavell rolled back, the chain slapped his neck and whipped around three times. The silver seared his skin when he unsuccessfully called his shade to flee.

Avoiding Detoa's poisoned dart, Calla dragged Mavell into a trace, aiming for the city. Halfway to the city wall, Mavell maneuvered out of the chain's hold and dove at the corpse of another collector, snatching a pistol from the holster at his hip. He pulled the trigger. The shot grazed Calla's stomach. Calla stumbled but hurtled toward the gate in a streak of dark mist, laughing as he disappeared through the lowered portcullis and into the city.

Detoa swooped to Mavell's side, her eyes widening at the blood soaking through his shirt.

Mavell fell to his knees, tossing the pistol and pressing his hands into his stomach. Gasping for breath, he grimaced. "That was a specter."

Detoa blanched. "Like Refsul? Like the Child Immortal?"

"I'm certain of it. We have no hope of tracking him. It seems the First Lord has agents far more dangerous than ordinary men. By now, the godkiller has greeted Fenris's people in Lorinth."

"That cannot be good for the force entering the Deep Wood," Detoa said.

Mavell hummed in agreement, the blood seeping along his pant leg as he struggled to his feet. "It is hopeless to warn them. Although I will not be sorry for a world without Fenris."

Detoa tilted her head but then lurched and gasped when Mavell sank back to his knees with a startled cry. She caught him before he toppled to the ground.

Mavell's vision blurred, his stomach churning with bile and blood. *Perhaps,* he thought as he slipped into unconsciousness, *the world would not be sorry for my passing either.*

*Rose*

The setting Mortemus moon shone through the foyer window of the Brimholt manor. It reflected across the crystal chandelier, dispersing flecks of red light in the entryway.

Rose perched on the bottom step of the staircase, focusing on the twisting arms of the light fixture and inhaling with labored breaths. Hale fidgeted while lying on a marble bench, hands cradling his head.

Both had remained awake all night. Since Ella and her suspicious Freelander comrades had left hours ago, Hale had spent most of the time pacing while Rose fretted.

"They aren't really going through that gate thing, are they?" Rose said.

Hale huffed and resumed his pacing. "Maybe."

A thud in the back hallway disrupted their exchange. They sprang and tripped over each other running to the rear entry, hoping to see Ella or her companions. But Calla and Joran stumbled through the back door.

"Calla!" Rose clasped his arm.

He cradled his side, and blood seeped along his shirt between his fingers.

Joran lifted him onto the bench. "The fool picked a fight with collectors."

Emerging from another room, Krishena pushed Joran aside, her face stern. "Do you have the brains of an unbound shade? What in Sovereign's name were you thinking going to the temple alone?"

"Huh?" Calla laughed quietly, smiling like he'd just received a great compliment. "Making sure our dear protégé and her fellows weren't followed."

"They sprang Jon," Joran said. "Mylis was there as well."

With pursed lips and crossed arms, Krishena listened. She peeled her husband's hand away to inspect his wound. "This is hardly a scratch, Calla."

"You overwhelm me with empathy," he said. "The gate is now broken. Permanently, I hope."

"That may be irrelevant," Krishena said, "considering the Drawls have managed to build one." She stomped to a nearby cabinet and rummaged through the stock of medical supplies. Apparently, Abad il'Dani was used to people stumbling through his back door with flesh wounds.

As Joran helped him strip his belt and shirt, Calla said, "I'm so glad you appreciate my effort, my dearest."

"I—" Krishena closed her mouth and scowled when Calla laughed.

"What happened to Ella?" Rose asked. "Where did they all go?"

Calla grimaced and examined his wound. "They passed through the wraith gate, as they'd planned. They should be in Zeree now. Your dear friend is far from danger."

"Well, I'm glad for that." Rose crossed her arms. "Meanwhile, we're stuck here with every Drawlen assassin in the world looking for us."

Calla smirked, leaning forward as Krishena dabbed his stomach with a cloth to soak up the blood. Using only the tips of her fingers, she wrapped another piece of fabric around his chest. "Worry not, little girl," Calla said. "The Drawls cannot afford to quarantine the city during the day when they know most of the infiltrators have fled. We'll be out of this place tomorrow."

"And go where?" Hale asked.

"Rotira," Calla declared. "Out of the Drawl's reach."

Hale paced again. "Rotira is still in Corigon. How is that out of reach?"

Krishena turned to him, the long vertical scar on her face shining against her dark skin. "Because it is my city. No Drawlen agent takes a breath in Rotira without my knowledge or allowance."

# 38

# THE BANSHEE

*The Deep Wood*
*July 25, 1195 PT*

*Nate*

For the first time since entering the Deep Wood a few days ago, Nate appreciated its wild beauty. Evening light cut across the trees, casting golden hues upon rocks and clusters of birch and pine. Instead of running for his life, he now stood on a ridge, rifle in hand, surveying the landscape and the steady procession of people below.

Every adult carried firearms. Mothers wore infants strapped to their chests and rifles slung across their backs. Hunchbacked men with canes and elderly women with sacks of rations also toted guns. They managed their loads quietly as they navigated the narrow path skirting the hill. Even the children held their tongues. However, in the silence, the attitude of the Ruvians abandoning their woodland home matched their warriors poised to defend it miles to the west: *We expected this. We're ready.*

Nate drew in that energy. He felt more like the fae citizens of the Deep Wood whom he'd seen at Halas's war camp, bewildered and unprepared.

Two bright chirps punctured the warm summer air. The sentinel further down the path checked in. Nate lifted his copper whistle—which hung from his neck on a heavy leather cord—and mimicked the signal. It echoed again and again eastward. He let the whistle fall from his lips, and it knocked against his green stone pendant.

Two short and two long chirps sounded from the west. Immediately, Nate raced along the ridge, checking his rifle as he ran. A sour taste threaded over his tongue as images of banshees making off with fierce but helpless Ruvian refugees taunted his imagination.

When he arrived at the source of the signal, he exhaled and relaxed. The only danger was the self-righteous temper of a short old man in a long fur vest.

"We cannot. We must not." Councilor Burnan fumed, flecks of spit flying from his mouth. "We are fleeing for our lives, and you thrust these trespassers upon us? They could be infiltrators!"

Burnan shook his finger in the face of the two Ruvian scouts. One scout, a man in his fifties, nodded in agreement with Burnan's protest. The other was Amara, lips pursed, hands fisted at her side.

Behind Amara, a woman huddled with two young girls. Unlike the Ruvians, blonde hair covered their heads, their skin pale as ivory. Dirt marred their once-fine clothes, and tears stained their cheeks.

"Nathaniel?" the woman gasped.

Nate blinked and peered at her. "Mrs. Creedle?"

"Please help," the woman cried in Palish. She hugged her girls closer as she watched Burnan spew at the two Ruvian scouts.

The old man waved his cane at Nate. "You know these Drawls?"

Nate leveled Burnan with a glare. "They're from Lorinth."

"Please, Nathaniel," Mrs. Creedle said. "The village . . ."

"I know." Nate's heart ached as he answered in Palish. "I'm glad you escaped."

"Who are these people?" she asked.

"They live in the woods," Nate said. "They're getting out before . . . before the Drawls do the same to them that they did to us." He turned to Amara and spoke in Ruvish. "Can they go with you?"

Burnan sputtered his disapproval, and the other scout cleared his throat as an elderly couple approached Mrs. Creedle and her daughters. As they put chunks of bread into their hands, the scout next to Burnan gaped.

The couple wrapped their green cloaks around their Tarish charges. They escorted them around Burnan with their backs toward him, their rifles bouncing on their shoulders.

Before she passed Nate, Mrs. Creedle grabbed his forearm. "My boy, my Philip. I couldn't find him."

Nate laid his hand over hers. "Where was he—when everything started?"

"On the roof of the mining office," Mrs. Creedle said. "Please."

Nate squeezed her hand. "I'll look for him. I promise."

When Mrs. Creedle and her girls moved out of earshot, Burnan barked once again. "The lives of thousands of innocent Ruvians are at risk if we let infiltrators wander here. They are not our people."

Cory joined Amara and the other scout. Amara's nephew, Roan, slept soundly, strapped to his mother's back. "Councilor, do not be afraid," she said firmly, dipping her head.

Councilor Burnan pounded his cane on the ground. "Secrecy and scrutiny, Cory. Those are our principles."

Cory lifted her chin. "Are not serenity and charity as well? What are we but a hidden pack of dogs if we leave women and children to the mercy of monsters because we are too cowardly to be kind? We must keep on, Councilor." She met Nate's eyes and nodded as she passed. Burnan crossed his arms and grunted.

Amara pointed to the ridge, and Nate gladly followed. When they reached the tree line leading to the crest, a form in the foliage far ahead caught Nate's eye. "Amara, look."

She crouched and stilled. "A banshee," she whispered.

Indeed, a ghostly pale figure with great black wings perched on a high bough of a pine, eyeing the last of the Ruvians moving along the hill. Nate knelt and raised his rifle.

Amara put a hand on the gun barrel and lowered it. "No. If you miss, it'll fly off," she said. "See what it's doing?"

Nate titled his head and squinted. It backtracked carefully along the branch, glanced at the people below, and sprang to the next tree, heading south.

"Why isn't it flying?" Nate said. "Is it injured?"

"It seems to be scouting. It must know we're watching the sky and the ground."

"I didn't realize those things were so smart."

Amara moved nearer the banshee. "It's a sapien, even if it seems like an animal." She blew on her whistle, signaling she was leaving the scouting post to track a threat. "The vines don't come this far east. We need to follow it."

Nate waited a few seconds and blew his whistle. After another moment, a reply signal sounded: permission to pursue.

As Amara had predicted, the banshee slunk through the trees, obscured in the canopy. Her keen eyes tracked it, despite Nate losing sight of it several times. She led him silently through the forest, using many game trails and clearings.

Night settled around them, and Nate wondered when the other scouts would worry about their absence. They slowly gained on the banshee, but the vegetation obstructed a clear rifle shot.

Amara reached her hand into a wall of thick brambles. She yanked on a branch, and a camouflaged canvas door opened, leading into a scouting path. "It's a sentinel trail," she whispered. "The fae use it to route Drawlen intruders. Hopefully they've kept it cleared. They don't use them much these days."

"They will now," Nate said.

The covered trail proved clear and quick, so they ran silently along the soft dirt. Through the slits in the canvas covering, the retreating banshee remained in their sights.

When they exited the tunnel, they landed near the tree where the creature moved above and in front of them. Rifles ready, they crawled along the ground.

Looking down briefly, Nate set up his shot. His pulse accelerated after losing sight of the banshee. "Where is it?"

"I don't . . ." Amara startled and screamed.

The banshee landed on top of her, grabbing her hair. As she swung her rifle, the creature tore the gun from her hands and tossed it.

Nate rolled away, avoiding the creature's foot, poised to stomp him in the neck. Fumbling, he raised his gun and put his finger on the trigger. The banshee screeched and placed a hand around Amara's throat. Nate couldn't make a lethal shot without hitting her. But banshees presented a large target.

*Bang!* His round shot tore a hole the size of his fist through its wing, and the creature dropped Amara. It lunged instead at Nate, who already had his knife in hand.

Nate dodged, his eyes widening at the banshee, who towered two feet taller than him, not including wings. Still, its skeletal structure wobbled, unfamiliar with moving along the ground. As it swiped at Nate, he ducked, lunged, and tackled it.

The banshee toppled easily. When Nate fell with it, he shoved his knife between its protruding ribs. But his hands were sweaty and shaking. Instead of a clean thrust, the knife glanced off bone and tore into the creature's stomach. It wailed and clutched at its wound. Nate steadied his hands and moved to stab again, only to make two more poorly aimed cuts. Nate choked out his own tormented cries.

Years ago, while David taught Nate to hunt, he had told him every hunter eventually must bear the guilt of a messy kill. Nate had shrugged off the proverb until his third deer, which he'd shot in the front leg and had to finish with a knife as it wheezed in anguish. All the while, the deer stared with horror-filled eyes.

In the present, the frightened eyes pleading with him belonged to a man. The banshee that had seemed so monstrous and so *other* now appeared indistinguishable from a human, regardless of wings and disfigurements. It wheezed and croaked, unable to move. Taking a shuddering breath, Nate thrust forward, stabbing it in the heart. He wanted desperately to close his own eyes but couldn't. Instead, he held the banshee's gaze until the light in its eyes died, its rasping and twitching gone.

Nate's stomach writhed as he staggered back. Tossing the knife, he fell to his hands and knees and retched. His head hung inches from the stinking, steaming vomit. Even so, he held his face low. He didn't want to meet Amara's proud, cautious gaze and hear her say, "You did well." Nate felt like he had regurgitated his own soul. Extinguishing the light in a person's eyes could never be "well done."

"Nate?" Amara placed her hand on his back.

He forced himself to look up.

Amara's calm expression revealed a mournful familiarity, rather than pride or relief. "I know," she whispered. Stepping over Nate, she knelt beside the fallen banshee and closed its eyes.

Nate stood, wiping the sour wetness from his mouth, but immediately sank to the ground, pulling Amara with him. Her raised brows questioned Nate without a murmur of surprise. Pointing cautiously over the brambles, Nate knew exactly where they were now. They crouched a hundred yards from the forest's edge bordering the Therman family's farm. And three silver-clad purifiers slunk among the trees toward them.

# 39

# INFILTRATORS

*Lorinth, Taria*
*July 26, 1195 PT*

*Nate*

Nate gripped his rifle.

"They heard the shot," Amara whispered. "We need to hide . . . we're no match for purifiers."

She was right. A second later, the purifiers appeared through a billow of shade smoke. One of them was a ralenta, but all three sported shaved heads and dark-gray robes, like the men Nate had witnessed in Lorinth before the horror had begun.

"Well, now," the ralenta said, his teeth glinting against his dark skin. The other two purifiers pointed pistols at Nate and Amara while the ralenta plucked a paper from his pocket and unrolled it. As Nate gaped at the surprisingly accurate sketch of himself, the ralenta tapped on the parchment. "That's the one, eh?"

A sing-song voice answered from among the trees behind the purifiers, followed by a girlish giggle. "That's the one."

The purifiers whirled around. Discarding the portrait, the ralenta flitted toward the voice, a shadow swallowing him. The other two purifiers trailed behind but collapsed, one with a crossbow bolt through the forehead, the other with a knife in the chest. Nate and Amara leaned back-to-back, unsure if these new intruders were benevolent.

A man entered the scene holding a crossbow. He yanked the knife from the dead purifier and wiped it across his trousers. The shadowy mass around the ralenta purifier dissipated, revealing his prone and bleeding body.

A woman with blonde hair, twisted in rag curls and tied with red ribbons, loomed over the body. Unlike her companion, hooded and wearing a wool coat, this woman was, in a word, flashy. Her black bodice with pink stitching accentuated her curves. Beneath that peeked a white blouse and a black, pleated skirt reaching her knees.

She propped her thigh-high boot onto the back of the fallen purifier, revealing a pink frill on her hemline. Planting her palms on her hips, she puckered her red lips, highlighting her pale skin.

Although Nate supposed she was pretty, he found her ensemble overdone. "A rogue if I've ever seen one," he mumbled.

"Why, thank you." The woman bowed. "And you must be Nate Therman."

Nate rested his hand on the hilt of his dagger and glared. If purifiers had come for his family, an ambitious rogue or two wasn't unreasonable.

"Oh, don't worry." The woman tossed her hand about. "We are the good guys. The Temple of Secrets put out death marks on you and your family. We've come on behalf of the Rogue Master, Krishena Dantiego."

"Thank Sovereign for that woman." Amara relaxed the grip on her rifle and stepped forward.

"That's right, dearie," the woman said, tilting her head with a smirk. "But it seems we're more than fashionably late."

Nate clenched his dagger. This woman's joke about a massacre infuriated him. "Who are you?"

"I'm Illania. This is Mikey." She gestured to the man with the crossbow. "We went to your house to see if we could help, but . . ." She glanced at the Therman farm.

"But you were late?" Nate retorted.

Illania crossed her arms, brows raised high. "We barely stopped to catch our breaths, thank you very much."

"Did you see more Drawls?" Amara motioned to the fallen purifiers.

"Well, there were plenty on the road." Illania shrugged. "We said hello to a few, but it seems the real party is here in the Deep Wood."

"What about the town?" Nate asked, sheathing his knife.

"We haven't had the pleasure yet. We'd just arrived when we saw these three prancing off into the woods. But the smoke was visible for miles before it got dark." Illania surveyed Amara's uniform. "You're from the neighborhood. What's going on here?"

"Fenris is attacking the Deep Wood," Amara said.

Nate straightened. "There's a wraith gate in Lorinth."

Illania winced, her mask of sinister amusement fading. She bit her lip and nodded to Mikey.

"My brother is Arimal Soral," Amara said. "He's gone into the town with a group of fighters to break the gate. We can certainly use your help."

"Of course, sweetheart." Illania sighed and adjusted her belt. "We didn't come all this way just to see the sights. Say"—she looked at Nate—"are your parents and brother hiding in the woods too?"

Nate frowned, his annoyance at the woman's nonchalant attitude replaced with the hopelessness he'd been successfully suppressing. "No. Like I said, there's a wraith gate in Lorinth."

Illania's eyes softened. "I see." She tapped her long fingernails on her mouth. "And you're heading there to break it?"

"No," Nate grumbled. "I wasn't *permitted* to go since I'm not a trained scout."

Illania wagged a hand at the fallen banshee. "I doubt that was the reason. You're Jon Therman's boy, right?" She propped her hands on her waist. "Since when has a Therman ever given a pile of ash about what's *permitted*?"

Nate gaped. Since putting on the Ruvian scout's uniform, he felt bound to whatever order he'd been given. But now his limbs quivered, adrenaline coursing through his veins. He grinned at Illania with budding, albeit reluctant, respect.

"Nate," Amara said. "Go help your people. You know the roads. You know the town and even the smuggling tunnels."

"I can't leave you here alone," he said.

"Don't worry, Hero Jr.," Illania said. "Mikey will go with your pretty friend. No gentleman lets a girl walk alone in the woods at night. You can take me on the grand tour of tiny town." She winked at him.

Nate scratched the back of his neck and faced Amara, whose eyes shone brightly while she nodded. She pointed to the field, and Nate's heart swelled.

He unbuttoned and shrugged out of the green uniform. Then he handed it to Amara. "Thanks. I'll make it up to you."

Amara smiled and flung her arms around his neck, whispering, "Sovereign watch over you, Nathaniel Riley."

Nate's tongue felt jumbled in his mouth. "Y-You, too, Amara."

Now clad in his brown shirt, Nate watched Amara and Mikey disappear beyond the trees. When he turned to Illania, she held her hand out, almost like offering a treat to a dog. "Ever trace before, Therman?"

"Riley," Nate said. "My father's Ruvian surname—it's Riley."

"Okay, sure. You ready?"

"What's tracing?"

Illania laughed, her voice musical. "Take my hand."

As soon as Nate touched the woman's hand, black smoke bloomed in his vision. For a split second, he felt like he'd been pulled through a pinhole. When the darkness lifted, he emerged on the road at the opposite side of his family farm.

"That's tracing." Illania straightened her necklace before planting her fists on her hips.

"That was awful." The words barely left his mouth when she sent them off again. Two more times, Illania traced them, a mile at a time. Nate bent forward, fending off his nausea with a forced breath.

"Okay." Illania fluffed her hair. "We're going the old-fashioned way from here. I gotta stay fresh."

They peered at the ditch on the side of the road. Five human corpses lay petrified and clinging to one another. Nate rushed by, sure he would recognize each of them. Not far away, a dead banshee sprawled on the road with a crossbow bolt through its heart. Nate had thought banshees wore metal necklaces to signify their order, much like the silver robes and shaved heads of purifiers. However, the corpse before him wore a collar welded around its neck with five links of chain dangling from it.

Once they passed the banshee, Illania dropped her casual demeanor, growing quiet and serious.

"There's a tunnel," Nate said.

"No need," Illania said. "I've got us covered. I'm sure we'll need those little mouseholes later, though."

Nate nodded. This may have been his first time tracing—which he never wanted to do again—but he knew a ralenta's cloaking capability, so he followed in silence.

When they entered Lorinth, they used the alleyways. Nate led the way around the back of the Loren Inn and Tavern, one of the more intact buildings. He imagined the tavern had been spared from Fenris's fire to allow Sir Doniva to search for Will. Most of the buildings in the town center had been torched. The stench of melted tar paint and burned wood lingered, a few buildings still smoldering. To Nate's relief, no bodies lay in the streets.

Scaling the fence and shed in the garden, Nate guided Illania onto the tavern roof. From here, they had a clear view into the town square and the field to the north.

Torches flickered in straight lines leading from the town to a small military encampment at the edge of the forest. Another row of torches marked the burned highway through the Deep Wood. Exploding powder flashed from the tree line, followed by gunfire. The bestial roar of a bear and the growl of a lion added to the cacophony.

In the town square, Arimal, Paul, and one other Ruvian scout engaged in a melee with Drawlen rangers. Another scout lay on the ground, immersed in a puddle of blood. More rangers also sprawled in the square, stony and still.

A heap of bodies, probably the fallen citizens of Lorinth, burned in the field. Nate searched the roof of the mining office behind him, as he had promised, but saw no one hiding in the dark. If Philip Creedle were smart, he would have run far and fast.

A woman in a bloodred dress laced with gold ribbons sat—no, lounged—on the roof of the first level of the Drawlen Temple. Propped on one elbow, she watched the scouts and rangers slashing at one another. Nate recognized her as one of the stage performers from two days ago.

She rose, pulled a pistol from the frills of her skirt, cocked the hammer, and aimed at Arimal. But Nate was ready. Before the woman could shoot, Nate pulled the trigger on his own gun. The round shot met her chest, and she toppled.

"Not too bad, Riley," Illania said with a smirk. She stared at the woman, unblinking, when the woman sat upright with no evidence of Nate's lethal shot.

"Ah, I thought so," Illania said. "Lady Crimson. A bit unimaginative, don't you think?"

"She's an immortal?" Nate asked.

Illania hummed. "The Mistress of Madness. Not well known, but plenty dangerous."

Nate gasped. "Aren't they all?"

Lady Crimson rose to her feet, searching for the source of her most recent, albeit impermanent, demise.

However, Nate's spot was well hidden. He and his friends had used it many times for pranks without being discovered.

"Mm, I wouldn't say so," the rogue said. "If not being able to die is all you have going for you, it only makes you annoying. Lady Crimson is dangerous because she's a grand master of poison." Illania propped a fist under her chin. "Here's the thing, sweetheart. You can't fight an immortal the way you fight anyone else. If you kill, they win. It's a restart for them. You've got to wear them down. Fight to wound, but not to kill. All you handsome woodland critters don't seem to get that."

As she said this, Paul felled his opponent and threw a knife at Lady Crimson. The knife sailed toward her chest, but she backflipped and pulled a black dart from her golden armguard. Pressing it between her fingers, she aimed at Arimal again. Nate hastily reloaded his gun.

Illania traced from the roof and reappeared in the square between Lady Crimson and the other fighters. Lady Crimson threw the dart, but Illania deflected it with her dagger.

Lady Crimson startled and barked, "Bitch!"

Illania bowed exuberantly. "Pardon me, lady cliché. You should pick on someone with a little more style. Shall we?"

Arimal, too, had dispatched his opponent and faced the pair. "Who are you?"

Illania curtsied. "I'm your knight in shining leather, dear. Isn't that obvious?"

For a horrifying second, Nate thought Illania's comical arrogance would get her killed. Lady Crimson had thrown another dart at her. But Illania vanished, dodging the poisoned projectile. She appeared directly behind Lady Crimson on the temple balcony and slashed the woman across the back before tracing away again.

The immortal screamed and swiveled, readying another dart. Since the rogue had disappeared, Lady Crimson aimed at Paul. Illania sped across the dart's path like a smoking round shot, deflecting that dart as well. This dance persisted, with Lady Crimson thrashing and screaming across the balcony.

The last ranger engaging Arimal and Paul succumbed to a deep stab in the ribs. Arimal's face dripped with sweat, and Paul bled from a gash in his side.

More rangers emerged from the field. Nate aimed, fired, reloaded, and repeated. Most of his shots hit their marks, though a few blazed harmlessly overhead as the rangers dodged to the ground or behind obstacles. He didn't have time to contemplate the depravity of his actions. It would probably plague him later, but presently, he resolved to keep his friends alive and break that cursed contraption on the temple stage.

The incoming rangers streamed in faster than he could reload, however, and soon Arimal, Paul, and Illania each fought, competently yet desperately, to defend themselves. Lady Crimson wagged her finger between the three infiltrators. Nate trained his rifle on her as she drew her arm back to throw another dart. He shot her in the shoulder. Fight to wound, he thought.

The immortal woman raged and ordered the men below, "Get the sniper, you idiots."

Just then, the rings on the wraith gate screeched and spun. Lady Crimson cackled while holding her injured shoulder.

Illania flung herself between Paul and Arimal. "Wanna get out of here, boys? I hear there's a big party in the woods tonight." She traced with them, appearing on the roof of the tavern behind Nate a moment later. "Now would be a great time for a tunnel tour, Riley."

Nate sprang toward the trap door when a preternatural buzz sounded from the wraith gate. For a second, a black cloud blanketed the platform. When it dissipated, a crowd of people appeared.

"Welcome, my fr—" the words faded on Lady Crimson's lips as she took in the new company. Whoever they were, they weren't Drawls.

# 40

# THE BATTLE AT THE GATE

*Lorinth, Taria*
*July 26, 1195 PT*

*Jon*

Jon expected the lung-crushing sensation of traveling through the wraith gate to Lorinth. He was prepared to see the aftermath of the Drawls' destruction in his town. When he and his comrades materialized on the temple stage, he was even prepared for a fight, crossbow held ready.

He was not prepared, however, for Ella's anguished cry behind him, following the crack of gunfire. He froze at the thought of seeing his daughter mortally wounded.

Dazed, he stared at the line of rangers surrounding the square in front of him. One ranger held a smoking rifle. From across the square, another shot sounded, and the ranger fell, blood seeping from his back. His firearm flew from his hands, red moonlight glinting off his bloody bayonet.

Jon refocused and fired his crossbow at another ranger. Remm and Bren traced past him, descending on the remaining soldiers like angry ghosts.

Shaking his head and pivoting, Jon lunged near Ella. She crouched with her hand clamped over a shallow wound across her upper arm.

"I'm fine," she said through gritted teeth. Jon tore off the sleeve from his shirt and wrapped her arm.

Tres lay prone next to her, struggling to sit. Beside them, Carris cradled Morgel around his shoulders.

"No! No!" she screamed. "Morgel!"

The glossy obsidian handle of Mavell's wraith blade protruded from Morgel's stomach. Gasping for breath, Morgel raised a quivering hand to Carris's face.

Shane's eyes still glowed red. His whole demeanor had changed, like some death-wielding specter had wandered into the waking world out of a legend. He studied the town, eyes narrowed and calculating, unaffected by the state of his companions.

Mylis knelt and pushed Haana behind her. The girl held her spent pistol like a war hammer.

"Where are we?" Mylis demanded.

"Watch out!" Rodden yelled. He lifted Mylis and Haana away as a black dart sailed from the direction of the temple. Jon flattened Ella against the floor, avoiding the flying dart.

A tall woman in a gaudy red dress balanced on the roof of the temple's first floor, arm outstretched from the throw. "Who invited you?"

"It's Prudence, the Lady Crimson!" Mylis yelled.

Jon knew the title—a minor immortal rewarded with her position after assassinating the Thuran Kaiser centuries ago.

"Kill her," Tres said as Jon helped him to his hands and knees.

Lady Crimson laughed. "You can try."

Remm materialized behind her. Grabbing her by the collar, he traced with her onto the wraith gate and shoved her at Shane. "All yours, godkiller."

Shane impaled Lady Crimson with his clawed hand.

Jon shielded Haana and blanched at the gut-wrenching violence. The woman convulsed pathetically, then fell silent. A buzz sounded like a fly hitting a windowpane. Lady Crimson stiffened on the ground, slowly graying with petrification.

Shane's arm dripped with blood. The deadly power, pulsing from him like a furnace, dissipated, and his eyes shone blue again. He gasped, sweat beading down his face and neck. His gaze landed on Morgel.

"Damn." Shane dropped to his knees beside him, going silent when Morgel grabbed his hand.

The ralenta held Shane's gaze and smirked. He raised his other hand, revealing the inner command ring from the wraith gate in Shevak.

Carris balked and drew him closer. "You burning, beautiful genius."

Grimacing and wheezing, Morgel tilted his head and winked at her. Shuddering, Carris pulled the wraith blade from his stomach. The blade smoked. The wound bubbled.

Heavy boots beating on cobblestone drew everyone's attention to the alleyway beside the temple. Jon readied his crossbow. A ranger sprinted toward them, raising his gun, but a round shot from across the square tore through his thigh. Jon finished him off with a bolt to the chest. In the moonlight, Jon spotted a thin wisp of gun smoke rising from the tavern's roof.

A crowd of soldiers swarmed past where the first ranger had fallen. Bren, Remm, and Rodden descended on them. Three more figures emerged from a swath of shadows, causing Jon's heart to soar—Illania Bradly, Arimal Soral, and Paul Greenwell.

A ranger escaped the melee and charged the platform, brandishing a bayonetted musket. On the third step, he stilled as Ella's knife lodged in his hip. After her second knife pierced his abdomen, he rolled to the ground. She cradled her injured arm, the linen wrap oozing with blood.

Jon hoisted his reloaded crossbow as several rangers thundered into the square. One of them on horseback fell quickly to the sniper on the tavern roof. Jon yelled to Mylis and Haana. "Take cover in the temple."

Mylis grabbed Haana's arm, but she pulled away. A ranger crawled onto the stage and lunged at Haana. He tumbled back when Jon's crossbow bolt sank into his ribs.

Another ranger jumped onto the gate. He shrieked and fell to his knees, dropped his rifle, and stared at Tres with terrified eyes. Tres leaned against the wall of the temple, his obsidian eyes gleaming with power. When he tilted his head, the man at Jon's feet fumbled for his pistol and shot himself in the gut.

Jon grabbed the fallen ranger's loaded rifle and felled another horseman who entered the square. With the bayonet, he parried the advance of another soldier. However, Jon toppled when the soldier thrust the butt of his gun into Jon's hip.

Carris barreled into the man and threw him to the ground. She leapt onto him with a murderous howl, slicing his chest with bloodstained claws.

A third wave of rangers entered the square. They stumbled and hollered, eyeing the beasts pursuing them. A grizzly bear and mountain lion descended on them with feral growls. They ravaged anyone in a Drawlen uniform. When the last of the rangers fell, this bazar group of defenders stood catching their breaths.

"Dad!" Jon heard the familiar sound of his son's voice. He staggered toward the Loren Tavern, where Nate waited at the door, a rifle slung over his shoulder. Jon pulled him into his arms.

Arimal approached. "You were supposed to stay with the scouts, Nate. What are you doing here?"

"Saving your ass," Illania said, brushing the dust off her skirt. "Not properly trained? Please."

"I'm glad you're safe." Jon pulled back and ruffled his son's hair. "Where's your mother? Where's Jeb?"

Nate's face twisted from relief to despair. Jon's stomach churned as he cupped Nate's face.

"They . . ." Nate sniffed. "They went through the gate. Kane had Jeb. Mom tried to rescue him. She did something to the gate—shoved a bayonet between the rings. They still went through, but it didn't work after that."

Jon closed his eyes. A scream raged within him but found no voice. He slumped to his knees and hung his head.

"Papa." Ella placed a hand on her father's back. He rose and pulled her and Nate into a gentle embrace.

"I told you she'd break it." Remm drew near, wiping blood from his face with his sleeve.

"Remm?" Nate said.

"Hey there, little trickster." Remm smirked.

Nate huffed, clasping Remm's wrist when his brother offered his hand. They side-hugged and slapped one another on the back.

A warrior's greeting. The camaraderie of men, no longer boys.

"What in the fires is happening there?" Shane watched the smoke rise in the northern field. A ranger's camp burned at the edge of the Deep Wood. Beyond, the trees gave way to a crude, straight road lit by flickering torches.

"Fenris is invading the Deep Wood." Arimal extended his arm to Shane, introducing himself. "We're grateful for your help. We were pretty desperate before you showed up."

The Freelander grasped his wrist. "Shane zem'Arta. We never pass up a good fight with Drawls."

Nate glanced around. "Where's Ezron? Where's my dog?"

Arimal smiled. "In the woods, tracking graycoats who broke away from the camp."

Carris brushed past Nate, scowling at Arimal. Blood covering her hair and clothes, she waved a clawed hand. "There are Drawls down there?"

"A whole army," Paul said, sitting on the edge of the dilapidated fountain in the middle of the square, holding his bleeding side. "Fenris the Fire Master and Paustus, Master of Chains are among them. There are rumors of one other immortal too."

"The Arch Purifier as well," Arimal added. He raised his sword to the temple stage, where Morgel's body lay with his hands over his chest. Now fully petrified, he looked like a stone monument of a Greqi samurai. "If you want vengeance for your friend, join us."

"You would be welcoming Freelanders into the Deep Wood," Tres said, pallid and sweating, while hanging onto Rodden.

"Normally, we wouldn't." A bear stood on its hind legs across from the fountain. It shifted into a wild-looking fae woman with a gray braid. She sported a wicked gash on her shoulder. "However," she said. "We can't turn down the help of a godkiller while immortals attack our territory."

Behind her, the mountain lion shifted gracefully into a golden-haired woman.

"What about him?" Shane patted Rodden on the shoulder.

"Who is he?" the gray-haired woman asked.

"Rodden Morrien," Shane said.

The woman tapped a hand on her cheek and squinted at the immortal fae. "I see."

Rodden pointed at the Deep Wood. "It seems the truce between Refsul and Halas is over. Normally, that old fox wouldn't be very pleased to see me. But I think he'll make an exception today."

"I truly doubt it," the woman with a braid said. "If it's a risk you're willing to take, you're welcome to enter though. I'm Sephora, captain of the border guard. This is Nyla, one of my lieutenants." She gestured to the blonde beside her. "I have the authority to grant you entrance into the Wood. Whatever quarrel Halas may have with you later is between you both."

"I'll vouch for you," Ella said. Everyone regarded her curiously. "Halas owes me a favor. I can at least make sure he doesn't hang you all from your ankles over a drake nest."

Remm laughed and placed his arm across her shoulder.

"What about the Drawls coming through this gate after you?" Arimal asked.

Carris held up the bronze ring Morgel had stolen in Shevak. "Not a problem. My husband grabbed this as we were going through. He . . . he took a wraith blade in the gut at the same burning time."

"My condolences, ma'am," Arimal said.

"We should take the burning thing apart," Nyla said.

"Not necessary." Nate grabbed three ranger's rifles off the ground and hopped on the stage. One by one, he jammed the bayonets between the rings.

"Will that hold?" Sephora asked.

Nate walked to the gate lever and kicked until it broke from its housing.

"We should still tear it to pieces," Nyla mumbled.

"We have other plans," Jon said. "If it can be moved and built in a few days, it can be stolen."

Sephora raised a brow. "Stolen by whom?"

"Consider it a gift of gratitude for our assistance," Tres said.

The border captain regarded Tres with narrowed eyes. "You're terrion. You look like a spire lord."

"Indeed." Tres straightened, pressing against Rodden. "I am Tres Romanus, Second Lord of Palim."

"With the World Burner? Really?"

"Rodden is our ally," Tres said.

"Brother-in-law, technically," Remm muttered to his father and siblings.

Sephora folded her arms. "And you're willing to fight with us?"

"Since I am . . . unfit for battle at present, my warriors are yours for the time being."

"Then we should go," Arimal said as he helped Paul wrap his wounded side. "Anyone too injured to fight can wait in the tavern, or perhaps the tunnels, just in case more Drawls return."

"I'm no warrior," Mylis said. Haana stood beside her in the square, glaring at the fae and Ruvian fighters.

Ella rose to her feet and grimaced. "I'll stay. I'm not in top form, but I can probably do a little damage still. Never leave a door unguarded, even a broken one." She lifted one leg, revealing an oozing puncture in her thigh.

"Very well." Sephora stowed her weapon and gripped her belt. "We should—"

Illania appeared in a puff of mist amidst their ramshackle company, a hand on her hip and twirling a bloody knife in her hand. "Sorry, kids. One of the graycoats ditched us for a walk in the woods and I had to say hi." She winked at Arimal, then sized up Shane and Remm. "Hello, boys. Been a while since we had a dance."

Remm huffed and rubbed a hand down his face, while Shane merely scowled.

Sephora beckoned her lieutenant forward. "Let's move."

Shane poked a finger at Tres's chest. "Get underground. I don't get paid if I have to bring your ashes back to Palim."

Tres nodded, but as Shane marched past, he grabbed the troll's arm. "Boy—Captain. There are at least two immortals out there."

"Yeah. Don't get all grouchy on me, flyer. I know the rules."

"No, zem'Arta. Listen." Tres leaned harder into Rodden, who had a supportive arm around the terrion's back. The spire lord put his right fist over his heart. "I, Tres Romanus, Second Lord of the Spires and Chief Lieutenant of the Freeland coalition, by the authority of the Ivory Throne"—he coughed, catching his breath—"command you, Captain zem'Arta of the Red Watch and Shard Keeper of the Mortari Order, that should you find any Drawlen immortal, if it is within your power, *kill it*."

A sinister smirk alighted on Shane's face. "Any and all?"

Tres raised his brow. "I'm sure my brother would prefer if you return to Palim alive as well."

"Fires, and you were starting to grow on me." Shane waved a hand to his comrades. "All right, idiots, let's go make some friends!"

# 41

# THE SUMMONS

*Palim, the Freelands*
*July 26, 1195 PT*

*Liiesh*

Once again, a memory of his father haunted Liiesh's sleep. The events never transpired in accordance with reality, but the result was the same.

*Liiesh, no longer kneeling nor bound by chains, stood atop the Romanus tower next to his great uncle, Rufius. His father, Tyris, waited in the middle of the tower platform. Liiesh willed himself to wake, but his body refused.*

*"Remove them," Rufius commanded. To his great horror, Liiesh bent over his father, who lay prone and wailing. Blood dripped from Liiesh's hand that held the knife. At his feet, his father's severed wings withered into ash. Rufius lifted Tyris by the hair and tossed him over the tower's edge.*

A mind calling interrupted his dream, and Liiesh bolted upright. For once, he welcomed the discomfort. Leaning forward on the bed, he rubbed his hands over his face. *'A moment,'* he called out in his mind.

*'Certainly, my lord.'*

Liiesh startled at the reply. In his stupor, he hadn't realized who initiated the mind calling. Praya Aldonus, although his betrothed, had never directed a mind calling or any form of mind craft at him. She avoided him like a rabbit evades a hungry fox.

Springing to his feet, he crossed the dim room. Embers glowed in the fireplace. The clock on the mantel ticked. Plucking his long red coat from the wire mannequin beside the hearth, he dressed quickly as the clock chimed three times. At the foot of the canopied bed, he sat on the bench, where a beam of silvery blue moonlight shone from the balcony doorway. Removing his limiter, he closed his eyes, then opened them to a wintery expanse.

"Lady Praya. I presume this is not a social call."

Praya pursed her lips and averted her gaze. Despite wearing her coral sleeping gown and hair tied, she poised with an air of elegance. "I have an urgent message from your brother."

"Can he not deliver it himself?"

"He is too far. He struggled to reach me."

"Where is he?"

"At the border of Taria and the Deep Wood."

Liiesh held his breath and clenched his jaw.

"He was successful in rescuing Rodden." She brushed aside a strand of hair. "However, the plan to travel to Zeree through the gate was not possible."

"Obviously."

Closing her eyes for a moment, Praya took a deep breath. "They are in Lorinth, the town where the Drawls built their new wraith gate. The Drawls used it to mount an invasion of the Deep Wood. An agent of Halas Gorvenah has granted Captain zem'Arta and his team permission to cross the border and aid in Halas's defense. Your brother has given his blessing in this endeavor. And also for zem'Arta to dispatch any Drawlen immortals he may encounter. There are at least two, possibly three, and he has already slain one."

"Who are they?" Liiesh crossed his arms.

"Lady Crimson has fallen," she said, briefly lifting her face. "Fenris the Fire Master and Paustus, the Master of Chains, will likely fall too. If zem'Arta uses that much power, he will need healing. The gate in Lorinth is not set correctly for him to travel to Zeree. I have arranged for the gate here in Setmal to receive him when the battle concludes. If Mona could get here—"

"No! My sister nearly killed herself saving zem'Arta's little groundling thief."

"He will be weak. Without a skilled healer, he will—"

"I will send someone else."

Praya's eyes flared, and her fists clenched, but she schooled herself. "No ordinary healer can work their power on a mortari."

Liiesh huffed. "He insisted on having Mona spend her power on some worthless outlander girl. Sovereign only knows if it did any good."

Praya's lips turned into a hint of a smile. "She lives, my lord. She was with Tres in his mind calling. He was weak from battle, and he brought her into the calling to ensure he stayed conscious. She secured the blessing of Halas Gorvenah's lieutenants for your agents to enter the Deep Wood, to go after Fenris. It is also she who petitioned for the Rogue Master Dantiego to aid in rescuing Rodden from Shevak, and it was her smugglers who got them into the temple. She introduced herself to me: Ella Riley, an emissary of Alistar Soral, Arch Traitor of Drawlen, who is also Protector of a secret Ruvian stronghold hidden in Halas's territory."

Breathing slowly for a tense moment, Liiesh tightened his lips and furrowed his brows. "I see."

Praya smiled fully now, straightening. "I don't think 'worthless' is quite the word you're looking for, my lord. And I'm sure Mona would be quite keen to know her husband is presently fighting alongside her mother's people against Drawlen invaders, don't you think?"

"She is suffering. It'll be a week before she can fly or use her power without threat to her life."

Praya inclined her head. "The timing should suffice. It's a long road from Dothra to Setmal, even if she uses the gate in Zeree."

"So be it. But when this is settled, I want to meet this emissary woman. Personally."

*Ella*

Glittering blackness filled Ella's vision as she and the Second Lord of the Freelands waited for Lady Praya's return to Tres's mind calling. When Ella was dying of wraith poison, she vaguely remembered lying in a bright expanse, feeling warm and safe. This time the psychic space felt unstable. Tres's head sagged, his eyes glassy with exhaustion. His eyelids closed, his head hanging lower.

"Hey." Ella jostled his shoulder, causing him to raise his chin, though he still slouched. "Maybe we should stop."

Tres shook his head wearily. "I can't make another mind calling. It was a miracle I did so in the first place."

Ella exhaled, but it felt as if she watched herself through a fog. Several more times, she startled Tres awake before Praya reappeared in front of them. She was a stone-faced young woman with glossy black hair twisted upon her head. In the strangeness of the mind calling, her beauty and clever eyes gave the impression of a painting.

"Mona will travel to Setmal." Praya's lips puckered, and a sparkle flashed across her face. "Liiesh was not particularly pleased, but he relented."

Tres sighed and smiled warmly at Praya. "Your persuasiveness wins again, my lady."

"I merely repeated your testimony, Lord Tres. He made his own demand as well."

Tres narrowed his eyes. "What demand?"

Praya locked eyes on Ella. "He was particularly interested in you, Miss Riley. He wishes to meet you personally."

"Me?"

"Did I not just say so?" Praya rolled her eyes.

"Why?"

"I'm sure he has his reasons." Praya bowed her head to Tres. "If there is nothing else, my lord, I should see to the gate preparations."

"Certainly, my lady."

In a blink, the staticky darkness of the mind calling dissipated, and Ella sat against the wall of the smuggling tunnel next to Tres with Mylis pacing anxiously. Haana had her ear pressed to the tunnel door, a hearth shovel in her hands.

"We hear people in the square above," Mylis said.

"I'll take a look." Ella pushed herself up, exhaustion dogging her. As she limped toward the hidden door of the tavern cellar, she cast a withering eye at Tres. "Well, flyer, was saving my life *worth the effort*?"

Tres glared with stoic intensity. "Perhaps. But you may soon find you'd have preferred to remain outside the interest of spire lords."

"Why is that?"

"Because you have been summoned to Palim. My brother wishes to meet you *in person*."

Ella raised a brow. "Pfft! He's welcome to pop in for a visit. I have other things to do."

"I don't think you understand the seriousness of this command, groundling." Tres crossed his arms and used a grave tone. "You've been called to the court of one of the most powerful and dangerous men on Ethar. It is not a request."

Ella stepped away from the door and propped her hands on her hips, shifting her weight off her injured leg. "By what authority does he require my presence? I'm no Freelander. And if you think you're going to kidnap me, I can promise it won't go well."

"He is not above threats and coercion."

Ella smirked. "Neither am I."

Tres raised his shoulders, exuding a strength not evident in the mind calling. "Tread cautiously, Miss Riley. We are not your enemy, and you and your comrades are dangerously short on friends. You have been instrumental in an unprecedented breach of security in the Temple Setvan and the forthcoming demise of more than one Drawlen immortal. I would not be surprised if Refsul himself curses your name by the end of the week. Consider how you might use this opportunity."

For the first time, wariness of the Second Lord sank in. Ella saw him more for what he was, rather than the unassuming disguise he wore. "I don't have the authority to negotiate alliances. I'm just a smuggler."

"You are a bridge between worlds, Ella Riley. You will be trodden on or you will be burned."

# 42

# BETWEEN BROTHERS

*The Deep Wood*
*July 26, 1195 PT*

*Nate*

Illania's tracing ended so abruptly, Nate slammed to the ground after the forest came into view. Sephora, the Woodlander captain, landed gracefully next to him. A second later, Remm materialized with Arimal and Nyla. They had traveled a wide, westward arc around Fenris's warpath, and now stood at the edge of the rocky landscape marking the defensive lines of the Woodlander forces along Sentinel Ridge.

"You're slowing down, Remmy," Illania said, fluttering her eyelashes at Nate's brother.

Remm glanced at the overdressed rogue with his chin raised. "It's been a wild night, Illy."

Nate shook the numbness from his feet. The childhood accomplice he remembered had been cocky, clever, and full of laughter. The man before him now seemed downright predatory. He certainly fit well among his Freelander companions.

"Ten minutes." Sephora gestured to the narrow stream crossing their path. "Fill your waterskins. Take your rations. We will reach the war camp in half an hour. After that, we won't rest until every Drawl in this forest is petrified."

Arimal and Nyla knelt by the stream, filling skins. Illania sprawled on a mossy patch of earth at the base of a spruce tree, tucking her hands behind her head.

Remm perched on a fallen log away from the group, biting into a portion of hardtack. He met Nate's gaze and held out the biscuit.

Nate plopped next to his brother and broke off a piece. "I thought you were in the Freelands."

"Hey." Remm held his hands up. "Half an hour ago you were happy to see me, trickster."

"How come you never write?"

Remm opened his mouth, then resumed chewing his food. His shadowed gaze flitted toward their companions for a moment, then found Nate again. The air quivered around them, as though steam rose from the ground. Nate raised an eyebrow at Remm, who shrugged.

"I'm just making sure princess nosey doesn't listen in," he explained. "What are you, now, fourteen?"

"Sixteen."

Remm fluttered his lips and tilted his head. "Right. Look, Nate, I don't expect you to understand. I'm not the same boy who left Estbye."

"No joke. That kid was an awkward bean pole who fumbled with a kitchen knife. You look like a walking arsenal." He studied Remm's outfit. Dark-gray sleeves extended from a leather vest padded with pockets securing numerous knives and darts. The armguards concealed retractable spikes, which Remm had employed an hour ago to rip into a soldier's neck. His patched pants sported a pistol holder around his thigh. Even his cracked leather boots bulged with hidden weapons around his calves.

"Where do you get a thing like that?" Nate gestured to a twisted, three-edged dagger on Remm's belt.

Remm chuckled, pushing aside two Kumuni-style swords, and patting the dagger.

"Some Thuran brute tried to stab me with it. Since he's at the bottom of the Shardling Sea, I figured he won't miss it."

Nate smiled. "I bet you have stories."

"Boy, do I."

Nate knitted his eyebrows and wrung his hands. "Maybe after this is over, you can tell me a few."

The smug smile melted from Remm's face, his eyes reflecting the red and silver moonlight around them.

After a moment of silence, Nate said, "I used to be jealous of you, ya know."

Remm's bright, hazel eyes widened. "Of me?"

Nate kicked a pile of acorns on the ground. "I used to think you were lucky, getting to live with rogues, then running around with Freelander mercenaries. I pretended I was off fighting pirates with you."

"Fires, Nate." Remm swallowed hard and closed his eyes. Caked with dirt and dried blood, he rubbed his hand over the stubble of his dark scalp. "I spent years dreaming I was back home with you all. When I fell in with Shane in Setmal, that was the first time I'd stopped hating my life."

"Really?"

"Rogues are a selfish lot," Remm said. "They're all about glamour and status: who steals the most, who knows what secrets about this noble or that. I didn't give a burning pile of ash though. A Drawlen cleric tortured and murdered my mother before I could even walk. I didn't know the full story until Krishena filled in the details when I was your age. From then on, I only wanted one thing." He stared at the break in the trees where a battle brewed five miles east.

"Revenge?" Nate asked.

"More than revenge, little brother. I want the whole Drawlen order to burn. When I'm done, only ashes will be left."

Since fleeing Lorinth three days ago, Nate's boyish longing for danger had wavered. He thought it had been extinguished but realized it had merely changed. No longer did he yearn for a place in one of David's stories. This struggle was now personal. It was about justice.

"Well," Nate said, "at least you won't have to worry about writing me letters."

Remm chuckled.

Nate drew himself up, tightening his grip on the rifle straps. "You saw what's left of Lorinth. Drawls have ripped apart my whole burning life. I have no home, mom and Jeb are gone, and there's no way I'm going back to pranks and petty smuggling jobs. Wherever you're going, Remm, I'm coming."

A smile tugged on Remm's lips, but his eyes remained stoic. "It's not an adventure, Nate."

"No. It's a war."

Remm smirked and placed a hand on Nate's shoulder. "Let's finish the fight in front of us before we go making any grand plans, all right?"

Nate dipped his chin, planting his hand on the hilt of his saber. "Okay."

The rippling around them dissipated when Remm called off his shade.

Illania watched nearby, one boot propped on a rock and arms crossed. "Is the family meeting finally over?"

Arimal tossed an acorn at her. "Weren't you complaining about needing more time to catch your breath?"

The woman batted her eyelashes and cocked her head. "Just trying to keep up some momentum here, sweetheart." Extending her hand to Remm, she said, "Shall we dance?"

"Only if you can actually follow my lead, Illy. This is a battle, not a contract."

Retracting her hand, Illania swayed her hips and skipped down the path. As she passed Remm, she brushed a finger under his chin. "Does that mean no after-party?"

Remm batted her hand and glared. "Not a chance."

Unfazed by his rejection, Illania swaggered ahead, twirling her finger in the air. "Come along, lovelies."

Nate huffed and followed, Sephora on his heels. Remm grunted, then clasped both Arimal and Nyla, conjured a torrent of mist around them, and traced past Illania, jostling her.

Illania stomped her boots and muttered, "Sore loser." She met Nate's critical gaze with a coy smile.

"You two seem close," Nate said.

Illania laughed and wagged her eyebrows. "Honestly, I thought he'd be a little less pleased to see me."

"What did you do?"

Illania looped her arms with Nate and Sephora, as if they were marching into a dance hall. "Well, let's just say I came between friends, and neither of them have gotten over it."

Sephora rolled her eyes. "Let's move on, please."

Tossing her hair off her shoulder, Illania said, "So, your tall, dark Ruvian friend—"

Nate cut her off. "Is married."

"Ah. Tragic." Illania then pulled them into a trace.

After two lung-crushing episodes of tracing and a mile of hiking through the craggy wilderness, they arrived at the rear command of a motley force of Woodlanders and Ruvians. Arimal waited at his father's side, prattling and glancing at Remm, who stepped off to the side with his arms crossed.

Alistar's calculating eyes landed on Nate, whose stomach dropped. Amidst the intensity of the battle in Lorinth, the consequences of leaving his post and the Protector's daughter had been far from Nate's mind.

Alistar loomed before him, lips pursed. Nate swallowed and met the Ruvian Protector's gaze apologetically.

"You left your post, Nathaniel."

"Yes, Protector." Nate had been consumed with recklessness and defiance when he'd departed for Lorinth earlier that night. He felt neither of those now.

"You abandoned a fellow scout," Alistar said in a sharp tone, crossing his arms.

"I—"

Remm stepped between them. He drew his short sword and pointed it at Alistar. Gasps and protests erupted around them. Swords and rifles encased Nate and Remm. Longing to undo the last minute of his life, Nate's stomach soured.

Remm narrowed his eyes at the guards and lifted his blade higher. From this angle, the word etched into the sword became clear: TRICKSTER.

"That your boy over there, Al?" Remm said.

Alistar's nostrils flared, and he gritted his teeth.

"Be grateful for Therman defiance, old man. It saved your son's life today, and probably your little war as well."

"Who the fires are you?" Alistar crossed his arms and widened his stance.

"Remm Therman—or Riley. Whatever we're going by these days." Remm withdrew his blade, stepped back and bowed, fanning his arms. "If you want to get at my little brother, feel free to try."

Whispers flushed through the crowd. Alistar looked to Arimal, who nodded in confirmation. Alistar motioned for his defenders to lower their weapons. A chorus of sheathed blades and rifles pulling back followed his command.

"You came through the wraith gate?" Alistar asked.

Remm cocked his head, flashing a hungry smirk. "With a few friends. We even closed it behind us."

"Where did you come *from*?" he asked.

"Shevak."

More murmurs of awe and skepticism rippled around them. Alistar unfolded his arms. "The Temple Setvan? How did you manage that?"

Remm twirled his sword and shoved it back into its scabbard. "The way Freelanders always do things where Drawls are concerned, Arch Traitor. By way of blood and burning."

Alistar assessed Remm. "I'm told you have others on their way."

Remm nodded and glanced at the crowd. "Where's the fox? Isn't he the one in charge?"

"The fox?" Halas's voice rang sharply over the crowd.

People shuffled, forming a narrow avenue between Remm and the red-haired man standing twenty feet away. Dressed for battle, Hallas sported leather armor, a shining cutlass, a rifle, and two pistols. Captain Sephora stood at his side, whispering in his ear.

He stepped toward Remm and nodded. "Freelander."

"Forest demon," Remm replied.

"You've come here at the risk of my wrath."

Remm peered at his surroundings, his gaze settling on the sunrock piles and campfires of the army gathered across the valley. "You're awfully cheeky for a man who's about to get burned off of Ethar."

Halas glared at the ralenta. "Captain Sephora says you've brought along an immortal."

Remm threw out his hands. "Well, we also brought a godkiller, so it seemed only fair."

The buzz of apprehension in the crowd erupted.

Halas scowled. "So you say. *Who* did you bring to my wood?"

Remm picked at his fingernails and said, "The World Burner."

One man screamed curses. Several fae women shouted, "To ashes with the World Burner!"

Halas bristled and hissed.

Remm shook his head. "Oh, come on. You're about to face the last real fire wielder in the world. Don't you think it's a bit poetic?"

"I don't care how burning poetic you find it," Halas spat. "If you brought Rodden Morrien here—"

"You'll what?" Remm asked. "Tickle me with your tail?"

Halas stepped forward, hand on the hilt of his sword. "You little . . ."

Remm placed a hand on Nate's shoulder, smiling like a boy who'd gotten away with a whole sweet cake. "Fires, El always makes friends with the crabby ones." Turning back to the Lord of the Wood, he said, "I've been told you have a debt to pay, and that allowing Rodden to crush a few Drawlen skulls will see it canceled in full."

"By whom?"

"Ella Riley."

For a moment, Halas stared blankly at Remm. Then he closed his eyes and howled with laughter. Nate sighed, relaxing.

"That sneaking little whelp," Halas said with a glimmer in his eye.

Alistar searched the crowd. "She's here?"

Remm cocked his head and winked at the Ruvian Protector. "Our dear sister is currently guarding the wraith gate in Lorinth and nursing a few battle wounds." He returned his attention to Halas. "I'm sure she'd be happy to hear all your grievances, Lord of the Wood, after we turn these Drawlen squatters into a parade of shades. Shall we?"

A grin alighted on Halas's face. "Cheeky and irreverent. I should have guessed you were related. Well, Freelander, the sun will rise soon, and with it a war cry. Come and tell me more about your friends, especially this godkiller."

Remm bowed to Halas with a flourish of his wrists, then approached Nate and patted him on the head. "Later, little trickster." He marched toward Halas with Alistar trailing.

A crowd of fae and humans gazed curiously at Nate as he stood beside Illania. When a gentle hand settled on his shoulder, Colas's warm, blue eyes greeted him. Nate mumbled an apology. After all, Colas had accepted his bid to join the scouts and assigned him to guard the exodus from Sidras.

Colas patted Nate's back. "Amara told me about the banshee and the rogues who came to warn your family. I've just heard from Arimal of your timely arrival in Lorinth. You've done well, Nate."

"I still left my post, sir. I had my reasons, but I accept responsibility."

Colas nodded. "That's very honorable. But you're not a trained scout, and you've taken none of the vows. You made a judgement call, and you did not leave your comrade defenseless."

Nate perked up and peered around. "Amara. Is she—"

"She's scouting to the east," Colas said. "Making sure no other Drawlen agents try to follow our refugees."

"I guess I was supposed to be there too."

"That would be a waste of your talent, sweetheart," Illania said. She linked her arm with Nate and beamed at Colas. "If I were you, whoever you are, I'd put this kid in a sniper's nest. He only missed two times in twenty shots."

Nate wiggled his arm, but Illania tightened her grip and continued. "How many did you get, little man? Twelve, thirteen?"

Nate slipped away. "It's not a contest."

"Suit yourself." Illania sauntered into the crowd.

Nate wiped his forehead. "Finally."

"Well, Nathaniel," Colas said, "that's the fourth person in ten minutes who's given you a glowing recommendation as a sniper. Go to the munitions cart. You'll be on the ridge."

# 43

# THE POISONED ROAD

*The Deep Wood*
*July 26, 1195 PT*

*Shane*

Shane breathed slowly, flat on his back, his nose inches from the wooden boards. Carris lay next to him in the smuggling compartment of Jon's cart.

"If this doesn't work," she said, "I'm gonna kill you."

"It won't work if you keep talking," Shane said. However, he couldn't blame the kobold woman's skepticism. Hiding in the compartment was an unconventional way to roll into battle.

The cart rattled as Jon maneuvered it over the rough road through the forest. The stench of wraith poison hung in the air, making Shane wonder if the fumes might be deadly.

"So, you've ridden in one of these before?" Carris asked.

Shane chuckled. "Yeah. Remember Kritcher?"

Carris huffed. "The banker who tried to blackmail Vernon vel'Tamer?"

"Yeah. I picked him up in Estbye."

"I'll bet that was a shock to him."

Shane clicked his claws on the boards. "Would'a been. Before I got a chance to make an entrance, El knocked him out with a kick to the face."

"The woman we left back in town? The one using Drawlen rangers like pin cushions?"

"Yeah."

Carris elbowed Shane. "That was five burning years ago. What was she, ten?"

"No! Fifteen, maybe."

"Fires, and you yelled at me for breaking Bren into the business."

Shane scoffed. "By using him for target practice."

Carris wiggled her shoulders. "I never miss."

"Pssht." Shane's throat constricted, forcing him to swallow.

Sorrow crept in through the lingering fog of battle. He could only imagine the heaviness for Carris, who, only two hours ago, had held her dying husband for the last time. A selfish thought arose: At least she got to say goodbye. After six years, knowing his wife, Nola, had died afraid and alone still tormented him. Shane wiped sweat from his forehead.

"Carris," he whispered.

"Don't you burning say it." She exhaled slowly.

"I'm sorry."

"Write it in Drawlen blood, grab boy."

Shane sighed. "That knife was coming for me."

"'Course it was. Do you think any of us would'a let it hit you, idiot?"

Shane put his hands over his face and growled. "Can't go losing the mortari right before a war, I sup—ow!"

Carris's elbow remained in his ribs. "Moron," she grunted. "Not one of us gives a pile of ash what kind of sorcerer's soup you fell into."

Shane laughed. "Are you trying to say something nice?"

"Screw you, zem'Arta."

Shane rapped a knuckle on the woman's ear. "Love you too, elf—oof."

This time, Carris flicked him on the nose.

Two stomps rattled the boards above, Jon's signal to be quiet. They stilled, breathing shallowly. As the cart halted, hinges creaked, and muffled voices rose.

In the distance, shots fired. The battle had begun. Shane itched with anticipation. The mortari shard burned inside his chest. It was going to be a rough but glorious day. If he wasn't careful, though, it would be a little too glorious.

When the cart moved again, Shane whispered, "Hey. If I go all red-eyed throat-biter out there . . ."

Carris's green eyes glinted in the dark. "I'll butcher you like a Grace Day ham if I have to. Just don't let it get that far. Last time was bad enough."

"Thanks," Shane mumbled. He would never forget the sensation of crashing from the violent high of mortari unrest. He could feel the blood on his hands, in his mouth, between his toes. The memory shook him. "Just . . . I think two more is my limit."

"What do we do with the third immortal, if there is one?"

Shane sighed. "Disable. Then hope the spire brat wakes up from his nap soon."

Carris chuckled. "If I didn't know better, I'd say you and Tres're growing on each other."

"Shut it."

The cart turned sharply and slowed to a stop. Three taps above Shane's head signaled it was safe to roll out. When he opened the side hatch, he choked on the bitter air. Suited in a gray uniform, Jon stood with a white rag tied over his nose and mouth. He shoved one into Shane's hand.

Heaving out of the compartment, Shane tied the cloth over his face.

"Burning hell," Carris grumbled when she slid from the cart. "Any chance all these flat tooth graycoats'll be dead from this air by the time we get to 'em?"

"It has to get in the blood," came a monotone reply from Bren, perched on the bough of a withering oak.

Carris blew out a long breath, then tied a cloth over her mouth.

"All right," Jon said. "We're past the rear guard. Are we set in there, Paul?"

Obscuring the inside of the cart, the canvas flapped heavily as Paul, the short Ruvian scout, emerged. He moved stiffly, holding his heavily bandaged side. He raised his thumb. "We're good to go."

Jon gestured at the forest with his chin. "Okay, Paul. Get some cover. You're in no condition to run if that's what it comes to."

"Banshee," Bren said.

Paul ducked inside the wagon. Jon squatted on the driver's bench. Bren used a shade to cloak himself within the trees while Shane and Carris crouched beneath the cart. When the cart dipped lower from the weight of something settling upon it, Shane lay flat.

"Whoa there, you two," Jon said. "Don't see your chain master around. Seems you're all alone."

A banshee screeched. Shane snapped his fingers. Carris rolled from under the cart, wielding a throwing knife in each hand. The zip of Bren tracing from the trees sounded at the same time, and within a few heartbeats, both banshees slithered off the roof of the cart, wide-eyed and silent.

"Well." Carris sighed at the bonnet of the cart. "You think the rangers'll mind if this thing rolls up with blood all over it?"

"Let's cover it," Shane said. He startled when Jon leapt from the cart and propped his elbow onto Shane's shoulder.

"Ya see"—Jon smiled—"this is what separates assassins from smugglers. You folk are always losing your crap over coverups. You gotta lean into the unexpected, use the mishaps in your favor." After Jon shared his plan, they hoisted the carcasses across the wagon top.

Shane, Carris, and Paul picked their way through the woods, watching Jon drive the cart as it hobbled along the burned, poisoned war trail. Bren sat beside him on the driver's bench. The two dead banshees sprawled across the bloodstained bonnet.

Carris snickered. "You know who that Jonny fellow reminds me of."

"Don't say it." Shane wrinkled his nose.

"Liiesh Romanus," Carris said. "Every bump in the road's another way to pull the rug out from whoever's on the other side of the table."

"Damn it, Carris." Shane rolled his eyes. He had privately thought the same thing on many occasions but refused to acknowledge his favorite smuggler and one-time surrogate father was anything like the ruthless Dragon of Palimar.

Another hundred yards down the road, a banshee passed over the cart. Its lamenting cry sounded equally tragic and revolting. Soon, two more circled overhead, mourning their fallen brothers.

"Burning brilliant, this Tarish bloke," Carris mumbled.

Riding a horse from the war camp, a Drawlen soldier wearing a bandana over his nose and mouth questioned Jon, who handled the conversation like a decorated stage performer. He convinced the ranger he'd found the banshees wounded and hanging on tree branches while he himself escaped a demon-possessed vine in the woods.

The ranger motioned Jon forward, then gave a commanding whistle to five other mounted rangers waiting ahead on the path. Together, the rangers trotted in the opposite direction of the cart. When the riders fell out of earshot, Paul blew on his whistle, mimicking a swallow. A twin melody echoed far behind them.

Amongst the trees, Paul ushered the Freelanders into a hidden tunnel of sumac brush and painted canvas. It blended well but allowed them to see the surrounding wood and the battle unfolding before them.

On the road, Jon steered the wood ox forward until a ranger held up his scarred hand to halt them. Jon and Bren exited the cart and followed the soldier for cargo inspection. When the soldier rounded the back of the wagon, Bren pulled Jon into a trace, disappearing in a swath of smoke. As they reappeared into the brush beside Shane, the wagon exploded.

Fire and debris scattered from the cart, knocking soldiers and priests off their feet in a deadly twenty-foot radius. Flames swallowed the four banshees circling the cart. Two of them flew out of the plume, their wings aflame. They dropped amidst the Drawlen fighters, furthering the damage of the smuggler's gift.

Riderless horses bolted through the thick of the Drawlen lines, and men with burned bodies wailed upon the poisoned ground. When some hit the soil with their open wounds, they inadvertently sucked up the wraith poison they had injected into the earth.

More banshees took flight. Once they crossed the tree line, animated vines swallowed them. Whoops and drums sounded from the defender's side of the battlefield. Their musketeers drew back, flocking behind long, slender cannons.

At the rear left of the Drawlen lines, several covered carts shuddered. Stationed at each one, chain masters tore off the black canvas coverings. From each cart emerged four banshees, all carrying lit balls of gunpowder. They flew toward the Woodlander cannons.

Raising their guns, the cannon operators shot at the banshees. Weighted nets rocketed from the cannons at the oncoming bombers. Several banshees and, consequently, their explosives, met the weighted nets and fell onto their own ground forces. Within seconds, the powder bombs exploded.

"So"—Carris looked at Shane—"we gonna cut some Drawlen throats, or what?"

Shane smiled, then whistled through his fingers. Bren disappeared in a trace. Paul pulled Jon into the cover of the canvas tunnel before leading Carris, Shane, and him farther down the path.

Bren crouched at the head of the covered trail when the four of them arrived. He nodded to Shane. "Fenris is at the front of the main force. He's easy to spot. Paustus is on the left flank. The third immortal is Turuz."

"Oh, fun," Carris chirped. "The Gate Guardian."

"That nasty Thuran is definitely gonna die today," Shane growled. "Where is he?"

"Right flank," Bren said. "In front of us."

Shane and Carris shared a sharp-toothed grin. Pulling out her curved knives, Carris twirled them. "Now can we cut some throats?"

A menacing horn sounded from the ridge across the field.

"Ah," Paul said. "Wait a moment. The Woodsmen have sounded the drake horns."

Sharp cackles and moaning burst from the field. Shane fingered the ivory fangs of his drake necklace, listening for the subtle differences in the wild cries. "Stone drake," he mumbled. "And—is that a shade crier?"

"Beats me," Paul said. "They live in the badlands northwest of here. All kinds, from what I know."

More cries drummed out of the field, the wails of men running from beasts. A stone drake burst into the area near the Woodlander's right flank. It stretched at least fifteen feet long, likely female, and looked about as angry as Shane had ever seen one with her nostrils flared and back arched. With a hide as hard as stone, her round head smashed rocks as she wielded her blunt-ended tail like a hammer. Three rangers fell under its first swing. She cast her gleaming gray-brown eyes on the foremost firing lines and charged.

Another drake, a shade crier, slithered onto the field. When the creature howled, a venerable cloud of black emerged from the corpses on the ground. Wild shades haunting an active battle could be a danger to anyone, not only the Drawls. Shane furrowed his brow at Paul.

The Ruvian scout shrugged. "Patience, my man. We all have shade immunity here."

The third drake, an earth eater, exploded from within the ground at Fenris the Firemaster's feet. It turned its ribbed head toward the immortal and opened its four-pronged jaw, showing off a monstrous mouth of saw-like teeth. Fenris scowled as he dodged out of its way. The drake dove over his head, shimmering blue and green, and slammed into a crowd of mounted rangers. The battlefield erupted into chaos.

Shane tapped Bren on the shoulder and nodded. Bren grabbed Jon and Paul by the arm and traced away, heading around the flanks, landing safely behind the allied lines.

Shane put out his fist, and Carris met it with her own.

"May you send a thousand souls to Sovereign's judgement today, warrior," Carris said, "And may your claws never dull."

Shane winked as he drew his cutlass and his last remaining dagger. The two of them ran into the Drawlen right flank, tearing into the enemy soldiers with feral roars. With the mortari shard alive and ringing in his blood, diving into battle was intoxicating. He and Carris cut their way to the open field before the Drawls regained themselves enough to fight back.

Unprepared for a melee, the Drawls paid dearly. Shane and Carris stayed tight near the right flank, allowing the Woodsman to focus on the left and center. They fought within the Drawlen troops so Fenris wouldn't burn them out.

Soon, Bren appeared at Carris's back, and Remm materialized beside Shane, laughing as much as he was killing. They performed this gruesome dance well, but Morgel's absence cut deeply. It drove them to fight harder, to kill faster, to serve justice for their friend.

# 44

# THE ARCH PURIFIER

*The Deep Wood*
*July 26, 1195 PT*

*Jon*

Jon crouched along a draw four miles north of Sentinel Ridge. Rodden sat next to him, a roll of powder sticks under his arm. Above them, Halas appeared in his fox form, poking his head over the ledge and glowering at Rodden.

"We're ready," the Lord of the Wood said.

Jon stepped aside and waited for Rodden, but the immortal fae continued scowling at Halas.

"If you two are going to glare at each other like scorned lovers, make yourselves bait at the mine instead," Jon muttered.

The two men turned from one another, rolling their eyes. Rodden pushed the powder sticks into Jon's hand and probed one end of the line through a crack in the rocks. He shifted into an alley cat and slunk beneath the rocks into the cave, stringing the cord inside. A few minutes later, he emerged from the entrance, resuming his sapien form.

"Like you guessed, Jon," he said, "Gorova and his little horde are trying to press through the mines. At least three earth speakers are with him. They're forming a new tunnel. Best case for us, they drop dead from the effort and leave the Arch Purifier and his troops stuck to backtrack."

Jon frowned, facing Halas. "How did they get this far into the woods without your scouts finding them?"

"Banshees and ralenta, I assume," Halas said. "They've clearly had this planned a long time."

Rodden tugged at his collar, moisture dotting his neck. "Chained fliers have been swarming your skies for days, and you didn't notice?"

Halas fixed Rodden with a glare so hateful, Jon feared they would come to blows. As a precaution, he swung an arm round their necks and drew them in like old drinking pals.

"All right, you pointy-eared furballs. We have a mine full of graycoats and sparkling throat cutters. Probably some chained bats too. Let's not get distracted by the leftover drama of your centuries-old boys' club. Take it out on the Drawls."

A twittering rang over the trees, prompting Jon to ready a match. Another whistle shrilled, and he struck the match against a rock. A fingerling flame sputtered, and Jon pressed the stick to the line. It hissed and smoke rose, snaking into the air and clogging the tunnel with silvery-blue fog and the heavy aroma of sulfur. He shoved a rock over the vent, locking the smoke inside the mine. Along the surrounding ridges, smoke rose from the other vent ports.

"Are we taking bets on which hole they crawl out?" Jon asked.

Halas threw up his hands. "I'm done making bets with Rileys."

"Do you really owe my daughter a debt?"

Halas smiled. "I lost to her at cards a few months back. I think I'm coming out ahead on this exchange."

Jon groaned. "That girl."

"I'm sure she meant to save time and lives," Halas said.

Rodden chuckled. "I'll bet a swipe at the fox's tail."

Halas growled, but the tension of impending battle settled on the three men, so the jabs between the two immortals ceased.

They hiked in silence to the entrance of the mine, where Halas's trackers had spotted footprints at the threshold. "Ten minutes or so until we see any runners," a tracker standing near the mine said.

They set up a barricade of pointed logs and sharp rocks ten feet into the opening, with twenty rifles propped along the face of the cliff.

Halas handed two rifles to Jon. "Let's make a pile of bodies before we collapse the tunnel. Once they breach the barricade, we'll fall back, let a dozen or two get into the open, then blow the mine. We can have ourselves an old-fashioned shoot-out to lessen their numbers in case they do make it out elsewhere."

As he waited, Jon's blood thrummed a heavy rhythm in his ears. He had limited battle experience but many shoot-outs with rival smugglers and pirates under his belt. At Halas's order, he ducked behind an earthen mound.

He checked his weapons—a cutlass and two pistols holstered at his side, various knives at his waist and boots, and two rifles against a rock. As he counted round shots, the drumming of boots reverberated under his feet. Near the mouth of the mine, the Woodsmen fired their first volley. Gun smoke obscured Jon's view. Anguished cries and the thud of bodies upon the barricade erupted through the haze. Following a third round of returned fire, a Woodsman toppled.

After several minutes of cross fire, the Woodsmen fell back, allowing the enemy soldiers to escape the smoke-filled tunnels. The Drawls poured into the clearing like rats fleeing flames.

Jon fired his first shot, hitting a purifier in the chest. Midway through readying his second rifle, the chill of a shade prompted him to draw his pistol. A silver-clad ralenta partially materialized before Jon put a round shot through his skull. He fired his rifle at another purifier, missing him but striking a ranger.

After reloading, Jon aimed for purifiers, the more dangerous of the Drawlen troops. The mine exploded, sending rock and bodies flying, and a ranger lunged over Jon's barricade. He struck the ranger in the shoulder with a shot from his second pistol. As the man scrambled for his gun, Jon put a bayonet through his chest.

Drawlen stragglers raced from the plumes. The Woodsmen met them with haphazard marksmanship. Close-quarters assault felled the last dozen enemies. The Woodsmen whooped, having taken few casualties.

Their elation ended when rocks flew like cannon fire from the cloud obscuring the mine. Debris remained suspended in the air, thickening instead of settling, as though a swirling wind held it up. The earth speakers had arrived, using their craft to clear the rubble blocking the tunnel, and turning the one-sided slaughter into an earnest battle.

"This just got fun!" Rodden shouted. He dodged an oncoming boulder, which toppled a spindly poplar.

Jon rolled aside, but a fist-sized rock struck his thigh. Blood pooled under his skin, forming a throbbing bruise. When the earth speakers crumbled his fortification, Jon grabbed his rifles and scrambled along the defensive line to flank them. He reached the far-left side of the clearing before crossing blades with a Drawl.

As he parried, he recognized the man—Berneas Gorova, Arch Purifier of the Order of Refsul. Gritting his teeth, Jon pulled his knife and sliced Gorova across the ribs. Gorova sprang back as he bellowed.

Behind the Arch Purifier, a woman in silver raised her hands, suspended rubble obeying her craft. Sweat dripped down her pallid face as her arms shook. Debris shot forward and crushed the skulls of two oncoming Woodsmen.

Jon threw the dagger at the fae earth speaker, hitting her ribs. She fell with a sputtering cry. A round shot from the trees blew through her chest. At once, the earth stilled, and dust settled.

Gorova lunged at Jon, who dodged and parried. Ducking under the next swing, Jon pulled another knife from his boot. Gorova slashed along Jon's elbow and forearm. Though shallow, it stung, slackening Jon's grip on his cutlass.

"You'll die screaming, Woodlander," the purifier said.

"I'll take you with me," Jon replied. "And I'm no Woodlander. I'm one of the Tarishmen you missed in your senseless slaughter. I returned the favor by making sure your burning gate never opens again."

Gorova gaped. He faltered in his attack, allowing Jon to step back and flick his knife. It sank into Gorova's gut and brought him to his knees. Jon knocked the sword from Gorova's hand and caught his other wrist, twisting until it cracked and the knife fell.

Seeing the Woodsmen nearing victory once more, Jon dragged Gorova around an outcropping of rock, out of view from the enemy. He kneed the man hard in the ribs and twisted the knife embedded in his abdomen. Blood poured from the wound like a weeping fountain.

"Where the hell are my wife and son, you burning monster?"

Gorova growled, and Jon snarled.

"You sent them through that damn gate after me, but they're not in Shevak. Where the fires are they?"

"You!" Gorova gasped. "You were sent to the Cellar."

"I didn't have time to hang around. So I broke out after making a nice pile of petrified spooks. I'll add you to it if you don't answer."

"And if I do?"

Jon smirked. "I'll let you run off into the woods. Maybe one of your deranged fliers can give you a ride to the border. Stay clear of town though. I've taken it back." He twisted the knife further, earning an anguished gurgle from his hostage.

"Where are they?" Jon demanded.

"How would I know?"

Grabbing Gorova's shaved head, Jon smashed it, temple first, into a rock. Gorova's eyes dulled, and his skin grayed. Still, Jon's blood-pounding rage remained.

A banshee shrieked above and dove for him. Jon ducked. Rodden's round shot blew through the creature's leg, knocking it into the cliff, blood smearing on the rock as it slid to the ground. When Rodden put his bayonet to the banshee's throat, it squawked and cowered.

"You might get to live," Rodden said, "if you do me a little favor. You're coming with us, and you'll deliver your friend here to Fenris."

The banshee glanced at Gorova's corpse, then nodded.

Rodden addressed Jon, resting his rifle over his shoulder. "I heard from a very compliant ranger that they planned to take the ridge from behind."

Jon heaved the corpse toward the banshee. "I'm all for dramatic entrances."

# 45

# FIRE WIELDERS

*Sentinel Ridge, the Deep Wood*
*July 26, 1195 PT*

*Shane*

Shane leapt out of the way as the shade crier plummeted to the ground. The banshees who felled it screeched while soaring to their chain masters on the left flank. Behind Shane, the earth eater sprang from the ground, amid the poisoned road. It roared, gurgled, and then collapsed. Black pockmarks dotted its scales, the sure sign of wraith poison.

In the eastern sky, the sun rose over a band of clouds when a burning heat erupted in the field. Fenris entered the fight by sending towers of fire forward, attempting to wrangle the stone drake. The creature faced Fenris, quivering with rage, a huge gash over her left shoulder.

On the right flank of the Drawlen lines, the immortal troll Turuz towered over the crowd of rangers. A horned drake skull sat atop his head. Shane plowed toward Turuz and plucked off the helmet. The man yelled and whirled around, brandishing a lit cannon. Shane dodged as the ball flew from the gun, smashing a giant pine.

Roaring with malicious glee, Turuz brandished the cannon like a hammer and ran at Shane. Waiting with a smirk, Shane twirled the helmet on his fist. When Turuz drew near, he stumbled and gawked as Shane disappeared. A low buzz vibrated. Shane then reappeared behind Turuz and reached forward with clawed fingers burning red, as if lava flowed beneath them. Turuz evaded Shane's slash, but he leapt back when his eyes fell on the glowing claws.

Through the full engagement of Shane's mortari blood sight, the shades haunting the battlefield appeared opaque, the dead nearly invisible, the living like bright lights waiting to be snuffed out. And immortals—they were black marks on creation, festering wounds upon Ethar that had taken too long to heal. Only one thing drove him: cutting them out.

Turuz stumbled to the ground. He sputtered and begged, but his pleas proved fruitless. Shane lunged, thrusting his hand at the black tumor of immortality inside Turuz's chest. Securing the heart in his grip, he snatched it out. Then he watched the cursed organ shrivel in his hand, admiring his accomplishment, craving more.

"Shane!" Carris screamed and clapped her hands in his face.

Shane squinted.

"Day's not over yet, boy," Carris said, shaking his shoulders.

He blinked as daylight flooded his sight again.

"You good?"

Shane nodded. "Yeah. One down." He stared at Turuz's body. In his shard-induced blood rage, he had ripped through the plate armor that once protected the immortal's chest. He shuddered. Winning this battle would cost him a year of his life or more.

People around him screamed. Drawlen rangers of every rank scrambled from Turuz's corpse as it petrified. A fire still burned at the center of the battlefield.

In a storm of flames, Fenris slayed the stone drake and moved in on the Woodsmen and Ruvian ranks. He raised his hands and threw his head back, laughing. Then he smashed his hands together over his head and thrust them forward. The flames responded like a red wave and hurtled at the center lines of the defending troops.

Shane reached for his dagger but found the sheath empty. For a few heart-rending seconds, he thought there would be no stopping this attack.

Then a cone of crystal-blue fire swallowed the red wave curling toward the throng of people, pushing the onslaught back. It split the sea of flames down the middle and surrounded Fenris. He sucked in a breath, eyes wide.

The Ruvian riflemen who made up the bulk of the center line stepped to either side. An elderly woman waded through the crowd and onto the field. The blue fire quivered and grew at a flick of her wrist.

By now, Shane's head had cleared enough to reassess the progress of the battle. He and his team had all but demolished the Drawlen right flank. Stragglers scurried to the center lines or, if they were stupid enough, into the woods.

The left flank of the Drawlen force dwindled. Paustus had a cocoon of banshees protecting him, but snipers picked them off in droves from every direction.

The central force of the Drawlen invasion remained strong, largely protected by Fenris's fire. However, now that the Woodsmen had deployed their own fire wielder, the tide of battle shifted.

Skin-changers screamed and clawed out of the forest on either side of the rear Drawlen lines. Shane counted two grizzlies, four mountain lions, a dozen wolves, a gigantic frost hound, and a badger who gnawed soldiers down at the ankles.

Shrieks sounded from the defender's left flank where purifiers cut their way into the lines. Swaths of black smoke and haughty laughter answered the assaulting purifiers when Illania joined that fight. Still, the purifiers progressed with deadly efficiency.

Shane snapped his fingers at Bren and Carris. When Bren's last adversary hit the ground, he grabbed Carris's wrist and traced across the field, appearing at Illania's side.

The elderly fire wielder now stood a third of the way into the field. Leaning on her wooden staff, her dusty blue robe shimmered around her. Her eyes locked on Fenris, even as a round shot flew inches from her cheek.

Fenris howled for his snipers to cease fire, then seethed at the old woman. "Sadiona. It seems your mortality has caught up with you."

Sadiona tilted her head, a twinkle in her eye. "Hello, little brother."

Fenris sucked in a breath and glared. "And where is your bushy-tailed minder these days, dear sister? Still using you to put out forest fires?"

Sadiona smiled. "In a manner of speaking."

Pacing in a narrow arc, Fenris threw his head back and sighed theatrically. "Why? Why must we do this? It never changes. He can't kill me. I can't kill him. It's a futile and vicious parade, don't you think?"

"Perhaps." Sadiona shrugged and tapped her staff on the ground. The tunnel of blue flames curled and crackled, pushing the red fire further back. "You're the one who came here, Fenris. What is it you hoped to gain? Surely, you cannot conquer the Deep Wood with this handful." She gestured to the remaining Drawlen forces.

The man smirked and twirled his hand. A slithering line of fire flew before him, curling randomly around the field. Abruptly, the flames changed direction, heading toward Sadiona. Tongues of blue flame bloomed before the woman, causing her robes to swirl and the red fire to shoot into the sky.

Fenris pushed his hands forward, laughing. The red flames leapt over Sadiona's head and targeted the riflemen behind her. At the same time, black figures appeared along the ridge behind the defending lines. From among them, a banshee took flight.

As the flames crashed closer to the scrambling crowd behind Sadiona, the banshee drew nearer. Shane spied a silver-clad figure in its grip.

With a grunt and a thrust of her hands, Sadiona routed the attacking red fire near the cliff, past the gathered Ruvian force. Fenris scoffed at Sadiona's success but glowed with sinister delight at the oncoming banshee.

"Welcome again, Arch Purif—" His greeting died on his lips as the banshee came nearer.

Bleeding from a gunshot wound, it carried the Arch Purifier, Berneas Gorova, who was fully petrified. When the banshee dropped the body, it crashed to the ground at Fenris's feet.

The Woodlanders on the ridge descended the switchbacks.

Fenris howled while fire burst from every part of him. Twisting flames spread in all directions. His own men scrambled away, breaking formation and fanning toward the flanks.

This put more soldiers in Shane and Remm's path. The two went after their new quarry with abandon. A volley of round shots sounded in Shane's ear. He felt their wind, the taste of red powder. If he was hit, he didn't notice, didn't care. The fury of battle ripened within him, fueled by the mortari shard lodged in his heart. Wielding his recovered sword, he used his free hand to tear at necks and faces.

When the enemy closed in, Remm traced Shane away. They landed among the chain masters and banshees on the west end of the battlefield. Paustus, the Master of Chains, lay near them with a wound in the side of his head. A dark pulse of power drummed around the immortal. His wound filled with a tarlike substance, and he jumped to his feet.

Shane's vision turned red, and he smirked at the immortal. Paustus screeched and rattled the chains hooked around his arms. Immediately, banshees flocked around Shane, squawking and scratching and biting. The world blinked, and Shane appeared a dozen yards away from his assailants with Remm huffing at his side.

"Burning coward." Remm shook his head at the group of banshees now flying high over the forest and heading south, their immortal master in their grip.

Fenris had moved halfway across the field to press Sadiona back. His concern seemed solely focused on overtaking the woman.

A booming, murderous roar permeated the deep rumble of fire rolling upon the field. Fenris hollered when a great brown and black hellcat sailed over Sadiona's head and pinned him to the ground.

Fenris raised his hand, only to receive a clawed swat across the forearm. The flames sputtered and dwindled, no longer fueled by Fenris's command. He struggled and cursed under the weight of the hellcat, screaming, "I'll kill you, you mindless beast."

"You'll find that a futile endeavor, Fenris," said a red-haired fae man now standing beside Sadiona.

"Halas! You coward," Fenris yelled. "Will you let your pets devour me instead of facing me yourself?"

"I'm sure Rodden wouldn't turn it down. Though I'd hardly call him a pet." Halas smirked, wiping the sweat off his brow.

The hellcat atop Fenris shifted into a sapien form, and the World Burner leered at his unsuspecting quarry.

Fenris stared into Rodden's harsh, yellow eyes and guffawed. He sputtered between bouts of crazy cackling. "You—you think it matters? Do you think—you can all hold hands and strike me down forever—with the sheer will—of your motives?"

"No," Rodden said.

"Then why go to such effort, Morrien?" Fenris spat. "Return to the fold. You can't kill me."

"True," Rodden said. "But he can." He lifted Fenris off the ground and threw him at Shane's feet.

Fenris scrambled upright. Shane's mind weighed heavily with the mortari shard's influence. He thrust his hand and crushed the black remnant of corruption that had replaced this foolish man's heart. When he pulled his hand back and Fenris fell, a thrill hummed in his bones. He wanted more. Scouring his surroundings, he spotted two other undying fiends. One stood close by and chattered to him.

What were the words of these cursed devils to him? He dropped the shriveled heart and lunged at his new quarry.

# 46

# REMNANT

*Sentinel Ridge, the Deep Wood*
*July 26, 1195 PT*

*Nate*

Nate lay atop a rise overlooking the battlefield before Sentinel Ridge. The surrounding rocks protected him from enemy fire while still providing a full view of the land. He gawked at the body of Fenris the Fire Master, who lay dead on the ground one hundred feet beyond him.

This was the third immortal Nate had witnessed Shane zem'Arta kill. It left him mesmerized and disgusted.

"What's wrong with the Freelander?" Aaron asked. The Ruvian boy leaned against the rocks beside Nate, holding a reloaded rifle.

Paul sat on Nate's other side, still nursing his stab wound from the Lorinth fight. But he could reload fast and proved to be a master at picking out strategic shots and predicting enemy movements. "His eyes—it's like in the square," Paul said.

They all shrieked as Shane dropped the blackened remains of Fenris's heart and lunged at Rodden. The immortal sprang and grabbed Shane in a headlock. "It's over, pup! Put it away."

Shane thrashed against Rodden. A buzz sounded, like an out-of-tune trumpet, and Shane vanished from Rodden's grip. In a blink, he reappeared behind Rodden, hand poised to rip through his comrade's body.

Nate prayed for mercy and squeezed the trigger of his rifle. Shane flew back and toppled.

"Where did I hit him?" Nate begged.

"Low on the thigh. Right in the muscle," Paul said. "It won't kill him, but by Sovereign's grace, I hope it's enough to stop him."

Shane staggered to his feet, growling. He stared in the direction of the gunshot, and Nate's heart leapt to his throat. Whoever this was, it wasn't the man who had written him letters every few months, who had told him of far-off cities and battles with pirates, who had assured him his brother was well and loved him.

This was a monster. His irises shone scarlet. The whites of his eyes had turned black, as though wraith poison soaked his brain.

"Stop him!" Carris screamed.

While Shane glanced from Nate to Rodden, Remm traced to his side and snatched him in a gray cloud of shades. Remm reappeared ten feet in the air, blood splattering from his side as he fell to the ground. He scrambled upright, cursing.

Shane landed in the middle of Drawlen riflemen. He fought the throng of Drawls like a scythe through barley. Remm fought at his back once more, yet they were no longer unified as they'd been throughout the day. Now, it seemed more like a feral competition. His mad appetite raging, Shane soon ran out of Drawls to kill. Many lay dead along the poisoned road; others had retreated. Shane whirled on the escaping graycoats.

Carris blocked his way, pistol in hand. "Don't you make me do this, zem'Arta. I gave Nola a burning promise. Don't make me break it."

He huffed, growling in a field of blood and petrifying corpses. If this was truly mortari power, all the stories were wrong.

Shane stepped forward but flinched when a shining metal dart struck him in the shoulder. He glanced at it, then stared at Jon, who was twenty feet away, holding a wrist-mounted sling aimed at Shane.

Nate scrambled for another loaded gun, sure this time he needed to choose between killing his friend or watching his father be torn apart like an animal.

For a moment, neither man moved. Then Shane staggered, losing consciousness and falling to the ground. Nate's heart wrenched.

"What was that?" Carris demanded.

"Essence of Allunen," Jon replied. "He'll wake up in an hour. Will that be a problem, Carris? Will he be himself again, or . . . ?"

Carris fell to her knees beside Shane and rolled him over, faceup. "You," she yelled to Jon, "are a burning good man to have 'round!"

Jon huffed, stowing the sling. "I've been called worse."

"Vanguard, scouts!" Halas shouted. "Anyone who can still run. We've got Drawls in our Wood. See that they don't reach the border."

A wave of Woodsmen charged down Fenris's war trail, parting around Carris and Shane. Nate followed Paul and Aaron down the rocky slope of their perch. He ran to Sadiona, who knelt before Fenris's body.

"I'm sorry, Sadiona," he breathed.

She peered at him with glassy eyes, her frown turning to a shallow smile. "Thank you, my dear boy. It is a wound that shall heal only when I come into Sovereign's grace. But still, I am grateful for this day. Sovereign is bringing together a people divided." She nodded at Carris and Remm, who lifted Shane's unconscious body onto a handcart. "He is repairing the torn fabric of Palimar, sewing together the remnants of his people."

*Ella*

Ella lay prone on the tavern roof overlooking the Lorinth square. She had spent many childhood hours here with Will and Nate executing pranks on unsuspecting citizens—mostly Edd Pran and Philip Creedle. Now, there seemed a morbid irony in Philip handing her a freshly loaded rifle. Battered, bloodied, and crazed graycoats stumbled into the square. Ella picked them off one by one.

Red-faced and shaking, Philip composed himself better than most of the other Lorinth survivors who had crawled out of their hiding places a few hours ago.

*'More are coming,'* Tres's tenor echoed in Ella's mind. *'They are being routed. Ruvians and Woodsmen at the rear.'*

The terrion lord hid somewhere in the field, too weak to fly but strong enough to pick off stragglers wandering through the grass. At first, Ella had found his mind speaking unnerving. Now it proved a comfort.

The sun sank low on the horizon. After three days of little sleep, her already-dodgy aim wasn't improving. She fired, missed, and swore, then took another rifle and fired again.

"Nice," Philip said when the round shot struck a man in the head. Ella didn't tell Philip she had aimed for the man in front of him. Their routine continued until one ranger spotted them in the draw of the roof.

"Fires," Ella muttered. "We need to go." She pulled Philip over the gutter. When she hit the ground, the ranger lunged at her, brandishing a bayonet. Ella winced when she put weight on her injured leg but dodged her attacker and shoved a knife into his belly.

"There's more." Philip fired their last loaded gun, striking an oncoming ranger in the shoulder.

Ella retrieved her knife and met two more rangers head-on. One stood more than a foot taller and likely a hundred pounds heavier. *You're a little thing, El,* her mother's voice chided in her mind. *Never fight pound for pound. Use it against them. Turn their weapons into their woes.*

Ella swallowed the bitter sorrow accompanying that memory. She flitted around the man, coming between him and the fence, and hesitated until he brought his fist forward. She dodged and sliced her knife along his inner bicep as his fist splintered the wooden fence.

The crack of gunshots startled her. To her relief, both rangers slumped over, and Nate emerged around the fence.

"Therman?" Philip said with surprise.

"Creedle!" Nate called back. "You're alive!"

Philip raised a brow. He opened his mouth to speak but remained silent.

Nate bounced on his heels. "Your mother and sisters are safe. They asked me to look for you."

Philip sighed. "Thanks. And I'm sorry, ya know, about your family."

Nate nodded, then placed his hand on Ella. "You okay? Where's that Romanus guy?"

"Here." Tres stepped into the opening of the alley, the pistol in his grip still smoking. He stood tall, but the heavy bags under his eyes betrayed his exhaustion. "Woman, your skills are required."

Ella raised her brows but followed as he walked into the square. Ruvians and Woodsmen swarmed the town, dousing fires and chaining the few Drawls still alive. Atop the wraith gate, cleared of Nate's makeshift locks, Shane lay on his back with Bren and Carris kneeling beside him.

Shane blinked heavily as though he'd just awakened. Bloodstains and a dozen wounds marred his body. None looked life-threatening, but they'd definitely pose a risk for infection.

"Fires, wolf," Ella said. "Did you take on the whole army by yourself?"

"Ha!" Shane attempted to laugh but instead coughed up blood.

"We're sending him to Setmal," Tres explained. "He needs a real healer."

Ella glowered, but the man seemed utterly immune to anyone's judgement but his own.

"If you could do something for the pain, in the meantime," he said.

"Right," Ella muttered. She pulled a vial of laudanum from her vest and a flask from her belt. After tipping a generous amount of the tincture into the whisky flask, she pressed the liquor to Shane's lips. He drank, then coughed violently.

As they waited for Nate and Jon to replace the lever beside the gate, more Ruvians and Woodsmen stumbled into the square.

At the temple door, Halas and Rodden faced each other. In their bloodied, weary states, they looked more like bitterly reunited brothers than enemies of ages past.

"I thought you were still wandering mindlessly in the Dead Lands," Halas said.

"I was," Rodden replied.

Halas folded his arms. "Did you get bored?"

"I wandered mindlessly into the crater mountains a few decades ago and got caught in a bear trap. I liked it so much, I stayed."

Halas chortled. "So, you're the First Lord's pet now."

Rodden put his back to the wall of the temple and assessed the square. His gaze lingered on Tres, who spoke with Alistar near the fountain. "Liiesh Romanus reminds me of someone," Rodden said, "before things went wrong."

"I see," Halas said.

Remm swaggered into the square, holding two Drawlen rangers by the collar. He deposited them in front of a startled fae man and traced onto the temple stage. "You in one piece, pussy cat?" he said to Rodden.

The fae immortal rapped him on the side of the head with his fist.

Ella jerked when Shane touched her elbow. "El," he said.

Ella peered down at him. His eyes glazed over, and his long, vertical pupils dilated.

"El. I think I'm in love."

Carris and Remm both sputtered and clasped their mouths. Bren looked on, curious and quiet.

Ella felt her cheeks might catch fire. "Oh, um . . . I think it might be the opium."

Shane rocked his head. "No. I really think—"

Ella closed her eyes and took a deep breath. "Shane, it's very sweet, but—"

"She's not like—anyone," Shane said.

"She? Oh, thank Sovereign."

Carris chuckled.

"She's incredible," Shane went on. "I just don't know—ya know—how to—"

As he started to go unconscious, Ella patted his cheek. "How to talk to her?"

"I love talking to her. I just—I was married once."

Ella felt torn. She knew vague bits of his story but had always understood his desire not to divulge it. On the other hand, he needed to stay awake. "Oh. Well, you have some experience then."

"No. I don't want an old man to put a gun to my head again."

Ella bit her lip to keep from laughing. Her brother and Carris bellowed. "Oh—that's probably prudent," Ella said.

"She's *so* pretty."

"That's nice."

"Like the kind that makes other women jealous and crabby. Ya know?"

Ella bit her lower lip.

"You're kinda pretty," Shane mumbled.

Ella choked on her own breath.

Beside her, Remm muttered, "Watch it, sharp tooth."

Shane's eyes fluttered and his head rolled from side to side. "Your mother is really—"

"Okay!" Ella declared. "How about we discuss the weather?"

Laughter drew her attention. Arimal and Nate doubled over, faces scrunched and red.

The moment's comedy was punctured by the sting of knowing Ruth—Ella's beautiful, capable, kind mother—was nowhere to be found.

Remm took Ella's hand. "We'll find her, Little Mouse. Don't you worry."

"Is it ready?" Tres stood at the foot of the temple steps, scowling. Bren nodded. "Very well," the Second Lord said. "Turn it on."

"Wait!" Mylis stepped before the fountain with Haana at her back. "The First Lord swore I would receive his mercy. How can I receive what I was promised if you send this godkiller away?"

"Do not make a scene, oracle," Tres commanded. "This man is in no condition to offer the mercy you desire. The effort of this battle has nearly killed him."

"I was promised—"

"I have what you seek, woman. Be patient." Tres drew his sword, a long, gently curved saber that shone a brilliant red.

It reminded Ella of the knife Shane had thrown at the Veiled Man in Shevak. Resting the blade at his side, Tres turned to Ella. "You, come with us. The child will need to be—handled." Without waiting for her answer, the spire lord walked into the field with Mylis and Haana marching behind.

"What a prick," Ella mumbled.

"You should go with him, El," Remm said under his breath.

"Why?"

"Mylis's deal with Liiesh was that she gets to die once she got Rodden out of the Cellar."

Ella's eyes widened at the seriousness in his gaze. Sucking in a breath, she ran after the terrion and the immortal woman.

Once away from the crowd, Mylis addressed Ella. Her narrowed eyes and smeared makeup gave her an air of tragic beauty. She placed a hand on the girl. "I entrust Haana to you, lady smuggler."

"Mylis," Ella said. "You don't have to do this, not yet."

"There is nothing in this world for me."

Ella shook her head. "I know people who can find a place for you."

"You sweet woman. You do not understand. You are beholden to no one. I am a foreseer. I am never free. You may find a place for me, but it will be yet another prison. I cannot live that way again. Liiesh Romanus is the first person to offer me what I truly want: an end. He could have demanded I serve him as every other king has done. I cannot squander this. Haana understands." Mylis faced the girl, who gazed at her with big, glassy eyes.

The girl nodded to her mistress and hugged her closely.

Mylis smiled and said to Ella, "Her life—it is the most important life in all of Ethar. You must protect her."

"I know she's important to you."

"No, regardless of that," Mylis said in a harsh tone. "Her destiny, the destiny of Palimar—they are bound. And you are bound to them as well. Protect her, please."

Ella drew in a breath. "I'll do what I can."

Tres waited in the distance, his sword still drawn.

Mylis cupped Haana's face and kissed her cheeks and forehead. "I love you, my sweet child. I entrust you to this woman and her family. They will be good to you. I have seen it. You will go on to do great things."

Haana flung her arms around Mylis's neck and whispered in the woman's ear. A single tear fell from Mylis's eye. When the oracle reached Tres, the two of them veered west and strode out of sight.

Ella took Haana by the hand and walked toward the town. The bloom of darkness over the platform confirmed that Shane had gone through the gate.

# 47

# MAKING PLANS

*Lorinth, Taria*
*July 26, 1195 PT*

*Ella*

As the sun angled low over the valley, Ella sat alone upon a flat boulder in the field west of Lorinth. A trickle of Ruvians and Woodlanders trudged between the town and the forest, carting supplies and the injured. The puncture in Ella's thigh burned, despite the laudanum she'd taken earlier. Reaching for her belt, she discovered her water flask missing.

"Water?" a voice asked behind her.

Ella yelped and teetered on the rock. Halas handed her a fat waterskin. Mouthing her thanks, she took a long drink.

"So," he said, sitting next to her. "What's this about a debt I owe you?"

"Ah . . ."

"Do tell."

Ella sighed. "While everyone argued over who was allowed where, Fenris marched through your woods like he owned it. I thought it would be helpful to expedite a workable solution."

"By lying?" Halas arched his brow.

She shrugged and held out her palm. "You owe me thirty marks from our last marauders game."

He batted her hand away. "Twenty. Which is hardly enough for my hand to be forced on the matter of who gets to march through my country."

"Yes. I can see how Freelanders handing you a decisive victory in an otherwise hopeless fight really puts a bug up your nose. You're welcome."

Hallas threw his head back and laughed. "So, that neck-breaking Freelander ralenta is your big brother?" Halas pointed to Remm who strolled toward the forest with Illania and a group of Ruvian scouts.

Ella puckered her lips and snickered. "What gave it away?"

With a glint of amusement, Halas watched Remm disappear in a trace. "You have a shared habit of being absolutely uncouth with authority figures."

She laughed. "A family pastime."

"Speaking of such, what are you going to do about this invitation you've received from Liiesh Romanus?"

Rolling her eyes, she scoffed.

Halas retrieved the waterskin. "Be very careful, Ella. This is not a situation to make light of."

She fidgeted with her coat and shifted her legs. "What do you think I should do, Halas? Would you go?"

He bobbed his head from side to side. The cut across his shoulders cracked and bled. "The opportunity is—unprecedented. I've not always been on friendly terms with the Freelands, especially when Rufius Romanus was in power. He was a terror. If anything, his great nephew is more dangerous, being a godkiller. However, Liiesh has made it clear that Drawlen, and not the whole of Palimar, is his enemy."

He plucked a long reed of grass from beside the rock and ran it through his fingers. "We are all scattered remnants of a once-unified land. Long ago, all of Palimar rose to meet the threat of Faust the Tyrant and the Devourer's horde. We looked to Sovelus Kane to lead us against our enemy. But he lied to us, trapped us in this undying curse, killed Faust, and became the new tyrant of Palimar—restyling himself as Refsul. He has succeeded because we who remain loyal to freedom have been too stubborn and too beholden to our prejudices to unite as we should. I—I am the guiltiest by far." As he spoke, the usual gleam of mischief behind his gaze dulled. Exhaustion, weighed down by centuries of struggle and regret, took its place.

"You really think Liiesh Romanus is more dangerous than you?" Ella asked. "You've kept Refsul out of your territory for almost seven hundred years!"

Halas smiled, but his eyes remained impassive. "I did say godkiller, didn't I? He has a mortari blade, Ironmaw. His brother carries Stonebreaker. Their swords do essentially the same thing your troll friend did today, although they don't turn their wielders into mindless, walking death. Even without his sword, however, the First Lord is worthy of caution. He has a spy network to rival any in history."

"The Red Watch," Ella said.

Halas hummed in agreement. "He is clever and ruthless on his own. He tricked the previous Greqi emperor into withdrawing his naval forces from Palish waters to instead engage in single combat. He killed Emperor Wai in thirty seconds, ending an invasion before it had begun. Emperor Kii is certainly greedier and more vicious than his father, but he will not dare to approach Palimar while Liiesh remains in power."

"Fires," Ella breathed. "I've heard rumors, you know, but it all seemed a little too glamorous."

"Perhaps you will see for yourself."

Ella huffed. "Whether or not I care to."

Halas placed an encouraging hand on her shoulder. "If it's any help at all, Ella Riley, I believe you are a worthy delegate. You could brush up on your manners, but your heart is true." He strode into the Deep Wood, passing Tres as the spire lord returned from the field. They nodded to one another but still held the guarded bearing of important men sizing one another up.

Tres stopped several paces from Ella. A subtle shadow of distress darkened his eyes. Of course, he'd just given Mylis a mercy kill. Ella had once thought the Second Lord cold and uncaring; however, it was clear he had a different way of communicating.

Earlier in the day, once he could stand, he'd been at her back, fending off retreating soldiers crazed with both fear and disregard for whom they shot. At one point, he stood between a boy and a bayonet. Afterward, he pursued the incoming soldiers with renewed fury.

She patted the rock next to her and nodded for him to sit. He hesitated, then perched an arm's length from her.

After minutes of silence, Tres said, "Where did you learn Kumuni Re?"

"What's Kumuni Re?"

"Your fighting style."

"I didn't know it had a name."

"You can't possibly be that proficient without knowing its name."

"Do I get an award?"

Tres scowled.

"My mother," Ella admitted. "I'd introduce you, but . . . I don't even know if she's alive."

Tres gazed at the Drawlen Temple. Its marble walls shone gold in the evening sunlight. "She disappeared from this gate," he said. "Which means she appeared somewhere else. One does not simply vanish from a wraith gate. You either go through or you do not."

"You know this for sure?"

"It has never been disproven."

Ella clutched her red stone pendant. "So she could be anywhere in the world?"

"Indeed."

Ella blew out a long breath, gazing at the lingering band of light on the horizon. Their silent camaraderie broke when Jon settled himself between them with a belch. He popped the cork on a brandy bottle, tossed the cap into the field, and took a long drink. Then he passed the bottle to Tres, who politely declined, and to Ella, who accepted.

She took a sip. "Did you pay for this?"

"Nope."

Ella leaned forward, studying her father. "Carl and Margaret? And Cameron?"

"They're with the Ruvian caravan," Jon said. "They don't know yet about Will." He passed the brandy around again, the hollow sloshing of the bottle puncturing the quiet.

This time Tres swigged the drink but pulled it away, scowling. As he handed it back, he surveyed Jon's arm. "Are you aware you're bleeding, Master Smuggler?"

Jon lifted his elbow, inspecting the blood-soaked bandage which covered the length of his arm. "So I am."

"Who gave you that?" Ella asked.

"The Arch Purifier."

She gaped at her father. "Papa!"

"What? You think only your mother's dangerous?"

She retied a loose strip of his bandage. "How did he fair?"

Jon took a gulp of brandy, then hunched forward, resting his good arm on his thigh. Glaring at the sunset, he said, "After we had a chat, he made permanent friends with a rock."

Tres sat propped on one arm with a leg drawn up while leaning toward Jon. "You're more a thug than a smuggler, I believe, Therman."

Jon huffed, swirling the bottle. "It's wise to diversify one's skillset, Romanus. Makes one more employable."

Tres tilted his head, narrowing his eyes. "How are you at grave robbing?"

"Rusty. Why?"

Tres adjusted himself and reached into an inner pocket of his worn traveling coat. He pulled out an antique square medallion. It had a chip in one corner and bore impressions of thin lines of varying lengths, with the tallest in the middle. Terrion spires.

"I may have a job for you," Tres said. "I need to dig something up without anyone noticing. It may interest you as well."

"Oh?" Jon said.

"There is an ancient map of all the wraith gates on Ethar," Tres said. "I think I know where to find it. It may greatly aid in your search for your wife and son."

Jon patted Ella on her knee. He had the hungry glint in his eyes that came whenever he found a chance to push boundaries, to pull off something big. "Consider me hired."

Nate and Remm approached from the wood line. Nate sank down next to Ella, with Remm settling on his other side. Jon passed the brandy to Remm. When Nate reached out, Jon pulled the bottle away. He hesitated, narrowing his eyes at Nate's pair of rifles resting against the rock. He sighed and held the bottle out for Nate, who grabbed it. He took an enthusiastic swig but immediately coughed and spit it out.

Remm chuckled and snatched the bottle from his brother's hand. "Hey, Pops."

"Remm."

"What're you gonna do now?"

Jon took the tarnished medallion from Tres's hand and tossed it to Remm. "Tomb raiding, apparently."

Remm examined the artifact and flipped it back to Tres. "You'll need a bodyguard, spire lord."

"That I will."

# 48

# A SCOLDING

*Setmal, Yvenea*
*July 26, 1195 PT*

*Venna*

Thunder overpowered Venna vel'Tamar's yelp as Gretta yanked her by the wrist. Venna skipped awkwardly to catch her balance, grimacing at the glossy puddle she missed on the sidewalk.

"You're as graceful as a bird after hitting a window, missy." Gretta smirked, the delicate lines around her lips and eyes accentuated by raindrops. She was notably tall for a terrion woman, sharing Venna's same height, nearly six feet. Even in Yvean finery, a velvet servant's jacket and trousers, her rigid posture and the scars on her neck marked her as a warrior.

Venna huffed and repositioned her book bag over her shoulder, stepping under the cover of Gretta's umbrella. "Only on my good days, Gretta."

The woman laughed in a warm tenor. "I can carry that, you know."

"It's fine." Venna patted the corset of her pleated green dress. "I always feel weird in these outfits. The bag gives me something to do with my hands."

"Why do you wear that stuff?"

"I was told I must. Apparently, all this political hullabaloo has made people twitchy. You'll see after you've been here a few weeks: Freelanders are either for gawking or mocking."

They turned into the carriage yard of the Freeland embassy. Two guards dressed in traditional Spire Watch uniforms stood before the stone pillars on either side of the drive. They caught sight of Venna and Gretta with ebony eyes, then returned to watching the road.

"Seems Yveans aren't the only ones getting twitchy." Gretta cocked her head at the guards near the gate. "We don't usually put mind renders on embassy doorsteps."

Venna glanced over her shoulder, observing the profiles of the guards. "How do you know who's a mind render and who isn't?"

Gretta tapped her temple. "I am one. Also, I did all my training with those two."

"Why didn't you say hel—oh, right. On duty."

Gretta smiled, shaking her head. "Fires, you're adorable."

"Well, you're much better for conversation than my last bodyguard."

"Who was that?"

"Marcus Tollsum."

"Ach!" Gretta flicked her wrist dismissively. "You poor little groundling. That old gun-slinger is boring, even by terrion standards."

Venna's shoulders shook as she covered her mouth, holding in her laughter. They approached the carriage port occupied by a team of doormen tending to a tall carriage.

"Someone important?" Gretta asked.

"There's always someone important coming and . . ." Venna trailed off when the side door of the carriage opened. Blood spatter marred the polished floor and blue velvet cushions. Venna stared, mouth agape while the rain beat down on their umbrella.

"Definitely a 'don't ask' situation," Gretta said, steering Venna toward the front entrance.

As they entered the embassy, facing the grand U-bend staircase, the normally calm energy dissipated. On the second flood landing, servants scurried along the corridors with towels and steaming pitchers.

"What's going on?" Venna asked.

"Something. That's for certain," Gretta said.

She tipped her umbrella upside down on the hallway floor and helped Venna remove her book bag and coat. Thunder rattled the windows.

A gruff, male voice shouted from the second floor. "Get it out, or I'll do it myself!" The person sounded familiar, but Venna couldn't see anyone.

"Miss vel'Tamar." Venna jumped as Praya Aldonus appeared in the entrance to the piano parlor. Wearing a fitted blue gown, her hair pinned in a coiled braid, she acted in her usual manner: reproachful yet polite. Praya narrowed her eyes at the pair of them, focusing on Venna's feet. Glancing down, Venna noticed the mud her boots had trailed on the rug. She raised her brow apologetically.

"I sent a message," Praya said, "for you to stay at the palace. We're in the middle of a sensitive matter."

"Oh, um, I'm sorry," Venna said. "I must have missed it."

Gretta stepped around Venna and bowed her head to Praya. "My Lady Ambassador, I assume the bad weather caused your messenger to miss us. We took a few shortcuts to dodge the rain. Shall we go back?"

Praya drew up her shoulders. "No. You're already here, and there's no sense wandering about with no dinner when there's a burning curfew to avoid. But Miss vel'Tamer must stay in her room. I will send for dinner service."

"Yes, my lady," Gretta said.

She ushered Venna to the back staircase next to the kitchen. At the second-floor landing, a tall, burly man stood in the hall. Dried blood coated his tangled copper hair, and bandages covered his arms and one leg. He leaned with his forearm against the open door of Shane zem'Arta's apartment, his torn clothes dangling at his sides.

He glanced sidelong at Venna, startling her with his sharp, yellow eyes. His gaze shifted, and he mumbled.

Carris's sharp voice bellowed from within the apartment, "So, ya think you should take a crack at it, Rodden? This mortari shit is still boiling in his blood. I ain't no doctor. But you come near him, zem'Arta'll rip up your other leg—or worse. And we only got two bottles of this Alunen crap left."

Gretta veered Venna away and nudged her up the stairs. When they reached the third-floor landing, she whispered, "Pretend you didn't hear that."

"But—" Venna sputtered.

Gretta spun her around and stared her down. The magnetic pull of Gretta's mind craft took hold, but it receded quickly. Gretta sighed. "Burning trolls and your stonewall brains. Look, there's a reason you weren't supposed to be here."

"What's happening? It sounded like Shane's badly hurt."

"I don't know, but you need to put it out of your mind."

Venna's mouth hung open. "They said mortari."

"It's nothing, just—"

"Nothing? I know what a mortari is, Gretta. That's not nothing."

"Forget about it. And Venna"—Gretta put a firm hand on her shoulder and guided her into her apartment—"try to keep yourself out of trouble." When

Venna cleared the threshold, the bodyguard shut the door, leaving her alone in the room.

Venna's mind whirled. For one thing, it sounded like Shane lay in the room directly beneath her, covered in serious wounds. But the word mortari sent her tearing through the overflowing bookcase in the room. She plucked *Legends of the Pillars of Palimar* from a high shelf and flipped through the stiff, illustrated pages. Finding her place in the book, she set it down on the pile of papers on her desk and read:

> *And so, Agroth became stone and slumbered a hundred years. When called, he awoke as a great beast of the sky, and obeying the spirit of the call, engaged for seven days and nights in battle with the Devourer. Upon imprisoning the undying horror, Agroth's life was spent. To pass on his power, he divided his heart three times and again. These shards were given to the second sons of the pillar kings and passed down in the order of the mortari warriors, those who watch with the red sight.*
>
> *Thus, the kings of the ground sought the Shards of Agroth, for the power of the mortari was known and revered. Thirty sons of kings and emperors sought the power, yet only one, a human archer, could endure its burden. All the rest suffered three days and perished. But for all who harbored a sliver of the dragon's power, their years were reduced, and their anguish increased.*

Venna reread the passage several times. A servant delivered her dinner tray. She set it aside, letting it go cold as she thumbed through a dozen other books, searching in vain for a more hopeful review of her friend's predicament. With the book on her lap, she fell asleep on the couch and dreamed of servants gathering Shane's ashes in the hall.

When she woke the next morning, her stomach clenched and growled. Finding the corridor empty, she snuck toward the kitchen. A servant with a covered tray passed her on the stairs. He ignored her and entered Shane's room.

Once in the kitchen, Venna grabbed a roll of bread and scurried up the stairs, lingering a moment at the second-floor threshold. Only meaningless mutterings met her ears. She returned to her room.

As lunch drew near, Venna crept down to the kitchen again and slipped a note into the covered tray on the prep table seconds before the maid scooped it up.

An hour later, Gretta knocked on her door. "The Lady Ambassador wants to see you, Miss vel'Tamer."

Venna followed Gretta to Praya's second-floor office. Praya motioned for Venna to sit as Gretta left the room. On the desk lay Venna's smuggled note:

I hope you're on the mend. Thinking of you. – Venna

She met Praya's disapproving gaze. No, disapproving was not sufficient. The woman's face pressed into a hard scowl. "*This* was in my meal tray. Venna vel'Tamer, this is not some boarding school where you can pass petty missives and think you're being sweet."

Venna pursed her lips and nodded. Heat rose to her cheeks, but only because she'd been caught. Her friend might be bleeding half to death! What did she care for this woman's approval?

Praya drummed her fingers on the arm of her chair. "Perhaps I should have you sent to the palace."

"Is it—" Venna stammered. "Is it not safe with him. I mean, being a mortari?" She immediately regretted opening her mouth.

Praya's eyes blackened, and her mind craft slammed inside Venna's head like a gong. "Foolish girl! You were not meant to know this. And you will pretend you don't. This information is one of the First Lord's most closely guarded secrets. Do you understand?"

Venna nodded vigorously. "Yes, Lady Praya. I'm sorry. It's just—"

Praya rose from her chair and paced around the desk. "It is classified information you will forget, Miss vel'Tamer. While I regrettably cannot force you to, being you are thurse, I must trust to your abiding loyalty and prudence. Certainly, you have enough of those to overcome your childish fascination with fairy tales."

Venna bowed her head, crimping her coral skirt in her grip. "Yes, my lady. I'll not tell a soul."

"Very good." Praya smoothed her dress with shaking hands and sank back into her chair. "Now, you've work to do, young scholar. Try to keep busy."

"Yes, my lady."

Venna spent the next three days either in her room or in summer term lectures at the university. In the evenings, she could hear muffled comings and goings downstairs. A few times, Shane's barking complaints echoed up the stairwell.

On the seventh night, Venna had finally developed a productive groove with her studies when she ran out of tea and her work light faded. She sighed and tiptoed into the empty hall to find a new work light.

In the darkness of the first-floor landing, she bumped into the broad back of a man propped against the wall. She shrieked, startled by the man's string of Karthan curse words.

A warm hand caught her forearm, and she looked into Shane zem'Arta's surprised blue gaze. They froze for a moment.

He wore only linen pants, but the number of bandages on his arms and torso could have counted for a shirt. Bands of black ink and olive skin peeked out between the white wrappings, and a bloom of blood grew along his lower left side.

Venna reached out instinctively. "Shane, you're bleeding."

When her fingers brushed his side, he stiffened. She caught a flash of red pass over his gaze. Knowing now what he was, she realized she'd seen this before. It both thrilled and frightened her.

He looked away and stumbled against the wall.

Stepping with him, she put her hand on his arm. "You should probably lie down, you know."

"Yeah." He struggled up the steps with Venna trailing him.

When they reached the top, she asked, "What are you even doing out of bed?"

Shane lurched forward, coughing and gripping his side. Blood spattered from his mouth, and he growled in unbridled frustration.

Venna slipped between him and the wall, forcing his arm around her shoulder, then straightened to support him. "Back to bed, gimpy."

To her overwhelming delight, Shane cracked a brief smile. In the golden lamplight, the convict marks on his cheeks stood out, along with the healing cuts on his neck and the dark circles under his eyes. His hair lay matted on his neck, and he seemed thinner. Still, Venna sagged under his weight. Even for a Zereen thurse, Shane was tall and stocky. Finally, she maneuvered him onto his bed.

The layout in his room was identical to Venna's: a sitting area, breakfast nook, bed, and hearth all generously proportioned. While her room had white trim and lace wallpaper, this one held stained wainscoting and a small balcony leading off the breakfast nook.

"No fair," Venna said. "You get a balcony."

"Hah. Makes it easy to sneak out at night for parties."

"And chasing assassins?"

Shane leaned into his pillow, coughed, and blew out a long breath. "I think I'm off the ticket on that one for a while."

"Hang on. I'll be right back." Venna scampered into the hall and down the stairs into the kitchen to assemble a tea tray. She tiptoed back, tray in hand, and mothered Shane into sitting up by stacking pillows behind his head.

He muttered his thanks and took a sip. Venna sat on the edge of the bed, fiddling with her hands while focusing on the bedside table. It held a crisp parchment, a fountain pen, and an open ink bottle. On the floor lay two wadded pages. She could read one sentence scribbled on a page: "I know it's been a while."

She wrung her hands and shifted her gaze to Shane. He glanced away like he'd been caught staring.

"So, mortari," Venna said in a casual tone.

Shane, who had just polished off the mug of tea, coughed and caught some of the liquid spilling from his mouth with his free hand. He regarded her warily, then shook his head.

Venna smiled warmly, patting the spilled tea with a cloth. "Is it a family legacy, or did you go to university for that?"

Shane gaped. After a moment, a little smirk appeared on his face. "I fell into it."

"I know it's supposed to be a secret," she said, running her hands through her hair.

Shane chuckled. "Well, maybe not anymore."

"Oh, no. I won't tell anyone. I promise." She pressed a hand to her chest.

Shane laughed quietly as he set the empty mug onto the tray. He leaned back and stared at the ceiling. "I'm not worried about you, Ven." He picked at the bandage on his right forearm. "I put on a little show in Shevak. I'm sure the Drawls are falling all over themselves trying to figure out how a thurse got hold of a Shard of Agroth."

"Well." Venna struggled to keep her imagination in check. "I'm glad you're okay." She plucked his hand away from the bandage. Laying it down gently, she said, "How—um—how did you fall into it?"

Shane stretched his arms overhead, wincing slightly, and settled his hands behind his neck. "I fell down a hole and found a shard at the bottom of an underground lake. I didn't know what it was."

"You didn't?"

"Well, I was nine."

"Nine? Oh, that must have been awful."

Shane bristled and turned his head away.

"I'm sorry," Venna said. "I get carried away a lot. It's just—it's *really* fascinating."

Folding his arms over his chest, Shane wrinkled his brows. "Fascinating? Most thurse find it pretty off-putting. Half the people in Zeree think I'm the harbinger of the apocalypse."

Venna scoffed. "Well, I don't put much stock in pagan superstition. They don't know their history very well anyway. Really, they should consider it an honor, not a curse." Realizing he was staring in disbelief at her still, she added, "Sorry, I got carried away again."

Shane studied her in silence. Venna fidgeted while staring back at him. She couldn't interpret his expression but was sure no one had ever looked at her that intensely before. Finally, he gave her a warm, genuine smile, and Venna thought her heart might catch fire.

"You know," Shane said. "I don't think I'm up for that dance I owe you at the moment."

Laughter overtook Venna's girlish nervousness. "You don't—" she began but went silent when Shane took her hand firmly into his and gazed at her with an expression she could interpret with utter certainty.

He shifted toward her, eyes warm, lips set in a satisfied smile. Venna let out a breath as his other hand rested under her jaw. She leaned in to meet him and closed her eyes when he pressed his lips to hers. It was the longest and shortest moment of her life. She wanted to drown in it.

Pulling back, Shane rested his forehead against hers, sighing heavily. "Does that make up for it?"

Venna searched for the right words. After a few fluttering heartbeats, she whispered, "Maybe a few more."

Shane met her quiet request with enthusiasm and wrapped his arm around her midback. When he winced, she pulled back, but he muttered, “Later,” and drew her closer.

*Shane*

Shane woke from a rare bout of peaceful slumber when a sensation burned in his abdomen. He sucked in a breath and lurched his head off the pillow, a feeble attempt at sitting up. Deep brown eyes and a warm, smiling face greeted him.

“Mona,” he whispered.

The woman hovered over him, working her healing craft along his torso with twitching fingers, as if she were playing a piano. She peeked past him with laughter in her eyes.

Venna lay curled next to Shane atop the bed covers. She slept soundly with her hand clasped in his. They had talked late into the night after Venna reapplied his bandages. Now, the gray light of early morning peeked through the seams of the shuttered windows.

Shane placed a hand across his chest, his eyes wide. “I was a perfectly behaved gentleman, I swear.”

An amused grunt from the door drew his attention. Rodden leaned on the doorframe, also in fresh bandages and a clean shirt. With a pang in his chest, Shane recalled the two slips he’d made into mortari unrest a week ago, both coming dangerously close to crushing the heart of the man standing in his doorway. Shane turned away, dropping his chin.

Mona’s gentle fingers under his jaw drew him back. “You’ve been reckless, again, Shane.”

He mumbled under his breath, “Only because your idiot husband got himself thrown into a Drawlen dungeon.”

Rodden chuckled. “Don’t worry, pup. I got my scolding.”

Humming in agreement, Mona re-engaged her healing craft, drumming her fingers in the air over Shane’s shoulder.

Beside him, Venna stirred. She opened her eyes, squinting, then jumped away from the bed, looking dubiously between Shane and Mona. “Oh, um—I really am not supposed to be here. Sorry.”

“Get us a breakfast tray, and we’ll swear secrecy,” Rodden said.

Venna blushed. “R-Rodden?”

He smiled, scratching at his bandage-wrapped elbow. "Make sure to put some coal in the pup's coffee."

"She may put some in yours if you keep on like that, dear," Mona said. She nodded to Venna. "Some honey cakes would be wonderful."

"Of course." Venna scurried from the room, sparing Shane a glance.

He chuckled.

"Well," Mona started, smiling at Shane, "Seems you both got something out of this in the end."

From the hallway came another deep voice. "Did we, indeed?"

Shane twitched and pressed his head against his pillow.

"I'd appreciate you not upsetting my patient, dear brother," Mona chided.

Liiesh Romanus appeared in the doorway, mirroring Rodden's posture. It had been over a year since Shane last saw the First Lord, but his appearance remained the same: Silk black hair framed his sharp cheekbones and fell loosely over his shoulders. His bottomless obsidian eyes shone cold and smug while his long red coat, embroidered in gold and ivory, hugged his tall frame. Liiesh nodded to his sister but returned his gaze immediately to Shane.

"Is it time for my scolding?" Shane asked.

Liiesh raised his chin. "We shall see." He held up an unfolded letter so Shane could see the back of it. It contained no seal, addressed only to "Spire Lord," written in blotchy script.

"What's that?" Shane asked warily.

"*This* is the first time I've read so many insults, accompanied by so many spelling errors, directed at me. Your smuggler friend has a temper."

Shane attempted to raise himself onto his elbows but collapsed when his shoulders spasmed.

Chuckling, Liiesh folded the letter and stuffed it into his coat pocket. "She called me an 'entitled overlord.' Does have a certain ring to it, don't you think?"

Beneath the spire lord's amused expression, Shane detected a shadow of danger. "*She*?" he said, blanching.

"Yes, the woman you insisted was worth saving. I must bow to your superior instincts, Captain. This development certainly has—potential."

"Why is El writing you a letter?" Shane demanded.

"It's an official answer to my summons."

"What summons?"

"To give account for involving my agents in her varied schemes. Fear not, zem'Arta," Liiesh drawled. "She declined. However, she will be making a delivery to Palim, so the point is moot. This"—he patted his coat pocket—"was her letting me know I am a petty monarch and she is merely gracing Palim with her *momentary* presence to ensure safe delivery of the wraith gate stolen from Taria. I am looking forward to how many insults she can muster when she looks me in the eyes. These outlanders are pathetic when faced with the simplest mind craft."

Shane recalled the fight inside the Temple of the Tree. Tres had attempted coercion on Ella—one of the strongest forms of mind craft—and she had responded by drawing a knife and telling him to back off. Keeping this to himself, Shane flashed his sharp teeth at Liiesh. "Suit yourself, Romanus. What in the fires are you doing in Yvenea?"

Liiesh tilted his head, sporting a self-satisfied grin. "I'm taking this opportunity to make the acquaintance of some of Drawlen's other enemies." At this, he pivoted and marched down the stairs.

Rodden cleared his throat. "You're not going to tell him Ella's a born savant when it comes to mind craft?"

"Fires, no," Shane said, settling his hands behind his head. "That jackass can find out for himself."

# 49

# UNINVITED GUESTS

*Cilé Faíl Palace*
*Setmal, Yvenea*
*July 28, 1195 PT*

*Orin*

Fredrick, the Novelen family steward, bowed to Orin with a grand wave of his arm. He exited the office with Orin's three wolfhounds in tow. When the door clicked shut, Orin sank into his chair and dropped his pen onto the desk. The letters he'd been pretending to write lay strewn on the polished blue surface. He brushed them aside.

Truly, he'd gotten nothing done today. The latest court spectacle had his mind spinning, his temper fragile. He drummed his fingers on the desk, trying to riddle out how things had gotten so out of hand in the Yvean court. Perhaps he should—

A rap at the door interrupted his thoughts. He stepped around the ornate desk and strode across the room. When he opened the door, a palace steward greeted him. Beside the steward stood Orin's father-in-law, the High Chamberlain of Yvenea, Taval Sesporan. The pale, sixty-eight-year-old man wore his usual powder-blue coat with understated embellishments and trimmed-down ruffles, a testament to his very un-Yvean pragmatism. Even his hair lacked the latest trend of being curled around the ears and powdered.

"Good morning, Arist Novelen." Taval clasped his hands behind his back and straightened his shoulders.

"High Chamberlain," Orin said, masking his surprise with a smile. "Ah, please." He motioned with his hand and moved aside to receive the older lord. As Taval crossed the threshold, the steward bowed and departed.

After Orin closed the door, he glanced anxiously at the state of his office. He would have tidied up before receiving such a guest. Taval leaned against the guest chair in front of the desk. His gaze lingered on the empty tea table before the hearth.

"My Lord Chamberlain," Orin said, "forgive the mess and lack of a proper tea tray. I wasn't told you'd be calling on me today."

Clearing his throat, Taval wrinkled his brow. "I received a request in your name to come at nine to your—"

The air chilled. In the corner of the room beside the door, a deep shadow formed. When it dissipated, a tall, dark-skinned man appeared in a bloodred coat. Orin tensed.

Liiesh Romanus stepped forward. A thin teenage boy with a shaved head and blank expression joined him—Bren, one of Shane zem'Arta's Red Watch agents.

Taval lurched and drew his pistol.

Liiesh put up his hands in mock surrender, his eyes flashing for a second. Orin felt the buzz of mind craft, and Taval lowered his gun, frowning.

"Gentlemen," Liiesh said. "I am the one who arranged this meeting."

Taval grimaced and raised his gun once more.

"Fear not, Arists," Liiesh said. "No one is here to kill you today." He inclined his head to the High Chamberlain. "Liiesh Romanus, First Lord of the Freelands. Pleased to make your acquaintance in person, High Chamberlain." He nodded to the boy, who disappeared with the air shivering around him.

Liiesh strode past the two arists with his chin raised and pulled a thick black envelope from his breast pocket. Fanning it, he lounged in Orin's favorite wingback chair. Orin glared at the man for this blatant territorial move.

Liiesh smirked. In Orin's mind, the First Lord's deep voice purred, *'See how you like uninvited guests in your house, boy.'* Out loud he said, "Arist Novelen, I'm sure you'll sleep much better at night knowing the most dangerous assassin's guild on Ethar is no longer interested in you." He dropped the envelope onto the tea table.

The parchment bore a broken wax seal with the impression of a war fan—the symbol of the Kumuni Cosazi.

Taval stowed his pistol and folded his arms. "It was *your* agents in Kumun!"

Liiesh narrowed his eyes at the chamberlain. "Yes, Arist Sesporan. I think it's time we stop getting in each other's way since we are clearly after the same thing, and it benefits neither of us to cancel out each other's efforts. I admit, I was very suspicious of you until recently. I assumed you sent agents to Kumun to counteract mine, not to bully the Cosazi into giving up their employer."

Huffing, Taval shifted on his feet. "It was a fruitless effort, First Lord. No offense, but your people proved very disruptive to my operation."

Liiesh snorted, and Orin thought no one could look more arrogant than the man sitting in his chair.

"None taken." Liiesh straightened and bent forward. "Especially since I have good news for you. The Arch Purifier of Drawlen, Berneas Gorova, was the personal sponsor of Orin Novelen's Cosazi contract."

Orin seethed when spoken of as if he were not in the room.

The High Chamberlain's eyes, however, widened, and he raised his voice. "That's treason!"

Liiesh shook his finger from side to side. "Technically, it is an act of war. Drawl and Shevak are sovereign city-states."

"I'm sure the Arch Purifier didn't intend to start a war," Taval said.

"No," Liiesh agreed. "He intended to frame me and diminish my influence on your nation."

"What is your evidence?" Taval gripped the back of the chair opposite Liiesh.

Liiesh pressed a finger into the wax seal. "My agents took this Cosazi contract from Gorova after he was interrogated and killed."

Taval furrowed his brow, his knuckles going white. "You murdered him?"

"He was a casualty of the failed Drawlen invasion of the Deep Wood. And it wasn't by me or my people." Liiesh gestured to the chairs near him. When Taval and Orin sat, Liiesh leaned closer. "It was one of yours, Chamberlain. The Master Smuggler, Jon Therman, ended the Arch Purifier's life. He recovered the contract and sent it along with my agents. He was kind enough to sign it."

He unfolded the parchment. Kumuni symbols appeared in vertical lines across the surface. At the bottom, four lines corresponded with different symbols. The first line was signed with a silver pen in a Kumuni character. The second was signed *"Berneas Gorova"* in red, contrasting the dark paper. The third line was blank, and the fourth was signed, *"Jon Therman"* in dried blood.

"I don't understand." Orin stroked his chin. "What does his signing this have to do with anything?"

Liiesh stared, remaining still for a moment. This terrion habit greatly annoyed Orin. Liiesh slid the parchment closer to the two men. "Cosazi contracts are made with witchcraft, Arist Novelen, with blood sorcery. They are binding until the target is dispatched or until the contract cancelation is signed. If the originator is killed, his authority passes to the one who took his life. If the originator or the inheritor signs the contract cancelation, all attempts on the target's life stop immediately."

Orin pondered this. If the Arch Purifier died in the Deep Wood at the battle of Sentinel Ridge, then he had only been dead two weeks. The knowledge of that confrontation wasn't widely known. And Kumun was three weeks' travel by ship from Palimar. "How would they know—"

"As I said, Arist, *blood sorcery*," Liiesh said. "You have a Tarish rock smuggler to thank for the lack of poison on your pillow."

"The Master Smuggler," Taval said. He ran a calloused finger over the name at the bottom of the paper. "I am acquainted with him, though not directly, I must admit. He's done work for my agents. He's not one of mine, per se. My people are chiefly concerned with the security and sovereignty of Yvenea, which makes me just as wary of you as I am of Drawlen, First Lord."

"Understandable. But this leads me to believe you are either unaware of all your agents' activities, or you're not being completely honest with me." Liiesh rested his elbows on his knees, mirroring Taval's posture. "Tell me, what is your relationship to the Arch Traitor, Alistar Soral?"

Taval studied Liiesh for a long moment. "You strike me as a man who doesn't ask questions until he already knows the answer."

The First Lord's lips curled upward.

Taval squinted, and he drew in a long breath. "Then you must already be aware that General Soral defected from the Drawlen Order over twenty years ago to join a remnant settlement of Ruvians. And likewise, that my daughter, Yvette, was kidnapped and held ransom in her youth by a tSolani rogue ring at the behest of Drawlen agents. Alistar himself rescued her."

With each of the High Chamberlain's statements, Liiesh nodded along, then added, "In partnership with the Rogue Master Dantiego."

"Correct," Taval said. "The Arch Traitor and I found ourselves in the same situation you and I are in now: wary of one another, yet with aligning ambitions." He tilted his head to one side and raised his brow at the First Lord.

Liiesh returned Taval's gaze with a shallow nod. "Well, Arist Sesporan, I can assure you I have no designs on the sovereignty of your great nation. Yvenea is the one thing holding Drawlen back from becoming the unchallenged theocratic dictator of Palimar. Your independence from both Drawlen and the Freelands is imperative.

"But you are weakening. Your dynast is unhinged, he has yet to confirm his heir apparent, and your citizens are on the brink of revolt. Not to mention, there are a dozen high-ranking Yvean officials on Drawlen's payroll. My people have been watching them for years. However, we don't have the overt authority to do anything about them."

He snapped his fingers. Bren appeared behind him, holding a bulging stack of papers and envelopes. Bren placed the stack over the Cosazi contract on the tea table. Bowing to the First Lord, he disappeared.

Liiesh placed his hand on the stack. "This is a list of their names and the necessary evidence to support my claims. I'm sure you'll find it a thrilling read. It is yours to do with as you please, High Chamberlain."

Taval ran his thumb along his jaw. "This won't help me combat the growing sentiment among the Court of Aristors. They say I'm after their seats like a hungry wolf."

Liiesh rapped his knuckles on the stack. "Wolves hunt better in packs."

Taval gathered the papers. "Then I should get to hunting. Good day, First Lord." He bowed his head to Orin. "Arist, a good day to you as well."

Orin escorted his father-in-law out of his office as Taval carried Liiesh's library of evidence. While the First Lord stood gazing out the tall bank of windows at the back of the room, Orin paced alongside his desk.

Waiting impatiently, he cleared his throat, and when Liiesh finally met his eyes, Orin said, "It seems your agents have been rather busy, First Lord."

"They certainly are not idle."

"Of course. No idle time to dedicate to finding my father."

The brightness of the south-facing windows silhouetted Liiesh's form so Orin could not read his expression when he spoke. "You assume Leron is an afterthought?"

Shifting on his feet, Orin clenched his fists. "You haven't seemed overly concerned."

Liiesh moved closer, allowing Orin to see him more clearly. Other than his unusually dark eyes, he could pass for a human in his early thirties. But Liiesh was around a century old, and his expression echoed lordly disapproval. "Oh?" he said, sneering. "Did you have time to evaluate my efforts in the midst of your political brownnosing, Arist?"

"I am trying to preserve the legacy of my house, Lord Romanus. Apparently, I'm doing it alone. I can't expect the great and unchallenged Dragon of Palimar to understand."

Liiesh's eyes grew completely black, and though his wings remained hidden, Orin felt them filling the room. The First Lord seemed more demon than man.

"Fool," he said. "Do you think my power and reputation were handed to me? If you believe you deserve the seat of the Celestial Hall, then prove it. Don't expect it to be thrown at you just because of your mother's blood and your father's heroics. I have turned over every rock and opened every cupboard from here to the Shardling Islands looking for Leron. But I can assure you it isn't for your benefit. There are darker forces in the world than the squabbling of politicians and priests."

As the First Lord spoke, Orin backed into his desk. He swallowed his fear, convinced it was manufactured by this mind-tampering tyrant. "Does that give you the right to use me to set up clandestine meetings with my betters?"

The ominous pressure in the room dissipated. Liiesh chuckled. After considering the Arist for a moment, he shook his head. "Your betters? Young man, if your chief concern is how you measure up to men in court, you will forever be stunted. Forever a pawn." He snapped his fingers.

Bren reappeared in the room next to his lord. He lay his hand on Liiesh's shoulder, and they both vanished.

Orin slapped his hands on the meaningless piles of paperwork on his desk. All frivolous gestures of statesmanship which would, in the long run, get him nowhere. He grasped the black parchment on the tea table: a testament to Orin's role as a pawn in bigger men's games.

A scream bellowed from his mouth, and when that didn't sate the fire in his chest, he picked up the guest chair and threw it across the room. It smashed into the hearth mantel, knocking the gold-faced clock to the ground. Orin's heart raced. After several minutes, his breathing slowed, and a moment later, he noticed the note that had been hiding under the mantel clock. He unfolded it and covered his mouth to muffle his anguished gasp as he read his father's stately handwriting.

'False flattery feels fair at first.
Wise words wound a wavering ward.'
Orin, the road before you will be full of both.

*Learn the difference, my son. It will save your life.*
*I love you.*

The first two lines were a proverb his father had often quoted when Orin accompanied him to court as a child and witnessed the peculiar interactions between nobles and officials.

Leron obviously meant it for comfort. Instead, Orin's bitterness swelled. His father had disappeared months ago, only leaving behind this cryptic note in a place Orin wasn't likely to look. Snarling, he crumpled the parchment and threw it among the hearthstones, where it smoked and shriveled.

# 50

# THE OTHER GATE

*July 23, 1195 PT*

*Jeb*

Jeb Therman woke to complete darkness. His mouth felt cottony, his head a ringing gong. Attempting a deep breath, he coughed. Light flooded his vision. He shut his eyes, whimpering.

"It's okay, sweetheart," his mother's voice crooned.

Her arm wrapped around him, and he fell into her embrace. Opening his eyes again, he squinted in the light shining from a blue sunrock on the stone floor beneath his feet.

The ground merged with more stone on walls and ceiling—a cave. Jeb shivered from the humid, cool air. The deep black of the cavern contrasted the gray and brown granite of the Tarish hill country.

When Ruth moved near the light, he gasped at the healing gash on her temple. His gaze flitted to her long, auburn hair bound high on her head, a style she'd never worn. She had reconstructed her brown healer's smock into separate pieces—a crudely sewn halter exposing her midriff, trousers reaching mid-thigh, and wrist wraps to her elbows forming a sort of armguard. She wore her same boots, but the silver hilt of a knife protruded from the top of each.

At her belt hung two other knives. One was her own with a leather-wrapped hilt, smooth and worn by frequent use. The glossy black handle of the other rested in a fine leather scabbard.

Altogether, the woman looked wild and dangerous, like a stranger who'd taken his mother's face but none of her warmth. Jeb scooted back, his gaze darting around her. Then, with world-shattering clarity, he recalled his last moment in Lorinth: scouring the crowd in desperation, seeing his mother run at the gate, feeling the rush of wind and the sudden change in the air. The town full of innocent people on fire transitioned to a rain-pelted valley of strange trees and impossibly tall ridges. Selvator Kane and two black-clad guards had arrived with them too.

"Mother," Jeb said in a raspy tone. "Kane. Those Drawls."

She shook her head and pulled her son into her arms again. "Hush, boy. The guards are dead. But Kane is out there, somewhere. We need to rest and stay quiet."

"But I saw him—" Jeb scrunched his brows. He wasn't certain what he had seen. He remembered the rain being very bright and feeling sunlight on his face. He remembered Selvator Kane screaming and writhing on the ground, as though he'd been on fire like the people in Lorinth.

"You saw a fiend of hell get knocked off his feet. Selvator Kane is a Cursed Immortal. I carried you here yesterday only hours after we arrived, then I searched for food. I saw him from the ridge, alive."

Jeb's eyes widened. "Won't he find us here?" His heart raced as he glanced around the cave. It seemed tall enough for them to stand and wide enough for them to lie down, with space in the middle for a sunrock pile and still room to spare. A narrow tunnel led off the main room, where a faint band of light shone.

Ruth sniffed. "Sovereign, help us. I pray not. I took the harder path and covered our tracks. Kane is desperate. And desperation makes people stupid."

"Why is he desperate?"

Ruth cupped his face in her dirty hands. "Oh, my boy. All I've wanted was to protect you from this cruel world. And now it's crashed onto your shoulders."

He swallowed and placed his hands over hers.

After a moment of silence, his mother said, "They want you because of what you are, Jeb." She pulled away and rolled the sunrock aside. In its place, she piled sticks and dried grass.

"I'm a ralenta, aren't I? I'm like Remm."

She paused, her eyes downcast. "It would seem so."

He barely remembered his oldest brother. He was four when Remm was smuggled away, Jon locked in Langry Prison, and Ruth sent to Lorinth with him, Ella, and Nate. Changing the subject to distract his mother from her mournful musing, Jeb asked, "Where are we?"

She shook her head. "I have no idea. It's a strange place. We're surrounded by cliffs. Some of the trees and plants—I don't recognize them. It's warm here too. It's not anywhere in Palimar, certainly."

He closed his eyes, recalling the bronze rings spinning at his feet on the temple stage in Lorinth and the same rings spinning on the ancient platform in the valley. "That thing we went through. The rings on the ground."

"A wraith gate," Ruth said with a frown.

"Is that like a world gate?"

"What's left of them." She arranged her pile of sticks.

"Why can't we just go back? Maybe Selvator already did."

"No. He tried. He seemed quite furious. He flitted off along the road. Like I said, desperate."

Jeb scooted closer. "If there's a road, it must go somewhere. Maybe there's a town nearby."

Ruth placed a stick upright upon a flat plank of wood and rolled it between her hands. She paused at Jeb's query and sighed. "The road is ancient, overgrown. Even if there is a town, if Sel finds it, there may well be no one left in it." She blew at the conjunction of the two pieces of wood. Soon, sparks flew, and in another moment, the tinder caught fire.

Other than when David lit the occasional Grace Day candle, Jeb had only seen Drawlen priests use fire. They called it a tool for destruction, an omen of death. David said it was a vessel for both good and evil, or for neither, like any tool. Jeb had always found it a little sinister. But when he watched the sparks dance into flames, the fire mesmerized him.

"I didn't know you could make one of those," he whispered.

Ruth smiled as she settled next to him. "I lived a whole life before you were in the world, Jeb. I learned a lot of things."

He noticed the worry in her gaze that she usually tried to hide. "Like how to tell if someone is a ralenta?"

Hesitantly, Ruth nodded.

Jeb warmed his hands over the fire and asked, "How?"

"Because I used to be one."

# 51

# A SPOIL OF VICTORY

*Lorinth, Taria*
*August 6, 1195 PT*

*Percy*

General Percy Duval paced along the border of the Deep Wood. Behind him, Lorinth lay in shambles. Before him, a towering pile of rock blocked the threshold of Fenris's war path. This earthen wall stretched east to west, like a wave frozen in place just before cresting. For several days, Duval had commanded his rangers to scale the wall and infiltrate the forest. Not a single man had returned.

The troops mingling nearby glanced, wide-eyed, between the barrier and their general: the bravest men in Palimar, all melting in fear over the prospect of a walk in the woods.

Percy signaled to Lieutenant Wesley Nylen, a short, stocky man in his forties standing to his right. "Have the fliers returned?"

Wesley shook his head. "No, General. We glassed them from our watchtower." He pointed between the town and forest at the sentry tower, built in haste using scraps from the town's destruction. "The Woodlanders appear to have fliers of their own. Silas's folk, we believe. They cut down our banshees before they even reached the battle site."

Percy gritted his teeth and swore, facing the border barricade. A foreboding phrase, made with red-painted stones, decorated the face of the wall:

**QUI HUC INTRASTI OMISSA SPE**

"What does it say?" Wesley asked.

"According to the purifiers, it says, 'Abandon hope, all who enter here.'" Percy turned to the lieutenant. "How goes the progress at the temple?"

"Slow, General. We've uncovered some larger pieces of rubble. They're harder to move, and the purifiers will not allow powder bricks. It will damage the gate."

"Hmph," Percy grunted. "Have the men take shorter rounds. They'll work faster that way. I don't care what the purifiers say about how long it takes. They can step up or shut up."

"Do you . . . do you want me to tell them that, sir?" Wesley's fingers twitched.

Although annoyed, Percy recalled the two rangers from a different battalion who had been put to the sword by the commanding purifier the previous day. But Percy was the commanding general of the Third North, the most feared of Odyssa's troops. "I will suffer no petty assaults on my men, Wesley. Make sure those glittering fools know it."

"Yes, sir." Wesley saluted and marched toward the wreckage of the town.

Percy surveyed the area and tapped his chin. "I knew this wretched hamlet was a stain on Ethar." From his pocket, he pulled the diary his men had discovered in a hill-house east of town. The writing on its pages was a prehistoric script, the origins of which no one could guess. But Percy knew to whom it belonged, who had previously occupied that dreary farmstead where his men recovered it. "I will hunt you down personally, Jon Therman," he grumbled. "And I will enjoy making you talk. You escaped the Cellar, but you won't escape a slow death."

Percy retreated from his musing when Wesley returned, huffing and shaking. "General, you must see this."

Percy followed him to the shambles of the Drawlen temple. Observing the stage, he blanched at the result of his soldiers' three days of work. A portion of the stage was exposed, revealing the deep grooves where, barely two weeks ago, the Drawls had cut into the granite structure. But the bronze rings and smooth, round wraith stones that completed the workings of the gate were missing. To the side of the empty grooves sat a square cavity where the missing lever mechanism to control the gate rings should have been.

"Fires and moons," Percy growled. "They've stolen it!" He clenched his fists and turned to Wesley. "Lieutenant, ready a regiment—no, two regiments—riders all and as many dragoons as we can spare. There is a wraith gate in those woods, and we cannot let them keep it."

Trembling, Wesley shouted at the surrounding men. Another soldier ran up and handed Percy an unpainted wooden shade box, open to display a folded parchment within. "This was in the gear cavity, General. It's addressed to you, sir."

"To me?"

"Yes."

Percy plucked the note from the box and unfolded it, his face growing warmer as he read.

To General Percy Duval or whatever graycoat piece of trash finds this letter

We have taken your lovely invention as a spoil of victory. For what you have done to the Deep Wood and to your own citizens, Sovereign's wrath be on you. You are heretics, and you have declared war on a people whose strength and resolve you cannot fathom. Desist now, and you may be spared your demise. Invade us again, and we will hold nothing back. Beware of the Wood, for we will take no prisoners and offer no mercy.

Signed,
Ella Riley
Apprentice to the Master Smuggler Jon Therman,
Who conquered the Wraith Cellar and your late Arch Purifier
Agent of Alistar Soral,
Godkiller and Second Arch Traitor of the Drawlen Empire
In partnership with Halas Gorvenah,
Godkiller, Lord of the Wood and of the Free Immortals
And with The Fiend and World Burner, Rodden Morien,
Godkiller and First Arch Traitor of the Drawlen Empire
On behalf of The Red Wolf, Shane zem'Arta,
Godkiller and Captain of the Red Watch
And of The Dragon of Palimar, Liiesh Romanus
Godkiller and First Lord of the Freelands

Fuming, Percy crumpled the letter and threw it to the ground. "Damn!" he snorted. "Damn that filthy whelp! Damn that burning traitor! Damn them all!"

He stomped on the letter. Along a curl of the paper, Ella Riley's spindly signature taunted him. He cracked his knuckles and muttered, "*They* have declared war, and the renewal of our hunt for the Arch Traitor is long overdue."

# INDEX

*Terms and characters are listed in alphabetical order, by first name, with section and page references for further exploration.*

**Abad il'Dani** – Character: Appendix C . . . . . . . . . . . . . . . . . . . . . . . .page 402
**Aginom** – Country: Appendix B . . . . . . . . . . . . . . . . . . . . . . . . . . .page 392
**Agitated Shade** – *(see Shade)* Entity: Appendix F . . . . . . . . . . . . . . . .page 416
**Agroth** – Character: Appendix C . . . . . . . . . . . . . . . . . . . . . . . . . . .page 407
**Alistar Soral** – Character: Appendix C. . . . . . . . . . . . . . . . . . . . . . . .page 403
**Amara Soral** – Character: Appendix C. . . . . . . . . . . . . . . . . . . . . . . .page 403
**Apostle** – Drawlen Occupation, Appendix D. . . . . . . . . . . . . . . . . . . .page 408
**Arbiter of the Spires** – Freeland Role: Appendix D . . . . . . . . . . . . . .page 409
**Arch Deacon** – Serenity Creed Role: Appendix D . . . . . . . . . . . . . . .page 410
**Archon** – Freeland Role: Appendix D . . . . . . . . . . . . . . . . . . . . . . .page 409
**Arik Leer** – Character: Appendix C . . . . . . . . . . . . . . . . . . . . . . . . .page 401
**Arimal Soral** – Character: Appendix C . . . . . . . . . . . . . . . . . . . . . . .page 403
**Arist / Arista** – *(see Yvenea)* Title: Appendix B . . . . . . . . . . . . . . . .page 394
**Aronos Hillmoran** – Character: Appendix C. . . . . . . . . . . . . . . . . . . .page 405
**Assembly Lord or Lady** – Freeland Role: Appendix D . . . . . . . . . . .page 409
**Beast Speaker** – *(see Speaking Craft)* Craft: Appendix E . . . . . . . . . . .page 411
**Blessed Immortal** – Drawlen Role: Appendix D . . . . . . . . . . . . . . . .page 408
**Blood Moon, The** – *(see Mortemus)* Celestial Body: Appendix F . . . .page 419
**Blood Sight** – *(see Mortari)* Sorcery: Appendix E. . . . . . . . . . . . . . . .page 412
**Blood Sorcery** – Craft: Appendix E. . . . . . . . . . . . . . . . . . . . . . . . . .page 412
**Blood Witch or Witcher** – *(see Blood Sorcery)* Craft: Appendix E. . . .page 412
**Blue Moon, The** – *(see Vitaeus)* Celestial Body: Appendix F. . . . . . . .page 419
**Bound Shade** – *(see Shade)* Entity: Appendix F . . . . . . . . . . . . . . . . .page 416
**Braella Romanus** – Character: Appendix C. . . . . . . . . . . . . . . . . . . .page 398
**Breaking of the Third Moon** – Event: Appendix F . . . . . . . . . . . . . .page 415
**Bren** – Character: Appendix C. . . . . . . . . . . . . . . . . . . . . . . . . . . . .page 399
**Bruce Hayden** – Character: Appendix C . . . . . . . . . . . . . . . . . . . . . .page 396
**Calla Dantiego** – Character: Appendix C . . . . . . . . . . . . . . . . . . . . .page 402
**Calron Maltez** – Character: Appendix C . . . . . . . . . . . . . . . . . . . . . .page 397
**Cameron Donfree** – Character: Appendix C . . . . . . . . . . . . . . . . . . .page 402
**Captain** – Red Watch Role: Appendix D . . . . . . . . . . . . . . . . . . . . . .page 410
**Carl Loren** – Character: Appendix C. . . . . . . . . . . . . . . . . . . . . . . . .page 401
**Carris Yan** – Character: Appendix C . . . . . . . . . . . . . . . . . . . . . . . .page 399
**Castor** – Character: Appendix C . . . . . . . . . . . . . . . . . . . . . . . . . . .page 396

**Chaplain** – Serenity Creed Role: Appendix D . . . . . . . . . . . . . . . . . .page 410
**Colas Noren** – Character: Appendix C . . . . . . . . . . . . . . . . . . . . . . .page 404
**Collector** – Drawlen Occupation, Appendix D . . . . . . . . . . . . . . . .page 408
**Commander** – Red Watch Role: Appendix D . . . . . . . . . . . . . . . . . .page 410
**Common Stone** – *(see Solinite)* Mineral: Appendix F. . . . . . . . . . . . .page 420
**Corigon** – Country: Appendix B . . . . . . . . . . . . . . . . . . . . . . . . . . .page 392
**Corruption** – Curse: Appendix F. . . . . . . . . . . . . . . . . . . . . . . . . . .page 414
**Corruptology** – Craft: Appendix E . . . . . . . . . . . . . . . . . . . . . . . . .page 412
**Cory Soral** – Character: Appendix C. . . . . . . . . . . . . . . . . . . . . . . .page 404
**Cosazi**– *(see Kumun)* Assassin's Guild: Appendix B . . . . . . . . . . . . .page 395
**Costa** – Country: Appendix B . . . . . . . . . . . . . . . . . . . . . . . . . . . .page 392
**Craft** – Magical ability: Appendix E. . . . . . . . . . . . . . . . . . . . . . . . .page 411
**Craft Healer / Physician** – *(see Healing Craft)* Craft: Appendix E . . .page 411
**Curse, The** – *(see Devourer's Curse)* Curse: Appendix F. . . . . . . . . . . .page 414
**Daeven Kritcher** – Character: Appendix C . . . . . . . . . . . . . . . . . . . .page 399
**Darï Priette** – Character: Appendix C . . . . . . . . . . . . . . . . . . . . . . .page 406
**David Therman** – Character: Appendix C. . . . . . . . . . . . . . . . . . . . .page 401
**Deacon** – Serenity Creed Role: Appendix D . . . . . . . . . . . . . . . . . . .page 410
**Dead Lands** – Country: Appendix B . . . . . . . . . . . . . . . . . . . . . . . .page 392
**Deep Wood** – Country: Appendix B . . . . . . . . . . . . . . . . . . . . . . . .page 393
**Deposed Immortal** – Drawlen Role: Appendix D. . . . . . . . . . . . . . . .page 408
**Deputy Rogue Master** – Criminal Occupation: Appendix D . . . . . .page 409
**Detoa** – Character: Appendix C. . . . . . . . . . . . . . . . . . . . . . . . . . .page 397
**Devourer, The** – Supernatural Entity: Appendix F. . . . . . . . . . . . . . .page 414
**Devourer's Curse** – Curse: Appendix F . . . . . . . . . . . . . . . . . . . . . .page 414
**Dispatcher** – Red Watch Role: Appendix D . . . . . . . . . . . . . . . . . . .page 410
**Door of Bamrian** – *(see Drawlen-Terrion Wars)* Structure: Appendix F . .page 415
**Dragoon Ranger** – Drawlen Occupation: Appendix D . . . . . . . . . . .page 408
**Drakelands** – Country: Appendix B . . . . . . . . . . . . . . . . . . . . . . . .page 393
**Drawlen** – Religion: Appendix F . . . . . . . . . . . . . . . . . . . . . . . . . .page 414
**Drawlen city-states** – Country: Appendix B . . . . . . . . . . . . . . . . . . .page 393
**Drawlen-Terrion Wars** – Event: Appendix F. . . . . . . . . . . . . . . . . . .page 415
**Dying, The** – Curse: Appendix F . . . . . . . . . . . . . . . . . . . . . . . . . .page 414
**Dynast** – *(see Yvenea)* Title: Appendix B. . . . . . . . . . . . . . . . . . . . .page 394
**Earth Speaker** – *(see Speaking Craft)* Craft: Appendix E. . . . . . . . . . .page 411
**Edd Pran** – Character: Appendix C . . . . . . . . . . . . . . . . . . . . . . . . .page 401
**Elf** – *(see Kobold)* Race: Appendix A . . . . . . . . . . . . . . . . . . . . . . . .page 390
**Ella Riley Therman** – Character: Appendix C . . . . . . . . . . . . . . . . . .page 402
**Emeral Ferren** – Character: Appendix C . . . . . . . . . . . . . . . . . . . . . .page 401

**Enforcer** – Red Watch Role: Appendix D . . . . . . . . . . . . . . . . . . . . . . . .page 410
**Eruna** – Character: Appendix C. . . . . . . . . . . . . . . . . . . . . . . . . . . . .page 397
**Ethar** – Planet: Appendix B . . . . . . . . . . . . . . . . . . . . . . . . . . . . . . .page 394
**Fae** – Race: Appendix A . . . . . . . . . . . . . . . . . . . . . . . . . . . . . . . . . .page 390
**Fallen Moon, The** – *(see Meridus)* Celestial Body: Appendix F. . . . . .page 418
**Faust the Tyrant** – Character: Appendix C . . . . . . . . . . . . . . . . . . . .page 407
**Fenris** – Character: Appendix C. . . . . . . . . . . . . . . . . . . . . . . . . . . . .page 397
**Fiend, The** – *(see Rodden Morien)* Title: Appendix C . . . . . . . . . . . . .page 400
**Fire Wielder** – *(see Speaking Craft)* Craft: Appendix E . . . . . . . . . . . .page 411
**Fires, The** – Event: Appendix F . . . . . . . . . . . . . . . . . . . . . . . . . . . . .page 415
**First Arbiter** – *(see Arbiter of the Spires)* Freeland Role: Appendix D. .page 409
**First Arch Traitor** – *(see Rodden Morien)* Title: Appendix C. . . . . . . .page 400
**First Moon, The** – *(see Vitaeus)* Celestial Body: Appendix F. . . . . . . .page 419
**First Lord** – Freeland Role: Appendix D . . . . . . . . . . . . . . . . . . . . . .page 409
**Flat Tooth** – *(see Human)* Race: Appendix A . . . . . . . . . . . . . . . . . . .page 390
**Flier** – *(see Terrion)* Race: Appendix A . . . . . . . . . . . . . . . . . . . . . . .page 390
**Foreseer** – *(see Foresight)* Craft: Appendix E . . . . . . . . . . . . . . . . . . .page 412
**Foresight** – Craft: Appendix E. . . . . . . . . . . . . . . . . . . . . . . . . . . . . .page 412
**Fredrick Devilos** – Character: Appendix C . . . . . . . . . . . . . . . . . . . . .page 406
**Freelands** – Country: Appendix B . . . . . . . . . . . . . . . . . . . . . . . . . . .page 393
**Furgus Baneson** – Character: Appendix C. . . . . . . . . . . . . . . . . . . . . .page 405
**Furnace Stone** – *(see Solazite)* Mineral: Appendix F . . . . . . . . . . . . . .page 420
**Garden of Souls, The** – *(see Life Harvest)* Place: Appendix F . . . . . . .page 417
**Garren Brodour** – Character: Appendix C . . . . . . . . . . . . . . . . . . . . .page 406
**Gaylen Hayden** – Character: Appendix C . . . . . . . . . . . . . . . . . . . . . .page 396
**Goblin** – *(see Kobold)* Race: Appendix A . . . . . . . . . . . . . . . . . . . . . .page 390
**Gravos** – *(see Old Waste)* Country: Appendix B . . . . . . . . . . . . . . . . .page 393
**Gregory Doniva** – Character: Appendix C . . . . . . . . . . . . . . . . . . . . .page 396
**Greq** – Country: Appendix B. . . . . . . . . . . . . . . . . . . . . . . . . . . . . . .page 394
**Guard of the Veil** – Drawlen Occupation: Appendix D . . . . . . . . . . .page 408
**Haana Wilde** – Character: Appendix C . . . . . . . . . . . . . . . . . . . . . . . .page 397
**Halas Gorvenah** – Character: Appendix C . . . . . . . . . . . . . . . . . . . . .page 405
**Hale Trevon** – Character: Appendix C. . . . . . . . . . . . . . . . . . . . . . . . .page 396
**Harriette (Harry) Harris** – Character: Appendix C. . . . . . . . . . . . . . .page 406
**Hazïr Noren** – Character: Appendix C . . . . . . . . . . . . . . . . . . . . . . . .page 404
**Healing Craft** – Craft: Appendix E . . . . . . . . . . . . . . . . . . . . . . . . . .page 411
**Heart Stone** – *(see Solazite)* Mineral: Appendix F. . . . . . . . . . . . . . .page 420
**Hearth Stone** – *(see Solazite)* Mineral: Appendix F. . . . . . . . . . . . . .page 420
**Henrick Lowe** – Character: Appendix C . . . . . . . . . . . . . . . . . . . . . . .page 405

**Hidden Strongholds** – *(see Scattered Tribes)* Nationality: Appendix B . . .page 393
**High Immortal** – Drawlen Role: Appendix D . . . . . . . . . . . . . . . . . .page 408
**High Lord Warden** – *(see Corigon)* Title: Appendix B . . . . . . . . . . . .page 392
**Hoven** – Character: Appendix C . . . . . . . . . . . . . . . . . . . . . . . . . .page 397
**Human** – Race: Appendix A . . . . . . . . . . . . . . . . . . . . . . . . . . . .page 390
**Jeb (Jebadiah) Riley Therman** – Character: Appendix C . . . . . . . . .page 402
**Jex ren'Turen** – Character: Appendix C . . . . . . . . . . . . . . . . . . . . . . .page 405
**Jon Therman** – Character: Appendix C . . . . . . . . . . . . . . . . . . . . . . .page 402
**Jonathan Riley** – *(see Jon Therman)* Character: Appendix C. . . . . . . .page 402
**Joran Wilde** – Character: Appendix C. . . . . . . . . . . . . . . . . . . . . . . .page 397
**Kartha** – *(see Dead Lands)* Country: Appendix B . . . . . . . . . . . . . . . .page 392
**Krishena Dantiego** – Character: Appendix C . . . . . . . . . . . . . . . . . .page 403
**Kobold** – Race: Appendix A . . . . . . . . . . . . . . . . . . . . . . . . . . . . .page 390
**Kumun** – Country: Appendix B . . . . . . . . . . . . . . . . . . . . . . . . . . .page 395
**Lady of the Spires** – Freeland Role: Appendix D. . . . . . . . . . . . . . . .page 409
**Langry Prison** – *(see Jon Therman)* Prison: Appendix C . . . . . . . . . . .page 402
**Lantern Stone** – *(see Solinite)* Mineral: Appendix F . . . . . . . . . . . . . .page 420
**Leo Harris** – Character: Appendix C. . . . . . . . . . . . . . . . . . . . . . . . .page 406
**Leonora Sesporan** – Character: Appendix C . . . . . . . . . . . . . . . . . . .page 406
**Leron Novelen** – Character: Appendix C. . . . . . . . . . . . . . . . . . . . . .page 406
**Lesser Immortal** – Drawlen Role: Appendix D . . . . . . . . . . . . . . . . .page 408
**Life Harvest** – Religious Ritual: Appendix F . . . . . . . . . . . . . . . . . . .page 417
**Light Stone** – *(see Solinite)* Mineral: Appendix F . . . . . . . . . . . . . . .page 420
**Liiesh Romanus** – Character: Appendix C . . . . . . . . . . . . . . . . . . . .page 399
**Lucas Riley** – Character: Appendix C . . . . . . . . . . . . . . . . . . . . . . . .page 404
**Maralyn vel'Tamar** – Character: Appendix C . . . . . . . . . . . . . . . . . .page 399
**Margaret Loren** – Character: Appendix C. . . . . . . . . . . . . . . . . . . . . .page 402
**Master Smuggler** – Criminal Occupation: Appendix D. . . . . . . . . . .page 409
**Mavell** – Character: Appendix C . . . . . . . . . . . . . . . . . . . . . . . . . . .page 397
**Mel van'Larus** – Character: Appendix C . . . . . . . . . . . . . . . . . . . . . .page 399
**Meridus** – Celestial Body: Appendix F. . . . . . . . . . . . . . . . . . . . . . . .page 418
**Mind Craft** – Craft: Appendix E . . . . . . . . . . . . . . . . . . . . . . . . . . . .page 411
**Minder / Mind Render** – *(see Mind Craft)* Craft: Appendix E . . . . . .page 411
**Mind Reader** – *(see Terrion)* Race: Appendix A . . . . . . . . . . . . . . . . .page 390
**Mona Morien** – Character: Appendix C . . . . . . . . . . . . . . . . . . . . . . .page 399
**Morgel Yan** – Character: Appendix C . . . . . . . . . . . . . . . . . . . . . . . . .page 399
**Mortari** – Craft: Appendix E . . . . . . . . . . . . . . . . . . . . . . . . . . . . . . .page 412
**Mortemus** – Celestial Body: Appendix F . . . . . . . . . . . . . . . . . . . . . . .page 419
**Mylis** – Character: Appendix C . . . . . . . . . . . . . . . . . . . . . . . . . . . . .page 398

**Nate (Nathaniel) Riley Therman** – Character: Appendix C .......page 403
**Nicos** – Character: Appendix C .............................page 396
**Necromancer** – *(see Corruptology)* Craft: Appendix E............page 412
**Nyla Elderen** – Character: Appendix C .........................page 405
**Old Waste** – Country: Appendix B ...........................page 393
**Ogre** – *(see Thurse)* Race: Appendix A.........................page 391
**Oracle** – Drawlen Occupation: Appendix D ....................page 408
**Orego Gorvenah** – Character: Appendix C.....................page 405
**Order of Odyssa** – *(see Ranger)* Drawlen Order: Appendix D ......page 408
**Orin Novelen** – Character: Appendix C.........................page 406
**Paganism** – Religion: Appendix F .............................page 418
**Paul Greenwell** – Character: Appendix C ......................page 404
**Percy Duval** – Character: Appendix C..........................page 398
**Petrification** – *(see Shade)* Physical Process: Appendix F...........page 416
**Philip Creedle** – Character: Appendix C........................page 402
**Praya Aldonus** – Character: Appendix C........................page 400
**Prophet, The** – Character: Appendix C .........................page 407
**Purifier** – Drawlen Occupation: Appendix D ...................page 408
**Ranger** – Drawlen Occupation: Appendix D....................page 408
**Raza Vizarr** – Character: Appendix C .........................page 400
**Red Moon, The** – *(see Mortemus)* Celestial Body: Appendix F ......page 419
**Red Watch** – Freeland spy network: Appendix D................page 409
**Red Wolf, The** – *(see Shane zem'Arta)* Title: Appendix C ..........page 400
**Refsul** – Character: Appendix C ..............................page 398
**Ralenta** – *(see Shade Craft)* Craft: Appendix E .................page 411
**Regem the Selfless** – Character: Appendix C....................page 407
**Remm Riley Therman** – Character: Appendix C..................page 400
**Richard Mathis** – Character: Appendix C........................page 404
**Rock Smuggler** – Criminal Occupation: Appendix D ............page 409
**Rodden Morien** – Character: Appendix C.......................page 400
**Rogue** – Criminal Occupation: Appendix D .....................page 409
**Rogue Master** – Criminal Occupation: Appendix D .............page 408
**Rolan Whittier** – Character: Appendix C .......................page 404
**Rose (Bellerose)** – Character: Appendix C .....................page 402
**Ruth Riley Therman** – Character: Appendix C ..................page 403
**Ruvia** – *(see Dead Lands)* Country: Appendix B.................page 392
**Scattered Tribes** – Nationality: Appendix B ....................page 393
**Sadiona** – Character: Appendix C .............................page 404
**Sapien** – Race: Appendix A ...................................page 390

**Second Arch Traitor** – *(see Alistar Soral)* Title: Appendix C . . . . . . . .page 403
**Second Lord** – Freeland Role: Appendix D . . . . . . . . . . . . . . . . . . . .page 409
**Selvator Kane** – Character: Appendix C . . . . . . . . . . . . . . . . . . . . . .page 398
**Sephora Elderen** – Character: Appendix C . . . . . . . . . . . . . . . . . . . .page 405
**Serenity Creed** – Religion: Appendix F . . . . . . . . . . . . . . . . . . . . . . .page 417
**Shade Craft** – Craft: Appendix E. . . . . . . . . . . . . . . . . . . . . . . . . . .page 411
**Shane zem'Arta** – Character: Appendix C . . . . . . . . . . . . . . . . . . . . .page 400
**Shape Craft** – Craft: Appendix E. . . . . . . . . . . . . . . . . . . . . . . . . . .page 412
**Shard Keeper** – *(see Mortari)* Craft: Appendix E . . . . . . . . . . . . . . .page 412
**Sid vel'Forr** – Character: Appendix C . . . . . . . . . . . . . . . . . . . . . . . .page 400
**Silas** – Character: Appendix C. . . . . . . . . . . . . . . . . . . . . . . . . . . . .page 396
**Sirahi** – *(see Dead Lands)* Ethnicity: Appendix B . . . . . . . . . . . . . . .page 392
**Shaman** – *(see Foresight)* Craft: Appendix E . . . . . . . . . . . . . . . . . .page 412
**Sharp Tooth** – *(see Thurse)* Race: Appendix A. . . . . . . . . . . . . . . . . .page 391
**Shayhem** – *(see Jex ren'Turen)* Freeland Prison: Appendix C . . . . . . . .page 405
**Skin-changer** – *(see Shape Craft)* Craft: Appendix E. . . . . . . . . . . . .page 412
**Sorcery** – Magical ability: Appendix E. . . . . . . . . . . . . . . . . . . . . . .page 412
**Sovelus Kane** – *(see Refsul)* Character: Appendix C . . . . . . . . . . . . .page 398
**Sovereign** – Deity: Appendix F . . . . . . . . . . . . . . . . . . . . . . . . . . . .page 418
**Sovereign's Heart** – *(see Meridus)* Celestial Body: Appendix F. . . . . .page 418
**Speaking Craft** – Craft: Appendix E . . . . . . . . . . . . . . . . . . . . . . . . .page 411
**Spire Lord or Lady** – Freeland Role: Appendix D . . . . . . . . . . . . . . .page 409
**Spire Watchman** – Freeland Role: Appendix D . . . . . . . . . . . . . . . .page 409
**Spire Watch** – *(see Spire Watchman)* Freeland Military: Appendix D. .page 409
**Sprite** – *(see Fae)* Race: Appendix A . . . . . . . . . . . . . . . . . . . . . . .page 390
**Shade** – Entity: Appendix F. . . . . . . . . . . . . . . . . . . . . . . . . . . . . .page 416
**Shade Bane** – *(see Solarite)* Mineral: Appendix F . . . . . . . . . . . . . .page 419
**Shardling Islands** – Country: Appendix B. . . . . . . . . . . . . . . . . . . . .page 395
**Shardling** – *(see Shardling Islands)* Term: Appendix B. . . . . . . . . . . .page 395
**Smith Stone** – *(see Solamite)* Mineral: Appendix F. . . . . . . . . . . . . .page 420
**Solamite** – Mineral: Appendix F . . . . . . . . . . . . . . . . . . . . . . . . . . .page 420
**Solarite** – Mineral: Appendix F . . . . . . . . . . . . . . . . . . . . . . . . . . . .page 419
**Solazite** – Mineral: Appendix F . . . . . . . . . . . . . . . . . . . . . . . . . . . .page 420
**Solinite** – Mineral: Appendix F . . . . . . . . . . . . . . . . . . . . . . . . . . . .page 420
**Solisite** – Mineral: Appendix F . . . . . . . . . . . . . . . . . . . . . . . . . . . .page 419
**Sun Tear** – *(see Solisite)* Mineral: Appendix F . . . . . . . . . . . . . . . . .page 419
**Sunrock** – Mineral: Appendix F. . . . . . . . . . . . . . . . . . . . . . . . . . . .page 419
**Taria** – Country: Appendix B. . . . . . . . . . . . . . . . . . . . . . . . . . . . . .page 394
**Taval Sesporan** – Character: Appendix C . . . . . . . . . . . . . . . . . . . . .page 406

**Terrion** – Race: Appendix A. . . . . . . . . . . . . . . . . . . . . . . . . . . . . .page 390
**Tessa Wilde** – Character: Appendix C . . . . . . . . . . . . . . . . . . . . . . . . .page 398
**Third Moon, The** – *(see Meridus)* Celestial Body: Appendix F . . . . . .page 418
**Thura** – Country: Appendix B . . . . . . . . . . . . . . . . . . . . . . . . . . . . .page 395
**Thurse** – Race: Appendix A . . . . . . . . . . . . . . . . . . . . . . . . . . . . . .page 391
**Torok Missien** – Character: Appendix C . . . . . . . . . . . . . . . . . . . . . .page 404
**Tree Speaker** – *(see Speaking Craft)* Craft: Appendix E. . . . . . . . . . . .page 411
**Tres Romanus** – Character: Appendix C . . . . . . . . . . . . . . . . . . . . . .page 400
**Troll** – *(see Thurse)* Race: Appendix A. . . . . . . . . . . . . . . . . . . . . . . .page 391
**tSolan** – Country: Appendix B. . . . . . . . . . . . . . . . . . . . . . . . . . . . . .page 394
**Unbound Shade** – *(see Shade)* Entity: Appendix F . . . . . . . . . . . . . . .page 416
**Unrest** – *(see Mortari)* Sorcery: Appendix E . . . . . . . . . . . . . . . . . . .page 412
**Vanguard** – *(see Archon)* Freeland Military: Appendix D . . . . . . . . . .page 409
**Veiled Man, The** – Character: Appendix C . . . . . . . . . . . . . . . . . . . .page 398
**Vernon vel'Tamar** – Character: Appendix C . . . . . . . . . . . . . . . . . . .page 401
**Venna vel'Tamar** – Character: Appendix C . . . . . . . . . . . . . . . . . . . .page 401
**Vitaeus** – Celestial Body: Appendix F . . . . . . . . . . . . . . . . . . . . . . .page 419
**Vulta** – Civilization: Appendix F . . . . . . . . . . . . . . . . . . . . . . . . . . .page 417
**Watcher** – Red Watch Role: Appendix D. . . . . . . . . . . . . . . . . . . . . .page 410
**Watchman** – *(see Spire Watchman)* Freeland Role: Appendix D . . . . .page 409
**Water Wielder** – *(see Speaking Craft)* Craft: Appendix E . . . . . . . . . .page 411
**Wild Shade** – *(see Shade)* Entity: Appendix F. . . . . . . . . . . . . . . . . . .page 416
**Will (William) Loren** – Character: Appendix C . . . . . . . . . . . . . . . .page 402
**World Burner** – *(see Rodden Morien)* Title: Appendix C. . . . . . . . . . .page 400
**World Gate** – Structure: Appendix F . . . . . . . . . . . . . . . . . . . . . . . .page 416
**Wraith** – *(see Corruption)* Curse: Appendix F. . . . . . . . . . . . . . . . . .page 414
**Wraith Gate** – Structure: Appendix F . . . . . . . . . . . . . . . . . . . . . . .page 417
**Yvenea** – Country: Appendix B . . . . . . . . . . . . . . . . . . . . . . . . . . . .page 394
**Yvette Sesporan** – Character: Appendix C. . . . . . . . . . . . . . . . . . . .page 407

# APPENDIX A

# RACES OF ETHAR

**Fae** – *(alt. sprite [mildly derogatory])* Fae are a long-lived race with a life expectancy of 300-400 years. They're considered adolescent by age 15 and adults by age 30. Shape craft is common among them, but they also possess the unique ability called speaking, which allows them to manipulate elements, plants, and animals. These abilities are common and sometimes incredibly powerful among the fae.

**Human** – *(alt. flattooth by thurse and kobold [mildly derogatory])* Humans account for just over a third of the population of Ethar. They generally live 100-140 years and are prone to possessing mild forms of mind craft, healing craft, and foresight. They are the only race capable of shade craft. They're considered adolescent by age 10 and adults by age 17.

**Kobold** – *(alt. goblin in Palish; sharp tooth; elf [derogatory])* No more than five feet tall, kobold have the highest strength to mass ratio, putting them on par with trolls and making them highly skilled at manual labor and combat. Kobold are generally treated poorly by other races. Like terrion, they have low fertility, so their numbers have dwindled in recent centuries. Kobold are highly sought after by slavers and generally ill represented by the governments where they reside. For this reason, some kobold settlements in remote areas are very hostile to other races upon contact. Kobold live 80-90 years, are considered adolescent at age 9 and adults at age 15.

**Sapien** – The encompassing term for all introspective, sapient races calling Ethar home. Under the Devourer's Curse, only sapiens petrify upon death and, if left uncremated for three or more days, produce a shade.

**Terrion** – *(alt. flier; mind readers [mildly derogatory])* Terrion were once the dominant race in Palimar. Low fertility, war and natural disasters have dwindled their numbers over the centuries. All terrion have a certain amount of shape craft and mind craft. Starting in adolescence, Palish terrion wear limiters, silver talismans meant to meter their mind craft. They manifest wings during puberty and can hide and conjure them at will afterward. They live 350-450 years, are considered adolescent by age 20 and adults by age 35.

**Thurse** – *(alt. troll in Palish; sharptooth; ogre [derogatory])* Second only to humans in population, thurse were the dominant power on Ethar until the last few centuries. They are generally taller and stronger than the other races. In Drawlen-controlled Palimar, thurse are generally unwelcome and mistrusted. Thurse live 90-110 years, are considered adolescent at age 9 and adults at age 16.

# APPENDIX B

# NATIONS AND REGIONS

## PALIMAR

*Palimar is the last inhabitable region of Urlas, a continent ravaged by an ancient and mysterious desolation called the Dying. As such, Palimar has become a land of diverse nations, creeds, and cultures. This vast peninsula is scarred by countless millennia of war, conquest, pestilence, and devastation.*

**Aginom** – *(ag-EH-nom)* A member of the Corigish commonwealth, Aginom is a politically unstable nation with abundant resources such as sunrock and copper. It has a tumultuous ancient history, having been the landing site for several successful foreign invasions.

**Corigon** – *(kohr-EH-gon)* Considered the most powerful nation on the peninsula, Corigon commands a commonwealth that includes Taria, Aginom, and (loosely) the Drawlen city-state of Shevak. Corigon has been rocked by civil war in recent decades. In 1153, the ruling dynasty was overthrown in favor of a new parliamentary system of government. This lackluster shift in power has begun to fall out of favor, however, as those who enacted it start to realize its flaws. The presiding executive ruler is titled the High Lord Warden.

**Costa** – *(KOST-uh)* The last independent human nation in western Palimar, Costa holds this position with an iron grip. They won independence in the civil war of 1153 and have maintained it through many of Corigon's efforts to take them back. The mountains of Costa are rich in resources such as sun rock, gold, and diamonds.

**Dead Lands** – Once the kingdoms of Kartha and Ruvia, these lands began to fall to the Dying in the first century after the Fires. Kartha fell first, many of its people falling to the sickness called Corruption, and others fleeing to various havens around the world. Most settled around the Howling Sea and became the city-states of Zeree and Thêen. Following the Drawlen-Terrion Wars, Ruvians fled the encroachment of the Dying upon their homeland, a desperate migration remembered as The Scattering. Most went into hiding upon their poor reception by the Drawls in Yvenea. One Ruvian tribe, the Sirahi, lingered in the Dead Lands for decades, ultimately re-settling near Dothra, a Freeland city.

**Deep Wood** – The last vestige of the ancient kingdom of Gravos, the Deep Wood is ruled by Halas, one of the original seven Blessed Immortals. There are no major city centers in the Deep Wood. It is a self-sufficient nation with incredibly secure borders and a long-standing truce with Drawlen and Corigon.

**Drakelands** – Once a part of the Devourer's Waste, the Drake Lands are a series of terrion settlements along the Drake Canyon ruled over by Silas, a former Drawlen banshee who rebelled and founded a haven for his fellow free slaves.

**Drawlen city-states** – The Drawlen church maintains three independent territories on Palimar. Two are large city-states—Shevak and Drawl—and one is a large temple surrounded by crop fields—the Temple of Ize. Beyond these three cities, Drawlen commands an incredible amount of economic power. They control much of the lumber and sunrock industries in the Corigish commonwealth.

**Freelands** – One of few regions in Palimar outside Drawlen influence, the Freelands are a coalition of independent city-states united by mutual prosperity and protection. The spire lords of Palim have ruled over the Freelands since their inception, and before that, over most of Palimar itself.

**Old Waste** – Gravos once spanned the northern portion of Palimar. The Old Waste is what remains of its eastern half. Once a part of the Devourer's Waste, it has returned slowly to life in the last three centuries. However, it has remained largely unsettled save for the Raegoths, a collection of nomadic tribes of kobold and humans. The ruins of the Gravosian capital, Mercena, sits near the east coast of the Old Waste.

**Scattered Tribes** – *(alt. Hidden Strongholds)* The seven scattered tribes descended from Ruvia settled in secret locations around Palimar to escape persecution from both Drawlen and the Freelands. The two most populous strongholds are Sidras, a sanctuary city in the Deep Wood, and Mumagra, a vast cave settlement hidden near Rotira in the Modrian Mountains. New Donness, the city Alistar Soral commissions Jon Therman to help supply in secret, is located near the ruins of Mercena in the Old Waste.

**Taria** – *(TAH-ree-ah)* A territory of the Corigish commonwealth, Taria has known peace only for the last hundred years. Before that, this region was torn between its southern and northern neighbors. Two hundred years ago, the nobility of Taria invited the Corigish crown to settle an inheritance dispute, and the Corigish king responded by taking the Tarish throne for himself. This sparked a decade of civil war, which was only settled when Drawlen priests came to negotiate peace. After that, Corigon and the Deep Wood attempted to invade one another several times before renewing their truce indefinitely.

**tSolan** – *(tSOH-lahn)* Not strictly a united nation, tSolan is the fiercely defended territory of a number of nomadic and settled tribes. They are the only remaining human people group native to Palimar. The others (now Corigish, Yvean, Ruvian, Aginomian, Costish) were brought in as slaves fifteen hundred years ago. The only people the tSolanies mistrust more than each other are outsiders, so they generally band together if their borders are threatened. In recent years, strong leaders have emerged within the tribes to make them more united. This resulted in pushing Drawlen influence out of tSolan and returning to their pagan roots.

**Yvenea** – *(yih-VEN-ay-uh)* One of the strongest nations on Palimar (both militarily and economically), Yvenea stands between Corigon and the Freelands. Throughout its five-hundred-year history, it has oscillated between loyalties. Three hundred years ago, it waged war on the Freelands. Now, they are each other's closest allies. Nobles are called Arist (male) or Arista (female), and the monarch is the titled Dynast.

## ELSEWHERE

*The planet of Ethar has been devasted by cosmic and supernatural calamities since time out of memory. Most notably, the Dying has rendered over half its lands uninhabitable, leaving what remains at the mercy of ambitious empires. The nations and peoples of Palimar contend with some formidable and persistent outside influences.*

**Greq** – Encompassing most of the livable lands of the Greqi continent across the Utheran Ocean from Palimar, the empire of Greq dates back thousands of years. Dozens of dynasties have held dominion over this human empire, some of whom have aspired to extend their influence over Palimar itself.

**Kumun** – An island nation off the coast of Greq, Kumun commands incredible economic and military power throughout the Utheran Ocean, especially given its size. Known for its brutal fighting arenas, extensive slave trade, and effective warships, this human nation is steeped in a violent history of civil war. For the last century, Kumun has been united under a ferocious shogunate. The infamous Cosazi assassin's guild, along with several others, operates out of Kumun.

**Shardling Islands** – A small archipelago halfway between Palimar and Kumun in the Utheran Ocean, the Shardling Islands have long served as a waypoint for trade and a haven for piracy. Historically, each island has been self-governed, if not anarchical. This changed in 1099 Post Tyrannus when Henrick Lowe, a notorious pirate captain, united the criminal factions operating out of the various islands. People from this area are known as Shardlings.

**Thura** – A thurse empire dominating the continent of North Mazagon, separated from Palimar by the Cathyn Sea and the Avaran Ocean. When the Dying conquered ancient Vulta, many of the resident thurse tribes fled west, eventually forming the Thuran empire. A brutal culture of cults and warlords, Thura has long harassed the nations of Palimar with conquest, slavery, and piracy.

# APPENDIX C

# CHARACTER DIRECTORY

*All stated ages are circa 1195 Post Tyrannus (after the time skip beginning in Chapter 8 of Remnant).*

### CORIGISHMEN

**Bruce Hayden** – *(94, born 1101 in Depbas, Taria)* The outgoing High Lord Warden of Corigon. He is known widely as a tyrant and a pedophile.

**Gaylen Hayden** – *(31, born 1164 in Pelton, Corigon)* One of Bruce's many illegitimate children, Gaylen won his legitimacy through treachery and cunning. He is the incoming High Lord Warden of the Corigish commonwealth.

**Gregory Doniva** – *(46, born 1149 in Pelton, Corigon)* Sir Gregory Doniva is a Corigish nobleman and loyal agent of Gaylen Hayden.

**Hale Trevon** – *(19, born 1176 in Pelton, Corigon)* Hale is one of many illegitimate children of the outgoing High Lord Warden, Bruce Hayden. He joined the Life Harvest in an effort to flee his father's agents and to keep his twin sister a secret from them.

### DRAKELANDERS

**Castor** – *(293, born 902 in the Drakelands)* Silas's firstborn son with Aurelia Romanus. Castor is Silas's heir and widely looked to for leadership by Drakeland citizens as his father ages.

**Nicos** – *(164, born 1031 in the Drakelands)* Castor's firstborn son, Nicos is a dangerous warrior with a special hatred of both Drawlen and the Freelands.

**Silas** – *(387, born 808 in Shevak)* Silas was born into Drawlen slavery as a banshee. He waged a successful rebellion after the Drawlen-Terrion wars and founded the Drakelands as a haven for other rebel banshees.

## DRAWLS

**Calron Maltez** – *(73, born 1122 in Shevak)* High Cleric of Drawlen, Calron acts as the mortal mouthpiece of the regime.

**Detoa** – *(29, born 1166 in Shevak)* Mavell's young and somewhat naïve partner, Detoa was born in the Drawlen harem. She was sworn in as a Drawlen collector at age 15, one of the youngest in history, and specializes in poison and hand-to-hand combat.

**Eruna** – One of the original Blessed Immortals, Eruna's history is shrouded in legend and confusion. Refsul claims her as his wife and that she was tricked by Rodden into leaving him. Therefore, Refsul claims, he was forced to curse her into becoming a petrified tree, which now stands at the center of the Temple of the Tree.

**Fenris** – *(217, born 978 in Shevak)* A sadistic and violent man even by Drawlen standards, Fenris is called the Fire Master. He is an elite military leader and often on the front lines of battle on behalf of the Drawlen regime.

**Haana Wilde** – *(HAH-nah) (11, born 3, January 1184 in Shevak)* Like many harem children of Drawlen, Haana is destined for the priesthood and treated as the property of her commanding immortal. Her father is unknown, but likely an immortal, since her mother is property of the harem and was not under Mylis's protection at the time of Haana's birth.

**Hoven** – The immortal leader of the Temple of Ize. Known for his shrewd political maneuverings and vile personal preferences, Hoven has helped Refsul hold sway over the Corigish commonwealth for three brutal centuries.

**Joran Wilde** – *(40, born 1155 in Oboran, Corigon)* The adoptive brother to sisters Ruth Therman and Tessa Wilde, Joran was conscripted into the Drawlen military at eighteen. Without much recourse, he embraces his new role, though he sours to it over the years. He makes a bold move transferring to the Temple Watch in Shevak. This maneuver may mask ulterior motives.

**Mavell** – *(muh-VEL) (41, born 1154 in Shevak)* One of the Veiled Man's most trusted and competent collectors, Mavell treads the line of blind devotion and self-preservation. He has seen the ugly underbelly of Drawlen and knows nearly every dirty secret of every immortal under its banner. He has the seemingly impossible task of finding Hoven's killer. But collectors are—if nothing else—endlessly patient.

**Mylis** – Called the Eternal Oracle, Mylis is the immortal matriarch of the Drawlen House of Prophecy. Unlike many immortals, she did not receive her immortality willingly. She is as much a slave to Refsul as any member of the Drawlen harem.

**Percy Duval** – *(64, born 1131 in Shevak)* An ambitious commander of the Third North cavalry division of the Drawlen military, Duval has a frightening reputation on and off the battlefield.

**Refsul** – *(REF-sool)* Leader and founder of the Drawlen religion, Refsul is considered by both his worshipers and his enemies to be the First Immortal. Starting out as a benevolent ruler, he quickly fell to his own fears and ambitions, morphing into a most terrifying and unpredictable tyrant.

**Selvator Kane** – Second in command of the Drawlen regime, Selvator is one of the most feared people in all of Ethar. Known—among other names—as the Master of Secrets, he is Refsul's chief spy and enforcer. He is also Refsul's biological son from the time before immortality and was named heir to their home kingdom before it fell to civil war and the Fires.

**Tessa Wilde** – *(44, born 28, August, 1151 in Depbas, Taria)* Tessa's life took a tragic turn when she determined to deceive Drawlen apostles in order to take her sister's place in the Drawlen harem. Clever and patient, she works her way into the protection of the Eternal Oracle, Mylis. Ever a protector, she works every angle possible to ensure the safety of her only child, Haana.

**Veiled Man, The** – One of the most influential immortals of Refsul's court, the Veiled Man is a creature of mysterious nature. His origin and race are unknown even to his fellow immortals, and he is often at odds with both Refsul and Selvator. Yet his temple endures, and he commands one of the deadliest of Drawlen's agencies—the Black Veil Collectors.

## FREELANDERS

**Braella Romanus** – *(297, born 898 in Palim, Freelands)* Braella is a master of many arts, including diplomacy, history, languages, and espionage. She is the First Scholar of the Spires and the head of the Alphius College of Industry at the University of Palim.

**Bren** – *(15, born 1180 in tSolan)* Born to a poor, nomadic tribe in tSolan, Bren was taken into slavery during a covert Drawlen raid. Discovered by Remm Therman on the slavers block in Drawl, he is recruited into Shane's Red Watch crew. Bren is one of the most powerful ralenta in the world, according to Remm.

**Carris Yan** – *(43, born 1152 in the Palim, Freelands)* A kobold fighter to her core, Carris is a member of Shane's Red Watch crew. She met Shane when he was in service to the notorious pirate Henrick Lowe. Her life is a string of tragedies, with her time in Shane's crew being a welcome bright spot. She is married to Morgel Yan.

**Daeven Kritcher** – An accomplished conartist who finds himself on the wrong end of a bad deal after unwittingly targeting Vernon vel'Tamar. He ends up in Jon's smuggling cart after being captured by Shane in Estbye.

**Liiesh Romanus** – *(lee-ESH roh-MAH-nuhs) (91, born 11, June, 1104 in Palim, Freelands)* The subject of many rumors and legends, Liiesh Romanus is the seated First Lord of the Free Lands. Having gained his position unwillingly after rebelling against his great uncle, Liiesh has settled into leadership with ruthless tactics. He is sly, intelligent, and sometimes heartless.

**Mel van'Larus** – *(46, born 1149 in Thêen, Freelands)* Mel is Liiesh's personal shield guard.

**Maralyn vel'Tamar** – *(59, born 1136 in Thêen, Freelands)* Wife of Vernon and mother to Venna and her sisters, Maralyn resents her husband's work. She understands its necessity but is determined to cement her daughters' futures with renowned men of high society.

**Mona Morien** – *(54, born 1141 in Sira, Freelands)* The half-sister of Liiesh and Tres, Mona was born to a Sirahi woman while her father and brothers were in exile. Being half terrion, she is sometimes treated poorly by the spire court. However, her skills as a healer are legendary. She is the modern-day wife of Rodden Morien.

**Morgel Yan** – *(38, born 1157 in Greq)* Once a world-renowned opera performer and assassin, Morgel was betrayed and enslaved, losing his tongue in the process. He spends his days under Shane zem'Arta's command and silently teasing his wife, Carris.

**Praya Aldonus** – *(57, born 1138 in Palim, Freelands)* One of Braella's most promising apprentices, Praya is cunning and stern. Her ambitions tend toward the academics and spy craft, and so she resents her position as Liiesh's betrothed. They make a deal not to fulfill their betrothal. But they must tread carefully so as not to anger their families and cause a political disaster.

**Rodden Morien** – One of the original Blessed Immortals, Rodden is known by many names: The Fiend, the World Burner, and the First Arch Traitor to list a few. Drawlen paints him as the villain of their religion. But the truth is more nuanced. Rodden lives under Refsul's curse, trapped in the form of either a hellcat or an alley cat most of the time, only able to take his sapien form a few hours each week.

**Raza Vizarr** – Another of the original Blessed Immortals, Raza is Liiesh Romanus's most entrenched spy. Fully devoted to undoing the mistakes of history, he lives in secret in the Temple Setvan, spying on Refsul and his agents.

**Remm Riley Therman** – *(24, born 12, December 1171 in Oboran, Corigon)* The son of Jon Therman and Luvena Dantiego, Remm was motherless by age one and a fugitive by age 14. He stopped agents of Bruce Hayden from kidnapping his sister but was discovered as a ralenta in the process. Fleeing from Drawlen collectors, he joins the rogue ring of his aunt, Krishena Dantiego. Some years later, he falls in with Shane zem'Arta's Red Watch crew and has been terrorizing Drawlen and Shardling agents ever since.

**Sid vel'Forr** – *(25, born 1170 in Thêen, Freelands)* Once the enforcer of Shane's Red Watch crew, Sid is transferred to Orin Novelen's personal bodyguard. He is a womanizer and connoisseur of whiskey.

**Shane zem'Arta** – *(27, born 3, April 1168 in Dothra, Freelands)* A captain of the Red Watch and nicknamed The Red Wolf, Shane is jaded and world-weary. Once a grab boy (one who tricks people into slavery) and assassin for the notorious Shardling pirate, Henrick Lowe, Shane now answers to a new master, Liiesh Romanus. Though Liiesh is a more benevolent minder, Shane is no less eager to be in his debt.

**Tres Romanus** – *(83, born 5, January 1112 in Palim, Freelands)* Younger brother to Liiesh, Tres resents every minute he spends in his brother's shadow. He is bitter about his position as Second Lord of the Freelands, mostly because he is forced to participate in politics. He has an infamous temper, which results in a ten-year sentence of reparation fealty to his brother.

**Venna vel'Tamar** – *(VEN-uh) (21, born 13, January 1174 in Thêen, Freelands)* The whimsical, bookish daughter of a Red Watch commander, Venna spends her time in university lectures and soaking up fairy tales. She is deeply infatuated with Shane zem'Arta. Her beauty often gains her unwanted attention.

**Vernon vel'Tamar** – *(64, born 1131 in Thêen, Freelands)* A commander of the Red Watch, Vernon is the shrewd but unassuming father of four incredibly beautiful daughters, including Venna.

## LORINTH TOWNSFOLK

**Arik Leer** – *(49, born 1146 in Lorinth, Taria)* A captain of the local temple guard, Arik is a decent and shrewd man.

**Carl Loren** – *(55, born 1140 in Lorinth, Taria)* The proprietor of the Loren Inn and Tavern, Carl is a gentle man with a love for literature and family.

**David Therman** – *(83, born 1102 in Sidras, The Deep Wood)* Determined to live openly and unafraid as a Ruvian, David took up residence in Lorinth in his late twenties. He was a close friend of Lucas Riley, later buying Jon out of slavery in service to his father. He housed Ruth and her children when Jon was sentenced to Langry prison. He teaches them his native language, culture, and religion. David suffers from a serious case of gout and other ailments common to aging.

**Edd Pran** – *(24, born 1171 in Lorinth, Taria)* Edd is a notoriously arrogant and lewd member of the temple guard. Believing he is destined for greater things, he is lax in his duty and a drunkard.

**Emeral Ferren** – *(70, born 1125 in Depbas, Taria)* The current principal of the Lorinth temple, Emeral's career has suffered due to his refusal to be cruel or corrupt. Sent to this backwater town by a disgruntled cleric, Emeral is content with his fate.

**Margaret Loren** – *(43, born 1152 in Lorinth, Taria)* Margaret is Carl's mild-mannered wife. Behind her gentle smile is a tragic past and the fear of an uncertain future.

**Philip Creedle** – *(17, born 1178 in Lorinth, Taria)* Son of the local slave master, Philip is known as the town bully. He is often at odds with Nate Therman and Will Loren.

**Rose (Bellerose)** – *(18, born 26, February 1177)* Rose came to Lorinth under mysterious circumstances. A novice priestess and likely the cast-off daughter of a nobleman in debt, Rose is determined to hate every aspect of life in Lorinth.

**Will (William) Loren** – *(21, born 1174 in Lorinth, Taria)* The son of Margaret and Carl, Will is completing his compulsory service as a town militiaman. The long-time love-interest of Ella Therman, he is eager to advance their relationship.

## ROGUES AND SMUGGLERS

**Abad il'Dani** – *(57, born 1138 in Corre, Aginom)* Jon's main business partner, Abad is the charming, profit-minded half of the pseudonym Master Smuggler.

**Calla Dantiego** – Calla is Krishena's cool-headed enforcer and husband. Possessing powers beyond any known ralenta, Calla's origins and motives are shrouded in mystery.

**Cameron Donfree** – *(71, born 1124 in Lorinth, Taria)* One of Jon's smuggling partners, Cameron is cautious and shrewd. The owner of Donfree's Trading Post, she keeps a brace of pistols close at all times.

**Ella Riley Therman** – *(20, born 11, April 1175 in Estbye, Taria)* Daughter of Jon and Ruth Therman, Ella is clever and good-natured. She is determined to help her father's people find their place in the world.

**Jeb (Jebadiah) Riley Therman** – *(13, born 12, March 1182 in Estbye, Taria)* Jeb is the youngest child of Jon and Ruth. Quiet and mild-mannered, he is content with life in Lorinth, especially when working in his garden. His mother believes he will become a ralenta, and so is a bit over-protective of him.

**Jon Therman** – *(50, born 12, October 1144 in Sidras, The Deep Wood)* Born Jonathan Riley to a Tarish mother and a Ruvian descendant of old Kings, Jon's life has been a string of tragedies, including a childhood of slavery and a four-year stint in Langry Prison near Depbas for failing to turn his ralenta son, Remm, over to Drawlen collectors. He harbors great resentment toward the Ruvians of Sidras, whom he blames for his mother's fate. Thus, he rejects his birth name (Riley) in favor of his adoptive name (Therman).

**Krishena Dantiego** – *(35, born 1160 in Quim, tSolan)* The sister of Jon's deceased lover, Luvena, Krishena is the notorious Rogue Master of Rotira. Once driven purely by revenge over her sister's death, she now concentrates her efforts on helping the Ruvians and weakening Drawlen's hold on Palimar.

**Nate (Nathaniel) Riley Therman** – *(16, born 17, August 1179 in Estbye, Taria)* Son of Jon and Ruth Therman, Nate dreams of escaping his small town life. He has a propensity for pranks and is nicknamed "trickster" by his brother, Remm.

**Ruth Riley Therman** – *(44, born 28, August 1151 in Depbas, Taria)* The twin sister of Tessa Wilde, Ruth lives with the heavy guilt of her sister's fate as a Drawlen oracle. As a result of hiding Remm's ralenta nature from the Drawls, Ruth serves a fifteen-year indenture as a healer in Lorinth, Taria. Along with her husband, Jon, she is determined to give her children a safe and happy childhood.

**RUVIANS**

**Alistar Soral** – *(57, born 1138 in Melgrove, Corigon)* Named the Second Arch Traitor of Drawlen, Alistar was once a general in the Order of Odyssa. He has embraced his wife's people (the Ruvains) as his own and earned the title High Protector of the united tribes. His singular goal in life is to build a city where Ruvians and Drawlen's castoffs can live in freedom and safety.

**Amara Soral** – *(17, born 1178 in Mumagra)* Daughter of Alistar, Amara sometimes resents her father's reputation but loves him dearly. She takes her duty as a Ruvian scout seriously, but still makes room to be the free-spirited girl she is.

**Arimal Soral** – *(22, born 1173 in Melgrove, Corigon)* Eldest of Alistar's two children, Arimal is level-headed and wise beyond his years. He is apprenticing under Jon to learn more about the world outside Sidras and the Deep Wood.

**Colas Noren** – *(43, born 1152 in Sidras, the Deep Wood)* Warden of Sidras, Colas acts as the head of the city's border patrol and liaison between the Sidrians and Woodlanders.

**Cory Soral** – (*24, born 1171 in Sidras, the Deep Wood)* Wife of Arimal and mother to the infant, Roan, Cory possesses significant healing craft. She acts as doctor to the citizens of Sidras and often gives wise counsel.

**Hazïr Noren** – *(27, born 1168 in Mumagra)* Colas's wife and mother to their three children, Hazïr is a talented engineer and architect, contributing heavily to the improvements of the Sidras settlement and the building of New Donness.

**Lucas Riley** – *(26 at death, born 1120 in Yvenea)* Lucas was the last descendant of the line of Mathis, the ruling house of Ruvia. He is Jon Therman's father. Lucas became obsessed with legends and artifacts. He was convinced the true Everstone was hidden somewhere on Ethar, a belief he pursued to his death.

**Paul Greenwell** – *(53, born 1142 in Sidras, the Deep Wood)* A captain of the Sidrian scouts, Paul is good-humored and kind. He is a great practitioner of shade charming.

**Richard Mathis** – *(1,228, born 1428 TA (Tyrannus Aetate)*, in Donness, Ruvia) The final member of the seven Blessed Immortals, Richard was once a king of Ruvia. He was instrumental in overthrowing and driving out Faust the Tyrant. After Refsul's betrayal and the spreading of the Dying in Ruvia, Richard has worked to preserve the culture and legacy of his people.

**Rolan Whittier** – *(34, born 1161 in Sidras, the Deep Wood)* Rolan is a Sidrian scout. He is most known for his skills in tracking.

**Sadiona** – *(219, born 976 in Shevak)* Once a child of the Drawlen harem in Shevak, Sadiona was trained to command fire in battle. Kidnapped by Halas as a youth, she turned on the Drawls and has fiercely defended the Ruvians of Sidras, her mother's people, ever since. She is a deacon of the Serenity Creed, and titled "Sadiona the Wise" by the Ruvians of Sidras.

**Torok Missien** – *(57, born 1138 in Thura)* Known as the Hound Man or the Master of Hounds, Torok is a Thuran troll whose reputation as a cunning warrior is known all over Ethar. He is a good friend to Alistar Soral and Krishena Dantiego.

## SHARDLINGS

**Henrick Lowe** – *(127, born 1068 in Shevak)* Henrick is a ralenta and the self-proclaimed leader of the Shardling Islands, a treacherous archipelago in the Utheran Ocean between Palimar and Kumun. He is a notorious pirate and slave trader.

**Jex ren'Turen** – *(43, born 1152 in Zeree, Freelands)* A pirate commander under Henrick Lowe, he currently serves a life sentence in Shayhem, a high security island prison in Palim.

## WOODSMEN

**Furgus Baneson** – *(17, born 1178 in the Deep Wood)* Furgus is a tree speaker, remarkably talented for a child of his age.

**Halas Gorvenah** – One of the seven Blessed Immortals, Halas maintains the safety and independence of the Deep Wood, the small region that remains of his homeland, which was devastated by war and the Dying. He maintains a fragile truce with Refsul with the understanding they will leave one another's territories alone. He is a skin-changer (fox).

**Nyla Elderen** – *(94, born 1101 in the Deep Wood)* Daughter of Sephora, Nyla is a skin-changer (mountain lion) and a Woodland border guard.

**Orego Gorvenah** – One of the seven Blessed Immortals, Orego is Halas' brother and deputy, much as he was when they were mortal soldiers of Gravos. He is also a skin-changer (hawk).

**Sephora Elderen** – *(153, born 1042 in the Deep Wood)* Sephora is a skin-changer (grizzly bear) and captain of the Woodland border guard. She also operates as a spy for Halas.

## YVEANS

**Aronos Hillmoran** – *(137, born 1058 in Setmal, Yvenea)* The ruling dynast of Yvenea, Aronos has held strong through many wars, assassination attempts, and periods of political turmoil. This latest season of civil unrest, however, seems to be eating away at his sanity.

**Darï Priette** – *(24, born 1171 in Mumagra)* Sister to Hazïr Noren, Darï is Yvette's shield guard and a fellow spy. She acts as liaison between Taval and Alistar.

**Fredrick Devilos** – *(52, born 1143 in Setmal, Yvenea)* Head steward of house Novelen, Fredrick takes his role seriously and makes sure others do as well.

**Garren Brodour** – *(43, born 1152 in Setmal, Yvenea)* Captain of Orin's personal guard, Garren leads with surety and respect.

**Harriette (Harry) Harris** – *(77, born 1118 in Palim, Freelands)* A commander of the Red Watch alongside Vernon and Leron, Harriette is unassuming and brutally efficient. She is married to a Yvean man, Leo Harris, with whom she had two daughters. Both girls died tragically.

**Leo Harris** – *(71, born 1124 in Niryen, Yvenea)* A gunsmith by trade and inventor at heart, Leo is gruff but personable. He is the husband of a Red Watch commander (Harriette) and resents whenever he is wrapped up in her schemes. His daughters both died tragically during an illegal Drawlen mining venture.

**Leonora Sesporan** – *(21, born 1174 in Setmal, Yvenea)* Taval's youngest daughter, Leonora is also Orin Novelen's fiancé. Beautiful and kind, she seems to lack the cunning that might be required for her future inheritance.

**Leron Novelen** – *(65, born 1130 in Thêen, Freelands)* A half thurse, half human scholar originally from Thêen, Leron went to Yvenea for research and got caught up in stopping a coup de ta instigated by rival nobility of the ruling Dynast. The incident was dubbed the Three Days Night. Leron's role in this confrontation earned him great fame and favor among those loyal to Dynast Aronos Hillmoran. He married Hillmoran's niece and remained in Setmal. He serves as the commander of the Red Watch until his mysterious disappearance in December of 1194.

**Orin Novelen** – *(24, born 1171 in Setmal, Yvenea)* The son of Leron Novelen and a Yvean noble woman, Orin is the heir apparent of the Yvean throne, being the closest living relative to the ruling Dynast.

**Taval Sesporan** – *(73, born 1122 in Setmal, Yvenea)* High Chamberlain of Yvenea, Taval is responsible for the country's finances. He moonlights as a spy master, commanding a vast network of agents and informants all dedicated to Yvenea's sovereignty.

**Yvette Sesporan** – *(28, born 1167 in Setmal, Yvenea)* Eldest daughter of Taval Sesporan, Yvette is also one of his best spies. She is a skilled archer and shuns many Yvean formalities and stereotypes.

## HISTORICAL AND LEGENDARY CHARACTERS

**Agroth** – A terrion warrior of antiquity rumored to be the first Mortari shard keeper. His origins, whether historical or mythical, are debated by scholars. Legend holds that he ruled as a spire lord in ancient Oboran. When the Devourer invaded Ethar, The Prophet gave Agroth the Heart of Mortemus, which transformed him into a dragon and allowed him to trap the Devourer in a crater, which later became the Howling Sea.

**Faust the Tyrant** – The titular villain of the previous age. When Faust finally fell, the proceeding era was labeled "Post Tyrannus" by scholars. A figure of mysterious origins and dangerous charisma, Faust first came to power by ousting the rulers of Ruvia before the Devourers Waste began its encroachment on Gravos in northern Palimar. Believed to be human, he rose and fell several times in his effort to dominate the peninsula, at one point escaping to Greq and sending his generals to Thura to breed and raise an army of thurse. He is credited with disabling the original world gates. He was a suspected necromancer, evidenced by his unnatural life of almost 500 years and his use of wraiths in his armies.

**Prophet, The** – A nameless messenger of Sovereign who, according to both Palish mythology and the text of the Creedan Psalm, came to Ethar through the first World Gate to preach the doctrine of Mysterious Grace, the foundational theology of the Serenity Creed, and to deliver the Heart of Mortemus to Agroth in order to imprison the Devourer.

**Regem the Selfless** – A human hero widely believed mythological and said to be responsible for breaking the World Gates and ousting Faust the Tyrant from Palimar during his first conquest.

# APPENDIX D

# ROLES AND OCCUPATIONS

## ROLES OF THE DRAWLEN REGIME

**Apostle** – Spies belonging to the Order of Secrets.

**Collector** – A spy responsible for finding and bringing in 'new stock' to the Drawlen order. They generally look for individuals with craft talent.

**Guard of the Veil** – The Veiled Man's personal military force.

**High Immortal** – An immortal who has significant political power within the Drawlen order.

**Lesser Immortal** – An immortal with less influence within the Drawlen order.

**Blessed Immortal** – The original seven immortals, including Refsul, who set out to defeat the Devourer and its chief agent, Faust the Tyrant.

**Deposed Immortal** – An immortal who has been removed from or left the Drawlen order.

**Oracle** – A foreseer of the Drawlen order.

**Purifier** – Priest-assassins of Refsul's order.

**Ranger** – The main cavalry force of the Drawlen military, belonging to the Order of Odyssa.

**Dragoon Ranger** – Elite rangers, considered heavy cavalry.

## ROLES OF THE PALISH UNDERGROUND

**Deputy Rogue Master** – The second-in-command of a rogue ring.

**Master Smuggler** – The pseudonym used by Jon Therman and Abad il'Dani. Most people outside their closest circle of confidants know the head of their business only as the Master Smuggler and do not know the real names associated with it.

**Rock Smuggler** – Someone whose main business is smuggling sunrock to evade taxation.

**Rogue** – A professional thief associated with a rogue ring.

**Rogue Master** – The head of a rogue ring, which is like a thief's guild.

## ROLES OF THE FREELANDS

**Arbiter of the Spires** – A member of a council of terrion judges. Their principal is the First Arbiter.

**Archon** – A leader of a city-state. Also a de facto commanding general of the Freeland Vanguard.

**Assembly Lord or Lady** – An official representative of a city-state to the assembly.

**First Lord** – The chief figurehead of the Free Lands. He acts as the commander in chief of the military, head of intelligence, and high protector of the Freeland borders. This is not a hereditary position, but rather an elected post which can be revoked by the assembly. Generally, the position has gone between the Romanus and Aldonus families. The First Lord must be a male terrion mind render with significant military experience. Only two First Lords of Palim have ever been deposed.

**Lady of the Spires** – Wife to either of the ruling spire lords.

**Second Lord** – The First Lord's second-in-command and first successor. He is often tasked with overseeing military operations.

**Spire Lord or Lady** – A terrion noble with an official seat in the assembly.

**Spire Watchman** – A member of the Freeland Spire Watch, typically terrion. Also referred to simply as watchman.

## ROLES OF THE RED WATCH

*The Red Watch is a spy network of ancient historical significance. Originally called the Order of Mortari, its mission has always been to combat the influences and consequences of the Devourer and its agents.*

**Commander** – The head of a division of Red Watch agents. A commander usually oversees operations in a particular region. Leron Novelen and Harriette Harris share command of the Palimar region. Liiesh Romanus is the modern founder and High Commander of the entire Red Watch network.

**Captain** – A leader of a crew or team of agents. Usually, a team numbers 4-7 agents.

**Dispatcher** – An assassin. Many crew members embody all three field roles: dispatcher, enforcer, and watcher.

**Enforcer** – The muscle of a particular crew. Usually in charge of interrogations.

**Watcher** – A spy tasked with observation and intel gathering.

## ROLES OF THE SERENITY CREED

**Arch Deacon** – The figurehead of the Serenity Creed. Candidates for the office are nominated at the Decennial Synod by a panel of chaplains and voted on by the attending congregation of deacons. The Arch Deacon's role is largely ceremonial and lacks doctrinal authority outside the consensus of the overseeing panel of chaplains and deacons.

**Deacon** – A spiritual advisor of the Serenity Creed. Deacons typically oversee churches or prayer chapels and minister to the local population of Creedan followers. Their duties vary depending on the local traditions, but typically involve preaching the Psalm and advising their local congregation. Depending on the theological order to which they belong, deacons hold to different ministry philosophies and minor differences in theology.

**Chaplain** – *(alt. missionary)* Chaplains generally attach themselves to secular institutions in an advisory or evangelizing capacity. Like all official representatives of the Creed, they do not hold political or private office at any of these organizations but are funded through congregational donations.

# APPENDIX E

# CRAFT AND SORCERY

## CRAFT

*Widely regarded as part of the natural order of Ethar, craft is generally inherent in different races and deeply ingrained in the fabric of society.*

**Mind Craft** – *(Minder and Mind Render)* The most powerful and dangerous of the crafts. Powerful mind crafters are called mind renders and usually occupy high ranks in terrion society. All of the First Lords in Palish history have been mind renders. Mind craft can detect lies, replay memories, detect feelings, and even influence the thoughts and actions of weak-minded people. However, mind crafters are vulnerable to mind fever, a phycological sickness that can cause extreme schizophrenia and suicidal thoughts. Limiters are used to mitigate the effects of mind fever. Silver can amplify a mind crafter's power and protect against mind fever while copper can deter the use of mind craft.

**Healing Craft** – *(Craft Healer or Craft Physician)* Considered one of the most blessed arts on Ethar, healing elevates the status of its practitioners in nearly every society. A strong healer can bring people back from the brink of death. Rather than truly healing, this craft undoes damage inflicted on the body. It comes at a cost, however, as it causes extreme fatigue and dehydration in its users.

**Speaking Craft** – *(Earth Speaker, Tree Speaker, Beast Speaker, Water Wielder, Fire Wielder)* The ability of some fae to manipulate elements, plants, or animals. This ability is exclusive to fae and relatively common. It requires very little effort on the user's part but can wear down the constitution of the element, plant, or animal in use.

**Shade Craft** – *(Ralenta)* The rarest form of craft and exclusive to humans. This craft is unique in that it is finite. It also requires the presence of a shade, which can be lost or stolen by other ralenta. Ralenta can accomplish incredible feats by using shades, including teleportation, hearing and seeing at great distances, and becoming nearly invisible. Powerful ralenta can solidify shades to a certain degree and use them as weapons. Ralenta can steal one another's power, a dangerous process called reaping.

**Shape Craft** – *(Skin-changer or flier)* Craft exclusive to fae and terrion, though in very different practices. Skin-changing is its rarest form and occurs only in those with strong fae heritage. Full skin-changing takes intense training and is difficult to maintain even for the strongest skin-changer.

## SORCERY

*Sorcery is generally seen as an unholy endeavor by followers of the Serenity Creed and Drawlen religions. However, many Drawlen immortals are known to practice it. Even immortality itself is rumored to be a result of blood magic. Sorcery is illegal in Yvenea and the Freelands and is contracted by many high-ranking members of the Corigish and Greqi governments.*

**Foresight** – *(Shaman or Foreseer)* There is a heated split among the philosophers of Ethar as to whether foresight is craft or sorcery. Most modern thinkers categorize it as the latter. It can be faked easily, making foreseers generally mistrusted. This talent is temperamental and nearly impossible to master or predict.

**Blood Sorcery** – *(Blood Witch or Witcher)* Blood sorcery is widely considered supernatural and even demonic in nature. It takes many forms, both benevolent and sinister. The Cosazi assassin's guild is famous for applying very sophisticated blood sorcery to their death contracts. It is widely unknown, outside its practitioners, how blood sorcery is powered and applied.

**Corruptology** – *(Necromancer)* Corruptology or necromancy is the act of attempting to control or manipulate corruption or other aspects of the Devourer (an ancient demonic entity which still has a presence on Ethar). It is considered the darkest and most vile of sorcery and is known to be very dangerous. Faust the Tyrant is the most famous necromancer in Ethar's remembered history. He is especially remembered for perfecting the art of reanimation, which is how he made and commanded legions of corrupted people, called wraiths.

**Mortari** – *(Shard Keeper)* An ancient and mysterious magic said to be the power of absolute death. Scholarly consensus holds that it originated with Agroth, a terrion lord of antiquity who battled the Devourer when it first assaulted Ethar. A cult of warriors, called the Order of Mortari, formed after Agroth's death. They came to be known as the Red Watch, but soon fell into obscurity. Little is known about the actual abilities of a mortari wielder, other than the power to permanently kill an immortal. Blood sight is the ability for a shard keeper to perceive things beyond the visible world, and unrest is a mindless state a shard keeper can fall into when overcome by Mortari power.

# APPENDIX F

# CULTURE AND ENVIRONMENT

## CONCERNING THE DEVOURER

**Corruption** – The term given to the physical manifestations of the Devourer's Curse. The Dying is what results in the geographic areas under the Curse. When sapiens fall to Corruption, they either die or become wraiths, seemingly mindless monsters with coal-black skin, white eyes, and a lethal allergy to sunlight and certain types of sunrock.

**Devourer, The** – A benevolent entity of ancient and celestial origin, the Devourer is credited by cultural and religious traditions around the world with responsibility for the Dying and the spread of Corruption. This entity has no sapien form, but many religious doctrines and mythologies assign it a sentient will. In many of these tales, the Devourer seduces and enables sapien servants to carry out its nefarious objectives, which universally revolve around consuming the lives of all living things on Ethar. In most accounts, the Devourer cannot tolerate the sun or light from solisite and solarite sunrock. Drawlen teachings hold that Refsul trapped the Devourer in the Garden of Souls and maintains that prison by using the souls of Life Harvest Journeyers.

**Devourer's Curse** – *(alt. The Curse)* The supernatural origin of Corruption. The Curse is referred to in many world-wide myths and professed by most religious traditions in Palimar to some degree.

**Dying, The** – The desolation left upon the lands touched by the Devourer's Corruption. Over the past several millennia, it has encroached on new territories around Ethar while receding from others. No traditions agree on or have successfully predicted how or why this happens. The progression is usually slow, taking years or decades to progress or retreat even a mile. Refsul credits the Drawlen Life Harvest practice with the stability of the Devourer's Waste over the last 700 years, and that the Dead Lands spread due to the Karthans and Ruvians rejecting his rule.

## HISTORY AND LEGEND

**Breaking of the Third Moon** – The legendary cataclysm that brought Meridus out of the heavens to fall upon Ethar, reshaping the landscape of Urlas and forever darkening the night sky. Palish mythology claims the Devourer, imprisoned in a deep abys, sent a demonic servant to trick a primitive stone mason into building three octagonal platforms around the world, and for a smith to fashion bronze rings upon them. The servant promised the mason and the smith immortality, achieved only by stealing Sovereign's Heart hidden within the Meridus moon. The two craftsmen convinced the dragon brothers Calix and Dimitrus to retrieve the heart. Despite the warning of their sister, Atonia, the brothers fulfilled this task. When the Devourer's servant touched the Meridus gem, the moon fractured and fell upon the land. In the resulting destruction, the demon lost the stone and his corporeal form, becoming the first shade and ushering in the Umbra Messis, the age of the shadow harvest.

**Drawlen-Terrion Wars** – A decade-long military conflict between the Drawlen territories and the Freelands beginning in 893 Post Tyrannus. When the Freeland vanguard laid siege to Setmal in Yvenea, Ruvia entered the fight and drove them back. The war ended in 902 with neither side gaining ground and the Dead Lands swallowing Ruvia in sudden deviation. Yvean and Freeland builders erected the Door of Bamrian to mark their border and signify a fragile peace.

**Fires, The** – In the first hundred years of the Post Tyrannus age, Palimar enjoyed abundant recovery under the leadership of the Blessed Immortals. The encroachment of the Devourer's waste into northern Palimar, called The Second Withering, brought famine, pestilence, and unrest into the proceeding century, triggering division among the growing ranks of immortals. Civil war between Sovelus Kane and Rodden Morien, his second-in-command, ensnared every livable corner of Palimar for over forty years. During this time, Eruna, Rodden's wife, lured Sovelus to a secluded place in the Modrian Mountains, supposedly to imprison him, only for Sovelus to trap her in the form of a petrified tree, which would later become the centerpiece of the Temple Setvan in Shevak. Drawlen tradition holds that, after cursing Eruna, Sovelus received a vision in which Sovereign commanded him to take a new name and build a temple over the ruins of the ancient world gate near the Syres River. Sovelus gathered his followers, built the Harvest Temple and the city of Drawl, and restyled himself as

Refsul, Sovereign's immortal prophet and priest. The Dying continued to encroach on Palimar, even as violent clashes between Refsul and Rodden persisted. They reached a tentative truce when a plague of wraiths poured in from the north, overtaking much of the peninsula. Rodden devised a solution: to use hundreds of fae fire wielders to burn the land infected by the Dying and overrun by wraiths. Initially a mutual endeavor, Rodden and Refsul used this tactic to turn on one another, initiating a ten-year total war that history would remember as The Fires. The Drawls emerged victorious after Refsul sent assassins to poison and slaughter Rodden's fire wielders. As a final blow, Refsul used the bronze rod with which he'd cursed Eruna to trap Rodden in the form of a hellcat.

**Shade** – An incorporeal entity that hatches from sapien corpses after the three-day process of petrification recedes. Shades are the subject of historical terror and mystery. Seemingly the real-world embodiment of an ancient curse, these phantoms haunt the dark corners of Ethar, as sunlight and certain sunrocks are lethal to them. A wild shade, one hatched from a sapien corpse and wandering without sapien interference, is generally benign. An agitated shade is one stimulated by sapien fear. A bound shade is one under a ralenta's control. If severed from that bond, a shade becomes unbound, leaving it in a permanently hostile state dangerous to all sapien and animal life. Terrion are especially vulnerable to shade menacing, while thurse and kobold are relatively resistant unless faced with an unbound shade.

**World Gate** – The predecessors to contemporary wraith gates, these ancient devices were said to not only connect to one another all over Ethar, but also to other realms and worlds entirely. Their invention is credited to many builders and civilizations with little consensus between the accounts. Palish mythology states the first three were built by a stone mason and a metal smith tricked by a demon. The demon's plan to use the gates to bring the Devourer to Ether failed when the Meridus moon broke. But the mason and the smith survived to build more gates despite lacking the power to open them. Convinced they would achieve immortality by constructing their network of locked gates, they attracted a cult of followers to help. Though the two craftsmen lived and died mortal lives, their descendants carried on their mission. Generations later, one such progeny recovered the fabled Sovereign's Heart. Three dragon siblings who had witnessed the fall of Meridus warned the man against using the heart. Ignoring them, he activated the world gates, ushering in the era of the World Walkers and inadvertently freeing the Devourer from its hellish prison.

**Wraith Gate** – Whether the World Gates truly opened to celestial realms or not, the physical evidence of their legacy is peppered across Ethar. Three millennia ago, a terrion scholar and inventor named Theonasis supposedly discovered their workings. Though he never put that knowledge to use, later inventors built upon his work until a human ralenta managed to open a gate using a shade. This method proved costly and tedious, with range limited to gates within a few hundred miles, but it changed the trajectory of the world, regardless.

**Vulta** – This vast empire, encompassing much of Urlas, including Palimar, reigned between the Breaking of the Third Moon and the First Withering, the initial spread of the Dying. Vulta is unique in both its longevity and its inclusion of many sapien races. Most prominently, terrion made up its religious and philosophical classes, thurse its political and military leaders, and humans its captains of commerce and industry.

## RELIGION IN PALIMAR

**Drawlen** – The dominant religious and economic power in Palimar, the Drawlen cult derives its history and practices from the Serenity Creed, with one glaring difference: the deification of Drawlen's immortal leaders. While the creed has strict philosophies about its officials refraining from political office, Drawlen blends religious and political power into a purely theocratic function. Drawlen immortals and clerics pull the strings of many political and economic interests in western Palimar. It controls much of the lumber and mining industries in the region, and played a crucial role in the outlawing of fire in many Palish countries. Drawlen's most sacred and entrenched practice, the Life Harvest, is a sacrificial eugenics festival professed to keep back the Dying and to keep shades from harassing the shadows of Palimar. *See Appendix D for Roles and Occupations of Drawlen.*

**Life Harvest** – The twice-per-decade Drawlen pilgrimage, culminating in the Festival of Souls in Drawl, requires the sickly and aged among the Drawlen devout to commit themselves to ritual eugenics overseen by the High Immortals. Drawlen doctrine teaches that Refsul collects these sacrificial souls within the Harvest Tower and brings them to a heavenly realm called The Garden of Souls. The Devourer's contemporary prison resides in the center of the Garden and must be reinforced with the power imbued to Refsul through the willing sacrifice of his followers.

**Paganism** – Dozens of pagan religious traditions exist in Palimar, some pre-dating the arrival of the Serenity Creed from Vulta. Each tSolani tribe has its own pantheon and practices. The Raegoth nomads of the Old Waste, while largely accepting the Serenity Creed, have their own pagan traditions and mythology.

**Serenity Creed** – *(alt. The Creed)* A monotheistic religion professing that all sapiens are dependent on the Mysterious Grace of Sovereign for their eternal salvation and on the teachings of the Serenity Psalm for their moral ethics. Before the rise of the Blessed Immortals and the fall of Faust the Tyrant, the Serenity Creed was widely practiced by all races and nations of Palimar. Its history dates to Vulta and the discovery of the World Gates thousands of years ago. Its chief sacred text, the Serenity Psalm, states that a prophet of Sovereign arrived on the first World Gate and preached the Mysterious Grace, the creed's central doctrine. The creed is practiced in diverse ways throughout the world of Ethar but originated in ancient Vulta on the greater continent of Urlas. *See Appendix D for Roles and Occupations of the Serenity Creed.*

**Sovereign** – The supreme deity professed by many monotheistic religious traditions in Palimar and other regions settled by descendants of Vulta. The Serenity Creed holds tightly to the teachings of the Serenity Psalm, which dates back thousands of years and has influenced cultural and religious traditions around the world to varying degrees. Drawlen doctrine states that Refsul and his immortal brethren are Sovereign's corporeal representatives, while the Creed interprets the Psalm's warning about "the undying horrors wearing the skin of the faithful" as a condemnation of the High Immortal and his ilk.

## THE THREE MOONS

**Meridus** – *(alt. The Fallen Moon, The Third Moon, Sovereign's Heart)* The moon known in Palimar as Meridus no longer graces the night skies of Ethar, if it ever did. Before the arrival of the Devourer, before even the age of the World Walkers, Meridus was said to light the night sky as proudly as the Sun ruled the day, save for the period of the new moons. Mythologies around Ethar, though varied, hold a similar thread: celestial visitors tore

Meridus from her heavenly seat and scattered her corpse across eastern Urlas and the Utheran Ocean. Her flesh became stone, but still possessed the power to steal the light and head of the sun. This is the mythological origin attributed to sunrock and to the power source of the original World Gates.

**Mortemus** – *(alt. The Red Moon, The Blood Moon)* The largest celestial body overlooking Ethar, Mortemus dominates the night with its red intensity. Said to fuel Agroth's power and fervor during his long battle with the Devourer, Mortemus is especially important to many religious and cultural practices amongst Palish terrion. In their apocalyptic mythology, Mortemus's fall from the heavens will be the final stroke of doom upon Ethar.

**Vitaeus** – *(alt. The Blue Moon, The First Moon)* This silvery-blue moon is dwarfed by its crimson neighbor, but still holds great gravitational influence on the planet, as well as cultural significance to the varied cultures of Ethar. The Drawlen tradition claims Vitaeus sustains the longevity and vitality of the Blessed Immortals and their lesser brethren.

## SUNROCK

*Sunrock, a dense mineral found mostly in eastern Urlas and islands dotting the eastern Utheran Ocean, absorb and emit heat and light. Most subsets of this mineral require exposure to sunlight to do so. Global mythology holds that sunrock is the fallen remains of the celestial body, Meridus. Contemporary geologists and philosophers have called the credibility of this ancient claim into question. Regardless, sunrock is an efficacious source of economic and industrial value. No other resource on Ethar has driven civilizations to as much conflict or prosperity. It is categorized into different grades pertaining to their varied attributes.*

**Solisite** – *(alt. Sun Tears)* The rarest and most valuable grade of sunrock and the only one that doesn't require exposure to sunlight. It emits intense golden light but almost no heat. It is just as deadly to shades as sunlight.

**Solarite** – *(alt. Shade Bane)* More common than solisite but still very coveted, this grade of sunrock does require sunlight exposure to charge and shines with a pale-yellow hue. It is still lethal to shades and is commonly used to deter these incorporeal phantoms. The largest known solarite mine on Ethar is in the Freelands and accounts for much of the wealth of the Romanus family.

**Solamite** – *(alt. Smith Stone)* Used in forges and industrial furnaces, solamite is a commercially significant mineral and heavily regulated by the Drawlen mining guild in most of Palimar. Heating it requires prolonged exposure to sunlight. It glows a soft red.

**Solazite** – *(alt. Heat Stone, Hearth Stone, Furnace Stone)* This relatively common grade of sunrock is a stand-in for the conventional bonfire, hearth fire, or furnace. It absorbs sunlight relatively quickly and emits enough heat to be suitable for most household uses such as heating and cooking. It projects light similar in color and brightness to a well-lit log fire.

**Solinite** – *(alt. Common Sunrock, Lantern Stone, Light Stone)* The most abundant subset of sunrock, solinite varies vastly in quality and color, depending on where it's found. Higher grades charge quickly in sunlight and emit a bright white or yellow light, while the poorest grades glow a dull, weak blue. Sunrock powder, a granular collection of low-grade solinite, is commonly used to light public lanterns.

# NOTE FROM THE AUTHORS

*Our Dearest Reader,*

Thank you for reading *Remnant*, our debut novel and the first installment of the epic fantasy series, *The Palimar Saga*. We're honored to have your interest.

This story began as a creative effort between mother and daughter when I (Kirsten) was a sophomore in high school. As a free-spirited, flighty, and quietly rebellious teenager, I didn't seem to have much in common with my steady, disciplined, hard-working mother.

The inspiration for this book brought us together under a common goal. Nothing mends a strained relationship like working together toward a unified vision.

The first spark for the premise of this book, which Carol had in a dream, was a question: *What would a world be like where fire was outlawed?*

The first completed draft of this novel was a combination of Carol's original idea and the wild imaginings of a teenage girl. However, that version felt juvenile and one-dimensional when I reread it many years later as a new mother in my late twenties.

So we hit the delete key on much of the content (although many of the characters remained intact) and added a different question to underscore the narrative: *What would a world become if broken people achieved immortality?*

At its core, *The Palimar Saga* tells the story of one family as they strive to reunite in a world fraught with danger. It's a story not just of this one biological family, but also of those they bring in along the way. So many stories in this genre revolve around orphans and protagonists who appear to stand alone. While there's certainly a place for these stories, we wanted to bring in a different perspective: a family that fights to stay together.

We hope this story resonates with you as it does with us. As indie authors, we rely on you as readers to spread the word about our book. Grass-roots testimonies like yours are the most powerful drivers of our success. **Will you tell a friend or two and write a review at any (or all if you're an over-achiever) of these sites?**

**– Amazon (amazon.com)**

**– Good Reads (goodreads.com)**

**– Barnes & Noble (barnesandnoble.com)**

**– BookBub (bookbub.com)**

We are incredibly grateful for you. We're working hard to perfect the next book in the series. To stay up-to-date about releases, go to palimarsaga.com and sign up for our newsletter. We look forward to seeing you there.

*All the best,*

K. R. Solberg & C. R. Jacobson

*To learn more about the authors, visit palimarsaga.com/authors*

*Sign up for our newsletter at palimarsaga.com or scan the code:*

# UPRISING

## BOOK TWO

The shock of losing several of their most powerful immortal leaders stirs the wrath of the Drawlen regime toward its enemies, who are, as of yet, fractured and vulnerable. Liiesh Romanus, First Lord of the Freelands and Drawlen's most deadly adversary, sets out to correct this. His best option for doing so, however, is working with a Tarish smuggler with a dubious reputation. But Ella Riley is not what she seems.

In Yvenea, the Freelands' only ally, Shane zem'Arta works to find his missing commander and to secure Orin Novelen's ascension to the throne. But Yvenea's aged dynast, acting on his severe paranoia, has turned his city into a prison, stirring up a resistance that threatens to become a nation-wide revolution and which sweeps the Red Watch into its tide.

On the other side of the peninsula, Jon Thurman races to find out what became of his wife and youngest son. Political unrest in Oboran complicates his efforts. He finds himself the guardian of a girl who is sought by both sides of the conflict.

Jon has left his son, Nate, to carry on with the mission to bring the scattered Ruvian people to their new city in the north. It is a difficult endeavor complicated by Drawlen cruelty.

All the while, Jon's wife, Ruth, and son, Jeb, must learn to survive in a strange land while avoiding its many dangers, chiefly the Drawlen immortal, Selvator Kane, who seeks Jeb for mysterious reasons and will use any means to achieve his goal.

# THE SMUGGLER'S DEAL

## A PALIMAR SAGA NOVELLA

*How Kritcher got in the cart...*

The relentless pursuit of a fugitive brings a reluctant hunter to a city rife with treachery, where he finds himself at odds with a jaded smuggler.

When a would-be swindler slips through Shane zem'Arta's fingers, he goes out on his own to track the man down. The Freeland spire lords do not forgive easily, and Shane has his reputation to protect. Leaving his crew behind, he chases the escaped con artist up the coast of Palimar to the quiet seaside city of Estbye.

There, he runs into old friend Jon Therman, a smuggler with his own dubious agenda. Their goals are conveniently aligned, but Shane's target is no slouch. With the help of Jon's clever daughter, Ella, Shane lays a trap his target is sure to fall for. But things never seem to go Shane's way, especially in this city.

*The Smuggler's Deal*, a companion novella to K. R. Solberg and C. R. Jacobson's *Remnant*, is an intriguing introduction to the world of Palimar, where immortals rule from splendid temples and their enemies lurk in grand towers. In this treacherous world of cults, magic, and guns, only the most cunning mortals survive.

Download the free eBook of *The Smuggler's Deal* on our website:

**palimarsaga.com/newsletter**

Paperback and hardcover versions are also available.

Printed in Great Britain
by Amazon

38837428R00238